taming of a rebel

EADA FRIESIAN

taming of a rebel

one

"Glad it's not me," Tori muttered.

Another loud scream reverberated through the aisles of the grocery store. She jerked and cringed with a start. Whichever toddler was blasting their lungs to test them out was throwing the entire building for a loop. Tori's lips curled at the thought. She had been there a time or two with Harley when she'd been younger. Thank God those years were done and over. *All right, back to shopping. Where was I?*

Eggs.

Milk.

Harley's cereal.

Tori mentally checked off the items left to add to her cart as she ran a hand through her shoulder length hair. She cringed at the feeling, adding conditioner to the list. She'd run out a week ago and hadn't managed to make it to the store to grab more yet. She'd had Harley all week, and when she had her daughter, she wanted to spend as much time as possible with her doing fun things.

She pushed the cart around the end of the aisle and something hit her right leg. That something was solid but not hard except for the top part that hit with force halfway up her thigh. Tori stopped short when pain shot through her knee.

A small cry came from the impact site. Her heart was in her throat as she stepped back and her heel hit something soft. Immediately, she lifted up on the pressure. Looking down, she saw a tangled mass of wild chestnut hair hanging over small legs that sprawled in front of a child. The child was on their backside, back curved into a C and head hung forward as though they had just bounced off someone's leg.

"Oh no." Realization hit. Tori dropped down, cart and list forgotten. Her entire world became about the kid in front of her, clearly hurt as big turtle tears raced down the kid's face. Her heart hammered as she scanned the bruised chubby legs, bare feet, and fisted hands.

"Are you okay?" She lifted her head over the girl's mop of hair, looking for the parents. Would they be worried? Frantically looking for her? Where were they? They had to be nearby, surely. Any parent would be.

At the sound of Tori's voice the girl looked up, big dark eyes peeping through strands of the wild hair that half covered her face. She was adorable, even in her tears.

"Hi." Tori smiled as a breath of relief escaped her mouth. "I'm Tori. What's your name?"

The child narrowed her eyes, her face reddening as if she was going to scream again. Only this time, it'd no doubt be a cry from the unexpected collision. Tori bit down on her bottom lip, trying to stop the laugh that bubbled up from her chest. The adrenaline and fear slid away at the sight of the defiance, replaced by a warmth and fierceness she felt whenever a child was involved.

"How about I help you find your momma?" Tori's smile relaxed as she offered her hand for the child to take.

But the girl's bottom lip trembled, and Tori's departing

adrenaline turned on its heels and returned to the scene of the crime, a gleeful expression on its lips.

"Oh, it's okay. You're okay, sweetie." Tori gently touched the girl's shoulder, but at the child's small flinch, removed her hand as though burned. She had worked with enough children to know when something scared them. The girl wore a shirt at least two sizes too small, with something crusted in various patches over it. She hoped it was food and hoped even harder that it was today's dropped offerings, but there looked to be layers of dirt caked onto her clothes. The green hem was ratty and torn, in addition to the small holes in the well-worn fabric. Tori's heart ached.

"Rebel?" The word cracked in the air like a gun being fired.

Tori flinched. With a steadying breath, she rested on her heels. A woman, stunning and oozing confidence in a dark pantsuit strode purposefully toward them. The *click click click* of heels against the linoleum raised goosebumps on Tori's bare arms. As the woman drew closer, Tori noticed the suit had a subtle white pinstripe through the fabric which drew all manner of attention to the definition of curved hips and generous breasts that filled the white shirt beneath. Tori blinked and moved on from the woman's cleavage and noticed that the accessories adorning her ears, neck, and even wrist looked more expensive than Tori's car. But there were no rings —none whatsoever.

The woman remained focused entirely on the small child in front of Tori as she drew closer. The *click click click* echoed in Tori's ears. She instinctively reached down and snagged the child's hand, clasping her small fingers to protect her. She had no idea who this woman was, but the two of them did not fit together.

Tori got the impression the woman hadn't even noticed her crouched down in front of the child. Which was disappointing as Tori definitely noticed her. Her eyes flicked between the child on the edge of tears and the woman in the power suit. Tori tensed as she waited to see what was going to happen, to see what this woman could possibly want with the two of them because surely it wasn't the kid, right? Tori's lips parted as she was just about to say something when a sob tore through the kid next to her.

The child glared at Tori's hand though her eyes still watered with unshed tears. Was this a real cry or a fake one? Because she still hadn't actually shed those tears that were building in her beautiful dark brown eyes.

A wave of nostalgia washed over Tori. Harley had had just the same defiant independence when she had been that small. She had seen her own fair share of grocery store time-outs throughout the years. Tori guessed the child to be around two, give or take a few months, because she still hadn't spoken.

"Rebel, you can't run away like that. I need to know where you are at all times." The woman's voice was harsh and loud as she spoke, still five steps away. A few shoppers nearby turned to look over at the colliding three.

Rebel looked over her shoulder and then back at Tori. Her bottom lip quivered once more, and Tori pulled Rebel into her side, pressing her gently against her hip. She would do anything to protect this child if she could, especially from someone who was coming after her when the two definitely didn't belong together. Who would talk to a toddler like that?

Tori might not be dressed to kill or be as drop-dead gorgeous as this woman drawing closer, but no way would she meet her on her knees. She shook her head slightly, stopping the wildly inappropriate thoughts growing in her mind.

She dusted off her own pants, plain and comfortable for her previous client's request to go for a walk during their session. By the time the woman stopped in front of her, Tori had her wide smile firmly back in place. Tori would kill her with kindness if she had to.

"Hi, is this one yours?" Tori flicked her finger on Rebel's wrinkled nose. Rebel clung to her side, which was unexpected, especially since Tori was a stranger. Apparently this kid hadn't ever met one.

"Why's she crying? What did you do to her?" The woman reached long fingers down to Rebel, who reached up and grabbed onto those fingers instantly. She shifted from Tori's side, reaching for the pristine woman with bright hazel-green eyes. Her jaw was set, however, the glare impenetrable as she turned it in Tori's direction.

Tori's skin burned as the woman's eyes ran over her from head to toe and then back up to her eyes. Had she just been checked out? Yeah, probably, but not in a sexual way. This was a dressing down, as if Tori had done something incredibly wrong by helping out a wayward toddler who had run into her.

The woman pulled her eyes away from Tori without so much as a fake smile, and spoke down to Rebel. "Let's go."

Rebel was on the woman's hip now, looking so out of place against her tailored suit. Tori's heart clenched at the sight. Was this woman really supposed to take her? Maybe it wasn't a case of this woman being Rebel's parent but a social worker? Though Tori had never seen a social worker look this made-up before. Maybe she was a foster parent? Tori snorted. That idea was ludicrous.

Before Tori could open her mouth again, the woman pivoted on her toe and took Rebel with her. She walked swiftly away, her ass swishing as she went, tight from the height of her heels as they made the same *click click click* sound they had when she'd approached.

Tori blinked as Rebel looked back over her shoulder, a small smile in place as she gave a half-wave. The turtle tears from before were completely gone, which was the only thing that eased the tension in her stomach. They did belong together, even if Rebel and the cold, icy woman didn't look like it. Tori gave a wave back, still blinking with her mouth slightly open.

What had just happened?

———

"Mommy!" The door opened with a flourish, and Harley jumped up into Tori's embrace. Tori wrapped her arms around her daughter's waist and squeezed her close and tight, taking a deep breath of the scent that could soothe her in an instant. It was the smell of home.

"Hey, Pumpkin." She let Harley wriggle out of her arms and back to the ground, then planted a kiss on a sticky cheek. "Go get your things ready."

Harley raced back into the house.

"And wash your face!" Tori called before Harley disappeared into her room. She was still off-kilter from the grocery store incident, but at least with Harley, she'd find her balance again. It would only take a bit of time to forget *that* woman.

"Hey, Tor. Do you have time for coffee?" the familiar voice echoed from the direction of the kitchen.

Tori smiled. There were worse things in this world than remaining close friends with her ex, the mother of her child. They had managed to find a nice balance after their divorce. It hadn't taken them all that long either.

"Oh, yes! You know how I can't resist coffee." Tori closed the front door and made her way through to the kitchen, stepping over abandoned toys and pieces of scribbled-on paper. It was much the same in her apartment when Harley ran rampant there.

"Hey." Siena smiled, warm and comforting with her proper greeting.

"Hey yourself." Tori took the offered mug with a grateful smile and kissed Siena's cheek. She'd never stopped doing that, even after being separated for years.

Siena eyed Tori over the mug, no doubt seeing everything Tori was trying to hide. "Where's the poop, Tor?"

"What do you mean?" Tori's heart skipped a beat. Was she really that obvious? She hated that Siena could still do that to her some days.

"Do you really think I don't know when you're flustered?" Siena laughed wryly as she slid onto a chair at the table.

Tori stuttered.

Siena prompted her again. "So?"

Huffing out a breath, Tori prepared to explain. She only hoped she would understand it herself by the end. The same indignation surged through her again, but full force this time now that she had someone to listen to her. "I just met *the* rudest woman I have ever seen in my life."

Siena sipped her coffee carefully, eyebrows raised, attention completely on Tori.

"Well, when I say met, what I mean is her child ran full-on into me, fell over, and then *she* stomped up like Ms. Miranda Priestly and all that. She had the audacity to accuse *me* of hurting her kid before snagging the kiddo from my arms, turning on her heels, and leaving before I could even answer the question in the first place."

Siena laughed and put the mug down gently on the table. "So she was hot, huh?"

Tori spluttered, doing a terrible job at hiding the blush that warmed her neck and cheeks. Why did Siena have to be so good at this?

"Oh yeah, she was hot. Was she dressed to the nines, too? You always do like a woman who takes care of herself. Those high-maintenance women." Siena chuckled.

"I hate you." Tori laughed as she pointed a finger at her ex-wife.

"No, you don't."

"For that I do."

"Whatever." Siena stretched her back.

Harley ran into the room, skidding to a halt with a bag attached to her side. It was the one bag that traveled with her from house to apartment. It held her most precious items— blanket and stuffie. Harley couldn't sleep without them, and both Tori and Siena had made late-night calls when they'd been forgotten.

"I've got to ask." Siena leaned in, lowering her voice. "Were you trying to meet the hot mom in the grocery store?"

"I'm not *that* desperate." Tori rolled her eyes, her cheeks burning again.

"But you are still determined to find your *soulmate* by your thirtieth birthday, right?"

Tori sighed. She regretted telling Siena that in a drunken stupor one night. Siena had teased her over the last two years for it, but a girl had to have hope, right? "I know it might seem crazy, but it really isn't. I just want to fall in love."

"I know." Siena smiled and reached across the table to squeeze Tori's hand, ruffling any upset she had caused. "You'll find her. I'm just sorry I wasn't the one."

"I'm not." Tori grinned broadly. "I found my best friend."

Harley crawled into Tori's lap with a giggle, putting her hands around the coffee mug, pretending to drink it.

"And we wouldn't have this tornado if we hadn't!" Tori dug her fingers into Harley's sides to tickle her.

"True, very true." Siena stood up, kissed Harley on top of her head, and took the now-empty cups to the sink.

"Can we go now, Mommy?"

"Sure can, Pumpkin."

"I'm not a pumpkin! I'm Batman!"

"Fair enough, though I really think you're my little Harley Quinn." Tori tousled Harley's hair, remembering Rebel's wild locks and how Tori had instinctively wanted to do the same to her. Sure, the woman had been hot, *super hot*. But why had the interaction remained lodged inside of her even after debriefing with Siena?

"Mommy?" Harley's hands cupped Tori's cheeks, her eyes staring intently.

"Yeah, sorry." Tori laughed and stood up. "Let's get going."

"Don't forget about Ms. Miranda Priestly!" Siena teased. "I bet you will have lots of wild dreams about her tonight."

"Oh, shut up." But Tori's cheeks were back to burning. "You go dream about her."

"Nah, I'm much more into Andy before she turns all fancy."

"You would be." Tori shook her head. "You'll pick Harley up Friday, right?"

"Yeah. See you then, baby." Siena opened her arms so Harley could run into them. "You be good for Mommy."

"Always." Harley giggled and ran toward the car.

Siena gently pulled Tori's arm to stop her. "It'll happen, Tori. But maybe you need to let it happen naturally instead of trying to force it, you know? Wanting something so badly can blind you to reality, and I want you to find someone perfect for you."

Tori cocked her head and looked at Siena. There was something Siena wasn't saying, something that pulled the air between them tight with tension.

"Thanks. And I know. I've just got to let myself go with the flow."

"You're the only one who put that deadline on yourself, you know."

"I know. And I guess it's just getting to me more as the time looms." Tori rolled her eyes to make her point and to ease Siena's obvious worry.

"You've got almost a whole year. Don't waste it worrying about finding the elusive true love. Promise?"

"I promise." The lie easily fell from her lips.

two

"You can't leave me with this kid much longer." Miranda Hart closed her eyes as soon as she was safely in her car with the Bluetooth on and Rebel strapped into her seat after a brief battle to get her arms through the straps. Rebel had escaped from her three times while in the store. It had been a disaster, and Miranda had left with the bare essentials she had needed, not what she'd initially gone in to get.

"Relax." Tierney's voice was calm and bubbly like it always was, but it grated on Miranda's nerves. She always sounded like she was talking to a baby. She'd never grown up. "I'll be home soon."

"When is soon?" Miranda wanted an answer. The call that evening to pick Rebel up from daycare had been unexpected, and she'd had to leave work early just to get to the daycare on time—which she hadn't quite managed. It had been a mess. But everything with Tierney was.

"I don't know." Tierney giggled. "He's picking me up at the airport in an hour."

"Picking you up?" Miranda shook her head wildly. "Where are you?"

"Dallas!"

"What?" Miranda clenched her fist tightly, her nails digging into her palm. "You didn't tell me you were leaving the state when you called. You said you had a date."

"I do have a date! He's picking me up in an hour."

"In a different state! Halfway across the country!" Miranda knew she was reaching screech levels, but did she really have another option? What mother would leave their two-year-old to go on a date with a man she'd never met halfway across the country? It was irresponsible. Though Tierney had never been responsible.

"But he could be the love of my life."

"You said that about Mike—Mark—Nick?" She could never keep up with them.

Rebel screamed from the backseat, letting Miranda know just how pleased she was with being strapped into the car seat. At least she had one of them in the car since Tierney had far too often not been reachable to pick up Rebel after hours.

"Nick." Tierney corrected. "And he wasn't the one. But Jason might be."

"Oh god." Miranda pinched the bridge of her nose. "You have to come home, Tierney."

"I'm going on my date."

Miranda groaned. "I'm not Rebel's mother. I can't be her mother. She needs you, not me. I have a job I work long and weird hours at. I can't possibly play parent to a toddler who runs wild through stores."

"What?" Tierney laughed, and Miranda could clearly hear the PA system in the airport through the phone. "What happened?"

"She ran away in the grocery store."

"Didn't you put her in the cart? Strap her in?"

"She screamed at me."

"She's two, Miranda! You can pick her up and put her wherever you want!"

Maybe you can. Miranda clenched her jaw tightly. How was she supposed to explain to her entitled, flakey sister that she didn't want to do that? That no matter how many times she picked Rebel up, Rebel tried to escape and pull away because Miranda wasn't Rebel's mother. Nor did she want to be. Parenting was something she never had a desire to do.

"I need you to come home."

"I can't do that."

Growling, Miranda shoved the gear shift harder than necessary and put the car into reverse. She really shouldn't be driving when she was so ticked off, but she had to get home and feed the monster in the back seat. That was the problem, right? They were both hangry. Well, Rebel might be. Miranda was just pissed.

"You can't abandon your child!" Miranda stepped a little too hard on the gas, jerking out of the parking spot. She gasped when she saw the front of a cart and came to a sharp stop. Blowing out a breath, she eased her way out of the spot this time. "She's yours. You deal with her."

"But this is real this time. I promise you," Tierney pleaded.

"You haven't even met Nick...or whatever his name is."

"Jason." Tierney sounded annoyed now.

Good. She could be in the same boat Miranda was, finally. "Yeah, sure. Jason." Miranda rolled her eyes, coming to the edge of the parking lot and waiting for a bright red SUV to go past her.

She jerked her chin up when she eyed who was in the car—the pretty brunette from the store. The one who had caught Rebel on her last escape. Miranda swore the glare could be seen through the windows, the deep glare and disappointment of being a shit parent. Well, she wasn't the parent. She wasn't even supposed to be in charge of a toddler—ever. She hadn't wanted that. She'd done enough when trying to raise her kid sister growing up because her parents had all but washed their hands of her.

And what a great job you did of that.

No, it wasn't her fault. It was her parents'.

"Miranda!"

Wrinkling her nose, Miranda blinked and came back to herself. She didn't deserve to be made a spectacle of. It wasn't her fault that Rebel didn't understand how to behave. It was Tierney's and her parents.

"When are you going to be done with your *date*?" She hated using the word, but it was possibly the only way to get information out of Tierney.

"Oh, I don't know. Two or three days, maybe? I think we're going to take a drive to Mexico."

"From Dallas?" The screech was back. She couldn't help it. Tierney had a way of pushing every single one of her buttons.

"Yeah! We haven't really talked specifically about what we're doing on our date."

Because it's not a date. It's a goddamned kidnapping. Miranda bit her tongue. She'd taken that tactic with Tierney before and hadn't gotten anywhere. The girl was as headstrong as she was oblivious. "Please let me know as soon as you do. I need to rearrange my schedule at work to watch *your* child." She put as much vehemence into her tone as possible, but she knew it would blow right over Tierney's head.

"Oh, I will! But how is my baby?" Again, Tierney's voice grated.

Miranda groaned. "Can't you hear her screaming?"

"Sounds like she's happy! Are you giving her McDonald's?"

Happy? Did Tierney even know her own kid? And thanks for the nod to the fast-food joint. Though she supposed one night wouldn't hurt, and since she hadn't managed to get much bought at the store, it would have to do for now. Miranda took a left instead of a right, heading to the nearest McDonald's that she knew of. They could eat it when they got home.

Home—to a place she didn't even have a crib for this kid. Did two-year-olds even sleep in cribs? Miranda cringed. She didn't know enough about this to do it well, and she hated that. She was always the one her family left holding everything together, wasn't she? "T?"

"Yeah?"

Miranda gripped the gear shifter like her life depended on it. "Since it seems like Rebel is going to be with me for a few days, do you mind at least telling me where she sleeps?"

"Oh, she sleeps with me. We bed-share."

Fuck. Miranda hadn't wanted that to be the answer, but she'd suspected it would be. Tierney didn't exactly have a house or apartment. She flitted from boy to boy in search of her soulmate, meaning Rebel had never actually had her own bed. The last thing Miranda wanted was to sleep with a toddler who would kick and punch her all night.

"And she still needs her bottle before bed, too."

"Bottle?" Miranda frowned. "She's two."

"Yeah, but you know me, I can't tell her no, and if it gets her to sleep, why not?"

Why not be a parent, you mean? But Miranda didn't say it out loud. She couldn't bring herself to get the answer because she wasn't going to like it. Tierney would no doubt get pissed off and hang up on her before she got the rest of the information she needed to care for a child that again—wasn't hers. She was going to have to let go of that grudge though, at least while Rebel was in her custody. She didn't want the kid to bear the brunt of her mother's mistakes.

"Right." Miranda didn't have a bottle. She would have to make do with whatever she could scrounge up because like hell would she go back into that store with Rebel. "What time does the daycare open? I know what time it closes." *Now.* She hadn't

known that until they called her the first time to tell her
Tierney was late and they couldn't reach her, or their parents,
and would be charging an astronomical fee of fifty dollars plus
one dollar for every minute she was late. The tardiness had
ended up costing her a hundred and fifty dollars, which
Tierney conveniently ignored when Miranda had dropped
Rebel off to where Tierney had been staying.

"Oh, I think they open at six."

"Good." That would at least ease Miranda's schedule a bit,
assuming Tierney was telling the truth, or had any idea of the
daycare's operating hours. She'd have to check online when she
got home to confirm the details. She didn't trust her sister to
remember anything useful.

"I've got to go. Jason's here!" Tierney squealed. "Wish me
luck."

"Good luck?" Miranda said as a question, but Tierney had
already ended the call. Letting out a sigh, Miranda gripped her
steering wheel. It was going to be a long, hellish night, that was
for sure.

Once they had the fast food and were home, Miranda
unloaded Rebel first. She had her on her hip before staring at the
car. How was she supposed to get everything inside with a kid that
would no doubt run when given the freedom? She pursed her lips
and narrowed her eyes at the bags of stuff she'd had to buy. She
had no food for a kid in her house. She had no diapers. Nothing.

Resigning herself to many trips back and forth, Miranda
gripped two of the bags after popping a French fry into Rebel's
hand.

"Seems like we're stuck with each other a bit longer," she
muttered to Rebel as she walked toward the house.

For only being two, Rebel was heavy. Miranda was used to
lifting bodies and moving them from one place to another, but
carrying around a twenty-pound kid on her hip was something

else. It took her five trips going back and forth and the entire container of French fries from the kid's meal to get everything inside.

She sat Rebel at the kitchen table with the rest of the food in front of her while she put away the groceries. She didn't even have clothes for Rebel for the morning. Miranda closed her eyes, leaning against the kitchen counter, nearly in tears. What had gone so wrong with her sister? Well, she knew the answer to that question but still hated it.

No one had raised Tierney. Just like no one was raising Rebel. Why did the kid think it was okay to run around a grocery store like a lunatic? Because no one had taught her that it wasn't okay. But that wasn't Miranda's job either. She was an auntie and that was it. She didn't want to be anything more than that.

Rebel screamed. Miranda jerked her head up, finding the milk spilled all over the tabletop and then dripping onto the floor. She clenched her teeth hard. It wasn't Rebel's fault. None of this was. She just had to keep reminding herself of that. Rebel was the victim here.

Grabbing paper towels, Miranda walked over to clean up the mess. She said nothing to Rebel as she did it, letting her cry and throw the fit. It wasn't until she rinsed her hands off in the sink that Rebel came over and wrapped her arms around her leg in a hug that Miranda stooped down and pulled her up into her arms again.

"What are we going to do? Hmm?"

Rebel leaned back, eyeing Miranda as if she held all the answers to the questions Miranda didn't dare ask. She couldn't ask them.

"Are you tired? I know I am."

Rebel gave her a blank stare. Miranda hadn't even heard her utter a single word so far. She should be saying something by age two, right? Reaching up, Miranda brushed her finger over Rebel's chunky cheek.

"Well, at least she's been feeding you even if she hasn't been teaching you." She sighed again. What was she supposed to do with a toddler? She had two funerals tomorrow, and three people out sick, which meant she had to work both of them and didn't have backup to call in. Her parents were out of the question. They were the ones who had made this mess in the first place. Miranda had seen the effects of generational trauma and abuse for years. This might not have been physical or mental abuse, but it certainly was emotional neglect.

"I guess we better find some clothes for you somewhere."

With weary feet, Miranda helped Rebel to finish her Happy Meal and then packed her back up into the car. They had to face the store again, only this time a different one. Hopefully it wouldn't be as bad as the last one. Because once again, everything in her family fell onto her shoulders, and she was the one who had to pick up the pieces. If only she could break the cycle of bad parenting. Maybe with Rebel she could —at least for the next three days.

three

"Aili, Aili, Aili!" Harley sang as though nothing else in the world would ever make her as happy as that moment.

Tori grinned as she stepped into the director's office at the daycare. She hadn't seen Aili in weeks, and she honestly missed her ex-girlfriend. Well, friend. They had broken up right after Tori's twentieth birthday, but it had been worth it. She'd started dating Siena a month later and landed herself the beautiful girl who was now sitting in Aili's lap, giving her favorite auntie a huge hug.

"Mommy! Aili's back!" Harley bounced with excitement and hugged Aili again.

"Hey," Tori stated, a sweet smile to her lips. "Glad to be back?"

"You know it. I missed this place." Aili flushed, her cheeks rosy.

Tori didn't miss that sly look and blush. "Did you meet someone on your trip?"

Aili shook her head. "More who I took with me. We'll talk later." She whispered the last part and covered Harley's ears.

Now Tori was intrigued, but she knew they couldn't talk

about certain things while in the center. She gave Aili a pointed look. "I expect a call tonight."

"Promises!" Aili giggled and turned her thousand-watt smile on Tori. "What have you been up to?"

The brunette in the grocery store flashed through her mind, the kid with the mop of curls clinging to her leg after falling and tears building in her eyes. Tori shook the thought. She needed to brush off the negativity she still carried around with her from *that* woman. She couldn't remember the last time something had stayed with her this long. Then again, that woman had been drop dead gorgeous.

"Things have been good. Business is booming lately. Something must be in the water because I've had more coaching clients contact me in the last two weeks than in the last two months. Everyone wants an emergency session with their favorite life coach." Truthfully, it did give her a boost of confidence every time she got that call, but she didn't have enough hours in the day to serve everyone.

Tiny thumping feet thundered through the hall. Frowning, Tori twisted around toward the door, her shoulders tense. She stepped toward the doorway and scooped up a small body with a familiar mop of tangled hair covering half her head and half her face.

"Rebel?" Confusion filled her.

At least this time Rebel hadn't run face-first into her. Tori popped Rebel on her hip as though she had done this every day of the young child's life. She tickled her stomach, eliciting a loud burst of laughter as Rebel tried to grab Tori's hand to make her stop. When Tori pulled away, Rebel bopped her on the nose with her chubby hand. Tori burst out in a laugh, uncontrolled and natural.

"You remember me!" She honestly hadn't expected that. They'd barely spent two minutes together in the grocery store aisle while she'd tried to find... Tori stopped short. Rebel's mother. The Miranda Priestly act-alike, though she certainly didn't look like her. At least in complexion. She'd certainly held the same air and tension and command in her shoulders. Strong. Sexy. Willful. Perfection wrapped up tightly in one smooth body with perfect curves. Tori gulped.

"Mommy." Harley pulled on Tori's pants near her other hip. Tori looked down and smiled at her daughter, though she was still struggling with the fact that *that* woman had to be nearby. "How do you know Rebel?"

"We met at the store the other day." Tori didn't need to look up to know that Aili's attention was glued to them. Tori held Rebel tightly, knowing she was a flight risk.

"Can I play with her?" Harley sounded so sweet when she asked.

Before Tori could say anything else, *her* bellow from the hallway cut Tori off. "Rebel!"

Oh that voice! It had featured in her thoughts far too many times. Maybe a dream or two in the last week as well. Because why the hell not? Tori could dream. Her panties were already wet just thinking about that voice.

"Where are you? Rebel!"

Tori stepped out into the hall, making immediate eye contact with *her*. With the Miranda Priestly act-alike. She shuddered, Rebel curling into her side on her hip. Tori instinctively put her nose into Rebel's tangled mess of hair as she eyed this woman over.

The woman stopped mid-step. Tori fought to hold back a smile as a soundtrack of screeching brakes played in her mind. This time it was her chance to catch *that* woman off guard. She held back her chuckle and straightened her back, keeping Rebel on her hip.

"Perfect," the woman muttered loud enough for Tori to hear her. She stalked forward, her steps quick and precise, but Tori missed the *click click click* of her heels since the floors were carpeted. *That* woman reached out when she was close enough, and Rebel all but jumped out of Tori's arms to fall into the strong hands that caught her. Tori admired that. Squaring her shoulders, Tori debated how to handle this, which way to approach the storm in front of her.

"I'm Tori, by the way." A pleasant introduction rarely hurt. "We never got to exchange names the other week."

The woman hesitated with a quick up and down look at Tori. Okay, this time it didn't hold the exact burning gaze as last time. Still it was far from checking Tori out in any way she might appreciate. "Miranda."

Blood rushed from Tori's face. *Bullshit!* She swiveled her head quickly around, searching for the cameras that must be recording this, because *holy shit* this woman's name could not actually be Miranda. She'd misheard, right?

"This is Rebel," Miranda continued in crisp words, almost as tight as the suit she wore today.

Once again, Miranda's outfit was dark, and the cut hugged her as firmly as the previous one, but this one gave Tori a better view of that generous bust that remained hidden beneath. So did the way she held Rebel, who conveniently shoved a hand down the front of the suit jacket as if she owned Miranda's breasts.

Fuck.

Miranda?

Really?

"Oh, me and Rebel go way back." Tori smiled, but her voice wavered unexpectedly. It was rare she was caught this off-guard. She forced her eyes and thoughts away from Miranda and her choice of clothing. Tori's cheeks warmed with embarrassment. She had one more chance to get a hold of herself. Tori winked at the child who giggled. "Don't we, sweetie?"

"I need to get to work." Miranda sent Tori a pointed look and turned on her toes. She stalked away from the office, her perfectly highlighted hair flicking over her shoulder as she went.

Tori leaned to the side, following the line that Miranda walked. The way her hips moved in that tight pantsuit, creating the perfect view of the curve of her ass. The dull clicking of her heels against the short carpet and all the power that came with it. The strength in her squared shoulders and perfection she probably strove for. She leaned a little more as Miranda turned toward the toddler room so she wouldn't lose sight.

"Uh-oh," Aili said, pulling Tori's attention away sharply.

Tori snapped her head up to see what the problem was, only to find Aili smiling and looking at her.

"Uh-oh?" Tori asked, confused.

"Oh yes," Aili swiveled in her chair as she nodded. "Definitely *uh-oh*."

"Do I get more than just uh-oh?" Tori let Harley's hand go as she pulled out of the grip and sat down in front of the papers and crayons that permanently stayed in the corner of Aili's office.

"You, love, have got it bad."

"What bad?"

"Don't be an idiot." Aili laughed lightly, her gaze flicking to Harley. She covered the side of her mouth so Harley couldn't see and pointed toward the toddler room. She mouthed the words *She's hot!* to Tori before laughing.

Tori's cheeks burned.

Aili devolved into a fit of giggles. "Oh my god. Add this to our conversation for tonight, will you?"

"I think I'll be skipping that phone call," Tori mumbled, now embarrassed. Not only had Siena called her out on it after a two-second retelling of the grocery store incident, but now Aili was calling her out on it.

"Oh, fat chance of that happening. I'll be calling now."

"Caller ID is a thing for a reason." Tori put her fists on her hips, determined to make her point. She did *not* want to discuss Miranda.

"Right!" Aili was still laughing lightly as she sobered. "But you did look good with another one on your hip."

"Oh, now we're talking about that?" Tori snorted and shook her head.

"Oh come on, you have always wanted more, and Harley would be an amazing big sister."

"Am I getting a baby sister?" Harley looked up, the joy covering her face.

So much for being subtle. Aili failed on that front, and she should know better. Also, why did all conversations lately have to go down this line? First her parents had mentioned it, and Siena had even hinted at it a few times. Tori couldn't get away from the fact that she was twenty-nine and hadn't found her soulmate yet.

"No, honey." Tori cringed as Harley pouted. She turned to Aili with a mock glare. "Thanks for that."

Aili gave an unrepentant shrug. "I've got a friend I can set you up with. You still have your before-thirty goal, don't you?"

"You and Siena!" Tori pointed at her. Her exes really were out to get her hooked up with someone. "But yes, I do still have that goal."

"Let me set you up, then."

"Uh. No. Do you remember the last time you set me up?" Tori did. Distinctly. And it wasn't something she wanted to ever repeat.

Aili pursed her lips, frowned, and then made a sour face. "You're right. That was a bad match. This one will be better."

"Uh...no thank you."

"You can't dream about Miranda forever."

"Aili!" Tori made a movement with her hand across her neck, telling her to silently cut the crap. The last thing she needed was Harley figuring out what they were talking about and then bringing it up for the next ten years. "Fine. I'll answer the call tonight."

"Thank you!"

"Harley, let's get you to class. You can bug Aunt Aili later, okay?"

"Yeah! Bye Aili!" Harley ran up to give her a hug.

"I'll see you later, kiddo. I think they are doing some dancing down in your room today."

"Come on, Mommy." Harley pulled Tori out of the door with more strength than Tori had ever thought a four-year-old could possess. Still, she missed those days when her baby had been a baby, with chubby hands to kiss and when she could prop her on her hip and carry her around. Maybe someday she would have another baby, but not any time soon, and certainly not with the cold Miranda.

Fuck, was that really her name?

———

"Oh shit. Not again, no." Miranda's voice was nearly panicked.

Tori got out of her car quickly. Miranda stood in the middle of the parking lot, her jaw tight and her eyes narrowed. "What's wrong?"

Fierce eyes like daggers pinned Tori with a look.

"Of course *you* would show up."

Taken aback, Tori put her hands up in the air. What had she done to deserve that? It must be something else bugging her, and Tori was the scapegoat. "What do you mean?"

Miranda scoffed. "How am I supposed to control a child who has never been told no in her life?"

"You mean Rebel?"

"Of course, I mean Rebel." Miranda ran a hand through her hair, creating a mussed look that Tori couldn't deny stirred her in a way it shouldn't. Not with the stupid quip Miranda had already made about her. "She's gone again. All I did was put her bag in the trunk. I turned around, and she was gone."

"It's okay." Tori met Miranda's eyes and nodded, trying to keep her calm since Miranda looked like she was about to go into a full-blown panic. "I'll help you find her."

"The road. What if she's gone out onto the road?" Miranda started walking toward the street, void of cars and kids.

"I don't think she's in the road. Let's check the obvious places first." A deep desire to ease Miranda's upset filled her. She'd question it later. For now, she had a kid to find.

They walked around, intermittently calling out Rebel's name. Tori walked faster than Miranda, who was still dressed like she worked on Wall Street or something. Maybe she did work in the government. Who knew? It wasn't like Miranda seemed to be into sharing information.

"I see her." Tori took a deep breath and let it out with a smile.

They had circled the entire building, and from Tori's position, she could see Harley holding hands with Rebel through the window of Harley's classroom. Harley encouraged Rebel to dance along to music Tori couldn't hear.

Miranda stepped closer, the scent of her perfume light but distinct, and it had an odd disinfectant undertone to it. Tori rubbed her finger under her nose as Miranda stepped away, the warmth of her body brushing teasingly against Tori's shoulder.

"How did she get back inside?" Miranda clenched her fists, walking swiftly toward the front door to the center.

"Looks like you may have your hands full with a mini Houdini." Tori tried to lighten the mood as she followed.

"Great, that's what I need." Miranda's voice was colder

than the afternoon. But at least it hadn't started pelting rain yet.

Tori didn't bother to reply as they punched in the code to get into the building. Forcing herself to take three deep breaths, Tori relaxed her shoulders and rolled her neck before following Miranda inside. She could understand being upset when losing a child. Harley had vanished a couple times on her, and it was the scariest thing on the planet.

Miranda pushed into the classroom and knelt down, her arms out. Rebel squealed and ran right for her. It was adorable. Tori had doubted Miranda's connection to Rebel before, plenty of times before, but this was a different interaction, more akin to that morning at drop-off. Tori didn't even try to hide her smile.

Harley came running toward her, wrapping her arms around Tori's waist in a furious hug. "Mommy!"

"Hey, Pumpkin." She bent and brushed a kiss into Harley's hair.

Miranda straightened up, Rebel firmly in her arms. The tension that had been in her cheeks and neck before was gone. She must have been more stressed than Tori had realized. Their gazes locked. Tori hadn't realized just how honeyed the browns in her eyes were until that moment. Miranda looked amazingly strong and steady.

Miranda came closer, and Tori couldn't rip her gaze away, not even with Harley tugging at her hand. Miranda stopped in front of her, crowding Tori into the doorway as they both stood in it. Tori's heart fluttered, her lips parted. What was she supposed to say?

"Thank you." Miranda's voice was calm, firm, sure. Maybe even a little vulnerable under the precision of each syllable.

Before she could reply, Miranda was already walking away. Tori still couldn't tear her gaze from her. She was completely enthralled. Holy crap, Aili was right. She *did* have a crush on Miranda.

"Mommy," Harley's voice interrupted Tori's thoughts.

"Yeah, Pumpkin?" She cleared her throat, finding herself again.

"Can I *please* have a little sister? I promise I'll be good. I really want one."

Tori smiled down at her. She had never wanted to have only one child, and that thought still made her heart ache.

"I'm working on it, sweetie. I'm working on it." But no way would that happen with Miranda. Nope. She was pretty to look at but so not relationship material.

four

"You ready for this?" Miranda stared at Rebel, still locked in her car seat.

Rebel giggled, her entire face lighting up.

"Glad you are. I'm not." Frowning, she reached in and pulled at the clips on the car seat. Tierney was supposed to be back over a week ago. Rebel had now been living with Miranda for two full weeks, and neither of them had slept well during that time, but they had found a rhythm. Mostly. Miranda had successfully gotten six full hours of sleep the night before, which was the only reason she thought she could handle this conversation with her parents.

Life wore on her.

With Rebel in her arms, she walked up to the house and knocked. Her mother, Sandra, opened the door, her brown eyes widening as she saw Rebel. "Oh, baby!"

Sandra opened her arms and took Rebel from Miranda. With the weight gone, she felt odd. When had she gotten used to that? Well, she shouldn't. Tierney would be home any day now and Rebel would be back in her hands. This was only temporary.

The house was pristine, like it always had been since Miranda was a kid. Her mother was fastidious about keeping everything in the place it should be. When Tierney had been born, it had been her job to keep the house clean to those standards until Tierney was old enough to help. Which of course she didn't because God forbid her parents ever actually parent her.

"Emmitt! Rebel's here!" Sandra called into the house as Miranda followed.

They were supposed to eat dinner, like a normal family, but Miranda was pretty sure she'd be the one cooking and that nothing had been prepped. It was like they had given up on doing the normal things households did once Tierney had been born. Maybe even a bit before then.

"Do I need to do anything for dinner?" Miranda asked as she stepped into the kitchen, finding nothing ready. Her mother didn't even answer.

She groaned.

She found her mom sitting on the couch in the living room with Rebel wriggling in her lap and her dad in the recliner, scotch in his glass and a book in his hands. He always was the quiet one. "Do you mind if we just order something in?"

She was too exhausted to cook. Parenting wasn't something that came naturally to her, and it wasn't anything she had ever wanted. Not after seeing the way her parents had handled it. They were the perfect example of a couple who just gave up, especially with surprise kid number two.

"Sure!" Sandra bubbled, baby talking to Rebel two seconds later.

Miranda hated it. It was probably why the kid didn't talk to begin with. She'd had time that week to sit down and talk with Aili, the director at the daycare center, about Rebel and some of her behaviors and lack of milestones. She wasn't quite two, but she was fast approaching her birthday and she should at least be saying some words. Her instincts on that had been correct. Sighing, Miranda moved into the kitchen to place an order from her parents' favorite restaurant.

When she sat down, she was ready for the day to end. But of course, she still had her almost two-year-old niece to look after. And with the problems she'd had that week, she wasn't even sure where to begin.

"Have you thought more about having your own?" Her mom asked.

Miranda frowned, her lips pressing into a thin line. "My own what?"

"Kids." Sandra's brown eyes, an exact match for Miranda's, locked on hers.

"Uh…no." Miranda clenched her jaw. She did not want children, and she'd been firm on that since she was sixteen and started to raise her sister because they refused to. The first three years, Miranda had been Tierney's primary caregiver, and when she'd gone to school to become a mortician, her parents had flipped. Not having that backup had been the end of their world. But Tierney had basically been in school by then, and they were as hands off as possible since.

"You should settle down, find someone, and have a family."

Because that worked so well for you. Miranda pinched the bridge of her nose. Her mom started on this line of conversation any time Rebel or Tierney showed up, as if the only value Miranda had was her ability to have a family. She hated that. She was worth the same as anyone who wanted a family.

Tori had a family. Maybe she already had a big one. Miranda was aware of the one girl who was hers, but she could be the youngest of a crew.

Crossing her arms, Miranda leaned back in the chair as Rebel crawled up into her father's lap, settling in to look at the book for a second before climbing back down. Tori was young, perky, and cute in every sense of the words. She was adorable really, and always had a smile on her face. Even when they'd thought Rebel might have gotten out into the road, Tori had smiled and kept her calm.

She seemed like the quintessential parent. Low key, down to earth, ready to get dirty with whatever idea her kid threw her way. And her daughter was adorable. The spitting image of her mother with those big sky blue eyes and shock of dark brown hair. Did she have more kids? There had only been one seat in her car when they'd met in the parking lot, but Tori seemed like someone who would want more than just one kid. A parent to her core.

Miranda jerked with a start when Rebel screamed. She cringed and stood up to scoop Rebel into her arms and comfort her, checking for whatever injury she had endured. "What happened, baby?"

Rebel screamed louder, tears falling down her cheeks.

"Did you hit your head?"

Running her fingers over Rebel's head, she searched for any kind of bump or redness. She didn't find anything. Instead, Miranda settled for holding Rebel against her side and cradling her until she was calm.

"Get her some ice, honey," her father called from his chair, back to reading his book.

Miranda walked into the kitchen to pull out a small ice pack. She handed it over to Rebel, who promptly threw it onto the ground. If she knew where Rebel had hurt herself, then she could show her how to use it. There was so much she didn't know about her, so much about Rebel that had been left out.

Her phone rang. Miranda frowned as she reached for it, seeing it was the hospital calling. She was on call. She had managed to switch everything around so she wasn't on call the first week she had Rebel, but it had been too long and she'd had to take a few nights. The phone call was quick, but she had no choice.

"Dad?" Miranda stepped back into the kitchen. "That was the hospital."

"Oh?" He barely glanced up from his book.

She glanced at her mother. "I have to go pick up a body. Do you think…" She wasn't even sure she wanted to ask them this question. But who else would she ask? The daycare was closed, and she didn't really have any friends she could call on such short notice, not someone who would be able to watch Rebel. And she didn't feel right asking someone else to do it. "Do you think you could watch Rebel while I go? It shouldn't take me more than an hour."

"Unless you get another call." Her mother's snide response slid in there. That had been why she'd asked her father instead. "You'll never find someone to marry if you're working all these crazy hours. Who wants to marry a mortician anyway?"

Miranda swallowed the retort. They'd been through this before, and despite telling Sandra that wasn't what she wanted, they never heard her. It wasn't ever about love either. It was about ticking off the boxes on the list they didn't think she was fulfilling. "Can you watch her?"

"I suppose that'll be fine." Sandra sighed heavily, clearly put out by the request.

"Thanks, Mom." Miranda slid Rebel into her mother's lap and left the house. She was going to miss dinner, but it was a small price to pay to help take care of someone's loved one.

———

It was close to midnight when Miranda finally got back to her parents. She was dead on her feet. Her mother had been right. One body had turned into three, and she'd started the process with them to ease up the workload on her morning crew. They had a busy week with services and an influx of bodies.

The lights were still on when she knocked on the door. She

had hoped, somewhere on the drive back, that her parents would have put Rebel to bed and she could get another six hours of blessed sleep. But the screams coming from the other side of the door told her otherwise.

"You could have called."

"I did call, Mom." Miranda pushed her way into the house, following the sounds of Rebel's cries to the living room.

The place was a disaster. Clothes were strewn everywhere. Books, magazines, the few toys that had been in the diaper bag.

"What happened?"

"We had a night." Sandra brushed her hand through her hair.

"Where's Dad?"

"Asleep. Where else?" She put her hands on her hips.

Miranda scooped Rebel up and bounced her lightly on her hip, trying to calm her down, but she knew from experience in the last two weeks that nothing was going to calm Rebel down this late at night. She was overtired, exhausted, and probably overstimulated.

"I'll take it from here." She wanted to cry. She couldn't leave Rebel with anyone, could she? It was hard enough at daycare, but somehow Rebel managed to sneak around that building too. She got in trouble routinely because she couldn't behave and listen.

Miranda started to pick up the living room with Rebel in her arms. She could barely look her mother in the eye. This had been a disaster. She had to figure out something better, but it wasn't like she could bring Rebel with her to pick up dead bodies. How did single parents do it? She wasn't a parent. She was single, but she wasn't a parent. Tori would probably have the entire situation under control.

When Miranda looked up, her mother was gone. No doubt off to bed like when Tierney was a kid. Plopping down onto the couch, Miranda held Rebel against her and rubbed a hand up and down her back. Why had they been decent parents with her and awful with Tierney? They weren't the greatest with her, but they'd been strict with expectations. Then sixteen years later Tierney had come along and it was like they had forgotten everything. And the same with Rebel.

She buried her face in Rebel's knotted hair. They really were going to have to work those out soon. Miranda pulled over the diaper bag, finding it empty and all the diapers and wipes used. Because of course her parents wouldn't know how to change a diaper in an efficient way. Frustrated, she put Rebel down and let her scream her loudest wail. She cleaned up as swiftly as possible, putting everything back.

It took a total of two minutes before she grabbed Rebel and left. Getting Rebel into the car seat was a battle in and of itself, but she won. She pulled out of the driveway and just drove. She wasn't ready to go home—not yet. And the car ride calmed Rebel into a quiet coo.

She couldn't leave Rebel with them again. That much was clear. They couldn't handle it. Well, they could. They'd done it with her growing up. But they were choosing not to, which was worse. What was she going to do? Every text, call, email that she'd sent Tierney had been ignored. She hadn't heard anything since her new *boyfriend* had picked her up at the airport. For all Miranda knew, Tierney was dead in a ditch in Mexico and no one would ever find her.

She could never do that to her family. Her sensibilities wouldn't allow it, but beyond that, she'd seen it happen time and time again. The druggie who was found stabbed in the street trying to get her next hit. The prostitute who was raped before being strangled. The woman who fell in love with the wrong guy.

"Please, Tierney, don't be her."

Tears ran down Miranda's face when she pulled up to her house. She wiped the tears from her cheeks. She would find

Tierney in the morning, or at least start working on that process. She wouldn't let her sister become another victim, and she wouldn't let Rebel be one either. She didn't want the family, the kids, but she would do it for her niece. Because who else would if not her?

five

"Hey Aili." Tori stopped in Aili's office doorway, hands on the frame either side of her, leaning a little forward on her toes.

"Hey, what's up?" Aili turned from her computer and smiled up at Tori.

"I have two huge bags of clothes that Harley has already grown out of and wondered if you knew who might appreciate some hand-me-downs? I can bring them to Goodwill, but I'd rather give them to someone who can use them."

"What are you feeding that girl?" Aili smirked playfully.

"Oh blood of virgins and goat sacrifices. You know the usual." Tori winked.

Aili let out a bark of laughter. "Excellent. So what were you asking?"

"If you know any of the parents of kids smaller than Harley who might appreciate some hand-me-downs?"

"Well." The smile on Aili's face dimmed a little. "You aren't going to like this suggestion, but I do think Miranda would benefit from having some extra clothes for Rebel. She doesn't have many."

Tori clenched her jaw tightly. What kind of parent didn't

have clothes for their child? Especially one who could manage to look like that every day. "I don't think—"

"She's had to come down with clothes more than once because of accidents. The situation isn't exactly ideal, and if it's one less thing she has to worry about, then I think that'll benefit Rebel."

"Ulterior motive?" Tori lifted her eyebrows until the top of her forehead pulled almost painfully. Aili did have a way to get her every time, and hitting her with the kid card was the way to go. Her chest tightened, and her curiosity piqued. What situation was Aili talking about? Did she assume Tori already knew?

"Absolutely none," Aili said, though Tori could have almost sworn the corners of her mouth twitched up a little. "I think she would be the best candidate for Harley's old clothes, especially if you have any winter ones since we're headed straight for the cold months. But if you're too chicken shit to offer them, then that's your loss."

Tori knew exactly what her friend was doing. She also knew she would never back down from a challenge, and Aili had deftly handed her one. Especially one she would have encouraged any of her clients to take up and push past their fear. Sometimes she hated when she had to take her own sage advice.

But was it fear? She wasn't afraid of Miranda.

Sure, the woman was intimidating and cold, and rude, and entirely gorgeous. But what was there to fear? It wasn't like she had a chance with a woman like that, even if she had wanted to. Which she didn't. Absolutely not. Even if the mere idea of combining her and Rebel into her small family made the corner of her own lips twitch up. But it was never going to happen. Gorgeous did not mean compatible.

"You're thinking about her again, aren't you?"

"About who?" Tori's cheeks burned.

Aili caught Tori's eyes with that knowing look.

"Fine, yes, I was thinking about her." She hated this. A crush was a crush, and she should just accept it. Then she should move on. Pretty things were nice to look at, and Miranda came with a whole personality that had rubbed Tori wrong since the moment they'd met. And again, why wouldn't she just buy Rebel clothes? She obviously could afford it.

"Excellent," Aili said, turning once again to her computer screen, that sneaky grin on her face. It infuriated Tori. For someone so obsessed with work, how did Aili know exactly what Tori was thinking about in relation to entirely unprofessional things?

"Right, I'll just bring the bags in."

"You should ask her first." Aili pinned Tori with a look. "That way if she doesn't want them, they're not just sitting in my office for years until I yell at you to get them out."

Tori sighed heavily. "Fine. Challenge accepted."

"Challenge accepted?" Aili looked amused.

"Yes. I'll talk to the icy beauty queen and ask if she needs help. Though I'm betting this will be a disaster."

"But a fun one to watch!" Aili pointed at the camera feed and the car pulling into the parking lot.

"I don't like you some days."

"You keep saying that, but I don't believe you! Now, get! I have work to do."

"Fine. Fine." Tori stepped out into the hall, her stomach a mess of knots. "I'll ask her."

"You do that." Aili's voice was far too singsong for Tori's liking. The *it's a trap!* refrain echoed through her mind.

She was completely distracted by how to approach Miranda. Until she stepped out into the parking lot. And saw Miranda. Or more accurately, she saw Miranda's shapely ass sticking out of the back seat of her car as she leaned inside. She even gave a small wiggle. Tori bit her lip, but the small groan escaped anyway. Thankfully she was far enough away that Miranda didn't hear her—she hoped. And far enough away from the cameras that she knew Aili was fastidiously watching.

Letting her smile settle on her face, Tori pushed her shoulders back and walked toward the car. She could do this. She could ask a question, offer a gift, and get out unscathed by that icy stare.

As she got there, Miranda's top half appeared from the car, a wriggling and giggling Rebel in her arms.

"You're such a wriggle monkey." Miranda chuckled as her fingers tickled Rebel's side while she popped Rebel on her hip.

Tori watched, the image playing far too easily into her previous unchecked thoughts. Rebel saw her and waved erratically. The movement made Miranda turn, and for a moment, she stared at Tori, honeyed eyes meeting Tori's in an intense stare. She would never get over that look.

Rebel wriggled again, and Miranda pulled her eyes from Tori. The spell broke, but Tori still couldn't manage to find her words again. Where had they gone? She was back to watching Rebel dig her chubby hands right into the V of Miranda's shirt, no doubt looking for boob milk. Harley did the same thing for years after she was weaned.

What the hell was wrong with her? She had to get over this crush on a woman who clearly wanted nothing to do with her.

Tori nodded. She could do this. She had attractive clients and had spoken to women just as gorgeous as Miranda. Not lately, but that was hardly the point. The point was, it was a fantastic day. A rare sunshine moment, and she wouldn't hesitate to take every opportunity to smile.

So she smiled and moved toward Miranda, who struggled to open the trunk of her car with the wriggling Rebel in her arms.

"Can I get that for you?" Tori asked as she drew closer.

"Oh. Yes. That would be appreciated." Miranda spoke

crisply and directly, but the sunshine kept any ice from landing on Tori.

"Great." She clapped her hands lightly together twice and then opened her arms. Rebel giggled and leaned toward the offered hands, giving Miranda no choice but to let her go to Tori.

"Hey, sweetie." Tori hugged Rebel to her chest. Wild hair brushed her nose, and the sweet scent of baby shampoo wafted from her. Relief washed over. She was sure Miranda was doing her best. The way Aili had mentioned her need for the clothes and some mysterious situation that Tori had no idea how to interpret tickled at the back of her mind.

Rebel pulled away and pressed her chubby hand on Tori's nose. Tori replied in kind with the familiar gesture.

"Down," Rebel said.

Miranda spun around, her eyes wide as she stared at Rebel and Tori. Tori frowned at her, trying to read what was under the intensity. The silence crackled between them.

It happened in a flash. Miranda softened, the lines of her face weren't as pinched, and the smile that had been there when she'd pulled Rebel out of her seat was back, but this time it went deeper, as though a weight had lifted off her shoulders.

This was the Miranda that Tori had longed to find in all their interactions, the woman underneath the armor she so effortlessly wore. Tori held onto Rebel tightly, completely entranced with the way Miranda looked right now. Perfect. Flawless. All herself.

"Down," Rebel repeated with a giggle.

Tori shook out of her reverie and rubbed a hand up and down Rebel's back before glancing back at Miranda. What had just happened?

"Down!" Rebel said louder this time.

"Okay, sweetie, down it is. But you need to stay with… um…your mom?" Tori knew as soon as the word slipped from her mouth that it was wrong. She could see small similarities between them, but the mom thing just didn't sit right. It never really had, though Tori hadn't been able to put her finger on why.

"I'm her aunt," Miranda corrected.

"Oh." Tori smiled wider, validation of her instincts boosting her serotonin even more on what was already a good day.

"Rebel, stay here please," Miranda said, her tone firm but still gentle in a way Tori hadn't heard from her before.

Rebel looked up at Miranda, laughed, and then raced away at lightning speed.

"Rebel!" Miranda called, but Rebel simply ran off laughing, chubby legs moving faster as the slap of shoes hit the concrete. "Shit."

Tori scanned her gaze over Miranda's pencil skirt, high heels with black toes and red heels, red blouse, and black blazer. No way was she going to catch Rebel before she vanished. Not in those shoes.

"It's okay," Tori said, already taking off after Rebel. "I've got her."

Tori's tennis shoes crunched on the asphalt as she picked up her speed. Thank God she'd gone to the gym that week. Rebel was faster than Tori remembered Harley being. No wonder Miranda struggled to keep up with her. She finally caught up on the other side of the parking lot, coming in hot.

Tori scooped Rebel up and swung her from one hip to the other to make it a fun game instead of a scary moment. She laughed as she once again plopped Rebel on her hip. She tickled her stomach. "See if I let you trick me into letting you down again!"

Her heart beat rapidly, and her breath came out in warm puffs. When she looked up, she gasped at Miranda's dark stare.

With as much joy as she could muster, Tori met Miranda in the middle of the parking lot.

"Wow, I've forgotten how fast they can be."

"She definitely is."

Tori handed Rebel over into Miranda's waiting arms. Her nerves caught up with her again, and the word *chickenshit* echoed in her ears. "Um…I have some clothes that Harley has outgrown. Aili mentioned you might be able to use them."

"What?" Miranda snapped, and the joy that had hovered around Tori all morning dimmed.

"They're all washed and in good condition. She's outgrown most of them before she had a chance to destroy them. Kids grow so fast at this age." Why was she rambling? This was a disaster.

"You think I can't provide for my niece?" Miranda hardened. Every inch of progress they had made in the last few minutes completely vanished.

"No, it's not that. It's—"

"You have no idea. You think you can come in and point out all the things I'm not doing right?" Miranda's voice was tight, the pitch high and tense.

"No." Tori put her hands up, trying to go back to wherever she had mis-stepped.

"I don't need your help." Miranda stepped past Tori and headed into the daycare. She didn't touch Tori, but the movement felt as though she had shoved Tori aside.

Tori watched in silence and shock. That had taken a way worse turn than she had anticipated. She was rooted to the spot in the parking lot, unable to move. Torn between checking out the sway of Miranda's hips and the utter disgust that seemed to radiate from the set of Miranda's shoulders, Tori was flabbergasted.

What the hell had she been thinking? What had Aili been thinking? Even entertaining the idea of friendship with *that* woman was ridiculous, let alone the fantasies of anything beyond that. She had to stop living in a fantasy world and remember who Miranda was. Cold-hearted. Impenetrable. Not interested.

Miranda might have been pretty to look at, but she was not what Tori needed. Tori needed to focus on her before-thirty goal, and there was no way she would spend a lifetime with a woman who was so fragile that Tori would need to step around broken glass to be in a relationship with her.

Thankfully, Tori's phone rang, pulling her eyes and her thoughts away from Miranda. She pulled the phone from her pocket and looked at the display. An unknown number. One more deep cleansing breath before she answered.

"Hello, you're speaking with Tori Frazee."

The voice on the other end was familiar beneath the sobs and hysteria.

So much for a nice morning.

At least Tori had something else to focus on, even if it was the death of Nadine's grandma.

"I'm so sorry. I'm on my way."

See? Now Nadine knew how to ask for help. Miranda? Nope. She couldn't even take it when offered. Tori couldn't be with a woman like that. Miranda would drive her crazy with her neuroses. Still, Tori was running short on time to find her soulmate before she turned thirty. She only had nine more months.

six

No way. No fucking way.

Tori stopped short right in the entryway to the funeral home. Nadine had invited her, which was odd, but with Tori's job, it wasn't abnormal either. But she had never expected to walk in and see this. Her heart was in her throat, and even though she knew she should be looking for Nadine, she couldn't stop looking at Miranda.

She had on a tight gray dress that flared with an edge at her hips so it looked more like a skirt and jacket. A black belt was tight across her waist, showing off her beautiful figure. Her long hair was plaited over her shoulder, and her makeup was on point today. Tori stuttered. She had not pegged Miranda for working at a funeral home, but it did make sense why she was dressed so nicely all the time.

What was she supposed to do?

Because turning tail and walking out wasn't an option. Nadine needed her, and Tori wouldn't let her go through this without strong support. Squaring her shoulders, Tori put on her professional face. She had to remember she was there for a job—mostly. Nadine was a friend too, but this is literally what she was paid to do with many life-coach clients.

Tori stepped up in the line, waiting for Miranda to hand her a program. It took a second, but her honeyed eyes registered Tori's presence the moment she stepped in front of her.

"What are you doing here?" Miranda's tone was frozen and sharp.

"Uh…I'm here for Nadine."

Miranda's lips tightened into a thin line, her gaze flicking over Tori's shoulder to something behind her. "Lee Ann's granddaughter."

"Yeah," Tori breathed out. "She's a friend of mine and asked me to come."

Miranda held her hand out with the program she was giving to every person who walked in. "The family has gathered together. You may take a seat with everyone else behind the reserved spots." She held her hand out toward the chapel.

"Oh…uh…" Tori glanced toward the chapel then back at Miranda. "Nadine wanted me to sit with her, I think."

"That's reserved for immediate family only."

"I…" Tori stopped. She glanced around her, more people filing in, most friends of Lee Ann based on their age. They wouldn't know half the drama with the family that Tori did. "Can I just say hello to her?"

"No."

Tori cringed. Lowering her voice so hopefully no one else would hear, she whispered, "Look, since I'm sure you've been dealing with the family, you understand them. I'm here for Nadine and Nadine alone. This is my job."

Miranda jerked her head slightly. "And my job is to protect sacred time with the family."

"Who's your boss?" Maybe this tactic would work. Surely if Miranda was handing out pamphlets she wasn't that high up in management.

Miranda flicked her gaze again. "Hannah, do you mind taking over for a minute?"

"No problem." There was a handoff of tasks as a young woman stepped into Miranda's place.

Miranda snagged Tori's upper arm and pulled her toward the offices just off to the side. They stepped inside, and she shut the door. "I won't have you making a scene in front of the family."

"Those are friends of the family. You just told me the family was gathered already." Tori wanted Miranda to stop touching her, but her grasp was firm, her hand warm. Tori looked down at her fingers, the thinness of them, the veins on the top of her hand. Why couldn't she stop *looking* at Miranda? This was getting ridiculous.

"I won't let you be here if you're going to disturb the services."

"I'm not going to disturb them." Tori stood her ground. "I'm here to support Nadine. I'm her life coach, and she asked me to be here because of the tensions between her and her family."

Miranda snorted. "Life coach?"

"Yes." Tori again looked at Miranda's thin fingers on her.

"This is insane."

"It is, because you're refusing to let me do my job." Tori slowed herself down. She couldn't let Miranda get under skin. "Can I talk to the funeral director?"

"You are talking to her."

Perfect. Tori's stomach swam with nerves. "Look, please just let me do my job. My goal is to help prevent drama today. I think we can both agree that's a reasonable and needed goal."

Miranda rubbed her lips together, as if she were mulling it over. Tori's hope ratcheted up a notch with each passing second. Finally, Miranda let go of her arm and stepped back. "Fine."

"Fine?" Tori raised an eyebrow. Had she really won that easily?

"I don't have time to argue with you today. We're short-handed, and I need to do the final viewing with the family and close the casket. You'll have to excuse me." Miranda was gone in a flash, a wake of frustration and confidence left behind her.

Tori blew out a breath, ruffling the baby hairs that haloed her face. Since one problem was out of the way, she could finally focus on Nadine. Finding her friend was easier said than done. But once Nadine had a hold of her hand, she wasn't letting go. Tori was glad she'd stood up for herself. Normally she would have backed down, and to be honest, she was surprised Miranda let her get away with it.

———

Miranda was fully in her element, and it could very well be one of the most beautiful things Tori had ever witnessed. She moved swiftly and efficiently, every sign of confidence in her actions and gait. Tori had to work hard to tear her gaze away from her.

As everything wound down and the reception started, Nadine let go of Tori's hand and gave her a moment to breathe. She flexed her fingers and took a steadying breath. She wasn't used to quite this intensity of emotions. She wasn't sure how Miranda managed it every day, but that could also explain a lot.

"I'm going to run to the bathroom. Will you be okay?" Tori whispered to Nadine, hoping for a bit of a longer break.

"Yeah. Sure."

Tori escaped down a hallway she hoped was the way to the bathroom but also the way outside. It was raining heavily, but she needed the breath of fresh, clean, crisp air. Anything to give her a moment of reprieve. Just as she was about to step outside, a sharp movement caught her attention. Miranda straightened her shoulders, dropping her gaze over the black A-line dress Tori had dug out from the back of her closet that morning.

"Not bad looking for a life coach."

"Excuse me?" Tori was instantly grinning. That sounded like a compliment, but she was almost afraid to take it that way.

"I like your dress." Miranda's eyes were locked on hers for a brief moment before dropping to her breasts and then back up. Was Miranda checking her out?

"Thank you." Tori faced her fully. "Are you relaxed now that the work is done?"

"Working in death means the work is never done."

"Same goes for life." Tori canted her head to the side, crossing her arms. This was quite easily the most relaxed she had ever seen Miranda.

"Seems once again we find ourselves at odds."

"Interesting turn of phrase." Tori had to hold back her smile this time. They were having an actual conversation! She was so elated. "Do you have a minute?"

"One, exactly." Miranda's gaze moved out the front door to the funeral home as if she was waiting on something.

"All right." Tori bolstered herself. "The other day...when I brought up Harley's old clothes...I didn't mean to offend you. Really. I was just trying to help, and it's not uncommon to get hand-me-down clothes because kids do grow out of them quickly." Her nerves got the best of her. "I'm butchering this. I really just wanted to apologize. I didn't mean to offend you."

Miranda stayed still, her gaze unwavering. Tori's heart was in her throat, clogging it up. Would her apology be accepted for what it was? Because she wasn't sure she could do that again. It had taken a lot out of her.

Eventually, Miranda's hard look turned into a brilliant

smile, her entire face transforming. She chuckled lightly. "I don't think anyone has ever apologized to me over something so benign."

"Benign?" Tori's eyes widened. "I thought you were going to take my head off."

Miranda wiped her palms on her dress. "No. We wouldn't want that, would we? Someone needs to be there for the living."

"I…" Tori was thrown off, completely. "I have no idea what to say to that."

"It doesn't require you to say anything. Sometimes there is more to say in silence than there is with words."

"Interesting line of thought." Tori leaned in again. "So what do you have to do after the service?"

"Oh." Miranda was looking back out the front door of the funeral home, distracted.

"Are you waiting for something?"

"Yes." Miranda cast a furtive look at Tori. "Rebel."

"Wait? What? Isn't she at daycare?"

"Not anymore." Miranda stepped forward and opened the door as rain pelted down.

In rushed two adults and Rebel, without a jacket, her head buried far down against the woman who carried her, and her clothes completely drenched. The woman was the spitting image of Miranda, and there was no doubt in Tori's mind that this was Rebel's grandmother.

"She tried to run away as soon as I put her down."

"You shouldn't have put her down," Miranda chastised as she reached for Rebel and ran her hands through her hair, brushing the damp strands from her face.

Tori's stomach clenched sharply. Rebel's cheeks were red, but the rest of her face was as pale as could be, ashen even.

"She should know better than to run."

"Mom, she's not even two yet." Miranda sighed heavily. "What did they say when they called?"

The man shook his jacket out, water droplets falling all over the floor and onto Miranda's foot. She didn't budge. "Fever."

"She looks pale," Miranda murmured. Rebel cuddled into her side. "I have a few more hours of work before I can leave for the day. Do you think you can take her until then?"

The woman's lips pursed in that exact way Miranda's usually did. Tori would have laughed had it been appropriate, but she'd finally gotten Miranda to smile at her, and she didn't want to ruin it by causing a scene where she wasn't wanted. She thought about leaving and heading back to Nadine, but the drama unfolding in front of her captured her attention.

"I need to finish this service." Miranda's tone was flat.

Tori shuddered at it and the chill her parents had brought into the entryway. She was pretty sure Miranda used that tone on a lot of the people who worked under her. It was the perfect *I won't take bullshit* voice. Except that rarely worked in these familial situations, especially when it was the child saying it to the parent. And sure enough, Tori's assumption was correct.

"I have an appointment to get my hair done."

"Your perm will be ruined in the rain. Reschedule it." Desperation edged its way into Miranda's voice.

Tori was about to step in, but Miranda's mom beat her to the punch. "I can't do that. It's a standing appointment."

"What do you expect me to do with a toddler in a funeral home? A sick toddler at that."

"She's not that sick." Her father stepped in, his face set. "She's been running a slight fever all week and you managed just fine."

Tori hated watching this. It was a train wreck happening in slow motion, and she couldn't do anything to stop it.

"Not today, Dad. We're already shorthanded. I told you that when you called."

"We can't watch her." Her mom threw her hands up in the air. "You're responsible for her. You deal with it."

They were out the door before anyone could say anything else. Tori's heart hammered as she stood with a stoically quiet Miranda, holding onto the obviously sick Rebel. Tori pressed her lips together tightly, looking the situation over in a new way. She could use this to make another connection with Miranda, maybe show her that she wasn't as alone as her parents had just made her feel.

"Well, that leaves you in quite a pickle, doesn't it?" Tori said, cringing at her own choice of words. Why did she keep messing this up?

Miranda said nothing, her jaw so tight that the muscles bulged at the sides of her face. Tori looked back toward the hum of voices filtering out of the room where the wake was being held. Nadine would be expecting her back any moment, and she had to be on her toes again, didn't she? Nadine had eased up on her need for Tori over the last hour or so, which had given her the chance to take a break. Maybe she didn't need Tori as much as she thought.

"Does she have the bug that's been going around?" Tori asked, running her fingers over Rebel's back to try and comfort her.

"I don't know." Miranda tilted her chin down awkwardly, looking into Rebel's face as best as she could. "They said she had a temp of ninety-nine."

Tori snorted. "I hate that they do that. It was awful with Harley that first eighteen months she was there. She was sent home so many times, and I had to cancel so many appointments."

"Her father couldn't take off?"

Tori raised an eyebrow at Miranda. "Harley's other mother

has a job with a crap boss who won't let her off work often, and my work schedule is more flexible than hers."

Miranda's gaze locked on Tori's. What just happened? Tori couldn't look away, falling into those honey-brown eyes with each passing second. Did Miranda not know she was a lesbian? It could entirely be possible because she'd been so wrapped up in herself, but Tori didn't hide who she was.

"Because you can schedule clients when you want."

"Yes, and at the time when Harley was really little, my business was just getting off the ground, so my hours weren't as filled as they are now."

Miranda hummed and pressed her nose into Rebel's hair. She was just about to speak when Hannah interrupted her.

"Ms. Hart, we need to prepare for the graveside this afternoon."

"Right." Miranda's shoulders tightened, her grip on Rebel firm. She looked wildly around, absolutely lost as to what to do.

Tori could read that look from a mile away. "You know what?"

Miranda jerked toward Tori.

Taking another risk, Tori held her hands out for Rebel. "My day was cleared for this, and Nadine is doing well enough at the moment. Let me take her."

seven

"What?" Shock ricocheted through Miranda's chest. She didn't want to put Rebel down. She'd never seen her this lethargic before, and even though it had been three and a half weeks of living together, she hadn't seen her this quiet. It worried her.

"Let me watch Rebel for you." Tori's hands were open, as if expecting Miranda to give in and just hand Rebel over.

"No."

"Please. It's the least I can do, and I know you have to work. No one can raise a child in a vacuum, and you're doing your part. Let me help a little. I have the time."

Miranda's stomach was in knots. She had so much work to do. She'd been falling behind more and more each day despite staying up late to work after Rebel fell asleep against her. She hadn't been expecting to be thrown full force into parenting. Hannah stepped in closer. They had a whole second service that afternoon, which would include going out to the cemetery in the pelting rain to do the graveside. She would be busy for hours, and she'd lied to her parents in hopes they'd agree and she could put off the inevitable frustration from them.

"I'm going to be busy the rest of the day," Miranda murmured.

"It's fine." Tori gave her a quick smile, something she always seemed to do. "I took the whole day off. I really don't mind. We can hang out in your office."

It wasn't ideal. But Miranda wouldn't be in her office for most of the day either since they were so short staffed. She'd be out in the cold. How could she do this without making Tori stay? She hated to ask her for help, not just because she was prideful but because she could do this on her own, couldn't she?

"Miranda." Tori stepped in closer, a hand on her wrist.

Miranda shivered at the touch. When was the last time anyone had touched her like this? Her heart skittered, especially knowing that Tori wasn't straight, knowing that those long looks she'd caught Tori giving her might not have always been judgmental ones.

"Let me help you. Just today. I can take her home if you want, too, but I get the sense you'll be more comfortable if I keep her here."

"Yes," Miranda squeaked out.

"Yes, I can watch her? Or yes, you'll be more comfortable if I stay here?" Tori still hadn't moved her hand. She rubbed her thumb along Miranda's wrist. It was a gentle, slight move, probably meant to comfort, and damn did it work.

"Yes. My office." Miranda turned to Hannah. "Give me a minute."

She walked straight into the main offices, past the front reception area and toward the back where her office was secluded. She kept Rebel against her chest, holding her tight. The need to put her down was strong, but the desire to keep cuddling her was stronger. With Tori inside the office with her, Miranda could let down one or two of the shields she kept up in front of her employees.

"I'll try to be as quick as I can."

"If she's only got a slight fever, we'll be fine. I know they have to send home for these kinds of things, but I really wish they wouldn't. The kiddos aren't sick."

"But she seems sick." Miranda ran her fingers through Rebel's mop of hair. She was asleep. She furrowed her brow. "She's sleeping."

Tori smiled. "It is about naptime at daycare, and she's probably into the routine."

"She doesn't nap at home."

"Really?" Tori stepped in closer, running her fingers over Rebel's back. "Here. I know this is hard, Miranda, but if you're going to allow me the honor of watching this sweet bean, then I need you to give her to me."

"I…" Miranda paused. "Anyone in this office knows how to get hold of me and where I'll be."

"We'll be fine." Tori's smile was placating, but Miranda was comforted by it. "I promise."

She hesitated again but eventually shifted. Tori pulled Rebel into her arms, cradling her in the same way Miranda had been doing. She brushed a kiss into Rebel's hair and took a step away. Miranda moved swiftly, putting her hand on Rebel's back and planting another kiss to the back of her head.

"I'll give you my number if you need anything."

"Okay."

Leaning over her desk, Miranda wrote her cell phone number on the back of her business card and handed it to Tori. Her stomach was still full of knots, but she knew her team needed her. There wasn't another option. Tori sat down in one of the chairs usually reserved for employees. Miranda had rarely seen families in here in the last couple years.

"Is there a diaper bag somewhere?"

Miranda paled. Cold washed through her. "I might have one in my car."

"That's all I need, then. We'll be right here when you get back."

Tori's beautiful smile was captivating. Miranda hadn't felt quite this at ease ever since Tierney had dumped Rebel with her. Tori was beautiful—young—but gorgeous in her own right. Her baby blue eyes were big and bold against her shock of dark hair. The black of her dress played up those contrasting colors.

Miranda said nothing as she left the office and hightailed it out to her car. She didn't find a diaper bag, but she did find diapers and wipes shoved into the pocket on the back of the passenger seat. She'd learned in the first week that she needed an emergency stash of those two items everywhere she went. She handed the items to Hannah and had her bring them in because she feared if she walked back into her office, she would never leave it. Tori was right. She couldn't do this in a vacuum.

———

Miranda's feet ached, and a chill had entered her bones that she hadn't managed to get rid of. The rain hadn't let up until they were leaving the cemetery well after the family had gone. It was nearing dinner time, and she knew she would have to get some food into Rebel soon. She'd gotten to the funeral home just after lunch.

Miranda went straight to her office, wanting to relieve Tori of Rebel before she started in on cleaning everything up and making sure they were set for tomorrow. She, luckily, wasn't working tomorrow, which would give her the chance to stay home with Rebel since she couldn't go back to daycare.

When she entered her office, Tori was sitting cross-legged on the floor, Rebel in her lap, as they read a children's book that she had pulled out of thin air. Miranda stopped short. This was what a family looked like. Not her running around trying to work and sending Rebel off with sitters, but actually sitting down and taking the time to spend together. She was awful at this.

She cleared her throat, trying to get that unnecessary shame out of her system. "How did everything go?"

"Perfect." Tori grinned up at her from the floor, not moving. "But I should be asking you that."

"Another service done."

Rebel squealed, jumping off Tori's lap and running over to Miranda, clinging to her legs.

"Hey, baby." Miranda combed her fingers through Rebel's hair, which seemed slightly less tangled than before. She bent down, picking Rebel up and putting her on her hip. "You're looking much better."

"She is," Tori agreed, pulling herself to a standing position. She bent down to grab the book and a few other toys Miranda hadn't noticed before. Not that she noticed them now because Tori bending over gave her a perfect view of her cleavage, the gentle swell and curve of her breasts, the creamy skin that had a smattering of freckles that disappeared under her dress. When Tori stood back up, her cheeks were flushed a gentle pink and their gazes locked. "Like what you see?"

Miranda swallowed the lump in her throat instantly, catching herself. "Thank you for doing this. You didn't have to, and I appreciate it."

"I see your sidestep, but I'll accept it." Tori grinned, her eyes glittering with amusement. "I really didn't mind. We had fun. We worked on the alphabet and numbers. She told me her diaper was wet."

"She what?" Miranda frowned, the stomach punch landing hard.

"She said her diaper was wet, so I changed her."

Miranda sighed. Why did Rebel's first few words have to be with Tori? Why couldn't they be with her? She sat in one of the chairs Tori had been in when she had left. Rebel wiggled, so she let her down after checking that the office door was shut.

"Rebel is behind in her speech. Aili was worried about it because since she came to the daycare, she's not said a single word." Miranda hated admitting that, but to hear that Rebel said two words in the last two weeks was huge, and she had no one else to share it with.

"Aili generally has a really good sense of those things." Tori slowly slid into the chair across from Miranda. "Did she suggest speech intervention?"

"Yes, but I don't..." Miranda clenched her jaw tightly. "I'm not Rebel's legal guardian. I can't take her to the doctor for a referral."

"Ah." Tori crossed her legs, smiling when Rebel came over for a hug. "Did Aili suggest anything to do at home?"

"Talk to her. Constantly." Miranda let out a wry chuckle. "Which I'm sure you can tell from the few times we've met isn't my norm."

Tori grinned broadly, shaking her head. "No, I can't see you rambling into the silence. But she is picking words up, so that's a good thing."

"I suppose." The tension in Miranda's shoulders eased slightly. "Her mother went on a trip. She was supposed to be back already, but extended it."

"Extended it?" Tori looked dubious.

Miranda flicked her shoe slightly so the heel came off. It relieved the pressure and ache in her foot. "Yes. I don't know when she'll be back."

"She can sign a form and the hospital will accept it, and any doctor associated with them, so that you can take Rebel in to be seen. It's really simple. Siena did that with her mom in case one of us couldn't be there to take Harley to appointments. She had a lot of ear infections when she was a baby."

"That's not a bad idea." Miranda would have to try and

get hold of Tierney, which was harder than she'd expected lately, and see if she could get something like that. Then she could properly take her to the doctor. Then again, she still held out hope that Tierney would be home soon. Because she hated being the only responsible adult in her family.

"Rebel is such a sweet kid, you know." Tori smiled at Rebel as she found the pile of toys and started to play with them. "She's full of energy and spice. I love seeing that."

"That's one way to put it." Miranda sighed heavily. "But I do need her to listen and not run into the street or run away from me every chance she gets."

"But she does love you. When she sees you, she comes running. That's what's important. She comes back to you."

Miranda's mouth went dry. Did Rebel really see her as that? She was so concerned about everything else going on that she hadn't even noticed that.

"I still have those clothes if you want them. I really didn't mean to offend you before."

Guilt racked her. She always did come off as a bit of a bitch when she first met people. It served her well over the years, but she could see why Tori would be concerned about it. "It's been overwhelming with Rebel."

"I can only imagine," Tori answered. "You've been doing amazing."

"I could...use the clothes. I don't have many for her, and I haven't had time to get more than a few necessities. Tierney—"

"Tierney?" Tori interrupted.

"My sister."

"Your parents named one kid Miranda and one Tierney?" Tori's brows drew together in confusion.

"Tierney was a surprise. I was sixteen when she was born, and Rebel was a surprise for her."

"So how old is she now?"

Miranda locked her gaze onto Tori's eyes, trying to figure out exactly why she was asking. "She turned twenty-nine at the end of August."

Tori's eyes widened, the shock evident.

"Are you surprised my kid sister is twenty-nine or that I'm forty-five?" She had a bite in her tone, but she wasn't going to apologize for it.

"Both? Honestly. For the record, you don't look forty-five, but also, I'm twenty-nine, and I can't imagine ever leaving Harley with my sister for a quick trip and not coming back."

"Well, that's Tierney for you. This isn't the first time she's done it, but it is the longest." Miranda's mind churned. She would have pegged Tori for being older. She acted older, mature, as if she had her life together and knew what she was doing. Which she probably did, but she was still so very young. Suddenly, guilt ate away at her. Miranda had checked her out! She'd actually looked her over with sexual interest. Miranda had been in high school when Tori was born. It was disgusting that she would even consider it, wasn't it?

"I really can't imagine doing that, not to mention the weight that puts on you."

Miranda knocked her chin up, centering herself. "She's always been allowed to do whatever she wants. Ever since she was born. If you don't mind, though, I do need to get ready for our services tomorrow."

"Do you need someone to watch Rebel tomorrow?"

"No." Miranda stiffened. "I can do it."

"Okay, just know if you do need an extra hand, I'm more than willing to help out."

"You have your own life to live." Miranda lifted herself up. "Where did the toys come from?"

"Oh, my car." Tori shrugged. "I always keep extra things in there in case we get stuck places."

It wasn't a bad idea. Miranda would have to add a few of

those to her vehicle the next chance she got, along with a proper backup diaper bag in there. Her to-do list was growing longer by the second.

"Let me know when you want those clothes. I can talk to my ex and see if she has any she wants to get rid of."

"Your ex?" Miranda's stomach tightened again. She'd thought Tori was safe to check out, that she was in a happy relationship with Harley's other mother, that there wouldn't be anything beyond simple looks. But ex?

"Yeah. Siena and I have been divorced a couple years now. Amicable." Tori grinned. "We parent really well together, but relationship? Not so much."

Miranda had no idea what to say to that. Tori was so open with everything in her life. Miranda was not. It had taken everything out of her to share what little she had that evening, and it had probably been the stress and exhaustion that had pushed her to do it.

"I'll text you my number. Just let me know when a good time would be to drop off the clothes."

"Oh. Okay." Miranda pulled herself from her thoughts.

"Maybe when that stinker—" Tori pointed at Rebel "—feels better."

"Yes." Miranda's throat was tight. What had she been thinking?

"Thanks for letting me watch her today." Tori was back to her bubbly self, the tension from the conversation earlier completely gone. How did she manage to do that?

"Thank you." Miranda nearly choked on the words, but it wasn't because she didn't mean them. It was the look Tori was giving her, open and appraising.

"Any time." Tori's grin flashed bigger. When she walked by, she touched Miranda's arm lightly and then bent down for Rebel to run to her and give her a hug. She dropped kisses into Rebel's matted hair before putting her down. Again, when she stood, Miranda got a wonderful view of her cleavage.

She inwardly groaned and closed her eyes. She *had* to stop doing that. They'd done well for today, but that was it. She'd get the clothes and move on. At least she'd have some back up if Tierney ever pulled something like this again. Tori walked out of the office, taking the warmth with her as she left.

eight

Miranda rapped her knuckles against the door four times in quick succession. She didn't really want to be there, but she needed the clothes, and Tori had been so sweet the other week. Rebel fidgeted on her hip, but she held on tight. She'd hoped that Tierney would be back by then, but she wasn't, and with the eviction finalized, everything in Tierney's apartment was a loss. There was nothing left of Rebel's.

"Hey!" Tori's bright smile was a refreshing change from the moods she normally dealt with. Death wasn't for the light-hearted and happy.

"Hi." Miranda mustered as much of a smile as she could, though she was sure it didn't reach her eyes. It never did.

"Hi Rebel!" Tori leaned forward and tickled her fingers into Rebel's belly. Rebel giggled and grabbed her hands.

Miranda couldn't prevent her smile at that. She was just about to speak when she noticed Tori's daughter pop her head around the curve of Tori's hip, peeking out to see what was going on. Tori instinctively reached behind her and cupped the back of Harley's—that was her name, right?—head.

"Can I show Rebel my room?" Harley asked, her voice

gentle and high pitched. Her words were precisely spoken, the consonants clear but still very childish.

"Oh. Um…" Miranda looked to Tori to try and find an answer. She hadn't expected to stay longer than necessary to get the items and leave.

"Harley's been talking about showing Rebel her room all day. If you don't mind, they can play and maybe we can go through some of the clothes so you're only taking what you want."

Miranda clenched her jaw, looking Tori over. She had no aversion to staying, no hesitation at the offer. She nodded sharply. Harley jumped up and down, clapping her hands. Tori stepped back and widened the door to the small apartment so they could all go inside. Miranda didn't dare put Rebel down on the freshly vacuumed carpet until the front door was shut and locked.

Harley grabbed Rebel's hand and led her away, Rebel willingly following. Harley chatted at her as they went, and Miranda had to resist the urge to follow and make sure everything would be fine. With Rebel being her responsibility now, she had to worry about those kinds of things.

"They'll be fine," Tori murmured next to Miranda's ear. "Harley was playing with some old Barbie dolls that her gram brought over. Siena's mom. They were Siena's toys from when she was a kid."

"You're awfully close with your ex."

"We co-parent, so yeah, we have to communicate a lot. I don't ever want Harley to feel like she has to choose between us." Tori walked around Miranda in the small entryway and sighed. "I have three bags of clothes and two bags of toys. I thought you might be able to use those too."

"Right." Miranda slid her sweaty palms over her tan pants. This was going to take much longer than she'd first anticipated.

"Want some wine while we sort?" Tori looked adorable, with the longing in her eyes.

Miranda wouldn't give in to it. She had enough on her plate with Rebel, and Tierney pulling another vanishing act. She didn't need to add any type of sexual relationship to it. But a glass of wine wouldn't hurt. "Sure, I'm not on call tonight."

"On call?" Tori called as she headed toward the small kitchen. "Red or white?"

"Red." Miranda sighed, still staring at the trash bags in the middle of the clean living room. She was willing to bet that Tori had massively cleaned knowing that she was coming over today. "I'm on call three nights a week to pick up bodies."

The wine cork popped. Miranda lifted her head to see Tori's reaction. Most people found it disturbing that she worked with dead people. Not everyone, but it had been a turnoff early on in many of her friendships and romantic relationships. Which had been in part why she hadn't tried lately.

"Makes sense I guess. Not everyone can die during business hours."

"No, unfortunately." Miranda squared her shoulders.

"I get late night calls too, sometimes, when people freak out over something." Tori came around the kitchen peninsula and handed over a glass of wine. "Though probably not as often as you do, and I get to charge twice my normal rate for it."

Miranda chuckled lightly. "That would be a benefit."

"Some days." Tori winked before plopping down onto the couch. "So I did sort them into sizes, or at least what size they kind of shrunk to in the wash. What's Rebel wearing?"

"3T for now."

Tori raised her eyebrows. "Then this bag is useless." She kicked one out of the way. "I'll see if Aili knows of anyone else or take it down to donation." Tori sat cross-legged on the floor, putting her wine glass on the side table. She started to open one of the bags.

Miranda didn't quite know where to sit or what to do. The apartment was clean, but it also had toys here and there. There was definitely a young child who lived here. It was nice to see. Her house didn't look anything like that except for one spot in the living room with the couple of toys she had for Rebel to play with at home. She was just about to sit down when Rebel came screeching out of the bedroom and down the hallway, running straight toward her. She was laughing.

Miranda managed to scoop her up with one hand and not spill her wine with the other, popping Rebel on her hip. Rebel laughed boisterously and buried her face in Miranda's shoulder before wiggling to be put down and running heavy-footed back to the bedroom.

"See? She's fine." Tori smiled up at her.

Miranda was still unconvinced that she shouldn't check on them, but she slid to the floor and followed Tori's lead. She sipped her wine, happy with the flavor, before setting it next to Tori's. "I don't know how long I'll have Rebel, so I'm not sure I should take too many clothes."

"Can Rebel's mom use them when she comes back?"

Pursing her lips, Miranda frowned. Probably. Everything they'd had was in the landfill by this point and Tierney would have to start from scratch again. "She might."

"Then feel free to take them all, or I can keep some of them here if that's easier."

Tori was so accommodating, with everything. What could have possibly made her that way? That never would have happened in her family. "I practically raised her, you know."

"Rebel?"

Miranda shook her head. "Tierney. I was sixteen when she was born, and she was an oops, massively. My parents were one and done. They liked their life, and when she was born, they wanted nothing to do with parenting, so I did it."

"I can't imagine how hard that was on you." Tori folded a small shirt, her gaze locking on Miranda's.

That was unexpected. People usually told her she was strong when she mentioned it—if she did at all—not that it was hard.

"I bet that killed whatever was left of your childhood."

"Not much there to begin with." Miranda pulled over some pants, checking the size before folding them again and putting them in a pile. "Tierney is convinced soulmates are a thing."

Tori stopped in her folding. "And I assume based on your tone that you aren't."

"Hardly." Miranda shifted her legs around to sit more comfortably. "But Tierney is trying to find her soulmate in the worst possible way. Even if she was only attempting to find a partner and second parent for Rebel, she could do it using her brain."

"That's harsh."

Miranda pinned Tori with a look. "It's really not when it's the truth. She flew to Texas to meet a man she's never met before, didn't vet, nothing. They drove to Mexico, where she has no cellphone coverage because she didn't pay for an international plan because she hasn't worked in months. So getting hold of her is dependent on him allowing her to use his phone."

Tori hissed.

"Exactly." Miranda reached for her wine and took a big sip. Why was she even talking about this? Tori was paid to listen to people, surely she didn't want to listen to Miranda complain on her day off. "Meanwhile, I'm left here, with Rebel. To pick up the pieces again."

Tori leaned against the foot of the couch, one leg curled under the other, and her wine glass in her hand. Her baby blue eyes were locked on Miranda, a curious question in her gaze.

"What? Too harsh?" Miranda clenched her jaw, ready for battle.

"No." Tori took a sip of her wine. "Sounds adequate."

Validated. It was the first time Miranda ever felt validated. "Is this your life coaching technique?"

Tori chuckled lightly and touched her foot into Miranda's thigh. "This is a friend technique, and I get the sense you could use one."

She could. Friends were always welcome. Miranda had a few friends from when she'd gone to school, people she'd kept in contact with when she'd moved home to take over the funeral home and run it the way she wanted to.

Rebel and Harley came out from the bedroom. Harley curled up against her mother's side, the spitting image. Rebel continued to try to play, attempting to pull Harley back to whatever it was she wanted. Harley pulled her into a hug, her small arms wrapped around Rebel's shoulders.

This was what family was about. Miranda remembered hugging Tierney like that when she was little, when she'd fall and cry, when she'd just wanted a random hug after Miranda got home from school. She smiled.

"What brought that on?" Tori asked.

Surprised she'd been caught, Miranda debated whether or not to share. Keeping it to herself, she shook her head and finished off her wine. "Any tips on getting Rebel not to run away?"

Tori laughed. "That one's tough."

"Seems like it."

"I wouldn't let go of her hand." Tori reached forward and tickled Rebel's stomach. Giggles erupted in the living room.

"I try not to, but she still manages it."

"What do you do when you catch her? Time out? Scolding?"

"Nothing usually."

"Try a time out."

Harley wrinkled her nose. "I don't want time out!"

"No, not you, silly." Tori brushed her fingers lightly over Harley's hair. "But if you do something against the rules, then you get a time out, right?"

"Yep. Four minutes!" Harley held out her hand with four fingers on it.

"One minute for every age," Tori supplied.

Miranda frowned. "She won't stay in time out."

"Make her stay." Tori winked. "You just keep putting her back until she stays."

"That sounds like torture." Miranda twirled her wine glass in her hand as Rebel came to sit on her lap. She snuggled against Miranda's chest, and Miranda couldn't help but wrap an arm around her.

"It can be."

Miranda's stomach was in knots with the look Tori was giving her. It was a joyful one, an easy one, but also one that was filled with so much meaning and connection. She'd longed for that for years and had never found it. She guessed she did have a friend now, someone she could come to with advice on this new part of her life. At least for as long as Rebel was with her. When Rebel went home with Tierney, their friendship would likely end.

Sadness ripped through her, and she wasn't quite sure why. They hadn't exactly known each other long, and it wasn't like they had gotten off to a great start. That was mostly Miranda's fault. Her cheeks burned with embarrassment from that.

"I'm sorry I was such a…" What word was she supposed to use with kids around? "…I'm sorry I wasn't nice when we first met."

"You were stressed. Reasonably so." Tori leaned over and took Miranda's hand and gave it a squeeze. "But thanks for the apology."

Miranda dragged in a breath of fresh air, the tightness in her chest easing a bit. "Thank you again for the clothes and toys."

"Any time." Tori seemed to take the hint. She took the folded clothes they had sorted and put them back into the bag. They hadn't even gotten a quarter of the way through it.

Shifting to help, Miranda had to stop. She glanced down, finding Rebel passed out against her chest, her body heavy and warm from sleep. She let out a small snort and brushed her fingers through the curls on her forehead, the ones she had managed to untangle. "I'm going to have to deal with that soon."

"Deal with what?" Tori raised her gaze.

"Her hair. It's been sorely neglected, and I haven't managed to get her to sit longer than a few minutes at a time to comb through it."

Tori hummed and then got Harley's attention. "Go get your detangler from the bathroom, Pumpkin."

"Okay!" Harley got up and raced off, her feet pounding heavily on the carpet.

"I don't know if it'll help because Rebel's tangles are massive, but Harley likes it when hers gets bad."

"Thanks. I really appreciate it."

Harley came back and handed the bottle over. Miranda studied it for a minute before setting it down next to her. She had to figure out how to stand up with a sleeping Rebel in her lap, and she wasn't as young as she used to be. While she routinely did heavy lifting, it wasn't usually from a sitting position.

Tori must have caught on, because she came over and leaned down. She scooped her hands under Rebel's body, across Miranda's stomach and chest as she lifted the sleeping toddler. Miranda's heart raced, not just at the touch but at the closeness. She missed that. Getting up, she took Rebel back and rubbed a hand slowly across her back.

"I'll help you out with the bags."

"Thanks," Miranda murmured.

They walked together, Miranda carrying Rebel, and Tori carried one of the black bags. As Miranda strapped Rebel into the seat, she let out a sigh of relief. Her back ached, her heart ached, and she wanted nothing more than to go home, curl up with Rebel in bed, and fall asleep for a good long nap.

"Here's the second bag." Tori put it into the trunk of her car and shut it. She stepped back, her hands on her hips, her young body taut.

Miranda had to stop thinking those things. Tori was the same age as her kid sister, and while they were both essentially parents, a family wasn't something Miranda wanted. Not then. Not ever. She had enough problems in her life at the moment. They couldn't be friends. What in the world had she been thinking? They had nothing in common. Once Rebel went back to live with Tierney, whatever flimsy connection they had would be gone, and Miranda would never see Tori again. She swallowed down the attraction and nodded her head sharply.

"Goodbye, Tori." Even to her own ears, it sounded final.

"Let's set up a play date some time. Harley loves to play with other kids."

The offer was tempting, but again, Miranda had no idea how long Rebel would be living with her. "We'll see."

nine

"Are they here yet?" Harley's sweet voice reached her ears.

Tori couldn't help but also be excited. When she'd texted Miranda to see if she wanted a playdate for the kids, she hadn't expected to actually be taken up on that offer. But they were due at the apartment in the next ten minutes, and Harley had been asking if it was time yet for the last two hours.

"Almost, Pumpkin." Tori brushed her fingers through Harley's hair. Siena had to switch weekends, which meant Harley was still at Tori's for the second one in a row. Miranda had seemed pleasant the couple of times Tori had run into her at the daycare center that week. It had been nice, like Tori was actually making progress getting through to her.

When they arrived and Tori opened the door, her stomach clenched hard. Miranda was back in her usual garb, the beautiful royal blue dress accentuating every single one of her curves. Tori's mouth went dry as soon as she laid eyes on her, and of course, Rebel, who wiggled on her hip.

"I'm so sorry we're late. I had some things run late at work."

"Don't worry about it." Tori found herself again, smiling

as she stepped to the side to let Miranda and Rebel in. "Harley is super excited to play with you." She tickled her fingers at Rebel. "We can do a late lunch and snack if you want. I'm sure the kids are going to be hungry in the next five minutes."

"That sounds divine. I haven't eaten today."

"What?" Tori locked her eyes on Miranda's honeyed brown ones. "Why?"

"We were running late all day. It's not abnormal for me."

"We'll have to fix that." Tori shut the door, and as soon as the lock clicked in place, Miranda bent to send Rebel off with Harley. When she stood up again, arousal tightened in the pit of Tori's stomach. She hadn't expected that. She thought after the last time they'd spent some time together that it would be gone.

Harley disappeared with Rebel, calling her sweet name and taking her by the hand down the short hallway to her bedroom. Miranda looked far more relaxed this time than the last, not sending worried glances toward the girls.

"I see some of Harley's clothes are coming in handy."

"Yes, thank you. It was just in time for the colder weather to hit."

Tori pressed a smile into her lips, tight. "Were you working a service this morning?"

"We had a simple memorial for a soldier. Graveside only with military rites and only a few family present."

"I always think it's a pity that more people don't show up for those." Tori stepped into her kitchen, ready to figure out what to feed everyone.

Miranda shrugged slightly, following her. She still had on those killer heels that she usually wore. Tori glanced at them, trailing her gaze up Miranda's shapely calves to her hips, the swell of her breasts, and then her mouth. She lingered there before flushing furiously. Miranda had caught her appraisal.

"Like what you see?" Miranda didn't move, her tone huskier than Tori had ever heard it before.

Her heart skittered as her brain tried to catch up with her mouth. Tori had to say something in response to that, right? Surely Miranda would be expecting it. But the real question was if she was offended by Tori's appraisal or not, and Tori couldn't quite tell from the pitch in her voice or the tension in her shoulders if she was.

"You're a very attractive woman." Tori cringed. She was awful at this.

Miranda's cheeks took on a rosy tinge. "Likewise."

"Hardly." Tori grasped the topic and went with it. "You're stunning. I'm your run of the mill soccer mom."

Humming, Miranda stepped in closer. "And what makes you think that's not attractive?"

Was this flirting? Tori's hand shook as she grabbed the crackers from the back of the kitchen counter. Miranda was coming on strong, for sure, but what had caused the shift? "I've dated a few women since Siena and I separated, but there's always been a hiccup somewhere in there."

"What's the hiccup?"

"Me...usually." Tori frowned. She opened the package of crackers and dumped them into a small plastic, kid-proof, bowl. "I usually want to jump into a relationship with both feet, and most women don't want that when I come with a kid in tow."

"Ah." Miranda slid in closer and took the bowl toward the small kitchen table. "Then perhaps you shouldn't jump."

"The problem is that I want a relationship. I want that settled and loved feeling again. I miss it." Tori had never quite explained it to anyone like that before, even Siena. She'd always just said she wanted to find her soulmate by her thirtieth birthday, but never the why. How had Miranda managed to pull that from her in such a short period of time?

"You can find that without dating." Miranda was back, standing far too close for Tori's comfort.

It was too damn tempting to lean in closer, to see how Miranda felt about her, if she felt anything at all. "Sure, I can, but I don't want to. I don't want to raise Harley alone."

"I thought you and Siena were co-parenting."

"We are, and it's going really well." Tori sighed heavily. "I'm doing an awful job explaining this, aren't I?"

"I have a biased opinion on soulmates." Miranda wrinkled her nose, and it was the most adorable thing Tori had ever seen. "Tierney wants a soulmate, remember? And she's willing to take all the risks out there to find the right man for her."

Tori frowned. "I'm not willing to risk Harley for it."

"Good." Miranda crossed her arms, pushing her breasts tightly against the dress she wore and giving a nice view of her cleavage.

Tori had to work hard to tear her gaze from Miranda's creamy skin and the line of freckles that littered Miranda's skin, no doubt from summers spent in the sun as a kid. "Have you ever been married?"

"No." Miranda took the small bottles of water that Tori handed over for the kids to drink. She moved toward the table to set them out. "I was engaged once, but it didn't last six months before I broke it off."

"Oh?"

"He wanted a barefoot, pregnant wife. I wanted a career and independence. The two don't mesh well." Miranda stopped in front of her, their fingers brushing when Tori handed over the string cheese. "We weren't compatible."

"He wasn't your soulmate then."

"Spoiler alert." Miranda winked. "I don't believe in soulmates. The concept that there's one person on this planet meant for one other person is asinine. I've seen so many relationships work and not work doing funerals, and I can honestly say none are perfect."

"I'm not looking for perfection." Or was she? Was that part of the issue? Would she have been able to make things work out with Siena if she'd spent more time working on herself instead of pointing out the flaws?

"Soulmates are perfection, which is impossible." Miranda seemed so sure of herself. "I was young when I was engaged, stupid, you could say. I mainly wanted to escape."

"Escape what?"

"Home." Miranda winced.

Heavy footfalls pounded as the kids ran into the kitchen. Harley skittered, trying to stop from her momentum and ran straight into Miranda's hip, pushing her in her precarious heels, straight into Tori. They were smooshed against each other, Tori's hands on Miranda's hips to steady her, Miranda's hands on Tori's arms. It was almost as if they were in the beginning stages of a sensual embrace.

Tori parted her lips, ready to speak, but when she looked up into Miranda's beautiful brown eyes, she couldn't find words. Again. She wanted to lean in and taste Miranda's red lips, touch her in a way that neither of them had dared before. Miranda blinked, desire running through her gaze. Tori was just about to move in when Harley's sweet voice reached her ears.

"I'm sorry! Sorry! Sorry! Sorry!"

Miranda blinked and that flash of desire was gone. "It's okay." Miranda shifted away, bending down to Harley's level, her knees pressed together as if she was used to being in awkward positions in fine clothes, which Tori supposed she was. "I'm not hurt."

Harley leaned in, wrapping her arms around Miranda's neck in a hug. It was a customary thing for her to do after she apologized, and she probably didn't think twice about it.

Miranda, on the other hand, hesitated before she returned the hug. But she did return it.

"I'm sorry," Harley repeated.

"It's okay, baby." Miranda smiled. "You didn't hurt me."

Harley leaned in and whispered, "You're supposed to say you accept my apology."

Miranda grinned. "I accept your apology."

Harley grinned and headed for the table of snacks, undisturbed by the incident that happened a few seconds before. Miranda stood up and shook her head slowly. The girls snacked for a bit before running back to Harley's bedroom to play. It was nice not to have to be the center of Harley's attention for the full day. It gave Tori a break but also Harley a friend.

"Do you have to go back to work today?" Tori gripped the handle on the refrigerator like it was her lifeline. She couldn't fall for this woman. Nope. They had just started getting to know each other and Miranda was closed off in a way Tori didn't appreciate.

"No, I'm done for the day."

Nodding, Tori reached for the bottle of red on the counter. "Want some wine?"

"It's lunchtime." Miranda's eyes locked on hers.

"Were you planning on doing anything that would require you not to drink?" Tori knew she was pushing, and her tongue usually got loose when she drank, but there was only half the bottle left from the other week, and she didn't want to waste it.

"No." Miranda squared her shoulders. Her gaze dropped over Tori, raking down and then up. Were they back to that already? Tori wasn't sure she could handle it. "I suppose one glass wouldn't hurt."

"Good." Tori let out a breath, happy to have something to do with her hands. The intensity behind Miranda's gaze was unnerving. "Have you talked to Tierney about dating with a kid?"

"What?" Miranda froze.

Tori regretted instantly turning the conversation that way. "I...I've talked to Siena some about it, and it's not easy. That's why Harley is here this weekend, so she can have a weekend away with her newest girlfriend." She flicked her gaze to Harley to make sure she wasn't paying attention. They hadn't really talked to Harley about girlfriends yet. "I wanted to give them the space they needed to explore their relationship without kids around."

"I supposed that's what Tierney does when she abandons Rebel with me."

Tori frowned.

"It's been about a year since I properly dated someone, but I suppose it would be complicated having a child added in the mix."

"It is," Tori agreed. "Forgive me, but I'm curious."

"About what?" Miranda sipped the wine Tori had given her.

"You said you were engaged to a man. So...there's no tactful way to ask this."

Miranda had a sly smirk on her lips, but she said nothing. No doubt she wanted Tori to spin her wheels trying to figure out how to get her question across.

"You...Do you...damn it."

"Just come out and ask, Tori." Humor lit in Miranda's eyes.

"Are you going to make me ask when you already know what I'm trying to ask?"

"Of course." Miranda took another sip, her tongue peeking out on her lips as she dashed the last droplet away.

Fuck. Miranda knew exactly what she was doing, didn't she? There wasn't a question in Tori's mind at all. It was stupid curiosity that she'd wanted confirmation for, but she already had it. Miranda had to like women. No one would give *that* look if they didn't.

"Never mind. I think I have my answer." Tori turned toward the counter to futz with something, anything, to distract her from *that* look.

Miranda chuckled low and slow. She set her wine glass on the counter and leaned in. "Chickenshit."

Tori's head snapped up, the phrase echoing in her mind. The same phrase Aili had used to get her to talk to Miranda in the first place. "Excuse me?"

"You should just ask a question if you want the answer. I won't be offended."

"I've offended you several times in the short few weeks we've known each other, Miranda. I'd rather not take another risk at doing that again." Why was her voice so tight? Why did she want to lean in and really test her hypothesis? But that would likely offend Miranda, and again, Miranda couldn't be her soulmate. They were too different, looked at the world from opposing viewpoints, and nothing about them was compatible. Except the sexual tension. That was definitely there.

"You won't offend me this time." Miranda nearly purred the words. "But since you're chickening out, I am attracted to both men and women, and anyone in between or other."

"Oh." Tori's lips formed a perfect O, her heart skittering again. "But—"

"There's no buts, Tori. That's just the way it is."

"No, I get that. I was just going to say, but you've never been married."

"No." Miranda frowned, the lines around her mouth and eyes deepening. "I never found someone who was worth the work, and I don't believe in happy marriages."

The unsettled feeling was impossible. Tori had tried and failed one marriage already, and Miranda was right. It was work. But to not believe in happily ever after? What a cold life to live. "I'd like to find my happily ever after."

"Then keep on dreaming." Miranda grabbed her wine glass again. "There's no reason you shouldn't."

There wasn't. Tori reminded herself of that as Miranda walked away. She followed into the living room, sitting next to her on the couch when the kids came back out to play on the floor. At the very least, Tori knew that Miranda wouldn't be interested. Not in anything. With a sigh, Tori changed the subject. She wouldn't let Miranda's doubts get her down. "How did that detangler work?"

ten

"Hey baby!" Tierney's saccharine tone floated through the speakers in Miranda's car.

Miranda cringed. "Rebel is napping."

"Oh." The surprise was shocking.

Miranda sighed heavily and brushed her fingers through her hair. She wanted to be done with today and this phone call. It had been a long day already, and she had spent more hours on her feet than she cared to admit. She'd managed to get Rebel from the daycare center in time, but barely.

"How is everything going in Mexico?" It was the only way she could nicely ask *when are you coming home* without being snarky about it and possibly starting an argument before she got an answer.

"It's amazing here." Tierney sounded wistful now. "Marcus is wonderful."

"Marcus?" She thought it was Jason. Frowning, Miranda turned onto the highway so she could head home. The daycare was nowhere near her house, which had been a disadvantage to Tierney picking it, but she hadn't wanted to move Rebel and upset her even more, considering she wasn't supposed to live with Miranda for long.

"Yeah, we met in Tampico last week. He's taking me to Cancun tomorrow."

Did Tierney realize just how risky her behavior was? Probably not. She could easily end up dead in a ditch somewhere and no one would ever know. Miranda bit her tongue, attempting to figure out how to get the most information out of Tierney before the phone call ended. "What happened with Jason?"

"Not my soulmate."

Miranda was instantly shoved back into the conversation she'd had with Tori. She hadn't lied when she said she didn't believe in soulmates, and Tierney was part of the reason why. That and her parents. She had never seen a more unhappy couple that somehow managed to stay married for years. "And Marcus is?"

"I don't know. But he could be."

The sun had already set. Miranda hated this time of year. It was always dark, and she never managed to get enough sunlight, especially with the rain clouds always overhead. "When do you think you'll be coming home?"

There. The question was out there. Now she had to wait for Tierney's avoidance.

"I don't know. Another week maybe?" Tierney sounded so unsure, as if perhaps the lie she was telling wasn't only to Miranda but to herself.

"Rebel needs you, T. Not me. She needs her mother."

"I know." Tierney pouted. Even though Miranda couldn't see her face, she knew that was exactly the look Tierney had on her face. She'd seen it too many times over the course of Tierney's life. It almost always got her whatever it was she wanted. "I miss my baby."

"Then come home," Miranda said as gently as possible.

Five weeks with Rebel was enough. She really needed her mother and not the aunt who resented having to take care of her. And she did resent it. Not because of Rebel but because of Tierney and the circumstances surrounding why Rebel was in her care.

"Oh! I got to go. Marcus is coming! I'll see you soon. Love you. Byeee!" Tierney elongated the last word of her send-off, putting emphasis on the last part of the word.

Before Miranda could say anything, Tierney had hung up and the other end of the line was quiet. She was so frustrated. She still didn't have an answer as to when Tierney would be coming back. And she didn't have an answer to why Tierney insisted on being an absent parent. Well, that one she knew. It was what she had been taught, and Miranda was determined not to continue that cycle.

She hit the button on her steering wheel and was about to tell Siri to call her mother when she stopped. Her mom had nothing to say. She'd brush it off as being another of Tierney's stunts. Which it was, but she wouldn't be any help in taking care of Rebel. No, Miranda needed to talk to someone who would actually listen, someone who could offer advice.

"Call Tori," Miranda said clearly into the microphone.

The call went through immediately. Miranda was stuck in traffic, stop-and-go, and just ready for a glass of whiskey or something to take the edge off her day.

"This is Tori Frazee. Leave a message and I'll get back to you as soon as possible."

Miranda hung up. What was she doing calling Tori? They barely knew each other, and what little time they had spent together didn't make them friends. Not someone Miranda could call for help or to vent to anyway.

The ringing through the Bluetooth startled her. She answered out of habit before seeing the name and cringed when it was Tori. Now she had no choice. "Hello."

"Hi!" Tori's voice was a breath of fresh air.

Now what? Miranda pulled her lips into her mouth, her shoulders tense and hard. What did she say now? "I just picked up Rebel."

"Yeah? Kind of late, isn't it?"

"I got stuck at the funeral home. We had a body come in."

"Ah." Tori didn't seem quite as happy as she did before.

A heavy weight rested on Miranda's chest. She'd called for one reason, and that was to complain. But did she really want to do that?

"I talked to Tierney."

"Do you want to come over?"

They spoke at the same time. Miranda winced. But not for the first time since she'd met Tori, she went with her gut. "Yes."

"Come over then. I'll have some dinner ready. We can have some drinks. Siena will be by to pick up Harley in a couple of hours after her date. Then it'll be you, me, and Rebel."

Rebel. Right. She was asleep in the back seat of the car. Miranda rubbed her lips together, debating whether or not to just go home and let her sleep. But she took the next exit on the highway and circled back toward Tori's apartment.

"I can be there in fifteen."

"See you then."

Miranda's stomach was awash with nerves. What was she doing? Tori wasn't her friend. Despite the few times they had gotten together and the conversations they'd had, times when Miranda had shared more than she had with anyone else in her life. It was just her, not Tori. It was because she was trying to contain so much in her life and couldn't keep it all bottled inside. That's all it was.

When she arrived at Tori's apartment complex, Rebel stirred. Thankfully. She pulled the toddler from her car seat and snagged the diaper bag at the last minute. Stashing that in the car had been a tip and investment well worth her time. She'd used it several times already.

Balancing everything, Miranda made her way to Tori's front door. As soon as she reached it, the scents from whatever Tori was cooking inside hit her. It smelled amazing. Tori answered the door in a pair of tight jeans, an even tighter shirt with a V-neck and buttons that showed off her ample cleavage, her dark hair pulled back into a ponytail, her eyes bright, and a dish towel hung over her shoulder.

"Hey," Tori said, her voice full of sunshine.

"Hey." Miranda shifted the bubbly Rebel on her hip. She was getting too big to be carried around everywhere, but Miranda hadn't found another way to contain Rebel so she wouldn't run off.

"Dinner's almost ready."

"It smells amazing." She put Rebel down, and immediately, she and Harley went to the living room to continue playing with whatever toy Harley had out. The girls chattered together, Harley talking and Rebel making noises.

Tori took Miranda by the wrist and led her toward the kitchen. She had a drink ready for her, and it wasn't wine. Miranda sniffed it. "What is this?"

"Vodka. You sounded like you could use something a bit stronger than wine on the phone."

"I can." Miranda sighed into the drink as she took her first sip.

Tori went back to work on dinner, her hips swaying as she moved to a rhythm all her own at the stove. "You said you talked to Tierney."

"That's a word for it. She talked. I avoided. Pretty typical." Why couldn't she take her eyes off Tori's ass? It looked perfect in those jeans.

"What did she say?"

"She's onto someone named Marcus. No clue who he is,

but she went down to meet with Jason. So, new man, new day."

"Oh." Tori threw a look over her shoulder with a frown on her lips.

"She's going to Cancun," Miranda added, dropping her gaze back down to Tori's ass. Would it be firm? Soft? The skin would be hot under her fingers, that much she could guarantee.

"Cancun?"

"Yeah." Miranda had to focus hard on the conversation because she was absolutely distracted. It was a good thing Tori hadn't given her tequila because that would be the end of everything. Clothes would be off, and all her barriers would be down. Nothing good ever came of drinking tequila, at least for Miranda. That was how she'd ended her last relationship. Swiftly. Stupidly. And with tequila.

"So where has she been the rest of the time?"

"No clue." Miranda finished half her glass. "Can I help with anything?"

Tori looked over her shoulder again, shaking her head. "It's almost done."

"Tacos?"

"I always love to eat a good taco." Tori tossed Miranda a heated look, one that said so much more than the words.

Miranda's lips formed a perfect O. She had no idea how to respond to that. Had Tori caught her intense gazes? Her leering stares? Why was she there again?

Laughing, Tori leaned in and touched Miranda's arm. "Calm down! It's a joke."

Miranda didn't think it was. She blew out a breath and leaned against the edge of the counter, her arms crossed and her glass between her fingertips. She really shouldn't finish the whole thing before she ate something. She'd missed breakfast and lunch that day, and she needed the food in her stomach to absorb some of the liquor.

"Oh my god. Your face!" Tori pointed at her. "Joke, Miranda, joke."

Maybe it was because she didn't want it to be a joke. She could so easily fall into Tori's lap, do anything Tori would let her do, and walk away the next day. It would be the perfect arrangement, except for the small fact that Tori was looking for something long-term. She wanted the relationship that came with the sex, not the other way around like Miranda.

Tori plated up food and set it at the small dining room table. The girls came to sit and were already digging into their meal before Tori came back and snagged Miranda's empty glass to make her another one.

"Did she say when she was coming back?"

"Who?"

"Tierney."

"Oh." Miranda brought her gaze back up from Tori's breasts to her face. "No, she didn't. She said she missed Rebel, and that was about it where it concerned us."

"Does that hurt? When she says things like that?"

Miranda took a full plate from Tori. "I guess it does. I never really thought about it before."

"I'm sorry she can't love you like you deserve."

That hit hard. Miranda stopped in her tracks while Tori walked over to the table and sat down, her own drink in front of her. It took her a minute to catch her bearings. She sat next to Tori, Rebel on her other side, and started to eat quietly. The food wasn't anything to write home about, but the company kept her nerves and dreaded thoughts at bay.

By the time they finished eating, the girls went to Harley's room to pack up her bag to go to Siena's. Harley had already begged three times over to stay because Rebel was there. Tori had reminded her that Rebel wasn't staying the night.

They were sitting on the couch, the girls clambering onto one side, which meant Tori had to sit in the middle, right up against Miranda. Their thighs brushed, sending fire raging through Miranda's body. She shifted to try and move away a bit, ease the discomfort between her legs, but that was a failure on all fronts.

Rebel climbed into her lap, then out of it, brought over a toy to show off and then went away to play with it again. Miranda struggled to keep up with it all. Tori rested her hand on the back of the couch, over Miranda's shoulders, taking up so much space. Miranda trembled.

"So have you thought about dating again? Since our last conversation?"

Miranda jerked her chin up, her eyes wide. "Excuse me?"

"Dating with kids." Tori's lips pulled up on one side. "I think Siena is trying to set me up with someone."

"Oh." Miranda took a long sip from her third drink that night. It would need to be her last if she stood any chance of driving home. "Are you going to let her?"

"Yeah. She's done it before. Sometimes she's better at finding people for me than I am. To be fair, she does know me better."

"You're going to let your ex-wife find your soulmate for you?" Miranda didn't quite believe it.

"Why not? She knows who I am, she knows the other person, that makes it easy. And if I want to find the love of my life by the time I'm thirty, then I have to use every resource available to me."

"Right. By the time you're thirty." How had she forgotten just how young Tori was? She certainly didn't act young, except for moments like this when she acted way younger than her actual age. "Then you should be on a date and not cooking me...tacos." Miranda added the pause, hoping it would come off as a joke. Two could play with fire, couldn't they?

"Yeah. I think Siena is planning on a big birthday bash, too."

"When is your birthday? For all I know you could have a month to find your soulmate. A real U-Hauler if that's the case."

Tori giggled and rested, turning slightly to face Miranda better. "I have some time."

"Fine, be skittish on sharing the day." Miranda swiftly finished her drink. Rebel was back in her lap, and she wrapped a couple curls around her finger and twisted it into shape.

"My birthday is in the spring. April fifteenth."

"Tax day." Miranda winked. Why did she just do that? Hell, the vodka was going to her head already. That definitely needed to be her last one. "You better get on some dating sites if you plan to find Mrs. Right in the next nine months."

"Yeah, already on it." Tori's cheeks were bright red. She was just about to say something else when there was a knock on the door.

"Mom!" Harley screeched, getting up and running.

Miranda tensed, every alarm in her head going off. She had forgotten Siena was coming. And she wasn't prepared to meet her. Then again, she had nothing to lose. It wasn't like she was dating Tori. It wasn't like Siena had to size her up or decide if she was worthy of her ex-wife. The door snicked open, and Miranda's stomach dropped. Siena was a bombshell, and also much older than Tori. What the hell had she been thinking?

eleven

"Hey." Tori pushed herself up from the couch and met Siena at the door. Harley was wrapped in her arms, her face buried in Siena's shoulder.

"Hey." Siena's smile was tight as she looked over Tori's shoulder and then back again, giving Tori a knowing glance.

"Ouch, Mom." Harley giggled. "Too tight, too tight."

"Oh." Siena blinked, surprised. "Sorry, Munchkin." Siena kissed Harley on the cheek and placed her back on her feet on the floor. Squaring her shoulders, she looked directly at Miranda, as if sizing her up.

"Harley, go grab your bag for Mom." Tori ruffled Harley's hair.

"All right," Harley raced off to her room.

"Come on in," Tori said. "You know how long she ends up taking to get her stuff, even though they packed it up ages ago."

"They?" Siena asked, keeping her eyes on Miranda and Rebel. Just what was she thinking? Tori wished she had some insight into that mind of hers. Siena had never shown any form of jealousy before now.

"Yeah, she loves showing Rebel everything."

Siena stopped Tori with a hand to her arm. "If you were busy, you didn't have to swap weekends with me." Siena looked pointedly at Tori with raised eyebrows and then a fast flick of her eyes to where Miranda sat comfortably.

"Oh no, this wasn't a planned thing. They just stopped by for a visit. Harley loves it when she gets to play with Rebel. They're like newfound best friends." Tori smiled, trying to both understand and ignore the tension that seemed to seep into the room. Uncomfortable, she checked in on Miranda silently to see just what was going on.

Siena turned a smile toward Miranda. It was as chilly a look as Tori had ever seen. Tori's breath hitched in her chest as her mind supplied Miranda's face over Siena's. They did look eerily similar in some ways. The same coloring, the same age. What the hell? They were nothing alike. The vodka must have been affecting her more than she had realized. The two she'd had should probably be her last before she did anything stupid.

Tori had better make introductions before this awkward silence continued between all of them. "This is Harley's mom, Siena. Siena, this is Miranda. She's looking after her niece, who goes to Harley's daycare."

"The aunt? The one you asked about clothes and toys for?"

Tori's cheeks warmed and a groan begged for release from her throat. Her spine stiffened. Offending Miranda was so easy to do. Walking on eggshells was tiring and painful. But she couldn't control what Siena said or didn't say.

"Yeah, I just wasn't sure if what I had here would be enough for what she needed."

"Uh-huh." Siena swallowed audibly and then stretched her smile, fake but wider. "Well, I'll grab Harley, and we'll be out of your hair."

"What?" Tori asked, her chest tightened, unable to ignore the energy in the room any longer.

"I won't be long, I promise." Siena didn't wait for an answer. She all but ran down to Harley's room.

"You asked your ex about the stuff for Rebel?" Miranda asked, and Tori had no idea what the tone in her voice meant.

Damn it.

What mess had she just put herself into the middle of? Miranda would be offended. Siena was acting odd. What was she doing? "Yes, but only because she has half of Harley's stuff anyway. I knew she'd have more to give you."

"Tori." Miranda's lips curled ever so slightly at the edges, a genuine smile that reached her eyes. "It's fine. Thank you."

"Of course. It's what friends do." The word caught in Tori's throat, but that's what they had become, hadn't they? Miranda had called her after a bad day and came over for a drink. It was a friend thing, *only* a friend thing. Tori ignored the part of her that scoffed at her reasoning. She was back to questioning what the strange energy in the room was all about.

"I should go. I shouldn't have interrupted your night," Miranda said. Did Tori detect sadness in her eyes?

"No, please. I'll just walk Siena out. Please don't go." Tori held her breath, waiting for Miranda to reply.

"Ready for the tickle train to depart?" Siena chuckled as she walked down the hallway.

Tori caught a glimpse of devastation in Siena's gaze as she caught her eye, the icy exterior she had greeted Tori with thankfully gone but replaced with something worse. Tori wished she knew what the cause was. Tori caught the apologetic look she threw to Miranda before Siena nodded her head down and reached the door.

"Come on." Tori grabbed Harley's bag that had slipped off of Siena's shoulder and hung it heavily on her forearm.

Siena threw Miranda another look. Her tone was back to ice when she said, "It was nice meeting you."

"Wait!" Harley said in a voice that stopped Tori in her tracks.

"What's up, Pumpkin?" Tori asked, searching Harley's face for the pain or panic. They hadn't had problems with her going from house to house in at least a year. *Please don't let this be the night she throws a fit again!*

"I have to say goodbye to Rebel."

Harley clambered up onto Miranda's lap along with Rebel, crushing the toddler in a hug. It was one of the most adorable things Tori had seen in a long time. She wished she could give Harley that, a sibling that she could play with and grow up with. An only child was never something she had in mind for her family.

"I need to give her a goodnight kiss," Harley said with such confidence Tori felt her chest swell with pride at the love and openness that came so naturally to her daughter.

Tori and Siena exchanged glances and small smiles. It seemed their parenting had rubbed off.

Harley wiggled in Miranda's lap to press her lips to Rebel's chubby cheek. She made an exaggerated *muah* sound before pulling back and laughing. Rebel reached forward, her arms around Harley's neck as she gave Harley a hug of her own. Miranda had a faraway expression in her gaze, and Tori couldn't put her finger on what it meant.

Harley let Rebel give her a wet kiss before giggling, and then she whispered something into Rebel's ear. Tori couldn't hear the words, but the tone held such sweet tenderness.

"Bye 'Randa," Harley said a little louder, turned on her heels, and bolted toward Siena. Siena opened her arms and swung her up to her hip.

"All right, we ready to go now?" Siena asked with a big bright smile, already moving toward the door.

Tori was torn between staying in the living room with Miranda and walking Siena outside to say her goodbyes to

Harley like she normally did. Something kept her rooted to the spot a moment longer than she expected.

Miranda gave her a curt smile. "Go on. We'll be fine while you tell her goodbye."

"Are you sure?"

"Positive."

Tori reached for the door and stopped again, looking Miranda over. She didn't want to leave. That's what this was. She wanted to stay in Miranda's presence for as long as she could and be the friend that Miranda so desperately needed. "I'll just be a minute."

"We'll be waiting."

Tori took Harley from Siena's arms for their goodbye squeezes. By the time Harley was strapped into her car seat, Siena was standing next to her, bag already stashed. It was a familiar dance. Tori was comforted by the routine though a little sadness lingered at the week she would miss with her daughter.

The look on Siena's face told Tori that the conversation they were about to have was one neither of them would enjoy. She shut the door firmly so Harley wouldn't hear anything. Protecting her from whatever argument was about to ensue had always been their primary goal. Harley didn't need to be privy to their disagreements.

"Tori." Siena spoke her name as though approaching a cornered animal.

"What's up?" Better to tear off the Band-Aid—it was a saying she often told her clients. And one she tried her best to live as well, without being cruel or unnecessarily harsh. She couldn't fix anything if unspoken questions lingered in the air. Miranda calling her a chickenshit came back to mind. Okay, she didn't always rip the Band-Aid so fiercely, but this wasn't Miranda. This was Siena.

"I didn't know you had a date. I could have changed my

plans." Rumbles of something unspoken stirred beneath Siena's words. What was that? Tori wanted to know.

"What?" Tori declared, though the heat in her cheeks belied her outrage. "I'm not on a date."

"I'm worried about you."

"Worried about me?" Tori laughed and shrugged. "Why on earth are you worried about me?"

Siena huffed out a breath as though needing to steel herself for her next words. "I'm worried you're chasing someone who isn't your type because you are so caught up on this ridiculous soulmate-by-thirty thing. She's twice your age!"

"Firstly…" Tori took a deep breath. She wasn't angry, not really. But the pain of Siena's flippant words about her belief in true love did hurt, just as it always had. "It's not ridiculous. And secondly, I'm not dating Miranda. It's not like that. She's been thrown into this shit situation, and she needs a friend."

"And that's all you are? Friends?" Siena didn't look like she believed her.

"Yes." Tori hoped Miranda really did consider her a friend, because she didn't want to lie. Even though she might be doing that to herself.

"And this wasn't a date?" Siena eyed Tori.

"Of course not. We both agreed no dates when we have Harley until something is serious and we're ready for introductions. That's why I was more than happy to take her tonight."

"All right, I know. I'm sorry. I know you better than that." Siena tossed a hand through her hair.

"Yeah." Tori laughed, but it didn't quite ring true. "You do."

"Okay okay, I'm being a jackass." Siena wrapped her arm around Tori's shoulder and pulled her in for a side hug, kissing her cheek.

"A little bit, yes, but I appreciate the concern."

Siena looked through the car window at Harley singing in

her seat, shuffling her body, her hands making actions for the words. She never could keep still. A lot like Rebel in that way. Tori grinned at her.

"She's such an amazing kid." Tori met Siena's eyes as they both pulled away. They were on even ground again. This was the way most of their arguments had gone since divorcing, and it had been blissfully uneventful. Tori called through the glass, "Bye, baby. Be good for Mom."

Harley waved and nodded.

"How did the date go by the way?" Tori asked as she walked with Siena around to the driver's side door.

"It didn't. If anything, she's more your type than mine."

"Oh god, not another setup." But Tori was smiling, relieved at the easing of tension between the two of them.

"Well, you need one, especially if you're not dating Ms. Priss in there." Siena pointed at the apartment window.

Tori stared longingly at it. She wanted to be inside with Miranda, not outside making idle chitchat with Siena. That should have been her first sign that there was more between them than just friendship. But they hadn't talked about anything beyond that. Or even that, really. "Why are you so sure Miranda isn't my type?"

"Everything about her." Siena knocked her shoulder into Tori's. "It's not that I think she's a bad person, but you need someone warm, and she isn't that. All she did was glare at me the entire time I was in there."

"She just expresses herself differently. And has a really bad case of resting bitch face."

"Riiiiight." Siena stopped at her door, making eye contact with Tori. "Just promise me that you'll be careful. We don't need a repeat of last year."

Right, last year, when Tori had landed herself on Siena's doorstep drunk off tequila and sobbing helplessly. That night had turned into a one-night fling between them, and they both swore it would never happen again. Though that was the second time it had happened.

"I'm being careful." Tori saw the doubt in Siena's eyes, but she bowled over it with a confident smile. Come hell or high water, Tori wouldn't admit that there was anything more between her and Miranda than friendship. Siena wasn't wrong when she'd said Miranda wasn't her type. She might be in looks, but definitely not in personality.

Tori didn't wait until Siena turned onto the road before heading back to the front door. Her stomach rolled into a flip as she stepped inside, Siena's concern swirling through her head. Tori knew Siena was right. She also knew that sometimes knowing something meant absolutely nothing at all.

"No, it means everything. She's not the one," Tori muttered as she stepped back inside to find Miranda singing softly into Rebel's hair as the child fell asleep in her aunt's arms.

twelve

Pulling out her phone as she stood in the hallway at the daycare after dropping Rebel off, Miranda sighed as she read Tierney's last text.

Sorry! The phone cut out. Call you soon! Love you!

The phone had cut out in the first two minutes of their call, and when Miranda had attempted to call back, it had gone straight to voicemail. She hadn't heard from Tierney in days since then. A war waged inside her whether or not to call her back. She didn't want bad news. But having Rebel in her custody for six weeks now, she was scared what good news would mean.

A gentle brush of fingers against her shoulder caught her attention.

"You seem lost in thought."

Miranda quirked an eyebrow, her lips pressed into a thin line. "Was I in your way?"

"No." Tori's smile was like the sun on her face on a warm day. She craved it.

But ever since their impromptu vodka—not tequila, thank the Lord—night, Miranda had worked hard to remind herself just how far out of bounds Tori was. She couldn't start a new relationship. Not now, and certainly not with someone searching for something that didn't exist. It seemed Tori had a similar epiphany as the innuendos and the ease they had cultivated became a thing of the past. Miranda hadn't seen or heard from her in the short week and a half since that night.

"I was coming to find you actually, or Rebel. I found this under the couch when I was vacuuming, and I think it's probably Rebel's." Tori held up a small toy that might have once been a bear or a dog or some other animal molded into a humanoid shape.

"Her stuffy." Miranda couldn't stop the smile as she snagged the toy. It would make getting Rebel to sleep in her own bed that night a cinch. It had been brutal the last few nights, and she'd all but given up on training her to sleep in the toddler bed she'd bought.

"I'm glad it's back with its rightful owner."

"Yes, thank you." Miranda looked into Tori's baby-blue eyes. Why had they not talked in the last week again? Miranda wasn't sure she could remember.

"Have you heard from her?"

"Who?" Confused, it took Miranda a second to pull her head out of the clouds. Sadness tightened in her chest. It was strange and yet almost nicer to feel that rather than the anger. "Oh. Tierney. She tried to call the other day, but the signal dropped as soon as it connected. I tried to call back, but I haven't been able to reach her."

"I'm sorry." Tori reached for Miranda's arm, wrapping her fingers around her wrist in a tender touch. Her warm hand burned through Miranda's shirt, despite the thick material. "That must be so hard for you."

She didn't know what to say to that. How had Tori picked up on her turmoil so easily? "Aili says she's happy with Rebel's improvements lately."

Walking toward the parking lot, Miranda broke Tori's touch. She had to put some distance between them. But she couldn't quite remember why.

"Oh that's fantastic. But I meant hard for you not being able to check if Tierney is okay."

Miranda hesitated a beat before following Tori outside. She'd known what Tori had meant, and she'd avoided the topic. No one ever thought about how much she loved her sister or how many nights she stayed awake worrying about her. But Tori seemed to always see beyond what others gleaned and picked out the parts that Miranda struggled with the most.

"I'm sorry. I didn't mean to overstep." Tori stopped near her car. She must have sensed something.

Why couldn't Miranda hold anything back anymore? "I'll try to call her again today. Maybe she'll be someplace she can answer this time."

"Sounds like a good idea." Something flickered across Tori's gaze, and Miranda wished she could make it vanish. It didn't look comfortable or good. "I guess I'll see you around, then. I'm glad I was able to get this back to Rebel."

"Yes. Thank you, again." Miranda locked their gazes together. Her heart raced. She didn't want to go to work. She didn't want to deal with Tierney and the phone call and what exactly they needed to talk about. It wouldn't be a pleasant conversation no matter which way it went. Tierney would feel like Miranda was overstepping. Miranda would struggle with lack of responsibility on her sister's part. It was that vicious cycle all over again.

"Was there something else?" Tori touched her wrist again.

Miranda's gaze locked on her fingers. Thin. Long. Two fingernails cut much shorter than the others. Even though she hadn't dated a woman in many years, Miranda knew exactly what that meant. She couldn't do this. As much as she wanted to, she couldn't do it.

"No." Did her voice just waver? What was wrong with her? What happened to the strong woman who knew what she wanted and got what she needed from no one but herself?

"Okay. Just…know you can call if you need something or just want to talk or maybe have some tequila."

Miranda inwardly groaned at that.

"Or maybe just some more vodka." Tori's cheeks had a rosy tinge to them, like she was blushing.

Was she hoping for more? Miranda panicked. She couldn't keep up with this. She leaned in. Why was she doing that? The misty morning dampened her cheeks, the fog sticking around in the streets longer than it probably should—or at least longer than Miranda wanted it to. She had to stop herself. But what would it be like to take exactly what Tori was offering?

"I'll think about it," Miranda finally said, her tone curt. "I have to get to work."

"Yeah. Right." Tori stepped away, releasing Miranda's wrist. "See you around."

She said nothing as she got in her car and drove off. She couldn't speak. Her mind was spinning with what she wanted to do.

———

"Tierney, thank God." Miranda let out a sharp breath she had been holding for the last three days. She had tried to call several times and hadn't gotten anywhere.

"What's wrong? Did something happen to Rebel?"

"She's perfectly fine. Are you okay?" Miranda asked, not entirely recognizing her own voice. She must have been more worried than she'd realized. Just hearing Tierney's voice put her at ease. Texts were one thing, but with the strange men Tierney hung out with, Miranda couldn't always be sure who was sending or receiving the texts.

"Yes, I'm wonderful." Her voice took on a wispy quality, the tone Miranda associated with teenagers and morons. "Marcus is a true angel."

Miranda needed to approach this carefully. But she needed information and to keep Tierney on track in the conversation. The downfall was that she could always hang up if she didn't like the conversation, which she often did. "So where are you now?"

"We're in Belize, and then I think Marcus is going to take me home to meet his family in Guatemala."

"What?" Panic hit Miranda hard. Her heart skipped, and she clenched her fingers, staring down at Rebel who was playing with the toy Tori had brought back to her. She wouldn't tell Rebel that, ever. She couldn't.

"It's okay. I promise I'm on my way back. Just another week or two." Why did she sound so confident in that? She shouldn't. She'd been saying just a few more days for six weeks now.

"Tierney." Miranda stopped herself from snapping out her sister's name, though she wasn't sure she was completely successful with that. She had to remember this was about Rebel, not their own past. "Did you get the notifications about your apartment?"

"Oh, yeah, but it's no big deal. I'll stay with Mom and Dad for a bit until I can find a new place." She didn't even sound worried. But she had more than one eviction on her record now, which would make it next to impossible to find an apartment. Not to mention she was jobless and had no income, and Miranda was pretty sure she'd spent the last of her money on that plane ticket.

"I was thinking that maybe when you get back, you can stay here with Rebel until you get things sorted out." It wasn't solely so that she knew Rebel would have housing, but it would be consistent housing for her at least, which would be to her benefit. But if she said it like that, Tierney would be pissed.

"Really?" Tierney's voice squeaked before a silent beat passed. "What's the catch?"

"There's no catch." Miranda took a breath, deep but as quietly as she could.

"You're going to take her away from me, aren't you?" Tierney's tear-filled voice warbled.

"What? No. If I was going to do that, I would have done it already," Miranda said quickly, though the thought had crossed her mind a few times. "I don't want her to be without her mom. She needs you, Tierney. I won't ever keep her from you. I just want to help you."

"You want to help me? What happened to soulmates being the stupidest thing in the world?"

"I still don't think soulmates exist." Miranda wanted to curse herself for letting the words spill automatically, but she pushed on. She wanted Tierney to understand. "But I know how hard it is to look after a child all on your own. And you need to be able to find someone for you, and for Rebel, without having to worry about it, or disrupt her."

"I'm a bad mom, aren't I?" Tierney's words were so raw that it threw Miranda, and she sat back on her couch as though pushed over by the emotions. "Marcus tells me I'm an amazing mother. I'm a good mom."

"I didn't say you were a bad mom." She might have implied it though, maybe not this time around but many other times they had talked. Miranda rubbed her temple. How could she keep this conversation going?

"Because I'm not."

"No, you're not." Except right now, Miranda thought she was. Choosing a man over a child any day put her squarely into that category for Miranda. She just couldn't say that. Not if she wanted to keep Tierney on the phone.

"Marcus is the one. We'll come home, and I'll show you."

"Okay." Miranda gave her standard one word answer, because what else could she say? She'd tried it all before and gotten nowhere. "I'm excited to meet him." Now she was lying? She was almost as bad as her sister. "When do you think you'll be home to introduce us?"

"Oh. I don't know." Tierney had that faraway tone in her voice, like she was going to hang up again.

Miranda cringed. She could have worked the conversation so much better to keep everyone talking and to get better answers. "Please come home soon. We miss you." That wasn't a lie at least.

"I miss you, too. I love you." Tierney's voice dropped and suddenly the phone went dead.

The silence was loud.

Miranda grabbed Rebel and cradled her. Tierney hadn't even asked to talk to her daughter this time. She was purposely putting distance between them because they both knew she wouldn't be home any time soon.

Kissing Rebel's sweet cheek, Miranda put her down to continue playing. Miranda paced her living room. With her phone in her hand, she hovered it over the call button several times before throwing it back onto the couch. Toys were scattered here and there, a pair of Rebel's shoes beside her own on the rack, an unopened package of diapers, and three packages of baby wipes sat on her kitchen counter. This was her life now. She was Rebel's stability. She was a parent again, filling in the gaps for someone who wasn't there, who wasn't present.

Tears threatened to fall, but she wouldn't let them. Not again. She'd done that enough.

"This is stupid." She picked up her phone and called before she could talk herself out of it.

After the third ring, she answered.

"Hey." Tori's voice came through the phone line like a ray of sunshine, and that craving was back.

Miranda shouldn't have called. They had put that distance between them, and Miranda was comfortable with it. At least she had been until Tori had given the stuffy back, until Tori had touched her wrist, until Miranda had wanted to kiss her. But if Siena was an example of Tori's taste, Miranda didn't stand a chance. She was too cold. Too aloof. And she was so bad at opening up.

"Hey." Miranda's lips spread in a smile. A real genuine smile, and it was wonderful and strange. She just had to remember why she called. "I got hold of Tierney. Finally."

"Oh? Is everyone okay?"

"I think so, but that's only for right now." Miranda bit her lip. Why had she called again? Oh right. "I asked Tierney to come live with me for a bit, whenever she gets back. It doesn't sound like it'll be soon."

"You did?" Tori sounded surprised.

"I thought it'd be the best way to give Rebel some consistency. She's clearly craving it."

"All kids crave structure. Adults too, to be fair." Miranda could hear the smile in Tori's voice. Did the woman ever not smile?

"Right. I mean it's not definite yet, but we spoke. I'm not sure how it will all work yet, but I know I can work it out." Was she rambling? Miranda couldn't remember the last time she'd gone into a conversation like this so unprepared. She always kept everything close to her chest, but Tori had a way of snagging it before she had it all figured out.

"Maybe you can both work it out." Tori's voice was soft and held no judgment, but Miranda noticed the unsubtle hint in the words.

"Yes, we can both sort it out."

"I'm so happy for you. Are you putting Rebel to bed soon?

I don't want to take away from that structure." Tori was nearly giggling.

Miranda looked over at the clock that hung on the wall between the living room and the kitchen. "Yeah, I suppose I will. She's been sleeping in her own bed, in my room still, but her own bed."

"That's amazing! Co-sleeping is not for the fainthearted."

"No, it's not. It's been easier to get her to sleep since she has her favorite stuffy back." Miranda's cheeks heated. *Oh my god, am I blushing?* Was she trying to flirt by talking about kids? Was this what dating with kids was like?

"I'm so happy to hear that! Enjoy some downtime without Rebel hanging all over you. It's invaluable."

"So I hear." Miranda smiled. "Thank you. I didn't really know who else I could call."

"I'm glad you called me."

There was an awkward pause between them. Miranda knew she should hang up, end the call, let Tori go about her night with Harley, and that she should get Rebel to bed, but she just couldn't make herself do it.

"Miranda?" Tori sounded hesitant.

"Yeah?"

"Do you want some company?"

Her heart skipped. Her throat clogged up. Miranda stared at Rebel, yawning as she played on the couch. For the first time in weeks she felt light, as if she wasn't carrying the weight of the world alone. Why was it so hard to breathe?

"Yes."

thirteen

"I brought tequila!"

Miranda's eyes widened like she had done something wrong.

"Or...not..." Tori frowned. "I did also get some more vodka. We finished off the bottle I had the other week. Thought I'd refill it."

"Vodka is probably the better option." Miranda's words were crisp.

"You don't like tequila?" Tori followed Miranda through the house toward the kitchen. It was huge compared to her apartment. Definitely three or four bedrooms at least, but her living room was the size of Tori's living room, kitchen, and bedroom combined.

"It's more that it and I don't agree well."

"Oh." Tori smiled. "I've had my fair share of horror stories with it. I guess we'll check that one off the list." She giggled as she set the two bottles onto the counter. "I was going out with this woman last year, and I misread all the signs."

"Somehow I find that hard to believe."

Tori eyed Miranda curiously. "Why do you say that?"

"Because you're so good at reading people."

"Well, it's my job, but that doesn't mean I'm perfect at it. And when it involves relationships? Romantic ones to be clear. I can be as dense as the best of them."

"I still doubt that." Miranda grabbed some orange juice from the fridge. "Screwdriver?"

"Yes!" Tori grinned. "Siena has Harley tonight. I hate being at home without her some days. Sometimes it's nice." Why was she rambling so much? Tori wasn't usually a nervous person, but since she'd pulled up outside of Miranda's house, finally seeing inside her world in a way Miranda hadn't ever let her in before, she wasn't going to take this in stride. "I mean. I love Harley."

"I get it." Miranda handed her a drink.

"How did Rebel go down tonight?"

"Easy as pie." Miranda sipped her own drink and raised it up in a *cheers* move. "Since she has her favorite stuffy back."

"I'm so glad I found it."

They paused, the tension pulling between them. Tori struggled to find something to say, anything to break that look Miranda was giving her because there was something under the surface she wasn't sure she wanted to experience. But another side of her wanted the full force of it.

"You didn't finish your story." Miranda's lips were perfect. Did she redo her makeup on and off all day to keep that look?

"What story?" Tori was so lost staring into her honeyed eyes that she would tell Miranda anything if she asked. She had no filters when Miranda gave her that look.

"With tequila? A year ago?"

"Right." Tori blew out a breath. She took a long sip of her drink, surprised by how strong it was. But she gulped down another swallow. "I thought she was going to propose. She definitely wasn't. She broke up with me. I died of embarrassment.

Ended up at Siena's, and well...things happened that shouldn't have."

Miranda paled.

Fuck. Tori shouldn't have brought that story up. Not if she wanted anything to happen. "It's the only time since the divorce, and there was lots of alcohol involved, and loneliness, and stupidity."

"I understand." Though it didn't sound as though Miranda did.

Tori touched her wrist again. Why couldn't she stop doing that? "It was a mistake. We both knew that as soon as it happened, and it hasn't ever happened again."

"Where was Harley during all of that?"

"With her grandparents for the weekend. We have a strict rule about bringing dates over when Harley is around if we're not ready for the next step." Tori let go of Miranda, though she didn't want to. She missed the touch.

"And did she meet your ex?"

"No, which should have been a pretty good sign of what I was getting into, right?"

"Perhaps." Miranda took a long drink. "Do you still want to find your soulmate by the time you're thirty?"

"Yes," Tori answered honestly.

"Then why aren't you dating?"

Chuckling, Tori followed Miranda to the couch. "Oh, because I haven't found the right woman yet."

"Dating doesn't require finding someone who is right first."

"True." Tori was halfway through her drink already. Miranda was brilliant, and navigating the undercurrents of the conversation was hard. "I've been on a few dates in the last couple months. Siena just had a breakup. That's what was happening the other night when she picked up Harley late, when we switched weekends."

"She was dating someone?"

"Yeah." Tori looked Miranda over. "Does that surprise you?"

"No. She's gorgeous. I imagine men and women fall over themselves to get to her."

Tori's stomach tightened. Was she even Miranda's type? Was she reading way too much into this? Miranda might not date younger women, and Tori could be walking into the wrong house. "I met Siena through Aili, actually."

"Aili?" Miranda furrowed her brow.

"Oh, Aili and I dated for a while way back when. Before I met Siena. But she's the one who introduced us. Thought we'd be a good match. I don't think she was wrong, but she wasn't exactly right either."

"Do all your exes just become your friends?" Miranda looked utterly appalled.

Tori chortled. "Yeah, I guess they do. I don't make a very good enemy."

"I don't imagine you do. Probably smite your enemies with smiles until they turn back toward you."

Tori's jaw dropped. She couldn't quite find her voice, wanting to say something to that. "Was that a compliment?"

"Take it however you want. It's odd."

"It's not that odd when you have such a sunny disposition."

"So you say." Miranda finished her drink. "Want another one?"

"Not if I'm driving home tonight." Tori set the cup on the glass coffee table. She was already feeling lightheaded and would have to hang out at Miranda's for another hour at a minimum, probably two, in order for that to wear off enough for her to feel safe driving home.

Miranda stood up and snagged Tori's glass as she walked back toward the kitchen. Tori stayed put, crossing her legs and resting into the couch. What was she doing there? She never could quite resist the call for help, but something had come between them the night that Siena had shown up. Was it just jealousy? Was Miranda insecure?

When she came back, she set Tori's glass, refilled, onto the coffee table. Tori eyed it, then she eyed Miranda. What was she saying? Excitement coursed through Tori, filling all the spaces in her stomach, her chest, and her heart. Grinning, Tori grabbed her cup and took a sip to prove to herself and Miranda that she would stay as long as she was welcome.

"Siena thinks I should go out with the woman she just broke up with."

"Why's that?" Did Miranda sound breathy?

"She says we'd be a better match."

"What would make a good match for you?" Miranda toed off her shoes and curled her feet under her. "What do you look for in someone?"

"Oh." Tori hadn't really ever put much thought into that. "I always just figured I'd know when I found someone."

Miranda let out a slight snort. "What attracts you to a woman?"

"I won't lie and say I'm attracted to every single woman out there, but being single is a strong contender."

Miranda laughed, the trill of her voice echoing through the living room. "Good to know you don't cheat."

"Always a good trait, don't you think?"

"Yes." Miranda moved in closer, their shoulders brushing before she stretched out her arm along the back of the couch, nearly cradling Tori in the move. She stayed there, closer than ever before. "But what else?"

"Tall, dark, and handsome?"

Miranda wrinkled her nose, her cheeks flushed from the alcohol. "What does that mean for you?"

"I love a woman who knows her worth and value. Someone who knows where she stands in the world and has already gone through the tides of figuring out who she is."

"So you like older women." Miranda didn't make it a question, her voice falling flat.

Tori swallowed hard around the sudden lump in her throat. "Y-yes." She'd never quite thought about it like that, but she did like women who acted mature, and if that came with age, it never came up as a second thought to her. "I don't like to screw around with the chaos of not knowing."

"I can understand that."

"What do you look for? In a soulmate, that is."

Miranda wryly laughed, moving even closer to Tori. "I don't believe in soulmates, and I'm not looking for love."

"I know that, but if you were, what would you look for?" Tori wanted to know, desperately, what Miranda would say. Who was she under that icy veneer?

"My ex-fiancé was tall, dark, and handsome." Miranda sighed into her drink. "We were very young when we got engaged. I had only just started working at the funeral home at the time. Hadn't been to school yet."

"But like you wouldn't let me get away with it, what else is there for you? You can't be attracted solely by looks?"

"Rarely from looks." Miranda locked her eyes on Tori. "Kind hearts. Bleeding hearts. I learned quickly that I can't be with someone who doesn't have compassion for another person."

"That's deep." Tori bit her tongue. She shouldn't have said that, but the vodka was pushing its way into her brain and making it hard to hold her tongue. "I mean...I don't mean anything bad by that. I just mean that it's hard to find someone without compassion."

"It's really not." Miranda leaned forward and set her empty glass on the table, but when she came back she was in the same position as before. "In my line of work, we have to balance compassion with professionalism."

"Mine too." Tori winked, putting her half-full glass down.

When she leaned back against Miranda's side, little sparks of electricity moved through her. What were they doing? Because this dance was drastically different from what she'd expected when she'd come over here tonight. "What else?"

"I love a woman who is confident in herself. And I won't be too deep and not say that I also enjoy a woman's body." Miranda's voice dropped at the end. "Her curves, her softness, her understated strength."

Tori's heart rate kicked up a notch. Miranda wasn't looking into her eyes anymore but dropping her gaze all down her body. She wanted to twitch and move, but she held as still as possible, afraid to break the spell.

"But I don't believe in soulmates," Miranda whispered, drawing Tori back to her lips. Those beautiful, half-full lips.

"But do you believe in love?" Tori couldn't tear her gaze away.

"Sometimes. I've seen many people grieve over lost love."

Tori's heart was in her throat, pounding away and making it so hard to speak. "Do you want to test something?"

Miranda's lips curled upward. "Test what?"

Tori took two seconds before she found that confidence Miranda had been speaking of. Moving swiftly, she pushed up on her knee and turned, straddling Miranda on the couch. She left enough space between them that Miranda could tell her to stop, to back away, get off, whatever she needed. But she didn't. Tori gazed down into her honeyed eyes, Miranda's lips parted as if surprised, but her gaze held an entirely different look. She'd expected this. Maybe even wanted it.

"Let's see if we're soulmates or not."

"I know we're not."

Tori canted her head to the side, reaching forward and curling a long strand of hair around her fingers. "But what if I can prove you wrong."

"You can't."

Tori knew instinctively that Miranda was right. No matter what she did, she couldn't prove they were soulmates, especially if Miranda was that opposed to the idea, but it would get them what she thought they both wanted. Even if this was a night of fun and nothing more, even if they just needed to get it out of their system. Tori would take it. She needed to get back on the horse of dating, and Miranda offered a perfect opportunity.

"Try me." Tori sat down fully, her knees pressing into the couch cushions against Miranda's hips.

Miranda's hands were on her thighs, fingers tightening. When had they gotten there? When had Miranda started touching her? God, Tori didn't want her to stop. Tori wiggled slightly, every sensation, every touch, every physical connection between them pooling between her legs, heat radiating from her crotch right into Miranda's lap. There was no denying anything now.

"Tori," Miranda growled her name. "I think we've had enough to drink tonight."

"Just as a reminder," Tori said as she leaned in, pressing her lips close to Miranda's ear. She closed her eyes and dragged in a deep breath, taking Miranda's scent in fully for the first time ever. "You're the one who refilled my drink when I said I wouldn't be driving home if I had another. Was that an invitation?"

Miranda's breath hitched. Tori could feel the dampness increase between her legs. This was exactly what they both wanted. It had to be.

"What do you want, Miranda? To test this theory or not?" Tori took a risk and sucked Miranda's ear between her lips. She twirled her tongue along the edge, sucking gently.

Miranda moved her hands from Tori's thighs up to her waist, to her breasts. She tilted her head to give Tori better access. Her thumb stroked Tori's hardened nipple. Tori moaned, kissing down the side of Miranda's neck to her collar bone.

"That's exactly what I want," Tori whispered. "But what do you want?"

"Tonight? You."

Tori grinned. She moved back to look fully in Miranda's face, to look into her eyes, making sure this was what they both wanted. Leaning in, she stopped a breath away from Miranda's lips. "Are you my soulmate?"

"No." Miranda tangled her hand in Tori's hair and pulled her down.

Their lips pressed together tightly. Tori leaned in, holding onto the back of the couch as she held her position against Miranda. This was everything she had dreamed of and more. She didn't want it to stop. She parted her mouth and slid her tongue out, ready for whatever taste Miranda would give her.

She had so lied when Siena had asked. She had lied to herself for weeks. There was always more between them. Tori wanted there to be more. She nipped at Miranda's lower lip, sucking it into her mouth before diving back in again. The kiss was wet and sloppy, Miranda's lips cold from the ice in her glass, the tang of orange and vodka on her tongue, but Tori loved it. She sucked in a breath and skimmed her hand down Miranda's shoulder to her chest, brushing as lightly as possible.

"Miranda," Tori whispered, kissing her again. She was falling and hard. "Tell me to stop."

Miranda held Tori close, her kisses turning feverish. She opened her eyes and pulled back slightly, her chest rising and falling rapidly. Her look was sincere. "No."

"Fuck."

"Exactly."

fourteen

Tori's moan echoed in Miranda's ear, a slight hiccup in her voice when Miranda covered her breast with her hand again. It had been so long since she'd been with a woman, too many years since she'd allowed herself to experience the wonders of a woman's body. Her heart raced as she ran her hands up and down Tori's sides, feeling the gentle slope of her curves, the strength in her thighs, the heat from between her legs.

Miranda's thumb brushed against the crotch of Tori's jeans, and she nearly lost herself there. But she wasn't ready for that yet. She needed more time to sink into the fact that they were doing this. They weren't holding back. Their mouths melded together as their kisses deepened and got sloppier.

Closing her eyes, Miranda felt with her body. She slowly shut down her brain, all the objections as to why they shouldn't be doing this, all the worries and fears that plagued her daily, the what-ifs she didn't want to entertain, and the anxiety about what would happen next. For tonight, she wanted nothing but Tori in her arms, bodies pressed together, and release. Release from so many things she couldn't even begin to count.

"Miranda," Tori murmured, breaking the kiss to go back to Miranda's neck.

Her tongue flickered against Miranda's ear in the same manner she had done before. Heat seared through her, warming her from what she'd once considered her cold, dark center. Maybe she wasn't as dead inside as she thought.

"Tell me…" Miranda trailed off, trying to catch her breath. She slid her hands up under the back of Tori's shirt, finding hot, smooth skin. She had to swallow the lump in her throat to find her words again. "Tell me what you like about sex."

Tori hummed, and it sent vibrations down Miranda's neck to her chest and straight to her nipples. They tightened instantly. They weren't going to be able to stop, were they? There was no going back now. Miranda had wanted this for weeks, but she'd never thought—after seeing Siena, she'd never thought Tori would want her like this. But the soft touches the last couple of weeks when they'd seen each other, the lingering gazes when Tori thought she wasn't looking or noticing—oh how could she *not* notice those?—had pushed them to this. She dug her dull nails into Tori's sides to get her attention.

"What do you like about sex?" Miranda repeated her question, needing some guidance as to what she would be doing next and some reassurance that Tori indeed wanted this as much as she did.

"I love the connection." Tori nipped at Miranda's collarbone, pulling the buttons of her blouse open one at a time to reveal more skin with each passing second.

That didn't surprise Miranda, but she wanted a non-emotional answer. She wanted to know where to touch, how to tease. She wanted to know everything Tori wanted so she could then do it. Tori had Miranda's blouse open, bending down to press butterfly kisses against her chest and over the tops of her breasts where her bra didn't quite cover.

Miranda's hand was in Tori's hair, tightening and holding

her steady against her breasts. Her mind was absolute mush, which was exactly what she'd needed after the last six weeks of almost constant stress. She released Tori's hair and pulled her T-shirt up, dragging it over her shoulders and head as Tori moved back to help. Instantly, Miranda unclipped her bra, revealing her gorgeous pert breasts.

One fit within her entire hand. Miranda was mesmerized by them, the softest skin she had felt in years, the fullness and weight, the darkened nipples already hard and ready for her mouth. Swooping in, she did exactly what she wanted and took one of Tori's nipples between her lips and teased her. Tori's breath hitched, and her hands came up to either side of Miranda's face and held Miranda against her body.

"Yessssss," Tori hissed, rocking her hips solidly. She writhed on top of Miranda's lap.

Miranda used her thumb against Tori's other nipple, teasing it in time with her tongue. Tori ground down against her thighs, heat searing through the fabric of their clothes and into her legs. Miranda nearly gasped when Tori did it again. Was Tori going to make herself come that easily? Miranda could only wish that were the case for her. She'd never managed that.

"Don't stop," Tori whispered, her voice catching.

Miranda pulled away slightly. She made her tone clipped and precise, hoping the demand would get her an answer this time. "Don't stop what?"

"Touching." Tori's murmurs were in time with the rhythm of her hips. "So many touches."

Leaning back into the couch, Miranda pulled Tori with her, forcing her to stop grinding down. She didn't want Tori to come yet. She wanted to be the cause and the reason, the person who was giving her what she needed. Flipping Tori onto her back on the couch, Miranda covered her.

Their chests pushed together as their mouths melded once

again. Tori frantically shoved at Miranda's shirt, trying to get it off, but it snagged on her watch. Miranda lifted up on her knee to help give them some space to get it off, tugging sharply until she had it free. Then she was back against Tori, skin against skin, mouth against mouth.

"What do you want?" Miranda asked again, moving down Tori's body with kisses and touches so soft she knew they had to be driving Tori crazy.

"You."

Miranda bit her lip to keep in the sharp retort. She needed to know how Tori wanted her to do this. It would make it that much better for the both of them. When she reached the hemline of Tori's jeans, Miranda stopped and pulled back up, making eye contact with those bright baby blue eyes.

"Tell me what you want me to do."

"Touch me like I'm your whole world." The wistfulness in Tori's voice startled Miranda.

She hadn't expected it. She was caught between continuing and stopping. Tori was so young compared to her. This wasn't just sex for her, was it? Miranda's mind raced, those walls coming back up even though she didn't want them to. She couldn't break her gaze away either. Tori started touching herself, playing with her breasts and pulling her lower lip between her teeth, enticing Miranda back to her body.

"Come here." Tori's voice was husky, filled with desire.

Miranda moved in, pressing their mouths together and trying to find that place again. The place where her mind didn't work, where only her body felt, where she didn't worry about what was happening beyond this one special moment. Tori had her bra off, hands on her hips, and the kisses deepened instantly.

"Start with your fingers," Tori whispered against her ear. She reached between them, undoing the button and zipper on her jeans and shimmying them down her hips. "Just start."

Miranda leaned back and helped Tori get completely undressed. She was stunning. The dark curls between her legs were already damp, the scent rushing up to meet Miranda's nose. Her heart raced as she used her thumbs to press against Tori's thighs and up to her hip bones. It seemed as if they'd finally figured each other out. Miranda was finally getting the directions she needed.

She had wanted this. She had planned delicately to move them in this direction if that's what Tori had wanted. Again, Miranda was stunned by Tori's youth, her toned body, the freckles that randomly dotted her skin. She trailed her tongue against the ones on her chest, up to her neck, tracing lines from one and then to the next.

Tori captured Miranda's hand and pressed it down between her legs, covering her fingers as she teased herself with Miranda. This was sexy as hell. Miranda followed every cue that Tori gave her, every press and tease, every swipe. Before she knew it, Tori gripped her hips and held her tightly, and Miranda was left on her own—mouth to Tori's breast, fingers knuckle deep.

"Just don't stop," Tori murmured, her hips rising to meet the occasion.

Miranda did exactly as she was told.

"I'm so close."

"Just let go," Miranda murmured against her skin, waiting for the tender pull against her fingers, the tightening of Tori's body, the pinnacle to be reached. "Let go," Miranda repeated.

Tori did just that. Miranda softened her touch but kept it going, easing Tori down from the high she'd found. She didn't want this to end. Miranda couldn't let her go, not just yet. Pulling back to sit, she dragged Tori up by her wrists.

"Come with me."

"Where are we going?" Tori giggled, her cheeks flushed with arousal, and her breasts still so damn tempting.

Miranda stood up and pulled Tori with her. "To a bed."

She almost went to her own bedroom, remembering at the last minute that Rebel was asleep in there. She pivoted and took Tori down the hall to the guest room that hadn't been used in months. She shut the door and pinned Tori against the wall, their mouths melding together with heat that had been missing only seconds before. Tori wrapped her in an embrace, groaning when Miranda touched her everywhere she could again.

Dropping to her knees, Miranda tugged Tori's hips to her. She nuzzled her nose into those damp curls, her heart thundering. She had longed for this. It had been so long, and this would be perfect. She cascaded her hands down Tori's legs and back up again, catching her breath before she began.

"Please," Tori begged.

Miranda didn't need to be told twice. She started with a kiss, a gentle delicate kiss right to Tori's clit. Then she nuzzled and worked her way lower, lapping up her juices, swallowing them before she truly started in again. She wanted Tori to come all over her, to think about nothing but what was happening in this one moment.

She teased Tori's clit with the tip of her tongue, flicking it hard before she covered it entirely with her mouth. Tori grasped her hair, pulling and tensing her fingers as she pressed into the door to keep herself upright. So much for the bed happening. The only problem Miranda found with using her mouth was that she couldn't talk, couldn't ask what Tori wanted or how she needed Miranda to do something different. She was stuck hyper-focusing on Tori's body, paying attention to every silent tell that she could take in.

Tori gasped. Her nails dug into Miranda's scalp sharply. Her entire body jerked suddenly. She was close. She had to be. Miranda held onto her hips, pushing in more as excitement coursed through her. This was amazing. She'd almost forgotten how good cunnilingus felt, the taste of another woman against her lips, the wetness that made her cheeks sticky, the thrill that ran through her knowing she was in complete control of Tori's pleasure.

Wetness pooled against Miranda's cheeks. Her heart racing as Tori cried out, the sound reverberating through Miranda's body and setting every one of her nerves on fire. She longed for this—the connection. Tori hadn't been wrong. That's what good sex was about, and she was only now willing to admit it to herself. Tori tapped Miranda's head twice, a silent ask that she stop. Miranda dragged her tongue through Tori's slit, gathering up as much of her as possible.

Standing up, Miranda kissed Tori's lips. She took and she gave whatever she had. She wasn't sure what to do next, where they would go from there, but in this moment, she really didn't care. This was about finding sanctuary in each other from the chaos that pounded them. Miranda wasn't willing to give that up.

Tori snapped the buttons on Miranda's slacks and pushed her pants and underwear down over her hips. Miranda pulled back, eyeing Tori carefully. She ran her fingers over Tori's lips, down her neck and over the swell of her breasts to her nipples. She was just about to lean in when Tori's voice stopped her.

"What do you like?"

"Hmm?" Miranda had to find her brain again. She'd left it somewhere in the living room, and it hadn't caught back up with her.

"What do you like about sex?" Tori was already working her hands over Miranda's body, skimming, touching, testing.

Her mind was a blur, and it was so hard to focus. Miranda rested her forehead on Tori's shoulder and dragged in a deep breath of cool air. She had to think. Tori expected an answer. Only two words came to mind, two of the most honest words she had ever said. "Losing control."

"Perfect," Tori murmured. She flipped them swiftly, crushing their mouths together.

The door was hard against Miranda's back, her head bouncing off it slightly from the force that Tori took her. Tori was everywhere. How did she manage to do that? She must have ten hands and three mouths at least. Miranda opened her eyes, staring at Tori and trying to catch her bearings. What was happening?

Tori laced their fingers together and then tugged Miranda away from the door. She walked toward the bed, a smile on her lips and her eyes full of mischief. She turned Miranda and encouraged her to get on the bed. Miranda cocked her head to the side. "What are you doing?"

"Helping you to lose control." Tori crawled on top of her, pushing her down as she went.

Miranda pulled herself closer to the center of the mattress, waiting to see what would happen next. She'd asked for this in a roundabout way, and it seemed as though Tori was going to deliver. Tori straddled Miranda's hips, the smile never leaving her as she bent down and placed the most tender kiss Miranda had ever received on her lips.

"Close your eyes," Tori whispered. "Trust me."

Miranda never trusted. She'd been taught throughout her life that she could only rely on herself, but this was Tori. She'd done nothing but be there when Miranda needed her. She hadn't torn down any trust between them yet.

"Okay," Miranda murmured. This was a risk, but it was one she was willing to take for now. Closing her eyes, she slowed her breathing and listened only to the slight touches against her skin. The brush of Tori's hair along her breasts as she moved. The shift of the mattress. The puff of hot air from Tori's lips against her neck.

"Let me do this." Tori's voice was a balm.

Miranda calmed even more. Tori pressed gentle kisses to the hollow of her neck.

"I love the lines of your body. You have so much understated strength in your shoulders, physically." Tori kissed her collarbones. "The emotional strength you have isn't something anyone could miss."

Miranda's breath hitched.

Tori kissed down the center of Miranda's chest before hovering right over her heart. The hot air from her breath sent shivers through Miranda, hardening her nipples again. "You have a heart of gold. I see that in the work you do, but in the love you show for your family mostly."

A kiss to her heart. Then Tori moved to her breasts, nipples, twirling her tongue and sucking. Miranda clenched her fingers into the blanket underneath her, struggling to keep her eyes closed. She wanted to know where Tori was headed next, what she would say.

The kisses moved down her stomach, over the slight swell she'd gained with age and poor eating habits. Tori hummed, lavishing care on every part of her body. "You carry so much of your emotions here, don't you?"

How could she know that? Miranda wiggled, uncomfortable at being called out.

Tori kissed her again. "I wish I could ease the ache."

The kisses moved swiftly down over her hips to her legs and thighs. "You carry the weight of the world on these legs, the weight of more than just your life."

Miranda's body clenched, longing for Tori's mouth or fingers inside her. She drew in a sharp breath, struggling to stay still and listen. Everything Tori was doing was so odd but so very welcome. She was seen. For the first time in her entire life, someone saw her for who she was.

Tori kissed the arches of her feet, then the tops, all the while humming. "You will go anywhere you want, do anything you want, because you so effortlessly push aside your doubts when you need to."

Miranda clenched her jaw, tingles swimming through her and pooling between her legs. She just wanted to open her eyes, to see Tori, to know what she was thinking. But she already knew. Tori was telling her. Miranda raised her hands above her head, grasping anything she could find.

Working her way back up Miranda's body, Tori stopped at her hips. Her tongue moved against Miranda's hip bone, tantalizing her. This was torture. It had to be some form of torture that Miranda had never been privy to.

"Tori." She breathed out her name. "I need..." What did she need? She couldn't even find words anymore. Miranda swallowed hard, her eyes fluttering before she realized it and clenched them shut again. "I need you."

Tori's hair tickled her thighs, and finally, she was right where Miranda wanted her. The touch of her tongue was firm and everything Miranda wanted. She was already so close. It was something she'd never experienced before. It usually took ages for her to be worked up this much, but Tori had managed it in a few short minutes. That's all it had been, right?

She spread her legs, digging her fingers into the pillow she managed to grab. Every swipe of Tori's tongue was slow and steady, as if she planned to make this the longest orgasm on the planet. Miranda keened, her voice careening through the room as it ripped from her lungs. She arched her back, clenching her eyes as she held on to the last few moments before pleasure consumed her.

"Tori," she said as her body jerked sharply, and she tumbled.

Holding onto her, Tori pulled her through, keeping her hands on her body to steady her and root her to the bed. Miranda lost track of time, not sure how long it took for her to come to and remember what exactly they were doing there.

Tori was still down by her legs, running her hands smoothly up and down Miranda's thighs.

"Come up here." Miranda held her hand out for Tori to take. She climbed up and lay down next to Miranda, the length of their bodies pressed together. Miranda gave in and kissed her, the tension from the entire week—and months—washing away in an instant. Tori couldn't have been right, could she? No, this was only about sex, nothing more. But damn, it felt so good. "I'm so glad you came over tonight."

Tori giggled lightly. "Me too."

Another kiss.

One more.

Miranda relaxed entirely. "Don't go."

"Wasn't planning on it." Tori brushed her fingers through Miranda's hair. "Want me to hold you?"

"Yes." Miranda buried her face in Tori's neck, breathing her in. Sex. That's all it was. She just had to keep reminding herself of that.

fifteen

"Fancy meeting you here." Tori kept her tone bright and bubbly, at least as much as she could. She was nervous approaching Miranda in the parking lot. They hadn't really talked about what happened earlier that week, and Miranda's texts had been fairly clipped and short. Not that she wasn't always straight to the point. Maybe Tori was reading something into it that wasn't there.

"Yes, indeed." Miranda straightened her back, Rebel on her hip as they stepped out of Rebel's classroom.

Harley tightened her grip on Tori's hand, as if sensing how uneasy her mother was. They walked side by side, Tori moving Harley to walk in front of them. Miranda was dressed perfectly again, this time in dark black slacks and jacket with a maroon V-neck blouse with long sashes on the front.

"How's work been?" Tori bit her tongue. Why was this so awkward? They'd had sex, an amazing night of wonderful sex, some of the best she'd ever had. It shouldn't be this weird between them. They were adults. Surely they could navigate this.

"Busy," Miranda responded, tightening her hold when Rebel tried to wiggle free.

"Down!" Rebel shouted loudly.

Miranda jerked her head back in surprise, stopping in her tracks.

Tori grinned broadly. "Seems she's getting better at words."

"Seems so." Miranda pursed her lips, lines forming around the corners of her mouth and her eyes. "If I put you down, you have to hold my hand."

"'Arley." Rebel reached toward Harley, hands outstretched.

Tori loved it. The two of them had become so close in the short time they had known each other, and she loved watching Harley interact with a younger kid. It really did give her hope that maybe she'd make a good big sister. That was if she ever found her soulmate to have another kid with. The nerves were back.

"You want to hold Harley's hand?" Miranda asked.

Rebel grinned, nodding enthusiastically.

With a deep breath, Miranda set Rebel on the floor. She stood silently next to Harley, hand in hand, and looked back up at Miranda as if judging what was to happen next. Tori gave Miranda a pointed look before moving her hands and sending the girls forward down the hall so they could leave.

Once they were in the parking lot, Tori was glad to see that Harley kept her grip on Rebel's hand tight as they walked together toward their vehicles. She opened the door to let Harley in before shutting it while Miranda helped Rebel into her seat. Alone, Tori snagged Miranda's hand. She was surprised when Miranda didn't instantly pull back.

"Do you have a minute?" Tori's voice wavered. She hated that. Why was this so hard? They definitely should have talked more before just jumping into the sack together. It was as though a cloud of fog surrounded her when she drew close to

Miranda, as though logic flew out of the window and she was driven entirely by instinct and emotions.

"I'm on call tonight." Miranda looked at her, without truly meeting her eyes.

What the hell? Okay, Tori couldn't expect Miranda to suddenly be a different person. She nodded as if understanding, but that still didn't answer her question. "So you can or can't talk?"

"I have a minute." Miranda frowned. "It's been a really busy week, I'm sorry."

The temptation to ask all about it was there, but Tori needed to play it selfish in this moment. She wasn't Miranda's life coach. They'd had sex, and Tori really needed some kind of answer instead of the quiet resolve of whatever this was between them. "Do you maybe want to do a playdate again? I guess...let me say that again. Do you want to get together without the kids around?"

Miranda's lips parted, surprise etching into her face. Her honeyed eyes locked on Tori's now, wide with a mix of emotions swimming through them. She dropped her gaze to their still-joined hands and then dragged her eyes up Tori's body. It was as if they were back on that couch, in that bed, naked together. Tori tried to hold back the shudder, but she didn't quite manage it.

"No." Her answer was so simple, said without the least bit of emotion, and it was unnerving to Tori.

What did that mean? Had she been used? She loosened her grip on Miranda's fingers, letting them drop from her grasp. "Oh."

"I'm not looking for a relationship, Tori. I'm sorry if I gave you any other impression."

She hadn't. Not really. They'd talked about the very fact that Miranda didn't believe in soulmates. But did that mean all relationships were off the table? Apparently. What a lonely life to live. "No, I just meant…" What the hell had she meant? Suddenly her resolve had vanished and she'd been tossed into the unknown. Tori inwardly groaned, the soundtrack from *Frozen 2* echoing through her brain. "I just meant that we could get together, that's all."

"For what purpose?" Miranda crossed her arms, pressing her breasts up against that V, and Tori had to rip her gaze from her freckled skin.

Her heart hammered so loud that she swore Miranda would be able to hear it. "To talk."

Miranda's jaw tightened. She relaxed her stance and stepped in closer, lowering her voice so no one else could overhear them. "It was one night, Tori."

"I—I know." Did she, though? She really wanted it to be more than one night. Didn't Miranda want the same?

"I told you that I don't believe in soulmates." Miranda's breath was hot against her neck and her ear as she whispered.

Tori had to close her eyes, not just against the onslaught of emotions but against the physical sensations running through her. Miranda turned her head, brushing their cheeks together. She clasped Tori's arm lightly.

"I know you don't," Tori murmured. "I didn't say anything about soulmates. But the other night…" Tori trailed off. The other night what? Why was she suddenly at such a loss for words? She was better than this. "The other night was amazing."

Miranda flushed, her cheeks brightening with a pink undertone to them. "It was good."

"I guess I was just wondering if it was going to happen again. We haven't really talked about it." Tori's heart was at a gallop. This was forward even for her.

Miranda's breath hitched. She pulled away slightly, looking Tori directly in the eye. Her face fell when she said, "No. It's not going to happen again."

"Why not?" Tori grabbed her hand again, needing to know.

"Because I don't believe in soulmates and you do. I'm not the woman for you." Miranda pulled her lip between her teeth, her gaze definitely dropping to Tori's mouth before flicking back up.

"That. That right there. What was that?"

"Good memories." Miranda stepped away. "I'm sorry if I implied anything else. I didn't mean to. But one night is all this ever was. I don't regret it, and I hope you don't either."

"Miranda."

"I'll see you around, Tori." Miranda stepped confidently to her car and got in.

Tori stood, too stunned for words. A cold misty rain fell on her, wetting her face and lashes. It was rare that the Portland weather suited her mood. She stayed next to her car as Miranda backed out of the parking spot and drove off. What was she supposed to do with that? If Miranda was going to be so cold after an amazing night, then she was probably right to back off.

Hating herself for giving in to temptation when it presented itself, Tori got into her car and let out a breath. Harley chattered in the back about something to do with school that day, but she struggled to pay a lick of attention to it.

———

"You didn't have to come over." Tori smiled nonetheless.

"I wanted to." Siena wrapped her in a huge hug, tightening her grip. "Something in your voice said you needed me."

"Mom!" Harley stampeded through the living room and weaseled her way in between them.

Tori stepped back and let them have their time. It was good they were still friends. It meant that Harley got to see each of them more often than other kids did. Even if it was hard. Tori blew out a breath. She couldn't tell Siena what happened because she would get the *I told you so* lecture of a lifetime, and then a scolding for letting Miranda be around Harley before they all had a chance to discuss.

"So? Drinks or just dinner?" Siena set Harley down.

"Definitely drinks." But Tori wasn't going to be stupid. She'd avoid tequila, and she'd only have one. She didn't need to make that mistake twice. Or was it three times, if she included her buzzed night of sex with Miranda? Tori sighed as she stepped into the kitchen to get everything going.

Siena played with Harley for a bit while Tori started dinner. When Harley finally had enough of being entertained, she snagged Siena's phone and went to her room to watch some videos. Siena touched her hand to Tori's back as she stepped next to the counter.

"Spill the beans."

"What beans?" Tori's back was up. She was awful at lying, but even worse at hiding things, especially from Siena. This was going to take some very careful maneuvering.

"What's got you so upset?" Siena stole a chunk of chicken from the stir fry right off the skillet and popped it in her mouth.

"I'm not upset."

Siena snorted. "Like hell you're not. Is it that Miranda woman? I'll beat her up for you."

"What? No."

"Oh my god, it is, isn't it?" Siena's eyes widened. "I was just teasing, but I'm right. What happened?"

"Nothing happened." Tori frowned and pulled the food off the stove top, plating it. "Crushes suck. Okay? Nothing's going to happen. I promise." Not with the conversation they'd had earlier that day. "But I have this crush on her, and she doesn't reciprocate."

"So now she's your new best friend?" Siena raised an eyebrow. "What have I told you about being friends with everyone?"

"Well, it seems to have worked well with you and Aili." Tori felt like a child pouting to make her point.

"Touché." Siena chuckled. "So you have a crush on your new friend. That's not all that odd, you know. I think most people crush on their friends at some point, even if they're not sexually attracted to that gender or sex. It's normal to really like the people you're friends with."

"Really?" Tori gave her a dubious look. It all seemed too easy.

"Yeah. How do you think we ended up dating?" Siena hip-checked her, bringing the plates to the table so they could eat. "Harley! Dinner is ready!"

Dinner was easy conversation, the silent understanding clear that they wouldn't talk about current romantic relation-ships in front of Harley. Siena tucked Harley into bed, and when she came back out, she flopped on the couch next to Tori with a heavy sigh.

"You're not the only one who's having girl problems."

"I'm not?" Tori settled her hand on Siena's thigh.

Groaning, Siena flopped her head back on the couch. "Haylee and I got back together again. Briefly. Like for a couple nights."

"To have sex." Tori laughed. "You make a bad habit of that, don't you?"

"Shut up." Siena knocked their shoulders together. "You do, too."

"Oh, no, I don't." She'd only ever gone back to one woman, and that was Siena. "So you two had sex again, and then broke up again."

"Yeah. Double breakups are rough." Siena was smiling

though. "I still think you two would make a much better couple than her and me."

"You just told me you had sex with her and now you want me to have sex with her?" Tori frowned. "That's just weird."

"It's really not."

"It really is." Tori relaxed. "I'll think about it. Will that make you happy?"

"It might help you to forget Ms. Priestly."

"You saw it, too!" Tori turned and pointed her finger at Siena. "She does remind you of her, right?"

"Yeah, I can see it. She's all prim and proper, well dressed, perfectly coiffed, and icy as hell."

"Thank you!" Tori threw her hands up in the air like she'd just won the lottery. "I knew I wasn't just making it up. Freaked me out when I found out her name was Miranda."

"Yeah, that's hilarious."

Tori wrinkled her nose.

"But it might help you forget about her."

"Maybe." But Tori was doubtful. It'd been hard enough to get Miranda off her mind from the moment they had met. Hanging out with her had only made it worse. Having sex with her—mind-altering sex—had been the clincher. She hadn't stopped thinking about her since. But she had to. Because as Miranda pointed out, they weren't soulmates. And if Tori really wanted to find her soulmate by her thirtieth birthday, she had to stop avoiding dating.

Not to mention, Miranda wasn't her type at all. She wasn't in touch with herself and was far too cold and distant for Tori's liking. She preferred warmer women, like Siena. Women who would be her best friends before, during, and after a breakup. That had to be a bad sign, right? That she was already anticipating her breakup with Miranda? It was stupid. They weren't even together enough to have a proper breakup.

"What are you thinking?" Siena asked with a yawn.

Tori chuckled lightly. "That you need to get home before you fall asleep on my couch. Again."

"Yeah. Yeah." Siena dragged her weary butt off the cushion. "Let me know if you want Haylee's number, okay?"

"Will do." Tori followed Siena to the door and kissed her cheek as she left with a goodbye.

Alone in her apartment, she had nothing left to do other than start again on finding her soulmate. Because Miranda had made herself crystal clear—she wasn't it.

sixteen

"So I need to get her two-year-old shots before she can come back?" Miranda ran her fingers through her hair—a habit she had long ago trained herself out of, and yet here she was, doing it all over again. She knew it wasn't Aili's fault. She tried to remind herself of that fact again and again.

The woman had been amazing with everything up to and even including this point. Rebel had turned two a couple weeks ago, and Aili had told her about it then. She had given her the two-week reprieve.

Miranda had tried, but without Tierney's written consent, she couldn't get Rebel her next shots, because she wasn't her legal guardian.

"I'm sorry, Miranda. I truly am. I know it's not ideal, but if I allowed her to stay and anything were to happen, the department could close us down."

"Fine." Miranda snapped. She wanted to apologize, to tell Aili it was okay and that she understood. But ever since that talk with Tori in the parking lot, even the most minor inconvenience set her off. And then there was the whole Aili being one of Tori's exes. She wondered if they had badges and annual meetings.

"Miranda?" The concern in Aili's tone was definitely something she didn't need. Nor did she need the pathetic *woe is me* thoughts running through her head. "I'll save Rebel's spot for another couple of weeks so you have time to get the immunizations."

Miranda frowned, casting her gaze over Aili. She did fit Tori's type, especially if she thought about herself and Siena. Tall, dark, and handsome. Perhaps she was a bit on the bigger side compared to the two of them, but Miranda couldn't imagine that would be something Tori would care all too much about.

Miranda wanted to vomit. She nodded sharply at Aili, acknowledging what she'd said, and then turned on her heels and stormed out of the office. She collected Rebel with as little conversation with the staff as possible. Even less than normal.

Miranda had managed to bite back her frustration at the teacher who told her they had allowed Rebel to sleep almost three hours at rest time instead of the conventional two. It would make bedtime a horror show. But she had not been as successful at stopping the growl that rumbled in her chest.

She swung Rebel up on her hip, her school bag flung over the other shoulder, and headed for the exit.

What the hell was wrong with her?

This wasn't an issue with Aili and the school. Miranda cringed. She'd had plenty of one-night stands. Almost all of her sexual encounters had been since she called off the engagement. They were that or they were long-term friends with benefits—mostly benefits since Miranda didn't really consider herself someone who had friends. People let her down, repeatedly, and she wasn't willing to give that trust to just anyone.

So why the hell did this one matter?

Rebel wriggled in her arms as she pushed open the front

door of the daycare. Miranda stopped and stared at the drizzling rain that hadn't shown any sign of coming in when she had gone inside.

"Sorry, Rebel. Looks like we are going to get a little wet. How about a nice warm bath when we get home?"

Rebel snuggled into Miranda, and she took a deep breath of sandy hair and dirty skin. She had been unimpressed with it the first time she had collected Rebel from the daycare, but now it held more than her nose could ever detect. It told her about Rebel's day, about what she did during the hours that she was there.

"Come on." Miranda made an effort to soften her tone. It would be a long night, but snapping at Rebel would do nothing to help the headache that pulsed at her temples.

They were halfway across the parking lot, the drizzle more of an annoyance than anything else, when Rebel bucked against Miranda's hip.

"What? What's wrong?" She stopped walking, oblivious to the danger of where they stood, her mind entirely caught on what had happened to make Rebel all but convulse in her arms.

"'Arley, down." Rebel met Miranda's eyes, face scrunching up before she screamed again. "'Arley, down now!"

Miranda's heart thudded rapidly. Harley? Cold raced over her skin, a cold that had precisely nothing to do with the misted drops that fell from her hair and slid beneath the collar of her shirt. Tori couldn't be there. Not today. She couldn't handle it.

"Where's Harley, Rebel?" Miranda asked, hoping her voice didn't carry to wherever Tori might be. As she waited for Rebel's reply, she scanned the area. Three cars lined up facing the door, waiting for the two of them to move from where she had stopped in her tracks.

She couldn't just stand there any longer. She never should

have stopped in the middle of the road anyway, especially not with Rebel with her. She should have known better, protected Rebel better from potential oncoming traffic.

"Okay, we'll find Harley in a second." Miranda's usual click of heels on the asphalt was drowned out by the puddles of water she traipsed through, unsure if she wanted to keep this promise to Rebel or escape without another encounter that would undoubtedly scar them both with the mood she was in.

"Rebel." Harley's small voice piped up from the car parked next to Miranda's.

"'Arley, 'Arley, 'Arley," Rebel sing-songed, swaying a little too far back and forth in Miranda's arms, requiring her to support the small but surprisingly strong child with her other hand. Visions of them both toppling to the ground plagued her. She couldn't lose their entire center of gravity if Tori was in the vicinity. That would be more embarrassment than she could manage right now. She was already embarrassed with the encounter with Aili and the disappointment running through her voice. Yep, this would be the last thing she needed.

"Oh hey." The voice that came from the car was not the one she expected.

Siena.

Miranda died a little inside.

This could potentially be worse.

Tori and Siena were best friends it seemed. So just what had Tori told her about what had happened?

Miranda had been so wrong, falling over was the second to last thing she needed. Miranda dared a look up and saw Siena's head poking up over the roof of her car. She had a bright smile on her face, her dark eyes excited about something. Miranda wished she knew what went on behind that mask of happiness, but it sickened her to think about it.

"Mom, it's Rebel and 'Randa," Harley screeched from the

back seat of the car, her face pressed up against the small crack of the window.

"I see that, Harley." Siena smirked and gave a small nod to Miranda. "Now buckle yourself in your seat, so we can get going."

"But Mom, I wanna play with Rebel," Harley whined.

"Maybe another time. We've got to get going." Siena tapped the top of the car, as if to get Harley's attention.

"Hi, 'Randa."

Miranda chuckled as Harley pursed her lips trying to smoosh the words through the crack in the window. She couldn't fault the girl for trying her best.

"Hi, Harley." Miranda smiled, and it hurt her to realize it was the first genuine smile she could remember giving all day. All week maybe. What was she doing? Because it wasn't life. She wasn't doing it well, anyway.

"Wanna come over and play?" Harley bounced in her car seat, still not buckled in.

"What your mom said. Maybe another day. I've got lots to work out for Rebel this afternoon."

"Everything okay?" Siena asked, genuine concern in her voice.

Miranda blinked and stared at the head that continued to float over the roof of the car. Why would Siena care? Was she hinting at something? Had Tori told her everything?

Miranda's cheeks heated up and burned. Of course Tori would have. Tori's secrets would be the shortest book in the entire world. She couldn't keep anything to herself, could she? Not one damn thing.

"Just some trouble with Rebel's enrollment." Miranda couldn't believe she had said that. She wasn't following too far behind Tori in that regard, was she? Meeting Tori had turned her into someone who would tell virtual strangers about her problems. "It's fine. I'll handle it."

"Oh yeah, sure." Sounds of Siena's feet sloshing around against wet pavement competed with her words.

A moment of silence and then another jerk from Rebel as she threw herself closer to the car where Harley chatted with pouting lips almost pushed through the window gap. The two made quite the pair as they continued to play through the crack in the window.

Siena stopped in front of Miranda, her arms crossed and a sour look on her face. She eyed Miranda up and down, judging her completely. This was what Miranda had been worried about. Now the rain coming down wouldn't just be from the sky. It'd be from the hellfire that Siena was about to unleash.

"Look, I know I shouldn't say anything, and I have no idea what actually happened, but it's obvious something has. Tori was very cagey the other night. So I get it if you don't want to call Tori." Siena lowered her voice, as if the girls couldn't hear her. They were probably too distracted anyway. "But she has heaps of contacts through her job that might be able to help with whatever issue is happening with Rebel's enrollment. Or I can go inside and beat Aili up for you. Wouldn't be the first time."

Miranda blanched. She shook her head, nearly losing her grip on Rebel as she tried to climb through the window. She remained speechless. This woman who had sized her up and obviously decided she was not good enough for Tori now stood there encouraging Miranda to call her? Offered to step in and do something for her? For what purpose? There had to be a catch.

"First time?" A droplet of water ran down Miranda's chin, dropping to her chest and running between her breasts. They really needed to get out of the rain.

Siena sighed. "Yeah, did Tori tell you about dating Aili?"

"Briefly."

"Right, I bet she gave you the nice version of the story, that Aili introduced her to me after they were done dating?"

"Yes." Where was Siena going with this? And what did it matter?

Siena snorted and scuffed her shoe against the pavement. "Yeah, that's the nice version all right. We were all kind of dating at the same time. It's true that Aili introduced us, but I didn't realize they were a thing—a non-exclusive thing to be very clear, no cheating involved—when I made my move on Tori. Let's just say I won, and Aili was not a happy camper, as you can expect, and in the end none of us won."

"Oh." Miranda tightened her grip on Rebel. "So um… what was the purpose of this story?"

"That I can still beat Aili up for you if you need me to." Siena winked. "Not really, but I'll have your back if you need."

"No, it's nothing you can help with." Not unless Siena could magically get Tierney to sign a single sheet of paper.

"Okay. Well, still, give Tori a call. I know it'll be awkward, but she does have a lot of contacts and might be able to help you out with whatever the problem is."

"Unless she can change laws at the snap of her fingers, unlikely."

"Miranda." Siena had a bite in her tone. She glanced at the girls and lowered her voice again. "Call her. I've got Harley tonight, so she's got the time."

Miranda nodded and pulled Rebel back to her own car, calling a goodbye to Harley as she did. She wasn't sure what to say to Siena's final statement, but she put Rebel into her seat. Miranda fussed around while getting Rebel buckled, and by the time she stood back up, Siena was already in her car, window rolled up, and backing out slowly. When she saw the taillights of Siena's car behind her through the rearview mirror, she slumped in her seat and let out a large breath of air. But she still gripped the wheel a little too tightly.

Looking for the taillights that were now gone, she flicked the rearview mirror so she could see Rebel as she drew with sticky fingers on the window.

"What do you think, Rebel, should we call Tori and see if she can help with our little dilemma?"

Miranda busied herself with starting the car and getting them to her parents' house for dinner that night. As she pulled into the driveway, she sighed, unable to fight the urge to find out exactly what Siena was talking about and even more importantly what exactly Tori had confessed to her ex-wife.

She hated herself just a little as she pulled up the contacts list on her phone and tapped Tori's name. The car's speakers kicked in, and with each ring, Miranda's heart beat a little faster.

"Hello?" Tori's voice sounded less sure than Miranda had ever heard it. Had she done that to her? No, this wasn't Miranda's fault. She was reading too much into an unsteady word, which could have just as easily been nothing more than the car's reception. It was raining after all.

"Hi." Miranda hesitated for a moment, and then, fingers gripping the steering wheel hard enough for her knuckles to turn white, she pushed on like she would have with anyone else. "I was hoping we might be able to catch up tonight. I'm having some problems with Rebel's enrollment, and it was suggested to me you might know someone who could possibly help."

"Oh, I can't tonight." Tori rushed out. "I have Harley with me, and I've promised her some one-on-one Mommy and Harley time."

Miranda froze. Never before had Tori lied to her, at least not that she knew of. But this was a blatant outright lie. Anger swirled in her stomach, and she tensed at the very thought. She had trusted Tori, and now she was breaking that connection between them. Maybe she had misunderstood. "You have Harley?"

"Yes." Tori's voice held a coldness Miranda had never heard. It shouldn't bother her. She had never lied or misled Tori about what she believed or her intentions. It was Tori's issue if she couldn't handle the reality of them having a one-night stand. But that didn't mean everything else had to fall away, did it?

Miranda looked up in the rearview mirror and met Rebel's eyes. Rebel smiled and waved, a small giggle filling the car. On the one hand, she couldn't believe that Tori had flat-out lied to her, and on the other...the other what? Miranda hadn't given her any reason to, had she?

"I guess I'll see you around then." Before Tori could respond, Miranda hung up.

She ran her tongue across her teeth as she stared at her parents' house. What was she even doing? She hated this. That night had been more than just sex, but that didn't mean they had to hate each other when it ended either. And she'd never told Tori it would be more. In fact, she made it very clear that it wouldn't be more.

Stepping into her parents' house, Miranda set her shoulders. She needed to sort this out. "Mom, I need to ask you to watch Rebel."

"Are you sure?"

Miranda had known they'd put up a fight about it, but she needed the time. She nodded. "Yes. I'm on call. It's going to be a late night, too. It might be easier if she just stays the night here."

Let them deal with the three-hour nap.

"Miranda, she's your responsibility."

"Actually, no, she's not. Because Tierney couldn't be the decent parent to make sure everything was taken care of." She knew she was being cruel, but she was worn down and tired of running around and doing her bidding. "I need to go out tonight, which means I need you to watch Rebel. Be the grand-parents you should be."

Miranda dropped the diaper bag from daycare with the extra clothes and everything in it at the front door. She kissed Rebel's pudgy cheeks and walked out of the house and back out into the rain.

"I'll get her in the morning." She just needed one night to get her head on straight and figure out how to solve this problem.

Miranda left the house, her mother too stunned to protest. They knew how to get hold of her if there were any disasters. They'd kept Rebel overnight before, although it had been when she was a baby and easier to watch. Slipping behind the wheel, Miranda clenched her jaw. She wasn't going to let Tori get away with this lie. Not without a good explanation for it.

seventeen

The knocking startled her. Tori was instantly tense as she stared at her apartment door, knowing exactly who was on the other side. She should have known better than to lie. Miranda was too smart to be duped by a simple lie like that, or really any lie. The question remained, however, did she want to answer?

Four sharp raps echoed.

Fine.

She didn't really have another choice, did she? Miranda knew she was home. Leaving her phone on the side table, Tori stood up and took her time going to the door. She flicked the locks and bolstered herself for the firestorm she had created.

Miranda was soaked.

Her clothes were drenched. Her hair hung limply against her head and shoulders. Her makeup was smeared. If Tori didn't know better, she'd say she'd been crying. But this was Miranda. She wouldn't cry, not over some woman she had fucked and left.

Tori gritted her teeth, standing in the doorway to prevent Miranda from coming in. She wasn't sure how this entire debacle was going to go, but she wanted as much control from the start as she could muster.

"You have a lot of explaining to do." Miranda's eyes widened with her accusation. Perhaps she was surprised by her own outburst of anger.

"I didn't want to see you tonight." Honesty. That should have been what she started and ended with, and it was her own stupid mistake for doing anything but. "I'm sorry I lied. I panicked, and I should have been better than I was."

Miranda seemed to stop cold. Her chest heaved, which meant her breasts pushed against the white, now sheer fabric of her blouse. Tori swallowed hard. They weren't going to do this again. She had to keep reminding herself of that.

"You lied to me about having Harley."

"I did, and for that, I'm sorry. I shouldn't have, and I know I hurt you in the process of trying to protect myself. That's my own fault."

Again, Miranda seemed stumped. Was she not expecting Tori to apologize? Frowning, Tori held the handle of the door and stayed put.

"This is absurd."

"I agree," Tori said truthfully. "I'll talk to you later, Miranda."

Just as she went to shut the door, Miranda flung her hand out, smacking it against the door and pushing it open. She cocked her head to the side, her eyes wild. "No, I'm not done yet."

"I am."

"No." Miranda straightened her shoulders, but she didn't step into the apartment, keeping that boundary line firmly in place. Her breathing was rapid, her lips slightly parted as she stared Tori down. "You lied to me. That's the first thing I'm ticked about."

"I did." Tori took a deep breath. How many times were they going to go through this? And what was the second thing?

"I saw Siena today, and she knew—" Miranda's voice broke. She gathered herself before continuing, "What did you tell her?"

"Nothing." Tori's heart raced. What the hell had Siena said? Also, that explained how Miranda had known she was home alone. "What did she say?"

"She told me to call you." Miranda's hands clenched into fists at her sides. "She told me she knows something happened, but the girls were right there, and I didn't get the sense she wanted to talk about it in front of them. What did you tell her?"

Tori sucked her lips between her teeth, deciding to get to the center of the issue. She was done pussyfooting around. "Why are we even having this discussion?"

"What?" Miranda's word had a bite to it.

"Why are we talking about this? There's nothing going on between us, is there?" She knew it was a ploy to get Miranda to react, but she had to know what was going on behind her well-honed resting bitch face.

Miranda took a step backward, putting space between them as if she was taken aback. Now was Tori's chance to tell her to back up and leave. This was the moment when she slammed the door in Miranda's face and told her she never wanted to see her again. But looking into her honeyed eyes, she couldn't. Because Tori wanted every part of Miranda. She wanted to peel back those layers and find out what was behind all the curtains that she put up to hide behind.

Tori pressed her lips together when Miranda took another backward step in retreat. "Miranda, what are you doing?"

"Talking." She sounded so damn calm all of a sudden. So in control.

When had they flipped roles? Tori's heart was in her throat, her entire body humming with arousal from that one damn look in Miranda's gaze. "Talking about what?"

"You betrayed me."

Tori flinched. "I broke your trust."

That was everything this was about, wasn't it? Miranda wouldn't have cared if she'd said no, or told her not to come over, or said she couldn't help. What Miranda cared about was the bond they had been building had not only been halted but snapped tenuously in two. And to add insult to injury, she thought Tori was spreading gossip about what they had done. For a woman who never shared anything, that was the straw that would break the camel's back.

Melting, Tori stepped out of her apartment and reached for Miranda, who had drawn closer. She said her name on a sigh, "Oh, Miranda. I'm so sorry. I didn't tell Siena anything, I promise. But she's not blind. I'm so sorry I hurt you."

"Don't do it again." Miranda stood right in front of her, water dripping off her clothes and down her face as the rain pelted both of them. Tori's shoulders were already soaked, her nipples hardening from the cold. Miranda took one step, coming into Tori's space, suddenly no longer on the defensive but the offensive.

Tori caught the drop of Miranda's gaze to her lips a second before their mouths connected in a brutal kiss. This was nothing like what the other night had been. It was all fire and heat, passion and anger. Miranda was on her, pushing her against the railing on the balcony, hands and fingers everywhere. Rain continued to pelt down on them, drenching them in its sorrow.

Groaning, Tori threaded her fingers into Miranda's wet hair and pulled sharply. "Miranda."

"Tell me to stop if you want me to stop," Miranda rushed the words before moving back in for another kiss.

Tori melted. She didn't want this to end. She had wanted

this to happen again the moment it had finished the first time. Wrapping her arms around Miranda's middle, she pulled Miranda into her. Water soaked into Tori's thin shirt and shorts, chilling her legs and arms, but she didn't care. She had wanted this just as much as Miranda had.

They were soaked through, but Tori didn't want to move. The cold air was the strong reminder that she needed. She'd hurt Miranda, and this woman was just as fragile as the next. Tori needed to take better care next time. She needed to be a better person. Because Miranda demanded it. Tori slid her hands up Miranda's back, realizing just how wet her clothes really were. How long had she stood out in the rain before knocking?

"Don't lie to me again." This time it sounded like a plea. Miranda dropped her mouth to Tori's neck, licking the droplets of rain as they trickled down Tori's body.

"Never," Tori murmured before tangling their tongues together. She had her hands under Miranda's blazer in a second, pushing it off her shoulders as she spun them around and walked them into the open apartment door. "We need to get you warm."

Miranda snorted, but the tension that she'd shown up with was gone. She pressed Tori into the entryway wall, their mouths still playing against each other. It was so damn hard to get the buttons on her blouse undone with her shirt soaked through. Frustrated, Tori leaned her shoulders against the wall, trying to pull a button. Miranda shoved Tori's hands away and did it herself.

Tori pulled her own shirt off in the meantime. As soon as Miranda was done and out of her shoes, Tori brought their mouths together again. She didn't want this slow like the first time. She wanted to get Miranda underneath her, against her, anything. Pushing Miranda backward toward her bedroom, Tori took the lead. She needed to make up for the trust she had broken, and she would do everything in her power to right that wrong.

Her fingers played at Miranda's slacks, needing to get the wet clothes off her entirely. Her skin was so cold to touch, a pale color with goosebumps running all over her arms and chest and stomach. She had Miranda on the bed and dragged her pants off. She was finally naked, her hair sticking to her chest as she gasped in deep breaths.

"What do you want?" Tori asked, remembering just how sexy that had been last time.

Miranda shook her head sharply and closed her eyes. "Just fast, dirty, and hard. Anything to get me off."

Tori shoved her shorts off and climbed onto the bed, settling her thigh in between Miranda's legs. "Not slow?"

"Fuck no," she said on a laugh.

Miranda gripped Tori's arms tightly before sliding her hand between them. She flicked her fingers between Tori's legs, finding her clit and rubbing. Groaning, Tori pressed her head down into Miranda's shoulder.

"God damn, you're freezing."

"Ignore it," Miranda demanded. "Make me feel everything."

Tori pulled back, staring down into Miranda's unmasked gaze. This was who she was, everything Tori had asked for. She only wished she could see her like this more often. Bending down, Tori pressed their mouths together, intending to go slow. Miranda arched her back up, her hand cupping the back of Tori's head, deepening the embrace and bringing things to a furious pace.

Tori had two fingers knuckle deep inside Miranda when she finally broke the kiss. Miranda moved against her, rutting her hips as she gripped onto Tori's shoulders to keep herself right where she wanted.

"You deserve everything," Tori whispered, dropping kisses to Miranda's collarbone and neck. "You deserve the world."

Miranda's voice caught in her throat, the smallest groan.

"I shouldn't have lied. I'm so sorry I did." Tori scraped her teeth against Miranda's neck, wondering if she'd leave a mark by the end of the night. What would Miranda do if she did? "You were right."

Miranda gasped.

"I should have taken better care of what we have." Tori kissed Miranda's chest, moving down to her breasts, keeping the steady rhythm of her fingers and thumb going. She sucked on Miranda's nipples, teasing them with the tip of her tongue before stretching back out on top of her. "You were right to call me out."

"Come here," Miranda slurred as she pulled Tori back down, their lips touching in a brief kiss. "Shut up."

"Never." Tori laughed lightly. "Because you deserve all the words and communication. That's how we move forward, isn't it?"

Miranda didn't answer. Her eyelids fluttered shut as her face pinched up. Heat rushed around Tori's fingers, wet adding to wet. A flush rose against Miranda's breasts and cheeks as she pulsed around Tori.

"There you are." Tori pressed delicate kisses to Miranda's cheeks, the corner of her mouth, her neck. "I want to mark you so bad."

"Do it." Miranda crumbled.

Tori scraped her teeth against the hollow of Miranda's neck, to the spot where her shoulder and neck met. She nibbled lightly, sucking the still-cool skin between her teeth. Tori took her time, warming Miranda inch by inch as she explored her body now that she had been given the time. She left bite marks here and there, all over her chest, her thighs, her hip bone. By the time she started back up, Miranda put her hand on Tori's head and shoved her back down. "Not done yet."

Chuckling, Tori raised her gaze up to meet those now amused honeyed eyes. "Care to tell me what you want now?"

"Your mouth on me. Don't stop until I can't breathe."

"Not something I'm willing to say no to."

Tori took her sweet time moving between Miranda's legs, pressing kisses here and there as she went, another hickey when she had a chance. Miranda tried to get her to move faster, but she refused. It may have been furious in the beginning, but now she was in complete control again.

"Tori," Miranda whined. "Enough of that already."

"I'm pretty sure you told me you wanted to feel everything. So either you lied to me, or I'm doing exactly what you wanted and you're just impatient."

Miranda huffed.

"That's what I thought."

Tori started again, just to annoy Miranda into another orgasm if she could. But when she finally nuzzled her face between Miranda's legs, the short-trimmed hairs biting into her cheeks and lips, Tori knew they were both beyond ready. She didn't even tease this time. She pulled Miranda's clit fully into her mouth, sucking, and swirling her tongue. She took in deep breaths, all her thoughts and senses consumed by Miranda.

"Tori," Miranda called, her back arching up again. "Tori, I don't think…" She paused. "I don't think…"

"Don't think then," Tori said quickly before diving back in. She wished Miranda would just stop thinking sometimes. It might get them both out of a whole lot of trouble—or into it—if she did.

Miranda curled up, holding her body up with one hand behind her. She held onto the back of Tori's head, pressing her firmly between her legs as she rode through her orgasm, crying out as she held on tightly. When Miranda finally eased her grasp, Tori slowed and moved back up her body with gentle kisses. Miranda flopped onto her back, her hands above her as she shook her head and laughed lightly.

"What on earth was that?"

"What was what?" Tori popped her head up, grinning when she saw the look Miranda was giving her.

"Don't think? Do you realize how hard that is to do?" Miranda was still trying to catch her breath.

"For you? Absolutely." Tori twirled her finger around Miranda's still erect nipple, continuing to tease her. She could go all night at this rate if she wanted. The burst of adrenaline from earlier was finally kicking her body into high gear.

Miranda stilled suddenly. She reached up, brushing the backs of her fingers against Tori's cheek. Tori leaned into the caress, so soft compared to anything they had done together before now. "I'm sorry I was angry."

"Angry or hurt?" Tori locked their eyes together, needing to see the truth behind whatever Miranda said.

"Hurt."

"I shouldn't have hurt you," she whispered. "And I'm so sorry that I ever did."

Miranda's thumb brushed her lips, then down her neck to her chest, barely touching her nipples. Tori sucked in a sharp breath, wanting to lean in and take her again.

"You did hurt me." Miranda frowned. "Because I trusted you."

It was so hard to see the hope through Miranda's despair, but Tori took comfort in the fact that Miranda had trusted her. She had been open to whatever was between them, and she hadn't shut it down. It nearly brought her to tears to see the pain behind Miranda's gaze.

"I hope you can trust me again," Tori whispered, taking Miranda's hand and kissing her palm and then her wrist. "I know how hard it is to trust."

Miranda hummed, her eyes heavy with emotion. "I'm beginning to wonder if you might be worth it."

Was that…? Was that what Tori thought it was? Was that Miranda's own hope shining through? Tori leaned in and kissed her, not sure what to say. She held the kiss, making it simple and pure, a true gift of what she was feeling in response to Miranda's sharing. It took a moment, but Miranda reached up, fingers tangling in Tori's hair as she pulled down to deepen the embrace.

Humming, Tori stayed right where she was, half-propped against Miranda's naked and warming body. She let Miranda take whatever she needed, giving and giving as best as she could. Eventually Miranda pulled back and smiled up at her. "We're not done for tonight, I hope."

Tori's lips pulled upward. "I can go all night."

"Hmmm, I'm not sure if I can. My body is jelly."

"I'll take that as a compliment."

Miranda smacked her lightly on the hip. "You're cocky."

"Only sometimes." Tori stole another kiss.

"Tell me what you want." Miranda started moving more, her strokes firmer and more sure. "Make it simple for my old body, will you?"

"Anything for you." Tori laughed as she pulled away from a pouting Miranda. "I'm coming back, just give me a second."

Miranda didn't move as Tori got up on her knees. She saw the second it clicked in Miranda's brain what was happening. Miranda settled flat on her back, pulling her hair under her shoulder so Tori wouldn't kneel on it accidentally. Straddling Miranda's face was something else entirely. Miranda didn't hesitate before pressing her tongue firmly against Tori, licking her completely.

Tori hummed and then chuckled as tingles rushed through her. "I was not prepared for that."

"Are you ever prepared for it?"

"With you? No. I think you like to surprise me."

"Always. Are you sure this is what you want?" Miranda asked, making sure they could see each other.

Tori was having such a hard time staying still, but she smiled down. "Yeah. All I want is you."

eighteen

Miranda's skin tingled as she brushed her fingers lightly over one of the spots Tori had marked on her. The skin rose in small lumps, like braille impressions. They could only be seen from certain angles, but Miranda ran the tips of her fingers over the marks again and shivered, pressing her thighs together. Tori had branded her as though Miranda belonged to her. She had never truly felt like she belonged anywhere, and certainly not with anyone.

She knew she should be concentrating, focusing on the files she opened on her home computer. But everything ached just a little and in the most delicious and distracting of ways. Miranda took a deep breath, forcing her fingers away from the branded skin and settled her hands back on to her keyboard.

"Are you okay, Rebel?" Miranda turned her head to check on Rebel, who played happily in the corner of Miranda's home office.

Rebel smiled up at Miranda, a small doll in each of her hands. She waved them around with a giggle.

"'Arley."

"Oh, they're ones from Harley?" Even that thought

warmed her. Harley had accepted Rebel into her life like they were meant to be. *Soulmates.* The word came crashing through her memory, stunning her.

Rebel sang, her entire body moving with the tilt of her head. "'Arley, 'Arley, 'Arley an' me."

"We'll see Harley again sometime soon." Miranda smiled and warmth grew almost painfully in her chest. She had said the words so easily and hoped she wasn't actually lying to her niece.

Rebel returned to playing, and Miranda enjoyed the sound of her chatting in words that Miranda still couldn't always interpret, but she was getting better. Pride bloomed in her chest that Rebel now had words that needed to be interpreted. Miranda stole another look at Rebel playing and shook her head slightly at all the toys that lay on the ground. There were now more toys in Miranda's house than she ever imagined necessary for a single child. But that was before all of this had started.

So much had shifted in her world. With a deep breath, she faced the reality that a lot had also shifted inside of her. It had now been two months since Tierney had left. Had it already been that long? Had it really only been that long? She almost couldn't believe that Tierney had missed Rebel's birthday. She'd thought for certain that would drag her flaky sister home again.

She returned her attention to the screen, but her mind wandered again as she signed off on one document and clicked on the next. In the back of her mind, she worried about not being at work this morning, but they had all reassured her that they had it covered. She had little other choice but to work from home until she got the paperwork sorted out for Rebel and got her immunizations done. The lack of control rubbed against her like sandpaper against her skin.

She had left three messages for Tierney already, but

resigned herself to the fact that it might be a while before her sister listened to them, let alone called back or signed the letter Miranda needed. It might push her to have to take more drastic steps when it came to custody, and that was something she had resisted for the two years since Rebel had been born.

She still couldn't understand how Tierney and Tori could be the same age yet so completely opposite to each other. Miranda knew without question that Tori would never leave Harley in search of her soulmate. Even though Tori seemed just as determined to find the elusive person as Tierney was, she had such an amazing balance and understanding of who she was.

The sound of her phone made her jump, the chair leaning back a little too quickly for her liking.

"Shit." The expletive came out before she could stop it.

"Shit, shit, shit," Rebel mimicked as she continued to play.

"Of course that's the word you pick up instantly," Miranda muttered as she lifted the phone and saw an unknown number. She sighed and hit the answer button.

"Miranda speaking."

"Hey sis!" Tierney's voice came through clear. Much crisper than she had heard over the last two months.

"Did you get a new number?"

"Yeah, I had to get rid of the old number."

Miranda bit back the question she wanted to demand an answer to. She could hear all about that later even though she knew what had happened. Tierney had completely run out of money. First, she needed to get Rebel sorted out.

"Did you get my messages?"

"I got one before my phone was turned off." Tierney's voice took on that giggly quality again.

Miranda bit the insides of her cheeks. She couldn't snap at Tierney, no matter how much she wanted to tell her to get home and finally act like the parent she was supposed to be.

"I'm going to the library today and will write up the letter and put all the details that you need for the doctor."

"Great." Miranda blinked, ashamed at her instant impression that Tierney would brush off the need for the letter. But to be fair, she had a pretty substantial track record of putting Rebel second on her list, after the search for her soulmate.

"So, when are you going to send me photos of her birthday party?"

"What?" Confusion swam through Miranda's brain. What was Tierney even talking about?

"It was her birthday, Miranda. Don't tell me you didn't have a party for my baby!"

"I know that, Tierney." Miranda tried to bite back her tone, but was Tierney serious? She hadn't bothered to even call on her daughter's birthday and now she expected photos of a birthday party Miranda was supposed to have had? No communication about it either.

"So what did you end up doing?"

"We didn't really celebrate it," Miranda said between clenched teeth.

"What? My baby turned two, and you didn't do anything?" Tierney's pouty whine came through the line, and Miranda had images of dogs in the neighborhood all looking up in search of the sound.

"Well, I didn't want you to miss out." Miranda slowed her voice with all the effort she could muster. "So I thought we could celebrate it a little later, once you get back home."

"Oh." Tierney squealed, and the imaginary dogs in Miranda's brain all whined at the sudden high-pitched sound. "Thank you! You are the bestest sister in the world."

Miranda made a non-committal sound that she doubted Tierney heard as she began talking about all the things she would do for Rebel when she got home. The party was apparently just the beginning.

"I need to go help Marcus now."

"With what?"

"With the car."

"You? Getting dirty working on a car?" Miranda scoffed, unable to even picture the scene.

"Well, you have to be willing to bend a little to make relationships work, Miranda. It's what you've never understood. Besides, I won't get to the library to write this letter if the car doesn't get fixed."

"Right." Miranda nodded to herself and sighed as Rebel climbed into her lap. It must be almost nap time. "Well, I better let you go. If you can please remember to send the letter as soon as possible, that would be good."

"Of course! I want to make sure my baby is safe and healthy. And the other daycares in the area aren't nearly as nice as that one. I don't want her to lose her place."

"Okay. Be safe." She did believe that her sister loved Rebel. She just wasn't very good at showing it sometimes.

"Bye-bye," Tierney sing-songed before she hung up.

"That was your mom," Miranda said, as she twirled her fingers in Rebel's hair. She had managed to tame it to an extent. But the tangles came back quickly if she didn't keep up with it.

Rebel's breathing slowed, and her weight grew heavier as Miranda continued to run her fingers through her hair.

Tori and Tierney couldn't be more different, and yet their goals remained the same. But was Tierney right? She had to be willing to bend for a relationship to work? Maybe all her experiences of chasing her soulmate had taught her a thing or two. But there was so much work to make a relationship grow, to allow the individuals to continue on their own paths without being drowned by the relationship. Was that something Miranda could even do? Her work meant the world to her, and she couldn't imagine not doing the late nights and the early mornings, the extra-long days and the draining conversations with the grief stricken.

Rebel's quiet snores filled her office.

And if she tried the relationship thing with Tori, it wouldn't just be the hard work of a relationship, it would involve parenting as well. Even if Tori wanted her to have only a minimal parenting input, there would still be times when she would have to step in. She couldn't name a single person she knew who remained happy in their relationship once a child was introduced to the equation. Tori was perfect proof of that. Divorced and a single parent.

Miranda knew all of these things. She had understood that she was not the relationship type. Workaholics rarely were. But she had never had someone like Tori to consider being on the other side of a relationship.

She kissed the top of Rebel's head and swiveled her chair slowly back around to face her computer.

Her insides churned. There was beauty in the falling pieces, but she had no idea where those pieces would land, and whether or not she would like the way it looked once they did. Besides, until Tierney returned, Rebel had to be her priority. She should have done something for Rebel's birthday rather than just making it like any other day of the week. Even the daycare had taken a picture and made a big deal about it.

Miranda managed to get through several more reports before Rebel stirred. When they returned to her office after lunch, Miranda sighed with relief to find an email from Tierney. The body of the email simply said. *The letter you need. Thanks sis.* But the attachment lifted a weight that had rested on Miranda's shoulders since Aili had first mentioned Rebel's upcoming shots.

With an answer in hand, she couldn't stop thinking about Tori. She had been so angry when she'd gone over there the other night. But all her anger wasn't solely at Tori. It was at

Tierney for abandoning her child. At herself for once again being the person who was parenting a child not hers. At the world for making it impossible for a single parent to function.

She really should apologize for her outburst. Snagging her phone, she called before she could find another excuse not to. Because she would find all the excuses if given the time.

"Miranda? Is everything okay?" Tori's voice came clearly through the line, a note of worry in it.

"Yes, yes, everything is fine." She found herself smiling, and enjoying the warmth that spread through her chest. "I was wondering if you and Harley wanted to come over for a play date."

"Just to be clear, the both of us?" Tori sounded hesitant.

Miranda could hear chattering in the background of the phone call and wondered if she needed to be careful of what she said because of who was in the room. She frowned. They really should have talked a bit more before she'd left the other morning. "Yes. Rebel misses Harley. I think having her home from daycare is making her regret only having me for a friend."

Tori chuckled lightly. "I feel like you could say the same thing about yourself."

But that's what she had Tori for, wasn't it? "So will you come over?"

"I can't stay the night," Tori whispered.

Miranda's heart skipped a beat. She frowned, but she understood. They needed to talk first, and as much as Miranda loved sex with Tori, she still wasn't sure she wanted any more than that. But for now, she would take what she could get. "That's fine."

"We can talk about it then. What day?"

"Saturday. I'll have a lot of catching up to do at work in the next few days. Rebel will be back at daycare tomorrow."

"Will she? That's so great! Tierney came through for you then."

"For her."

"For you, too. I've got a client coming in, but I'll see you Saturday."

Miranda smiled as she hung up. For the first time in years, everything was going right. Even if it was just for a few days. She would take it.

nineteen

Warmth filled Tori as soon as she stepped into Miranda's house. The feeling was so different this time. Toys littered the living room, and Rebel came screeching toward the front door, arms out wide as she raced for Harley.

Harley laughed as she picked Rebel up and swung her in a circle. "Rebel! I missed you."

"'Arley!"

Tori laughed and shut the door behind her. Miranda stood close. Tori tensed. She hadn't talked to her about what it would mean to have the kids around. She was an idiot. She should have done that. She'd mentioned it before, but Miranda wasn't a parent, despite essentially being that for Rebel. She wouldn't be thinking about it.

Miranda leaned in. Tori panicked. She shifted her stance and wrapped an arm around Miranda's side, hugging her awkwardly. She knew Miranda had gone in to kiss her. Tori's heart pounded rapidly against her rib cage, her nerves over the top.

"I need to talk to you," she whispered.

"So talk."

Tori straightened up and looked at the girls. She locked her gaze back on Miranda and shook her head. "Not with them around."

"Okay…?"

Tori snagged Miranda's hand and squeezed lightly. "It's nothing bad, I promise. Just some ground rules."

"Ground rules?" Miranda's brows drew together in confusion.

"Come here." Tori dragged Miranda toward the kitchen while the girls played with all the toys scattered around. She stepped through the doorway and immediately her hands were on Miranda's hips, pushing her back into the counter, their mouths locked in a kiss.

Tori melted into the embrace, holding Miranda as close as she could and trying to make the kiss as quick as possible. She didn't know when the girls would lose their attention and come to find them. She nipped Miranda's lower lip as she groaned and pulled back with a smile.

"Sorry, it was really hard to wait for that," Tori whispered.

"Why did we have to wait?" Miranda dug her fingers into Tori's sides, holding on tightly.

"Siena and I have a rule that we don't date in front of Harley. At least not until it's really serious."

Miranda nodded slightly. "I remember you mentioning it."

"So unless we're going to introduce you to Harley as my girlfriend, and a serious one, then I think we need to keep this —" Tori kissed Miranda's swollen lips "—just to ourselves for now."

"Probably good thinking." Miranda pulled her in for another kiss, running her fingers up and down Tori's sides.

They should have done a play date without the kids. Tori groaned, her hips rubbing into Miranda's as they smooshed together against the kitchen counter. She didn't want to move if she had to.

"Mommy!" Harley called.

She broke the kiss instantly and backed away, shooting Miranda a serious look before spinning around to find Harley in the doorway. "What's up, Pumpkin?"

"Rebel has a stinky diaper."

"Oh." Miranda's voice was full of surprise. "I'll take care of that."

She walked right by Harley and snatched Rebel up, taking her to the back bedroom. Harley eyed Tori suspiciously, then she wrinkled her nose and ran out to the living room laughing maniacally. That was a close one. She definitely had to be more careful from now on.

Sitting on the couch, Tori waited for Miranda to come back with Rebel in tow. It wasn't long, and when Miranda sat next to her, it was right next to her, their thighs touching, Miranda's hand resting gently on Tori's knee, her thumb drawing designs on the outside of her thigh. Tori sucked in a breath, eyeing Miranda suspiciously. Was this just to torture her?

Miranda's raised eyebrow back confirmed that suspicion. She clenched her jaw. Well, two could play at this game. She just had to figure out exactly what she was going to do next. The girls picked out some dolls, and Rebel started lining them up one by one. Harley kept trying to make some school game out of it, but they babbled on, not paying a lick of attention to the adults in the room.

"What were we doing for dinner?" Tori asked, leaning in to whisper to Miranda, making sure that her breath would flutter across the open collar of her blouse. She was still dressed up from work that morning, and Tori couldn't resist toying with her since the opportunity presented itself.

"Did you want to order something?"

"Why don't we go see what you have in the kitchen?"

Miranda's lips parted, her cheeks rushing with red. She

slowly moved, using Tori's leg to push herself off the couch. As soon as she stood up, Tori glanced at the girls, figured they weren't looking, and pinched Miranda's butt as she walked by. Miranda squeaked and moved her hand down sharply.

"That, Tori, wasn't nice."

"Right, because I'm the only one playing tonight."

"Touché."

Tori laughed as she clambered off the couch and followed Miranda into the kitchen. They made it into the room, and Tori skimmed her hand down Miranda's shoulder to the small of her back. "Do you actually have anything to cook?"

"I cook." Miranda tossed a look over her shoulder. "Why does that surprise you?"

Tori shrugged. "I don't know. You seem like a workaholic who eats out often because she can and needs to."

Miranda shook her head slightly. "I rarely eat out. Well, present company aside."

"Smooth move, Miranda." Tori laughed. "What do you cook then?"

"Anything. I have some pasta we can make. The girls will probably actually eat that."

"Harley loves pasta. Got marinara and cheese? She'll love you forever if you add in that combination."

"I can see what I can come up with." Miranda opened a cabinet. She pulled out the ingredients slowly. Teasingly.

Tori couldn't tear her gaze away. Miranda was winning this one, that was for sure. But the worst part was that Tori couldn't decide if she was doing it on purpose or not.

Rebel screamed. They both jerked with a start. Harley started crying instantly, and Tori raced out of the room, her heart in her throat until she could adequately figure out what was going on. Harley had her hand clutched over the side of her head. Rebel was back to playing like normal.

"She pulled my hair!" Harley whined.

Tori held her arms out while Harley ran into them. She checked her over, but aside from red and tear-stained cheeks, she didn't look worse for wear. "What happened to instigate Rebel pulling your hair?"

Miranda had Rebel in her arms, staring at the two of them and waiting.

Harley started sobbing harder.

"Harley Quinn, you tell me what happened."

"I took her toy."

"Right, and so she pulled your hair because you took her toy without asking, am I right?" Tori wanted to sympathize with her kid, but there was no denying that she was somewhat at fault here. At Harley's nod, Tori sighed. "I think you should apologize. You know better than to take toys without asking."

"She should apologize to me!"

"Probably, but Rebel is two, and can't really talk yet. You might have to settle for a hug and smiles."

Harley pouted. Tori glanced up at Miranda who set Rebel onto the floor again. It had taken long enough for it to happen. She was surprised it hadn't happened before now, honestly. They were both small kids, and Rebel was a wild child who didn't have a lot of rules or structure.

The girls apologized, and when they were done, Tori stood up and stretched her back. "You two can either go back to playing together or play separately for a bit. Miranda and I are going to make some dinner, all right?"

"Can I help?" Harley asked sheepishly, as if she was unsure of where she stood after being scolded.

"Sure." It would put a crimp in her style when it came to subtly flirting with Miranda out of view, but they were going to have to contend with that at some point. Now was just as good a time as any.

They had the girls wash their hands and stand against the kitchen counter. Tori sent Miranda an apologetic look before she helped Harley fill the pot with water. Miranda stood awkwardly, as if she didn't know what to do.

"Have her break the spaghetti up," Tori suggested. "That way the kids can eat it better."

Miranda did as she was told, her movements rigid as she held Rebel's hands to break the spaghetti in half.

"What now?" Harley asked.

"Now we wait for the water to boil, which can take a while." Tori put her hands on her hips. "Why don't you and Rebel go play in the living room, and we'll call you back in when it's time to put the spaghetti in."

The girls skittered away. Tori crossed her arms and leaned back against the counter, dropping her gaze to the floor. They needed to calm down whatever they were doing until they had some more definitions in place. But damn, she didn't want to. She wanted Miranda against her any chance she got, and it had gotten harder over the last few days.

"What ended up happening with Tierney?" It was the safest conversation Tori could come up with that would keep her hands off Miranda. Unless she started another argument, but the last time they had argued, it hadn't exactly gone that way either. In fact, it had gone exactly the opposite way. Yes, sticking with Tierney as a topic was a good way to avoid all the *other* thoughts running through her body—er, mind.

Miranda's jaw tightened. So did her throat, straining against whatever crappy emotion Tori had forced her to relive at the moment. "She signed the papers so I could take Rebel to the doctor. Aili held her spot until I could get her in."

"Well, that's great news."

Miranda grimaced. "It's not."

"Why not?"

Crossing her arms, Miranda leaned against the counter. She stared out at the living room, seeing something only in her mind's eye. Tori wished she was privy to whatever was going on behind her gaze.

"Miranda?" Tori touched her arm lightly. "Why isn't that a good thing?"

"It means she's not coming back any time soon." Her tongue dashed across her lips, her eyes watering.

Tori desperately wanted to turn and give her a hug, wrap her up in a tight embrace to show her that the world would be right again.

"I haven't told anyone that." Miranda laughed lightly. "Not even our parents. They still think she's coming back tomorrow. Every day they think she's coming back tomorrow, but it's been two months, Tori. She missed Rebel's second birthday, and it didn't even phase her. I thought, of all things, *that* would bring her home."

"You miss her, don't you?"

Miranda shook her head, her arms across her chest tightening. "Of course. But imagine how much Rebel does."

Tori couldn't. Just the thought of leaving Harley for more than a week at a time like she already did was overwhelming, and even then she still got to talk to her every day. Siena made sure of it. They worked so well together when they were apart. It was odd in a lot of ways. "She'll come around."

"I don't think she will," Miranda whispered. She shrugged slightly. "She gave me medical rights to get her child treated. What's next? Temporary custody?"

"What is she doing out there anyway?"

Miranda turned slowly, locking her eyes on Tori's. "She's looking for her soulmate."

"I remember you said that, but at the expense of her own kid? Are you sure that's all she's doing?"

"Yes. Some people will go to the extremes for a belief in something that doesn't exist."

Tori tensed. She'd nearly forgotten that Miranda didn't

believe in soulmates. Maybe she didn't even believe in love. Still, they had been so warm toward each other lately. "You believe in love, right?"

"Romantic love?"

Tori nodded.

"Of course." Miranda straightened her back when the water boiled. "Rebel! Harley! It's time to add the pasta." She threw in a dash of salt before the girls got there, climbing up on the chairs they had dragged over so they could reach everything.

Tori was unsettled by the tone the conversation had taken, but she'd gotten the confirmation that she was looking for. Miranda might not believe in soulmates, but she did believe in love. There was more in that one statement than she could imagine, and it was the essence of what Tori was looking for.

By the time they sat down to dinner, the conversation had dropped. Tori pressed her hand to Miranda's knee, squeezing lightly to offer whatever support she could. Rebel made an absolute mess of herself, and they all giggled over it.

Before she knew it, it was time to go. Rebel was overtired and cranky, and Harley was too. Tori had stayed way too late. She got Harley into the car, buckled in and safe with the engine running before jogging back into the house. She'd forgotten one of Harley's toys. Miranda cradled Rebel next to her, but she was already asleep.

"That was quick," Tori commented.

"She's been tired since her shots."

"Harley does the same when she has to get hers." She snagged the toy and held it awkwardly in her hands.

"Do you have a minute?"

Tori glanced out at the car in the driveway. Harley would be fine, and she could see her from there. She nodded to Miranda, who walked toward the bedrooms. When she came back, Rebel wasn't with her. Miranda said nothing as she walked straight into Tori's arms and kissed her. Passionately, Miranda teased and tested, pushing the limits of Tori's resolve.

"When can I see you again?" Miranda murmured. "Without Harley around."

Tori hummed, kissing Miranda again and keeping her eyes closed. She wanted to say tonight. And tomorrow. And the next day. She groaned. "Next weekend."

"I can wait." Miranda cupped her breast, squeezing delicately before sliding her thumb gently over Tori's nipple.

Tori sucked in a sharp breath. "You're evil, woman."

Miranda chuckled, the sound low in the back of her throat. "I think you like to be teased."

"Some days." Tori kissed her again, pulling Miranda's lip into her mouth and scraping her teeth against her. "When you can follow through on what you're promising."

"Oh, I can follow through." Miranda dug her fingers into Tori's sides. "You're the one who has rules."

"Good rules." At least she kept telling herself that. Though right now, she wanted to damn the rules and bring Harley inside, put her to sleep next to Rebel, and take Miranda into the other room.

"So you keep saying." Miranda kissed Tori's neck. "Seven days is a long time."

"Friday," Tori choked on the word. "I'll come Friday."

"Yes, you will." Miranda kissed her again, lingering this time before pulling away slowly. "See you in six days, Tori."

What had she gotten herself into? Tori had to calm her racing heart, and libido, and force herself to walk out that front door. It was harder than it should have been. On her drive home, she couldn't help but think about that final interaction. Maybe she hadn't been wrong about Miranda at all.

Maybe Miranda really was her soulmate.

twenty

"I know! I'm sorry." Miranda tried to speak in the soft tones she often used for the families she worked with.

Right now, the tone did nothing to soothe a cranky and overtired two-year-old. She was late again to pick Rebel up, and her screaming let Miranda know in no uncertain terms her opinion on the matter.

"Okay, let's get some food in you before we head to bed." She swung past the fast-food place again, and while Rebel was almost dozing in the car, the minute Miranda took her out of her car seat, she screamed.

Food eaten and tears dried, Miranda finally breathed a little easier as Rebel's weight slumped against her chest so close to but not quite asleep. By the time Rebel snored in her arms, Miranda was ready for a bath and a drink, her muscles were tight, and her nerves were frayed to a wire.

She had just started running the bath when the doorbell rang.

"Oh, you've got to be fucking kidding me." She slapped off the water, dried her hands roughly on the towel, and stormed to the front door. "If you wake up the baby…" She muttered beneath her breath, unsure what threat she would like to throw at this uninvited visitor.

She yanked open the door, ready to give the idiot a piece of her mind, and then stopped, mid-swing of the door, the anger rushing from her chest down to her feet and disappearing from view.

"Tori." She breathed the name, and wondered who the hell she was, a lovesick teenager? Love? No, definitely not that.

"Hi." Tori's energizing-as-the-sun smile dulled at the sight of Miranda. "I've come at a bad time, haven't I? I knew I should have called first. I'm so sorry."

Miranda heard the hint of fear, and perhaps a little jealousy in Tori's tone.

"Come here." Miranda found her voice. Thankfully the teenager had gone back to the past where she belonged.

Tori stepped over the threshold into Miranda's house, arms open and welcoming.

After the last few days of Tori's naked body playing on repeat in her mind, Miranda imagined them going in for another hard and heavy session before either of them said a single word. But Miranda wrapped Tori up in her arms, breathing deeply of the faint citrus scent to her hair. Tori's arms wrapped around her, arms bent and hands pressed against her shoulder blades. It was an unusual embrace, but Miranda sighed and relaxed into it.

Despite not wanting to, Miranda pulled back and looked into Tori's eyes. "What are you doing here? Is Harley okay?"

"Yeah." Tori smiled and gave Miranda a chaste kiss on the lips. "Harley is perfectly fine. Siena called and begged to have Harley for the night because she got some unexpected tickets to a kids' show early tomorrow morning. I didn't ask too many questions. I'm more than happy to have an unexpected free night *before* Friday." That sexual gleam was back, Tori's cheeks reddening with arousal.

Miranda cleared her throat from a sudden influx of emotions she didn't know how to name, but knew she was unfamiliar and uncomfortable with them.

"Do you mind me just dropping by?" Tori asked. "I know we'd talked about Friday…but I thought…well, with the way last weekend went…"

"It's fine." Miranda led her toward the couch, the place they had already gotten themselves up to so much trouble. *In for a penny…* "I'm glad you came over. It's easily the best thing that has happened all week."

"Uh-oh." Tori sat, one leg bent with her knee pressed against the back of the couch, and gave a small understanding smile. "Want to talk about it?"

"No, that's not what you came here for." Miranda mirrored Tori's position and tried to conjure the images of their flirting from last weekend, but Tori's open blue eyes kept her trapped in the here and now.

"I came here to see you," Tori said as she entwined their fingers along the back of the couch. "Whatever that means."

Warning bells went off in Miranda's head. But she tamped them down. There was nothing going on between them but mere sex.

"Are you sure?" Miranda's mind screamed at her to stop talking and start fucking. Okay, that might have been her body more than her mind, but either way, she had an overwhelming desire to unload. And for the first time, she thought Tori might actually understand. The woman had had a certain ability to see what no one else ever had.

"Of course." Tori's smile lit up the room.

Miranda searched for disappointment or annoyance but saw none in that open gaze. "I'm going to have to fire one of my employees."

"That's hard."

"There have been far too many complaints. And originally I thought it had to do with the company we use for the coffins, but after some investigation, it doesn't look that way."

Tori shifted a little closer toward Miranda, their legs touching. Her fingers, now freed from Miranda's, ran over her lower arm in a slow soothing motion. It sent shivers through Miranda's body, but it wasn't exactly arousal. She was comforted, safe.

"I can't imagine anyone thinking it's an easy job."

"You'd be surprised." Miranda scoffed, reliving memories of her parents' rolled eyes and snide comments about her playing with the dead. They'd called her a freak of nature. Told her she should end up in an asylum instead. Those had been some of the most painful moments with them, but it was all in the past. Decades in the past.

"I'm sorry, Miranda. No one should ever be made to feel less for following a path that's right for them."

Tori's hand slid up higher on her thigh, her fingers playing against her leg. If only she would move her hand a little farther up, that would really get Miranda going. She looked into Tori's gaze, and a knot of guilt tightened in her stomach.

She had thought the exact same of Tori when they'd first met. "I'm sorry. That's how I made you feel, isn't it?"

Tori blinked and looked taken aback at the apology, but also confused.

"I guess so, a little bit. But I'm used to it. People think I'm an airhead because of my job. You tell someone you're a life coach and they think all you do is sit on your ass and get paid."

"You aren't an airhead." Miranda's voice dropped as she conveyed the truth of her statement. Tori was anything but, and Miranda wanted to make sure she got her point across. Miranda leaned back into the couch, stretching a little as the nearly always present ache in her back persisted.

"Is that a compliment, Ms. Priestly?" Tori grinned, then frowned, then her eyes widened and her mouth parted in fear once the realization of what she'd said hit her.

Miranda swallowed hard, her gaze never leaving Tori's face. She wanted to feel insulted by that comment. She wanted to scowl and give a snide response worthy of the name, but when she thought about it, Tori wasn't too far off.

"Oh my god, I'm so sorry." Tori looked horrified, and unfortunately, she raised her hands to her face to cover her mouth, which meant that delicate pattern on Miranda's thigh had stopped.

"You're adorable, even when you're a smart ass." Miranda took Tori's hand firmly in her own and brought it right back to her thigh, albeit a little closer to the place where she wanted Tori to feel her.

"Oh really?" Tori leaned closer, her cheeks still red from her stunning moment of embarrassment.

Miranda held the tension between them, waiting to see what Tori was going to do next. They had set up their next get together for the entire purpose of sex, And it was about time they got to the reason Tori had shown up. Miranda dropped her gaze to Tori's mouth, hoping that would push her to do what they both so desperately wanted. Tori moved in slowly, brushing her lips across Miranda's in a soft, gentle kiss.

"Yes." Miranda breathed out, leaning in when Tori tried to pull away. She had waited too long since Tori's arrival for that. She wasn't going to let it go.

"Thank you." Tori's breath tickled Miranda's lips.

"Thank you?" She asked, not moving away but needing to understand.

"For telling me what was upsetting you. For letting me know what's going on in your life."

Miranda's stomach did something funny, and there was a fluttering in her chest. She had nothing else to say, so she leaned in, lips meeting lips as hands slipped closer, running gently under clothes and brushing skin.

"Can we take this to your bedroom?" Tori asked.

Miranda didn't answer. She wasn't entirely sure she could. Instead she stood up and, hand entwined again with Tori's, led her to the guest bedroom. Tori would probably assume it was hers anyway, but she hadn't had a chance to train Rebel to sleep completely by herself yet.

Words felt unnecessary as they stood at the foot of the bed, kissing and undressing each other slowly, taking time to caress breasts and skin.

"I…" Tori began but stopped herself almost instantly.

"I'm glad you're here," Miranda said, finally ridding Tori of her underwear and kneeling in front of her. She ran her fingers up the inside of her thighs.

"Oh, me too." Tori's words were breathy.

Miranda pressed her smile against the inside of Tori's thigh, just above her knee, right where Tori's finger had made that irresistible pattern on her. Tori's hand found Miranda's head and wove her fingers through her hair as Miranda kissed her way up Tori's thigh, closer to the glistening dark curls that beckoned her. With a chuckle, she finally moved her mouth far enough up to where Tori's legs met and took in a deep breath of the pure scent that was Tori, the scent she had fantasized about for days now.

She flicked her tongue out and tasted, humming in elation. This had been exactly what she'd needed: Tori in her arms, face planted between Tori's legs. This would relax her more than the damn bath she wasn't going to get. Miranda tightened her grip around the backs of Tori's thighs, holding on for dear life.

Tori's legs shook, and her grip on Miranda's hair tightened, encouraging Miranda to suck harder on her clit while her tongue flicked out in irregular intervals, making Tori gasp and moan. Miranda wasn't going to stop. She never wanted to. She needed Tori to come apart against her, vulnerable in her sexual haze in the same way Miranda had just been moments before. They would be even in vulnerability then. Whether it was a weakness or not, she would catch Tori if she fell. But almost more importantly than that, Miranda trusted that Tori would catch her.

"Oh, fuck. Miranda." Tori panted as her legs shook harder, and her grip in Miranda's hair tightened so much it hurt.

"Come for me," Miranda demanded between licks, her cheeks slick with Tori's juices. She dove back in, only brief seconds between licks when she spoke. She dug her nails into the backs of Tori's thighs, not letting go.

"Yes," Tori screamed, then collapsed forward cradling Miranda's head to her stomach.

Miranda was enveloped in warmth and the beautiful scent of Tori's orgasm. Lapping her up, Miranda didn't stop. She slowed, dragging out as much pleasure as she could for Tori, wanting to give her everything she possibly could tonight. She could so easily fall asleep every night wrapped in these arms and surrounded by Tori.

She stiffened.

Tori's arms loosened a little around her, and Miranda was able to back up to look Tori fully in the face. She pulled herself together, putting on her *Miranda Priestly* mask so Tori wouldn't know what she was thinking. Tori couldn't find out.

"Are you okay?" Tori laughed.

Miranda focused on the pulse of her clit.

"I need you," she said, hoping the roughness of her voice could be mistaken solely for arousal, because that's all this was. Her mind was confusing the chemicals of sex for something else. Miranda shuddered.

"Good." Tori helped Miranda to her feet and kissed her, moaning into Miranda's mouth. Tori's sound and taste pushed away all other thoughts. "Now lie on your stomach."

Miranda did as she was told, thankful Tori was taking control when she was so very close to losing it. The tenuous lines of control were slipping from her grasp so unexpectedly. She'd never been this close before. As uncomfortable as she was with all of that, losing control with Tori felt like a dream come true.

The bed moved as Tori climbed on after her. The first kiss at the base of her spine made Miranda jerk slightly, twitching from surprise. Tori's warm breath tickled her back as she laughed and kissed her way up Miranda's body. When a kiss touched the base of Miranda's neck, Tori's weight pressed against her side, and Miranda moaned.

Short nails scraped teasingly, following the path of the kisses, up and then back down where they continued beyond the base of her spine. She groaned as Tori kneaded her ass cheeks, first one and then the other. Miranda lifted her hips automatically as she ached for Tori to relieve the throbbing pressure. This was what they were there for, right? Not to make love but to fuck.

Miranda inwardly snorted. Since when had she ever thought there was a difference?

Still, this time felt so different from the last two. The tension between them was gone, eased into a comfort of knowing each other, of being safe together.

Light touches danced down to the top of her right thigh, back up to her buttocks and then down to the left. Miranda groaned louder, lifting her hips higher, almost panting with need. Tori had to take her. Touch her. Anything to give the growing ache between her legs some relief. Even though Miranda instinctively knew that the ache in her heart wouldn't be eased by anyone other than Tori.

Tori's laugh caused her to clench more, her hips circling, desperate for a release of the pressure.

"Tori, please."

"Please?"

"Yes, oh god, please."

She could have sworn she heard Tori smile, felt the warmth of that beaming grin brush her skin before Tori's body rested against her back. Tori's knees tapped Miranda's thighs, and she opened them obediently. Tori's kisses grew harder along her shoulder blades, nipping and sucking as finally, finally she slipped a hand between Miranda's legs and found her ready and waiting.

There was no way for Tori to know just how much she loved being taken this way, how much she loved the feeling of pressure all over her. Miranda groaned as she ground against Tori's fingers as they slipped inside of her.

"More," Miranda begged, a near sob of release escaping with the demand.

Tori's fingers slipped out of her and returned with an extra one.

"Yes, Tori, yes, yes." Miranda fisted the sheets, giving her a hold as she rocked harder and faster.

"Rub yourself for me."

"What?" Miranda didn't stop rocking on Tori's fingers, but the request made her breath hitch. Her brain was too slow to catch up to the command.

"I want to feel you rubbing your clit while I'm inside you."

Miranda couldn't answer, even if she had known what to say. Instead she pried her fist from the sheet and lifted her hips a little higher, which pushed Tori's fingers even deeper inside of her. Miranda gasped as pleasure pulsed though her. It took her a second, but she rubbed her own clit just as Tori had told her to.

"Yes, just like that." Tori breathed into her ear and bit gently on her ear lobe.

"Oh God," Miranda panted. She was so close she might actually shatter into a thousand pieces of glass and all of them would reflect the dazzling light she had always associated with Tori.

"Let go of all that control for me," Tori cooed, her voice so soft and confident.

And she did. In a scream of ecstasy Miranda came, her body shuddering as she collapsed onto the bed, her knees no longer capable of holding up her hips. Tori's fingers remained buried inside her, and she clenched and throbbed around them in the aftermath of pleasure.

"Oh fuck."

"Indeed." Tori laughed, rolling off Miranda and onto her back.

"Give me a few minutes." Miranda wasn't even sure that was her voice. She didn't sound like herself.

"It's okay." Tori smiled that kaleidoscope of colors Miranda had just been shattered into.

"Oh no, it's definitely not okay. We aren't even remotely done yet." Miranda shuffled over and lay half on Tori, one leg thrown over Tori's and her hand cupping Tori's breast as though they were made solely for her.

Miranda blinked at her train of thought. What the hell was she thinking? Her hands weren't made for anyone. What would be next? That she loved Tori and believed in soulmates?

Her heart, which had just begun to slow, beat faster again as neither of these ideas inspired the jeering disgust that usually accompanied it.

Tori's breath slowed and deepened, and Miranda looked up from where her head rested on Tori's shoulder. Her eyes were closed, and her face looked even younger in the post-orgasmic bliss.

Miranda smiled, and her heart felt all manner of oversized within her chest.

Oh fuck!

twenty-one

Miranda had no idea why she was even there. Everything told her to turn around and leave, but she went against that gut instinct. Rebel rocked against her side as Miranda clutched her so she didn't escape. As she went to knock on Tori's door, Rebel leaned in and pressed her palm to it, as if she was knocking.

"Yeah, that's right. We knock when we want to let someone know we're here."

Miranda's cheeks flared with heat. She had definitely knocked the last time she'd been at Tori's. Hard. Repeatedly. And when she'd been let in? Let's just say it was well worth her anger. Though none of that would be happening tonight because Harley was around.

Speaking of, Harley opened the door and busted out in a grin that matched her mother's million-watt smile. "Rebel!"

"Hey, Miranda," Tori said with a sly smile on her lips.

Miranda could so easily melt into that look, but she hesitated to let herself do it. This was what was holding her back. This was why she hadn't wanted to come tonight. Something was off, but she couldn't put her finger on what it was other than her. But so much had changed in her life over the last two and a half months. She'd been off her game starting then.

"Hey." Miranda set Rebel down and let her run off with Harley.

Tori glanced over her shoulder before stepping out of the apartment and pulling Miranda in for a hug and a kiss. As soon as their lips touched, Miranda sighed. And it wasn't because it felt good. It did *feel* good. Anytime Tori was in her arms was amazing. But it was the undergirding of devastation that overwhelmed her.

What was wrong with her?

"I'm really glad to see you again." Tori took Miranda's hand in her own and led her inside. As soon as they were through the doorway, she dropped it and straightened her back as if nothing was going on.

The hot and cold threw Miranda every time. She couldn't keep up with it. Mostly, she didn't want to. This wasn't a relationship, so she didn't have to force herself to pretend to hide what wasn't there from the kids. She just had to keep reminding herself of that.

"Aili will be here in a few minutes."

Miranda's shoulders tightened. "Aili?"

"Yeah." Tori's eyes shifted to Harley and Rebel as they raced back into the living room. "I thought we could go out—properly."

Miranda's stomach sank. This was a date. Not only was this a date, but she was pawning Rebel off on Aili, the director at her daycare. Everything in her was a live wire, just waiting to be let loose to electrocute whatever came nearby, preferably Tori who thought this idea was anywhere near what Miranda wanted.

"Is that okay?"

What was she supposed to say? Miranda glanced down at

Rebel as the two of them played together on the floor. "What did you have planned?"

"Just a dinner out where we didn't have small eyes watching us."

"Siena won't mind?" It was the best defense she could come up with at the moment that didn't involve her being rude, angry, or too bitchy for her own good, because she wanted nothing more than to tell Tori no, grab Rebel, and walk away.

Tori shook her head. "No, because we won't be here."

Panic wheedled its way into her chest, wrapping around her heart and lungs making it so hard to breathe. Miranda clenched her fists against her sides, wishing someone from work would call and beg her to come in tonight and deal with a body. Anything that would get her out of what was about to happen.

The knock on the door was sharp. Tori grinned as she went to answer it, leaving Miranda rooted to the spot nearby, not prepared for anything that was happening.

"Aili!" Tori wrapped her arms around Aili's shoulders and dragged her into a hug. "I didn't make you give up a date night for this, did I?"

"No." Aili winked. "But that is going well, thanks for asking."

What fresh hell was this? Tori was way too close to all of her exes. Talking about current relationships as if there was nothing wrong about spilling every detail and secret out there. Miranda couldn't breathe. She was so close to being pushed into a panic and running. It would be the best way to get out of this, whatever *this* was.

"Aili! Aili! Aili!" Harley shouted and ran forward, wrapping her arms around Aili in a huge hug. Rebel followed Harley's cue and did the same.

Miranda swallowed a lump in her throat. She needed a

minute to sort through all of this, and it seemed like she was going to get it because everyone else was ignoring her silent meltdown.

"Did you have fun at daycare today?" Aili picked Rebel up, sliding her onto her hip and tickled her belly. "I bet you did with all that dancing you were doing."

Dancing? Miranda truly had no idea what Rebel did day in and day out. Nap, eat, sleep—yes. But what else? Did they practice writing? Do crafts? She came home with drawings every once in a while, but not every week.

"Dance!" Rebel clapped her hands and giggled.

Miranda should ask. She should know, shouldn't she? What Rebel was doing...what she was eating...how long she was napping each day, not just on the ones when it was more or less than normal. Her heart was in her throat. Tori grabbed her arm and pulled her toward the front door of the apartment.

"We'll be back in a few hours. Give a call or text if you need something."

Miranda walked, dumbfounded, and unable to parse exactly what she was feeling. When she was outside, the cold air biting at her cheeks, she closed her eyes and listened to Rebel's cries through the door. She wanted nothing more than to walk back inside and take Rebel home. Put an end to what was happening.

"What's wrong?" Tori had a hand on her elbow, holding still as their eyes locked together.

Miranda shook her head, no idea what to say. "I don't think Aili should have to watch the kids at night too."

"She's my friend. And she's more like an auntie to Harley, anyway. They haven't had special time together in months since Aili started dating Birch."

"Birch?" Wasn't that Rebel's teacher? Miranda's stomach dropped. Miranda clenched her jaw. How could she get her point across? "I'm not comfortable leaving them."

"They'll be fine. Rebel knows Aili. That's why I asked her."

"You didn't check with me first." Miranda's words cracked through the air like lightning.

Tori stilled, as if suddenly realizing the chaos she had forced Miranda to walk into. "I'm so sorry. You're right. I didn't. I just thought…it doesn't matter what I thought. I didn't check. I should have."

Miranda crossed her arms tightly, still standing in place. She was calmer now, more rational thoughts migrating through her brain, but she still didn't quite know where to start. "I won't stay the night."

"No, just dinner," Tori said slowly. "Unless you don't want to anymore. We can always go back in." She pointed awkwardly toward the door.

Miranda stared at it. Rebel's cries had already quieted, no doubt because she knew Miranda wasn't going to walk back inside. But oh, how she wanted to.

"Have you ever had a sitter for Rebel?"

"Just my parents, on occasion."

"So in the three months you've had her, she's been with you or at daycare?"

Miranda nodded sharply.

Compassion filled Tori's gaze, and it churned Miranda's stomach. She didn't want that. Taking care of Rebel was her responsibility, and she'd accepted that burden when Tierney had left this last time.

"Do you still want to go? I really don't mind staying. This is all my fault." Tori rambled on.

Miranda only picked up on about half of what she said. She had to get herself together. Leaving Rebel wasn't the issue. She was fine with that. Well, it wasn't that simple either. It wasn't leaving Rebel with someone she trusted, it was leaving her when it should be Miranda there.

"No, let's go," Miranda murmured, stepping toward Tori's car.

"Are you sure?" Tori touched her arm again to get her attention.

"Yes." But she wasn't. Not for the first time that day, Miranda wasn't sure what she was doing and why she was doing it. Tori had thrown her into total and complete chaos. Which meant she was stuck either staying and making a scene or going and never doing this again. And Miranda was someone who never made a scene if she could avoid it. She'd been taught from birth that it would get her nowhere.

"Miranda."

"Let's go, Tori." She had a bite to her words, and she wasn't even sorry about it.

The drive to the restaurant was silent. Tori kept sliding her looks, and she wished she could push her discomfort from the day away, but she couldn't. She should have canceled at the first sign of not feeling right about this. She needed to put a stop to what was happening so she could collect herself.

They were seated in record time, Tori having already made reservations. She had gone all out on the dinner for sure. It was a nice place, fancy but not so much that jeans were unacceptable. Once they were seated, Miranda ordered wine. Maybe that would help her get through this meal and put her back on the right track.

"Tell me what I did," Tori pleaded as soon as the waitress left.

Miranda pursed her lips. No matter how she said it, it was going to hurt, and it wouldn't come out right. "It's my job to raise Rebel."

"Right..." Tori dragged out the word. "Maybe I'm confused, but you're doing that. Quite spectacularly, if you ask me."

Miranda warmed slightly at the praise, but then darkened

again as soon as she met Tori's gaze. She was going to have to get specific, wasn't she? She hated this. It always made her feel awful and drained at the end. Avoiding that was normally easy, but with Tori, it was hard to want to.

"If you're not comfortable with Aili—"

"It's not Aili." Miranda tightened again. "My parents— God love them, who knows why—didn't really raise Tierney. I did." There. She'd said it. That would explain everything, right?

"I'm not following."

Miranda cursed inwardly. She was so bad at this. "Our parents raised me, mostly. But Tierney is sixteen years younger, and she was an unwanted surprise. When she was little, they didn't bother themselves with an infant or a toddler."

"So you did it," Tori said it like a statement, not a question, but Miranda could see the question in her gaze.

She nodded. "I did it."

"You were a baby raising a baby." Tori's eyes softened, as if finally understanding. "That must have been so hard."

"Right, it was, but that's not…" Why couldn't she just say it? It was like something plugged up her throat, refusing to let the right words out. It frustrated the fuck out of her. She was forty-five years old, damn it. She should be so much better at this by now. "It's my responsibility to raise Rebel."

Now she was just repeating herself. This was going to get them nowhere. She fell into silence as their meals were set in front of them. She had zero appetite now. The food looked amazing, but she couldn't even bring herself to take one bite of it. Tori hadn't eaten anything either. Instead, she reached her hand across the table, palm up, as if expecting Miranda to grasp it.

She didn't.

She couldn't do that.

Miranda tensed again. She was going to need the longest,

hottest shower after this to loosen the muscles in her shoulders. She dropped her eyes back to the table, unable to keep holding Tierney's—no…Tori. She was here with Tori—gaze. What was wrong with her? She shouldn't have let herself get mixed up in something that was nothing more than a fantasy. Tori sounded like she had everything together, but she didn't. She couldn't.

"Miranda." Tori's sternness cut through Miranda's chaotic inner monologue. "Talk to me."

"Rebel is my responsibility, and she should be with me."

"Always?" Tori raised an eyebrow.

Miranda gave the slightest, almost imperceptible nod. "Tierney won't do it, so I have to."

"That doesn't mean you don't deserve time for yourself." Tori slid her hand back into her lap, but she didn't look sad about it. In fact, it seemed as if she finally understood. "You're not doing anything wrong by going out without her, you know."

"She needs stability."

"And she has it with you. You know that. Aili knows that. But you need to take care of yourself, as well."

Miranda's lips parted. "No, I don't."

"How can you think that?" Tori frowned. They sat in the silence for a second longer before she blew out a breath. "Look, I used to think that too. Especially right after my divorce. I thought that every moment Harley was with me that I needed to be there because she deserved it. And she does. But she also deserves a mother who is happy. And I can't be happy if Harley is my life. I love my daughter, don't get me wrong. But I am more than a mother."

"I'm not a mother." Miranda's stomach churned. The emotions running through her were so foreign that it was taking everything in her to keep them straight and to find words that matched them. "I'm her aunt. And I'm the only one willing to take care of her."

"And that's honorable."

"It's not." Miranda locked her eyes on Tori. "It's not honorable. But I won't make the same mistakes that my parents did or that Tierney is making."

"So that's what this is about." Tori's lips quirked slightly. "I don't think you're making the same mistake by going out for dinner one night out of the nearly three months you've had Rebel living with you."

But it felt that way. Why couldn't Tori see that? She wouldn't understand, and Miranda was just going to have to accept that. With every last ounce of energy and gumption she had, she started to eat. The sooner she could get the dinner over, the sooner she could get back to Rebel. She wouldn't make the same mistake again.

twenty-two

"Tori, are you all right?" Aili's voice cut into Tori's numbness, and she stopped walking, looking around at the walls covered in colored artwork. When had she gotten to the daycare?

"Hey." She forced the smile into place, knowing it was unlikely to convince Aili but hoping her friend knew the signs well enough not to push, at least not right then. "I'm fine, just in my own little world I guess."

"Uh-huh." Aili and her familiar knowledge of Tori. Not to mention Tori's absolute pitiful excuse for a poker face. Aili pinned Tori with narrowed eyes and a raised eyebrow.

"I better go get Harley." Tori perked up enough for Aili to lower the eyebrow but not enough to soften the glare.

She had missed her little girl even more than normal this week.

The high expectations she had at the beginning of the week vanished quickly as Miranda responded to her texts with longer time between and fewer words.

She knew Miranda wasn't the most verbose—really she did —even though she thought more than once that Miranda had found quite a lot of words to say at the restaurant. Still, Tori couldn't shake the feeling that there was something else going on. She told her clients to trust their instincts, to believe in their gut feelings, and to learn that not feeling okay about something was enough to move away from a situation.

But Tori felt the insistence of time pressing down on her shoulders, and the need to find her true love weighed more than the earth itself. She was further from it now than before.

She slowed her steps as she drew closer to Harley's room. She couldn't carry this energy in with her, not when she hadn't seen Harley for an entire week.

She had to look at the facts.

She and Miranda had eventually returned to a more comfortable silence and conversation. It had still been a little stilted, but it was okay. They had even ended the date with a kiss, not chaste per say, but the moment Tori had deepened the connection, the moment her fingers had made their way up Miranda's neck and buried themselves in Miranda's hair, Miranda had pulled back and said her goodbyes. She had thanked Aili, cradled a sleeping Rebel in her arms, and left without a backward glance.

Tori had convinced herself that Miranda just needed a day or two to process the fact that having a date night did not equal abandonment. Not everyone processed things as quickly as she did, and Miranda had proven herself slower at times. Tori had always managed to keep going no matter what the world threw at her.

"Mommy." Harley's voice pierced Tori's spiraling thoughts, and she grabbed Harley up in her arms and spun her around. Harley's laugh brought a ray of sunshine back into her mood.

That was what she needed. She had to focus on the positive things, and nothing was more positive than Harley. Miranda was worth giving more time to. There was still time. Perhaps not a lot, but enough to give her a little longer to settle into what her life had become. Miranda had a lot to deal with, and being a new parent, whether she considered herself one or not, was damn tough. Tori remembered the struggles she and Siena had gone through that first year of Harley's life.

"Hey, Pumpkin." Tori put Harley back on her feet and then crouched down to her level. Meeting her daughter's eyes, Tori's smile stretched naturally over her face. "How about we go out for a special dinner tonight, just you and me?"

"'Arley! 'Arley! 'Arley!"

Tori's heart stuttered at Rebel's excited voice. She wanted to turn around and see Miranda, she wanted to look into those honey eyes and know that all the short texts were about work and new parenting.

Taking a deep breath, she spun on her heels and saw Rebel running full force toward her.

Rebel didn't stop as she bowled Tori over, knocking her onto her butt. Tori's arms flew out, grabbing Rebel around the waist and lifting her up in the air. Their eyes met, and Tori smiled at the excitement filling Rebel's face, the squeal of delight unmistakable.

"Hey, Rebel." Tori was mesmerized by how similar Rebel's eyes were to her aunt's. Golden flecks mixed in with dark ones made her eyes look bigger than they probably were. Her hair was no longer matted and had nice cute ringlets to it. Tori couldn't resist curling one around her finger and giving a very gentle and light hug.

"Rebel." That voice, cracking like a whip around Tori, made her arms shake slightly and her heart beat faster. Oh, how she had missed that voice. "You can't keep running off. We've talked about this."

Tori helped Rebel back to her feet and stood up, brushing off her clothes as she did. She needed the extra time to gather herself and figure out just what she was going to say. Miranda giving her the cold shoulder the past week was putting it lightly, but everything had been off since Tori had planned that date night.

"Hey." She smiled, the mere sight of Miranda making her heart beat a little faster and her cheeks heat enough that she knew the pink would be visible. In some ways, she didn't care. Let Miranda see that she was still interested in something between them. Let her know how much this was hurting her.

"Hello." The corner of Miranda's lips lifted for a moment before dropping away, her eyes following suit. She could barely maintain eye contact.

Okay, so much for the returned iciness not being about her. An ache, raw and burning, throbbed in her chest. She couldn't possibly have read everything so wrong. That moment she had been allowed inside of Miranda's walls was real. It had meant something for both of them. Didn't it?

So much for being a great life coach, she couldn't even get her own life together. No, Tori couldn't accept that it had all been a lie, a miscommunication. She stepped forward, ready to tackle this difficult topic. With Harley next to her, she reached out as if to touch Miranda's arm in the way that had become so commonplace between them.

"Miran—"

"Come on, Rebel." Miranda held out her hand, and Rebel squeezed Harley in a big bear hug before running and taking the offered hand.

"Bye Rebel-bug," Harley called, arm waving as though she was sending Rebel off on a trip around the world and might never see her again.

Tori's chest ached for a whole other reason now.

How had she allowed herself to get so distracted that she hadn't thought about the friendship growing between the two girls. She had noticed it, and she had loved it. But not once did she think about what would happen if things didn't work out with Miranda. Is that what Miranda saw, a similarity between Tori and Tierney? After all, she had put her focus on Miranda being her soulmate above the possible damage to her daughter.

"Come on, Harley." Tori led Harley over to collect her items, the bubble in her chest rising painfully, threatening to burst and spill over in gasping, heaving sobs.

Was Miranda right?

Tori followed a skipping, singing Harley out of her room and down the corridor of the center. The colored artwork that had always looked so uplifting suddenly felt garish against her black mood. She wanted to crawl into a pit and sort out the internal drama in her heart before even beginning to attempt to reconcile with Miranda again. She needed her head on straight for that conversation.

"Aili," Harley squealed as she ran into Aili's open arms.

Tori hadn't even seen Aili standing outside her office.

"You, in here, now." Aili jerked her head toward the office and waited for Tori to obey before following her. She closed the door behind her with a definitive click and set Harley up in the kids' corner.

"Sit."

Tori did as commanded. That old sensation of being sent to the principal's office washed over her, and the tears she had held back threatened to burst through again. She was miserable.

"What's going on?" Aili, direct and to the point, never disappointed.

The first tears slid down Tori's cheek, and without taking her eyes off of Tori, Aili reached behind her and snatched up a box of tissues, offering it along with a pitiful expression.

"I don't know." Tori grabbed a tissue and swiped roughly at her face. "Just me having a breakdown, or a midlife crisis."

"Pfft." Aili scoffed. "You're not even thirty."

"But I'm close, too close. And I don't know what to do. Am I just wasting my time?"

"Ah." Aili leaned back in her chair, the shoe seeming to have dropped. "Miranda?"

"Yes, Miranda."

"And the soulmate thing?"

Tori rolled her eyes, at Aili or herself she wasn't entirely sure. "Yes, the soulmate thing."

"Is she?" Aili asked.

"Is she what?" The tears stopped as Tori blinked, trying to follow the jump of questions from Aili.

"Is Miranda your soulmate?"

Tori opened her mouth and shut it again. She looked over at Harley who lay down on her side, comfortable on the carpet of Aili's office, making an elephant stomp back and forth in front of her.

"I don't know," Tori whispered, and wondered what had happened to her this week. She felt as though hope and sunshine had been drained from her. She had just gone through the motions, but from the start she and Miranda had different ideas of what they wanted from their relationship—friendship. Damn it, Tori had to remember. They'd never actually said they were dating. In fact, Miranda had told her that wasn't what she was looking for. Tori had messed this up royally by putting expectations on them that she shouldn't have.

"Then maybe it's time you find out for sure." Aili raised those eyebrows again and looked at Tori with all the power of a woman in charge.

"Now why didn't I think of that?" Tori asked, sarcasm dripping from her lips.

"Seriously, Tori." Aili laughed, shaking her head. "This woman has you all twisted up. It's been years since I've seen you conflicted. And when you came back from your dinner the other night, something was…off."

Tori nodded. Aili was right. She hadn't let anything or anyone get her down like this for years. She only had a couple months left until she turned thirty, and she wasn't going to waste any more time wondering.

"Thanks, Aili." She stood, strength returning to her limbs. It felt good to make a decision.

"Thanks?" Aili asked, eyebrows furrowing.

"Yes. Thank you." Tori smiled and felt the weight lifting from her shoulders.

Why was she moping? She knew what she wanted, and if Miranda couldn't give it to her, she needed to know and then she needed to move on. She'd been a chickenshit, as Aili had so fondly called her on more than one occasion. She'd avoided as well as Miranda did, instead of just confronting and getting an answer. Enough was enough.

Once Harley was clicked into her car seat, Tori closed the car door and pulled her phone from her pocket.

Her fingers trembled as fear and pain washed over her. She didn't want to know that she wasn't enough for Miranda, but she respected herself too much to drag any of this out any longer. Her goal remained the same, and though she suspected confirmation of the fact would shatter parts of her that might not heal for a long time, or forever, she would be able to move on more easily and find someone who wanted the same in life.

She closed her eyes, took a deep breath, and sent the message flying out into the ether. Slipping it back into her pocket to stop herself from seeing if Miranda had read the message or not, she got into the driver's seat and twisted to look over her shoulder at her daughter.

"Ready for a Mommy-and-Harley special night out?"

"Yeah!" Harley threw up her arms and legs, and Tori laughed.

She would get back on track, and she would reach her goal. Even if Miranda wasn't part of her future, she had been right about one thing—Harley needed to be her focus no matter what.

twenty-three

"Got a minute?"

Aili startled Miranda as she bent over Rebel's cubby to pull her stuff together. She straightened her spine immediately and nodded with a silent, firm look.

"Rebel can come too. I've got stuff she can play with while we talk." Aili held her hand down for Rebel, who took it and walked side by side with her.

That was a skill Rebel had only just now started learning. Miranda appreciated it, honestly, because carrying around a wily toddler was getting to be a bit much. She stiffened her shoulders as she followed, carrying the diaper bag in her hand as she went. They walked down the hall and stopped in Aili's office, Aili shutting the door as soon as they were all inside.

"Rebel, there's toys and crayons if you want to color something." Aili pointed to a small corner of her room.

Rebel toddled over and started to play.

"Have a seat." Aili pointed to a couch against the far wall as she sat in the rolling chair by her computer. "I wanted to talk about some of Rebel's improvements."

"Oh?" Miranda's teeth unclenched a little.

"Tierney started Rebel with us maybe a month before..." Aili trailed off, glancing over at Rebel.

"Before she went on her trip," Miranda supplied. That was how she explained it to Rebel, not that Rebel asked where her mother was or why she'd been abandoned. She was two. She didn't have words for that yet, but it was going to be a conversation that came up later, especially if—Miranda wasn't sure she could think about that.

"Right." Aili gave a pitying smile. "Anyway, Rebel was...*wild* is honestly the only word I can think of."

Miranda swallowed the lump that formed instantly. As much as she wanted to throw Tierney and her lack of parenting under the bus, she couldn't. Tierney was still her sister, and she wasn't going to dish gossip on someone she was supposed to protect. Someone it was her responsibility to protect. That familiar lump formed in her stomach. She continued to do a shit job of that, but she would break that cycle with Rebel. She had to.

"Anyway, in the last four months since she's been in your custody, she's like a whole new child." Aili raised her eyebrows. "Perfect example."

Rebel calmly played with the toys and colored, going back and forth between the two. Miranda cast her gaze into the corner, fondly looking at Rebel and recognizing fully all the changes she had made and how much she had learned in the last few months. Okay, so maybe she wasn't doing too badly. The lump found its way to her chest.

"I'm honestly amazed by how rapid her improvement has been. It's a huge part of why I was willing to hold her spot for you while you sorted out her doctor appointments."

Miranda still hadn't spoken, absorbing everything Aili said. It really confirmed what she'd already been thinking, and perhaps she really was in the right to do more than think it. With Tierney still gone and onto boyfriend number four—

three didn't last more than a week—and no sign of coming home, she might just have to file for temporary guardianship and start the process of being Rebel's legal home.

"I think she's ready to start potty training, too. We can help here. Just let us know whatever method you want to use and we'll continue it."

Method? Miranda hadn't even looked into that, but it would make life a whole lot easier, wouldn't it?

"I'm really impressed with everything Rebel is doing. I wanted you to know that. She's such a joy, and Birch loves having her in class. She and Harley like to play together when we go outside."

Miranda's stomach tightened. She had loved watching the girls play together, best friends despite their age differences. But they hadn't spent any time with Harley or Tori since the whole surprise date debacle. She hadn't managed to bring herself to talk to Tori about it.

"Let me know if you have any questions or concerns. I want to make sure that we keep an open line of communication with all parents." Aili frowned. "Or adult figures in our kids' lives."

Miranda nodded. "Thank you."

Aili turned to Rebel. "See you tomorrow, cutie!"

Rebel grinned and ran straight to Aili, giving her a hug. Then she took Miranda's hand as they walked out of the office.

The entire drive to her parents' house, Miranda couldn't stop thinking about the future and what it might look like for her and Rebel. The lump in her throat eased as she focused on how she might begin the process to file for custody, temporary or not. This was better. She had always been better at action than emotion. The conversation with Aili only confirmed that she was right to start thinking about all of this. Miranda knew the state recognized that at six months of no support a parent had abandoned their child. It was how Tierney got Rebel's father out of the picture. But did she really want to do that to her own sister?

Pulling Rebel out of her seat, Miranda watched as her toddler—wait, *her* toddler? She shook her head and corrected her thoughts—Tierney's toddler ran up the stairs to the house. Cold washed through her. What would her parents think? They'd talked about Tierney every time she'd come over and more in between, but they always held strong behind Tierney, particularly their mother. But that could just be a defense mechanism.

"Hey!" Sandra scooped Rebel up and gave her kisses all over her cheeks as Rebel giggled. Eventually she put the child down, and Miranda stepped into the house. "You look like you've seen a ghost. Then again, in your line of work…"

Miranda shook her head. "I had a conversation with the daycare director when I picked her up."

"Oh?"

"She's very impressed with Rebel's improvements lately."

"That's good." Sandra crossed her arms as they walked into the house.

Miranda immediately went to the kitchen to get started on cooking dinner. Her mother followed her in, snagging a wine glass and leaning against the counter as Miranda worked.

"So why do you look like you've just received devastating news?"

Tori flashed to her mind. The awkward conversations they'd had in the last couple weeks. The silence she had encouraged to grow between them. Then she went to Tierney. Also silent, and with the same amount of tension.

"Have you heard from Tierney this week?"

"She's going to Puerto Rico with Jaxon? Or was it Hunter?"

Miranda hadn't heard either one of those names before, so Tierney must be onto boy number five or six already. She frowned. "She hasn't talked to me in over a week, and she hasn't asked to talk to Rebel in close to a month."

Sandra remained silent. Miranda eyed her carefully. The bomb she was about to drop would no doubt explode wildly and leave scars years deep.

"I'm thinking about contacting a lawyer and filing for guardianship. It may lead to terminating parental rights in the end, but I'd like to avoid that if possible."

Sandra's face remained impassive. Miranda wished she knew what was going on in her brain, that she didn't have to parse through all the drama between everyone to try and figure out where they stood. Then again, her parents would undoubtedly be torn between their two daughters, something Miranda had attempted to prevent.

"Mom?"

Sandra cleared her throat, looking Miranda in the eye.

"Mom, what are you thinking?"

Sandra sighed, setting her wine glass down and picking Rebel up when she screeched into the room. "I think you need to do what's best for Rebel. I just wish you had someone to support you through it."

Isn't that what you're for? Miranda hated that her mom didn't see her role that way. She went back to chopping the vegetables for the saute, her jaw clenched tightly. Tori had a perfect support system, even if it was made up of all her exes. She had people she could rely on. Sandra wasn't wrong. Miranda needed someone to help her through it all, but she also knew that her mom meant a husband and not just a support system of friends.

"You need balance, Miranda." Her mom just wouldn't let it go, and it took all of Miranda's strength to bite back what she really wanted to say.

Instead, she jerked her chin up, locking her eyes with her mom's. "What do you mean?"

"Parenting can be all consuming, and you need to have a balance. I don't want to see you throw your life away for a child."

"You mean one that isn't mine?" She bit back.

"No. I mean a child. Having a kid doesn't mean you can't also be you."

The words seemed to echo some of the sentiments Tori had been trying to say on that fateful night, didn't they?

"Sandy!" Emmitt bellowed from the other room.

"Dad wants his night libations."

Her mother walked out of the room as if she hadn't just dropped her own bomb, leaving Miranda confused and uncertain where to land.

More than anything Miranda was stunned. Had they actually had a decent conversation for once? Rebel tugged on Miranda's skirt.

"'Elp?"

"Yes, you can help." She dragged over a chair and started to teach Rebel how to cook some of their dinner. If her parents weren't going to help, at least Rebel would.

After a dinner that was rather uneventful, where no one brought up the fact that Tierney was still gone, Miranda had a weighty decision to make. As she got home with a sleepy Rebel, Miranda put her to bed in her own room and then collapsed on the couch with a glass of wine she wasn't sure she wanted to drink.

Her phone was in her hand, her mother's words ringing through her mind since she'd said them. She breathed out a sigh and closed her eyes. She didn't have a support system. And right now, she had no one to talk to. The only person who kept coming to mind was Tori.

On a whim, Miranda unlocked her phone. She hadn't read any of the texts Tori had sent in the last week. She'd used busyness as an excuse, but after Rebel had knocked her down and their awkward moment at the daycare center, Miranda couldn't bring herself to figure out what was going on between them.

She called without reading them. Tori picked up on the third ring, a curious, "Hello?" ringing through the phone.

Warmth spread in Miranda's chest at just the sound of her voice. "Hey."

Stilted silence filled them.

"Um…I talked to Aili today."

"Oh?" Tori didn't actually seem all that interested.

"She said Rebel is making a lot of improvements lately. She's been really impressed."

"That's good."

Miranda bit her lip. Why had she called again? This wasn't going well. She had been the one to stop talking, she knew that, but she'd been overwhelmed with everything. She still was.

"I haven't heard from Tierney in a while. Mom has. She's on boyfriend number five or six I guess. Hasn't found her soulmate." She let out a wild and weird chuckle. Why was she so nervous? Miranda had to get better control of herself. "I've been doing a lot of thinking lately."

"I don't think you ever stop thinking," Tori teased, but Miranda could tell her whole heart wasn't in it.

And it brought up a memory. One of Tori with fingers inside her, mouth against her, telling her to stop thinking while she convulsed with pleasure, the only thought in her mind at the time was Tori. Nothing but sweet, sunny Tori. Against her wishes, Miranda's body heated, pleasure growing between her legs, and she had to shift on the couch with how uncomfortable her body had become.

"That's probably true." Miranda found herself smiling slightly. "I know Rebel misses Harley."

"Harley misses her."

Why was this so hard? Miranda smoothed her fingers over

her leg. It shouldn't be this hard to talk to someone when it had been so easy before. "I need to make Rebel more of a priority in my life, especially if Tierney isn't going to come home any time soon."

"I think you're already doing that." Tori's voice cracked, but she caught it. "You've been wonderful for her."

"Aili seems to think so. I just worry about her."

"You worry about Tierney."

She did. Every day she wondered if Tierney was going to resurface or if she'd vanish into the ether. "And I don't want Rebel to have to worry about that."

"She doesn't."

"She's two. She doesn't know better."

"True, but even two-year-olds are very astute about their surroundings. They're aware of what's going on even if they don't understand it."

Miranda pondered that. She relaxed onto the couch, bringing her feet up and resting into the arm. She was so tired. Exhausted from running around and trying to keep up with everything, with early interventions for Rebel's speech, for doctor appointments when she was sick, and with work. That had been the sole focus of her life for the last four months, and she couldn't see it being any different in the near future, especially if she was going to fight Tierney.

"I think I'm going to try to get custody." Her voice was so quiet when she said the words. It was only the second time she'd said them out loud, but to say them to Tori meant they had to be real, right? There was no backing away from it now.

"That's going to be brutal."

"I know." Miranda closed her eyes, soaking in Tori's voice and all that she could of the conversation. "But Rebel deserves to be someone's priority, and since I'm the only one here, I'll make her mine."

"Sounds like you know what you're doing, then."

"Maybe." Miranda's body ached for sleep. "I'm so tired."

"Go to sleep." Tori's lightness was still there. Miranda envied it.

"I think I will."

"See you around, Miranda."

"See you around, Tori."

Why did hanging up seem so final? Miranda curled onto her side, pressing her forehead into the couch and imagined the firmness was Tori's body against hers. Tori would wrap her up and hold her, keep her right where she needed to be if only until she could be on her own again. Miranda cringed. What was wrong with her?

twenty-four

"What the fuck?" Tori smiled, bewildered by Miranda's sudden call. So much distance, and yet a touch of warmth. Well, Miranda's version of warmth. Tori stared at the phone in her hand, trying to push away the lump that almost closed her throat at their goodbyes.

"Mommy, that's a no-no word."

Tori spun around to find Harley sitting among a castle of multicolored Duplo blocks they had been building before Miranda's unexpected phone call.

"You're right." Tori shook her head and smiled at her pouting daughter. "I'm sorry, Harley, I shouldn't have said that."

"I miss Rebel." Harley sighed, shoulders heaving up and down in the true devastation that only a four-year-old seemed to be able to achieve.

"But you get to see her every day at daycare, right?" Tori sat down with Harley and continued to build the walls of her princess's castle.

"Yeah." Harley joined in, added a red block, and then a

green one. "But we only see each other a little bit. I wish we were the same age. Kids my age are silly."

"I know, honey." Tori couldn't bite back the amused smile that spread across her face. "Can I tell you a secret?"

Harley's eyes grew wide, and she nodded excitedly.

"I don't like many people my age either."

"What about Mom?" Harley's eyebrows pulled in together, and Tori saw the distress that threatened on the horizon.

"Oh, I like Mom. But she's not my age."

"What?" Harley's hand, her short fingers gripping a blue block, dropped down from the wall she had been about to add it to.

"That's right." Tori laughed, leaving a gap in her wall for a window. "Mom is a few years older than me."

"Like I'm older than Rebel."

"Yeah." Tori didn't think going into just how many years there were between Siena and her would be productive just yet. Though it definitely brought home the fact that she had a type. She hadn't been lying when she'd told Miranda *tall, dark, and handsome*. Then again, she probably should have also added *older by a good sum* to that mix as well.

Harley nodded and returned to building.

The tower was done. Four walls that went only to Harley's shoulders when she sat in the middle.

"That's all the blocks, Harley."

"Oh good." Harley looked relieved. "Because there's no door, and I need to go potty."

"Oh no, we didn't think about a door!" Tori laughed and offered her hands toward Harley.

Harley lifted up her arms, and Tori scooped her up, swinging her over the walls of her castle.

They had dinner, and the night routine only had a few tantrums, most noticeably the one where Harley didn't want to wash her hair.

"Good night, Pumpkin." Tori kissed Harley on the forehead, closing the second bedtime book she had been conned into reading.

"Mommy, why don't I get to see Rebel and 'Randa anymore?"

"Sometimes it happens, Pumpkin. People get busy."

"Is 'Randa your age?" Harley said it with such disgust and just a hint of pride at figuring out what was going on that Tori couldn't hold back the laugh.

"No, Harley, Miranda is not my age. She's closer to Mom's age."

"Oh." That perked Harley up instantly, relief washing over her face. "So you still like her, and I can see Rebel and 'Randa again when you aren't so busy?"

"Yes, now go to sleep." Tori hated lying, especially to her daughter. She hoped she hadn't really told her something that would never happen.

No, she just had to get used to Miranda and appreciate who she was. The spark between them was too strong to let the distance stop what they had. Despite the seeming finality to the end of their phone call, Tori couldn't deny that merely hearing Miranda's voice had sent a shiver up and down her spine.

For the rest of the week, Tori kept herself busy, as though it would make the potential lie to her daughter more true.

By the time she said goodbye to Harley for another week, Tori was just about tearing her own skin off with the itch to hear Miranda's voice again, to see her honey eyes, and feel her skin against her own.

She paced her floor, all remnants of her daughter packed up neatly in their proper places ready for her return.

She lifted her phone, and Miranda's name and number lit up the display. Her finger hovered over the call button. She dropped her hand by her side again and kept pacing. After three paces, she stopped, lifted the phone, hesitated, dropped the phone again.

"This is ridiculous," Tori growled out loud to herself.

This time she didn't stop pacing. She lifted the phone and pressed the call button immediately, not waiting for the twist in her stomach to make her hesitate at the sight of Miranda's name.

The ringing sounded like a warning bell in her ear. Damn it, when had she become so melodramatic?

"Hello?" Miranda's crisp voice came down the line. In the background, Tori could hear the sound of running water.

"Hi." Tori smiled. The nerves still twined in her stomach, but just hearing Miranda's voice settled them a little. "I thought I'd see how things are going with Rebel and Tierney. I haven't had a chance to catch you at daycare this week."

"It's only been a few days," Miranda spoke as though she were distracted.

"Oh, so you haven't looked into it yet?" Tori asked, hoping her own personal reservations about Miranda's plan didn't come out in her voice. She had a terrible poker face, she knew that, but sometimes she could manage to keep her thoughts better in check over the phone.

"Honestly?" Miranda sighed down the phone line, and Tori's heart yearned and her arms twitched, wishing she could wrap them around Miranda. "No, I've barely had a chance to do anything but get through the week."

"Did you want to talk about it?" Tori smiled at the ease of her question. After all the anxious energy of the week, she finally felt a little more like herself. She sat down on the couch, leaned her back against the armrest, and stretched her legs out on the cushions.

"It's been a really tough week." The sound of running water stopped, and Tori heard some shuffling happening in the background.

"What are you doing?" She asked with a laugh.

"I'm taking a bath." The soft sound of lapping water made Tori press her thighs together, imagining Miranda's naked body submerged, the drops of water sluicing over her breasts and neck for Tori to lick up, following the trail as they moved against her skin.

"That's a good self-care activity." Tori nodded to the empty room, her voice tight.

"It's the first time I've had one since I've had Rebel."

"Why's that?" Tori closed her eyes and bit back a groan. Why was she slipping into work mode? Especially now of all times.

"It's been hard. Rebel still sleeps on me several nights a week, and even when she doesn't, I'm usually too busy to worry about taking the time."

"I'm glad you're taking the time for this now."

Silence lingered for a moment over the phone line, and Tori's feet wriggled on the couch.

"So, did you want to talk about why this week's been so rough?"

"Rebel's been home with an infection."

"Oh no. Is she okay?" Tori sat up a little straighter, tension stiffening her back.

"She's mostly better now. It's just been hard juggling work. And my parents."

"You could have called me. I could have helped."

"It's not your responsibility," Miranda snapped. Another beat of silence crackled over the line. Miranda sighed heavily.

Tori's stomach twisted at the tension she heard in the quiet. She wished she could see Miranda's face, understand better what she was thinking and feeling. Her heart broke for her. Tori bit her lip and stayed silent, however, not sure where to begin that part of the conversation.

Miranda started again, softer this time, "I didn't want to

bother anyone. She's my responsibility, and my parents need to realize she's theirs as well. And I still haven't heard from Tierney. I don't know what to do about custody."

"Have your parents heard from her?" Tori wanted more than anything to wrap Miranda up in a hug and relieve the tension she imagined was in those perfect strong shoulders.

"They haven't."

"Are they worried?"

"No." Miranda scoffed. "Of course not. They are all about Tierney finding the right husband to help her raise Rebel. They also just brush it off as *Oh, that's our baby!*"

Tori could almost hear the eye roll in Miranda's voice.

Settling back into the couch, Tori tried to find that calm ground she'd had when she made the call in the first place. This was the Miranda she had gotten to know, the one who cared so much about her niece, about her family, even when it seemed all they did was put everything on Miranda's shoulders. And yet there was so much more to her than that. Tori played with the edge of her shirt as nerves worked into her belly.

"Rebel is so lucky to have you." Tori smiled and nestled farther into the couch. It had been a bad week, that was all.

"I don't know if I'm enough."

"We all think that. Remember what Bon Jovi says."

"Living on a prayer?" Miranda's words were delivered so deadpan that Tori burst out laughing, feeling the last of the tension between them sizzling away.

"No man is an island." Tori half-sang, half-laughed down the phone line.

"That's why I need my parents to start helping out more."

"And what about friends?"

"None of my friends have kids." Miranda's words were crisp once more.

"I do."

"Yes, you do," Miranda said.

Something cracked inside Tori. Was that what they were? Is that all they would ever be?

She wanted so much more with Miranda, but her birthday was creeping up, and if this was all Miranda could ever give her, this *maybe* friends-with-benefits arrangement, she needed to stop fooling herself. Because that wasn't what she wanted. It wasn't what she needed.

"I'll see you around, Miranda."

"See you around, Tori."

Tori didn't move when she hung up. The phone sat in her lap, and she stared down at it. That hadn't been what it was supposed to be. Tears brimmed in her eyes as the realization settled into the hollow of her chest.

Soulmates weren't supposed to make each other crazy, soulmates weren't supposed to fight to have that connection and promise of happily ever after.

So what were they then? Miranda didn't think of them as friends, but Tori did. It was normal that certain people picked up friends easier than others. She was one of them, but that didn't mean they hadn't had a connection, did it? She was confused. Beyond confused. And it hurt to even begin to think about everything. What they were. What they weren't. What she wanted them to be.

She still hadn't managed to ask the question, the one that was clawing its way through her. Tori brushed her cheeks and shook her head. If Miranda wanted nothing more than sex, then that's what they would be. She could do that. Maybe not beyond tonight, but that's how she would label it when she looked back on her past. Still…it stung. She needed a good venting session, someone who could listen and set her right.

Tori huffed and picked up the phone again.

"Hey." Siena's voice answered on the first ring.

"Hi." Tori's voice sounded wrong, even to her own ears. "Do you have a few minutes to talk?"

"Of course." A loud noise, something metal dropping to stone came down the line. "What's going on?"

"Did you drop something?"

"Just put the pan back down."

"Oh, I'm interrupting." Tori rushed the words out, unable to say them fast enough. "I shouldn't have called, I'm so sorry."

"Tori, I'm emptying the dishwasher." Siena's voice cut through the roar of Tori's blood. "Now, stop stalling, and tell me what this is about."

"Miranda."

twenty-five

"What are you doing here?" Miranda's shoulders tensed instantly, her stomach dropped, and her heart raced. She hadn't expected this. Not with the way their last conversation had gone. "I didn't expect—"

"Rebel left this at daycare." Tori rushed the words and grimaced. "Aili asked if I could bring it to you."

"Why would she...?" Miranda's jaw tightened when she realized what she was saying. Aili thought they were a couple, which would be why she asked Tori to bring Rebel's most prized stuffy to the house because everyone in this conversation knew that Rebel couldn't sleep without it. Miranda took the stuffy and clutched it to her chest. "Thank you."

"Yeah, no problem." Tori rubbed her hands against her hips. "I guess I'll just see you around."

"Where's Harley?" Miranda asked before she could stop herself.

Tori froze, looking Miranda over for a long time before she dropped her shoulders. "She's in the car."

Miranda glanced over her shoulder, finding Rebel sitting at the coffee table with a piece of pizza in her mouth and her eyes glued to the television. She had no idea what made her do it, but when she turned back around, she asked, "Do you want to stay for dinner? I ordered pizza, and Rebel's watching *The Little Mermaid.*"

"Harley loves that movie." Tori smiled, genuinely.

Miranda missed that look. She missed the radiance and warmth that came with it. "Stay. Please."

She could see the hesitation. And she hated that she was the cause of it. Miranda reached out, wrapping her fingers around Tori's, tangling them for a brief second before she broke contact. "Rebel misses you."

"Rebel does?"

Miranda lifted a shoulder slightly and dropped it, not giving a verbal answer. She couldn't even make those thoughts in her head, let alone say them out loud to the woman in question.

"You sure there's enough?"

"I have leftovers I can eat if there isn't."

"All right. Harley keeps asking about Rebel. Apparently everyone in her class is silly and boring."

Grinning, Miranda waited as Tori walked to the car to get Harley. Once they were all inside, the house seemed so much warmer than it had before, so full of life. Miranda sat in the middle of the couch most of the night, Tori on her right and the girls running around before settling in for a second movie.

The girls fell asleep on each other, Harley stretched out with Rebel curled up against her side. Miranda touched Tori's knee to get her attention and pointed at them. Tori cringed.

"I hate to move them."

"Me too," Miranda murmured. "Rebel hasn't been sleeping well lately."

"Harley either. Must be something in the air."

Miranda hummed. "Come with me."

She didn't wait as she stood up and left the girls sleeping.

The last thing she wanted to do was wake them up and have to deal with cranky kids. She needed the break. It had been so long since she'd talked to another adult who didn't need something from her. No employee, no parent, no sister. She started down toward the hallway, Tori right behind her. She didn't want to talk though. She wanted to forget all the stresses she had today. Sighing, she stopped when they reached the entry to the hall.

"Miranda?"

What was she supposed to say? *Yes, let's fuck. I need your fingers inside me?* She dropped her gaze to Tori's breasts, imagining their firmness in her palms. She had missed that recently. It had been too long since they'd taken from each other, and that was exactly what she wanted.

"Stay the night," Miranda said confidently. She stepped in closer, pushing Tori's back against the wall, their breasts brushing together through fabric. Reaching up, she curled her hand around Tori's neck and then trailed it down over her chest lightly. "Let the kids sleep, and stay."

"Miranda…" Tori trailed.

Pulling her lip between her teeth, Miranda couldn't stop looking at Tori's mouth. She wanted to kiss her, to lose her thoughts in an embrace that she knew could do that. She needed to be distracted from the thoughts weighing on her.

"What are we doing?"

"Fucking," Miranda whispered. "Preferably on a bed with a locked door between us and small children."

Tori chuckled lightly. "That's not what I mean."

Miranda knew that. But she ignored every warning bell going off in her head, preferring to listen to Tori's words and give her a truthful answer. Lifting her hands, Miranda reached for the edge of her shirt, taking the chance. She pulled it off, clutching it tightly in her fingers as she leaned into Tori's body.

Tori clasped her hips, pulling her in tighter and looking

over Miranda's shoulder, no doubt trying to see if either of the girls had woken up yet.

"Miranda." This time her name was a growl.

Before she could say anything, Tori's mouth was against hers. Their tongues tangled as Tori flipped them, pushing Miranda against the cold wall and shoving her thigh between Miranda's legs. This was exactly what she had wanted. Everything. Tori, her willing body, and something that wasn't going to hurt.

Miranda carded her fingers through Tori's hair, tugging on the tie holding it up so that her dark locks cascaded around her shoulders, curling wildly now that it was set loose from its confines. Pure chaos tightly controlled. Tori palmed her breast and ground against her. Miranda groaned, her eyelids fluttering shut as she focused on everywhere Tori touched.

"Thank god you came over tonight." Miranda sucked on Tori's neck, scraping her teeth as she pushed her hands up under Tori's shirt. "I don't know what I'd be doing without you here."

"Co-sleeping."

Miranda chuckled. "Probably."

Tori kissed her cheek, then behind her ear, then rocked her hips hard. Miranda's breath left her as pleasure coursed through her. "We should probably get to your bedroom."

"Mm-hmm." Miranda agreed, but she didn't want to move at all. She wanted Tori to stay plastered against her and never leave. She gripped Tori's ass, keeping her right where she was and pressing her crotch down harder onto Tori's thigh. If she did that enough, maybe she wouldn't fall apart.

Tori had Miranda's bra off, her lips closed around Miranda's left nipple. Working her hands between them, Miranda undid the button on Tori's jeans and slid her hand between her skin and the barriers of fabric. Tori was already wet, her slit hot against her fingers. She pressed two fingers, knuckle deep, into her, swiping and teasing as best she could with the awkward position they were in.

Tori bit into Miranda's shoulder, keeping her moans to a minimum at best. Miranda kept the pattern going, rocking each time Tori's body involuntarily jerked. She must be closer than Miranda thought she was. Turning her cheek, Miranda caught the lobe of Tori's ear between her teeth and sucked, flicking her tongue rapidly.

"Imagine my tongue on you." She did it again.

Crying out, Tori folded against Miranda. She still writhed, not quite there, but so close. Miranda clutched against her back and held her as close as she possibly could.

"Almost there," Tori muttered and grunted.

"I wish I could taste you."

Tori didn't answer. They rutted in the silence, the music from the movie echoing down the hallway toward them. Miranda tried to tune it out, clenching her eyes shut as she rested her head against the wall. Tori careened through her orgasm and pulled Miranda's hand from her pants, pressing her palm against the wall above Miranda's head as she held herself steady.

It took Miranda a minute to catch her breath, to really look Tori over and see the strain on her face. She was just about to speak when Tori interrupted her.

"How close are you?"

"Oh. Um…" Miranda pulled her lip between her teeth and ran through her body. She wasn't close at all. She should be. With the fantasies she had been coming up with and the fact that Tori was against her, fully clothed still, but pressing her up into the wall.

"Bed," Tori stated.

"Right." Miranda moved slightly as Tori stepped back and gave her space.

She bent down and grabbed her shirt and her bra, taking it

with her to the guest room that Tori led her to. Tori must think it was her bedroom. To be fair, any time they'd been together before had been in there. Miranda almost corrected her, but instead let Tori lead the way. It would be easier like this, wouldn't it?

Tori shut the door after her, and Miranda threw her clothes on top of the dresser. She sat awkwardly on the edge of the bed and pulled her slacks off, getting naked as Tori did the same. It was like they were practiced at it by this point, nothing more to it than getting business done.

Miranda pulled herself backward on the bed, and Tori was on her in an instant. Their mouths locked together in a heated kiss, one that should get her going. She dug her fingers into Tori's sides, clutching her as once again Tori slid her thigh between her legs, this time starting a rocking motion that Miranda ground against. That was what she needed, more friction.

She took it upon herself to keep the motion going while Tori teased her breasts with her tongue and lips, while she tried to concentrate.

Clear my mind.

Why is this so awkward?

What did Tori mean?

You know what she meant.

Stop thinking!

Miranda ground her molars against each other and huffed out a breath in frustration. "This isn't working."

"Hold on." Tori moved, sliding down Miranda's body until her face was planted between her legs.

The swipes of Tori's tongue did hardly anything. Miranda gripped the blanket and closed her eyes. What was wrong with her? This shouldn't be so damn hard, but it was. She put all of her attention on Tori's mouth and tried to shove her frustration with her own body out the door they had come in. They didn't need it there.

She was sure Tori was getting tired, that her tongue was wearing down. Miranda finally felt the pull of her orgasm, the blessing of it almost bursting before it was chased away. Cursing under her breath, she went back to focusing on her body to find it.

Just come already.

Tori hadn't taken this long. She'd practically come in seconds. Miranda wanted to cry. *There!* There it was again. She chased the pleasure through her body. As soon as she had hold of it, she wasn't going to let it go. It still took longer than she would have liked, but her orgasm washed through her like gentle waves on the beach.

Tori didn't even stay down there to pull out the last legs of it. She crawled up the bed and lay on her back next to Miranda's shaking and weary form. Miranda brushed her hand over her mouth, turning slightly to look into Tori's eyes.

"What are we doing?" Tori stared at her directly. "What are we to each other?"

Miranda blew out a breath. She couldn't have this conversation. Not now. Not when she had so much else on her shoulders. Miranda stared up at the ceiling. "I need to focus on Rebel. She's my responsibility."

"That doesn't mean you can't be in a relationship."

"It does." Miranda bit back the tears. "I can't be distracted, not if I'm fighting for custody, and I know all of my attention is going to be on Rebel and Tierney. This is going to be a mess."

Tori's lips pressed together. She threw a hand over her eyes and shook her head. "Do you even want more?"

"Honestly?"

"Yes." Tori wrinkled her nose, making eye contact again. "Please just be honest."

"I don't have the mental capacity to think about this right

now." Miranda was backed into a corner. She hadn't anticipated that Tori would force her to answer this, not tonight of
all nights. "I wish you would stop pushing me on it."

Miranda sat up and slid off the bed. She grabbed her
clothes and started to pull them on roughly. Getting dressed in
her aggravated state probably wasn't a good idea, but she had
to move. Anything to get Tori's pained expression out of her
line of vision.

"Well, I guess that answers my questions."

"What questions?" Miranda snapped. "This was never
more than this. You knew that going in."

Tori raised her eyebrows in surprise before she nodded.
"You're right. I did."

Why did she feel so shitty? Miranda stood up straight. Even
though she was telling Tori to leave, she didn't want her to go.
She didn't want to watch her walk away again, to wonder if
she could call or text. Her heart raced, her mind spinning. She
should take it all back. She should stop her own defensiveness
and self-destruction.

Tori stood up and picked up her clothes. Miranda stared at
her, dumbfounded. All the words tumbled through her mind at
the same time, but she couldn't force a single one of them past
her lips. Tori was dressed in seconds. She leaned in and pressed
a sad kiss to Miranda's cheek.

Miranda almost turned to make their lips touch. Maybe
that would snap her out of whatever this was. But it didn't
happen. Tori squeezed her hand, whispering, "I'll see you
around, Miranda."

The words from their last few conversations clenched
tightly against her heart, dragging her to the bottom of the pit
of despair she thought she'd avoided. But she hadn't. She
hadn't even managed to come up and breathe fresh air. The
world tumbled down around her as Tori left, walking out of

the room and probably out of her life. But this was what she wanted, wasn't it?

No relationship.

No complications.

No soulmates.

Miranda shuddered as Rebel cried, awoken no doubt when Tori moved Harley away from her. She buttoned up her pants and left the guest room, making the long walk down the hallway. By the time she reached Rebel, Tori and Harley were gone, the lights of her car flashing through the window as she backed out of the drive.

Rebel ran to her, clutching to her leg as she sobbed. Miranda picked her up, cradling her and pressing her nose into Rebel's hair.

"Yeah, baby. I get it. I feel the same way."

twenty-six

"Hey." Siena smiled from two tables away and tried to be perky. Tori saw it in her extra-wide smile and the worry in her eyes. But she knew Siena too well, and the same could easily be said the other way. She just hoped Siena wouldn't get stuck in the details of their previous conversation over the phone. She regretted it more than she regretted just about anything.

Tori watched the sway of Siena's hips and the ease of how she walked into a room and the eyes that gravitated toward her. She rarely noticed the heads turning in her direction for a second, or even a third look, and never seemed too concerned by the pairs of too-curious eyes roving up and down her body.

Siena leaned in and kissed Tori's cheek before she slid into the seat at the cafe table, once again proving Tori's exact point. She hadn't noticed a single one of her instant admirers.

Tori had chosen the cafe because she didn't want to break down. She'd had her time to wallow, and she could feel the fizzing energy of excitement bubbling beneath her skin. There may also have been fear and trepidation, but she was sticking with the excitement.

Siena nodded at the coffee that had already been ordered for her. "Thank you."

"Of course." Tori smiled, knowing it wasn't up to her usual level of energy and brightness, but it was getting there. She was getting there. "Thanks for meeting me."

"Is everything okay? Something to do with Harley?" No wonder Siena hadn't noticed a single other person in the cafe.

"Oh, no." Tori reached out her hand and quickly squeezed Siena's fingers for a beat before pulling back again. The touch felt nice, a little too nice.

Another reason the public place was a very good idea. It had also been why Tori had waited a few days, allowing herself to grieve in a far healthier way then shagging her ex who, with her own recent break up, probably wouldn't be opposed to the idea.

"Okay, so this is definitely something else." The square of Siena's shoulders drooped a little, and she relaxed back in the chair.

"I'm sorry, I didn't even think that you might have worried it had to do with Harley." Tori hadn't been on her toes. She had even lost a potential new client because she hadn't been focused enough, and the thought made her sick. She prided herself on giving every client her full attention. She hoped she could find a way to make it up to the person.

"That's okay. Part of me figured you would have just told me, but then I thought other horrible things." Siena slowly rolled her eyes upward while a small frown creased the corners of her mouth.

Tori burst out laughing, and oh how the sound made her feel alive again. And it wasn't just the sound. The rumble within her chest as it built its way up to her throat was divine. She had missed this. Not just Siena, but the ease of what a relationship should feel like. Any relationship, not just the soul-mate type.

Her thoughts brought back to mind the reason for the catch-up and took some of that joy along with it. Which made absolutely no sense. She had made the decision, and she knew it was the right one.

Miranda wasn't her soulmate.

She accepted that, as much as it hurt to do so. The worst part was that her birthday continued to tick down like a bomb primed and ready to explode. If she really wanted to meet someone by then, even if they didn't get married and ride off into the sunset by then, she had to get herself back out there.

"My birthday is coming up." Tori bit the bullet. She locked her eyes on Siena, hoping she would understand what wasn't being said.

"Yeah, just a couple months away now." Siena smiled patronizingly, like she would ever forget when Tori's birthday was. "Have you decided if I'm allowed to plan a party for you or not?"

"Not yet. I don't know, do whatever you want." Tori's heart sank. That hadn't been what she wanted to talk about, and Siena had missed the cue. Which meant she was going to have to speak far more bluntly.

"Okay." Siena opened her mouth as though she wanted to say something else but closed it, still unsure until her lips were pressed tightly together, all color drained away.

"And you know I am searching for my soulmate before then." That was as nicely as Tori could manage to say it.

"Yes." Siena drew out the word. "But I thought..."

"Miranda isn't my soulmate," Tori said in a rush, avoiding Siena's gaze. It still hurt to say that, because somewhere, deep inside her, she had hoped that Miranda was. She'd thought that just maybe she had stopped her search because she'd found the right one.

"Oh, all right. I think I understand now."

Tori looked up, and Siena's eyes pinned her to the spot.

She might have also stopped the world from spinning as it seemed to tremble beneath Siena's unforgiving glare. What was that all about? Tori shuddered, trying to parse through what she had said that would set Siena off like that.

"Do you?" Tori wanted so badly not to say the words.

"You need some dates to go on while you search for your elusive soulmate." Siena smiled, not entirely back to its usual shine but definitely closer.

"Am I crazy?" Tori pushed her untouched coffee away from the space in front of her and leaned forward, arms folded on the tabletop, resting her head heavily on her arms.

"Why would you think that?" Siena reached out and ran her fingers through Tori's hair.

Tori loved it when she did that. It was so soothing and comforting. She groaned and closed her eyes, trying to find the right words that would pierce through the chaos she was feeling.

"To be so determined to find my soulmate by the time I'm thirty…it just seems so…unrealistic, doesn't it?"

Siena didn't respond immediately. Instead, Tori heard the faint chink of Siena's coffee cup being lifted up from its saucer.

Tori lifted her head slightly from her arms, peeking over but still managing to avoid looking her ex in the eyes. She watched as Siena sipped slowly from her drink. Tori focused on the lipstick-stained white ceramic rim as Siena set it back down on the saucer with just the tiniest hint of a clatter.

"No, I don't think you are crazy. Most people, even those who believe in love, don't believe in soulmates, but you always have. You've always interchanged the two, and it's one of the things I've found so beautiful about you. You are never without hope."

"I'm not beautiful," Tori said, knowing she sounded more like Harley than her mother. But what Siena said warmed her thoroughly. This was why she'd called her for a coffee date.

She needed the positive support that only Siena could give her.

"Now you're actually scaring me a little bit." Siena nervously chuckled.

"Why?" Tori lifted her head farther away from her arms, and her eyes met Siena's.

"I don't think I've ever seen you question yourself like this. So please." Siena reached over, rising slightly from her chair, and tucked a stray strand of hair behind Tori's ear and smiled. "Tell me what happened with Miranda?"

Tori huffed. *In for a penny…* "I did what I tell all of my clients never to do."

"And what's that?"

"I thought she didn't mean what she said. But she did. And I stupidly thought her opening up meant more. Because I *wanted* it to mean more, not because she did. And I placed so much hope for my future on her, and I shouldn't have."

"It probably did mean more." Siena was gentle, and Tori reveled in that.

"But not what I thought." Tori took a deep breath and sat up straighter. At least she hadn't cried. The few tears that slipped out unbeknownst to Siena while her head was buried in her arms could hardly count.

"So, got anyone you think who just might be my soul-mate?" Tori smiled, and it felt good to confess her mistakes, but Siena's continued unwavering view of her was what brought that home.

"Are you sure you're ready for that?" Siena squeezed her hand again before releasing Tori to her own devices.

"I have to be." Tori grimaced through her smile, wishing Siena wasn't so good at reading her. "I mean, yes, I am."

Siena shook her head slowly. "Don't rush into something because you're trying to meet a deadline."

"I won't. I promise. Scout's honor!"

"Fine." Siena straightened her back. "I still think you and Haylee will absolutely hit it off." Siena tilted her head, furrowed her brows slightly and tapped long fingers against the sides of her cup. "But are you absolutely sure, about Miranda I mean?"

"You're the one who told me not to waste my time with the ice queen right at the start." She was pouting. She knew it the instant her lips pushed together and her gaze dropped, but damn it, it still stung that she'd let herself get so stupidly wrapped up in someone who wasn't even interested.

"And you're the one who told me she wasn't so icy after all," Siena parried back.

"She isn't." Tori smiled, a small, sad laugh of resignation slipped from her lips. "But she's also not my soulmate."

"Okay, well I'll get in contact with Haylee and give her your details. Is that okay?"

"Thank you." Tori hoped the words conveyed all the ways she was grateful for having Siena in her life.

"I'm always here for you, Tori." Siena smiled and leaned back in her chair, and for the first time, actually looked around the cafe. "Next time don't hesitate, yeah?"

"Yeah okay." Tori felt her cheeks warm a little, but also felt that welcome pull of a genuine smile tugging at her lips.

Her heart still felt raw and tender. She wasn't sure going on a date with Haylee would really be fair to either of them, but she refused to give up on her goal just because she fucked up so badly, wasting her time with Miranda.

Guilt twisted her stomach. She hadn't wasted her time. Apart from their last attempt at connecting, Tori didn't regret a moment she had spent with her own real-life Ms. Priestly.

"This would be a great first-date place." Siena spoke as though she had forgotten Tori was there.

"For me and Haylee?" Tori furrowed her brows.

"Oh no, you two definitely need longer than a coffee catch-up. I have no doubt she'll have some suggestions for you on where to go."

"You are assuming she'll want to go on a date with me." Tori laughed.

"Of course she will. You are adorable, and you deserve your happily ever after."

After this past week, Tori wasn't so sure about that. But she was willing to try again.

"You know what?" Siena asked.

"What?"

Siena got a wicked gleam in her eye as she snagged Tori's phone and dialed. She pressed it to her ear and winked. "Hey, It's Siena. What would you say to me setting you up on a date with my ex-wife?"

Tori's stomach clenched hard. Siena wasn't doing this. She was *not* making the date right now. Her cheeks burned, flames of embarrassment coursing through her.

"Yeah. She's right here. Want to talk to her?"

Siena held the phone out, expectantly. Tori shook her head, waving her hands. She wasn't prepared for this.

"You asked."

Tori wrinkled her nose with a silent curse. She took the phone and pressed it to her ear. "Hello?"

"Hey!" Haylee's smooth voice was a balm.

Siena laughed and stood up, leaning over the table. She kissed Tori's cheek and whispered, "Don't forget to get Harley in an hour."

"Yeah. See you. Love you!" Tori went back to focusing on Haylee.

For the next hour, they chatted, the conversation never dying until she pulled into the parking lot of the daycare. Talking to Haylee had such an ease to it. There was a constant flow of conversation as they talked for far longer than Tori had expected.

She hoped they hadn't taken up all the first date conversation on their phone call but somehow she doubted it.

She was excited again, for the first time in weeks, since that messed-up date she'd taken Miranda on. She stretched as she got out of her car, ready to tackle parenting Harley with a renewed energy. She had gotten back on track with her life and her goals.

She headed inside to get her baby.

"Sorry," Tori said automatically as she pushed the door a little too hard, trying to get in out of the rain.

"It's fine," Miranda's voice was crisp and sharp. It reminded Tori of when they had first met. Why had she not trusted her instincts then? She'd gotten way off course for sure. But now she was on the right track.

"Oh, hey." Tori smiled and gave a small nod. Rebel was asleep over Miranda's shoulder, and Tori couldn't hide how beautiful it all was. "Didn't forget the stuffy today, did you?"

Miranda stiffened, freezing on the spot. "No."

"Just checking." Tori smiled as she ran her fingers over Rebel's back. She turned her cheek, locking her eyes with Miranda's honey ones, breath leaving her in an instant. She wanted to lean in, kiss her, take her mouth in the way they should have done days ago. Touches, heat, connection—it all flashed through her. Tori staggered backward. She hated that Miranda still had that power over her. She'd hoped with a new date lined up that it would stop. But Miranda had so much influence in her life.

"Well, I better get going. Nice to see you." Tori's voice wavered when she spoke, and she despised that she couldn't keep herself together.

She left Miranda in her wake as she scurried out the way and went into the daycare. The bounce Tori had finally gotten back deflated as she slowed her steps in the hallway to Harley's classroom.

"Tori?" Aili stood in the doorway of her office, leaning against the frame.

"Hey, Aili."

"Everything okay?"

"Yeah." Tori nodded and forced herself to bounce once more.

She wouldn't let anyone, not even Miranda, take her happiness away again. So then why did she feel so awful? She fought down a nearly overwhelming desire to race back outside into the rain and stop Miranda. To do the dramatic romantic-movie big-scene thing even though she knew Miranda would fault her for it and have some sharp retort if she tried anything. Their kiss would be so much like that first rain-soaked kiss, the one outside her apartment. The kiss that ended all kisses. Tori's pussy tingled just from the memory.

Aili cleared her throat.

"Uh… just got a lot going on."

"Uh-huh." Aili wasn't fooled.

Tori knew it, and Aili damn well knew that Tori knew. But for once, Aili didn't push.

Tori got Harley from her room and headed on out. She would focus on tomorrow night's date with Haylee. She hoped by then the heavy weight in her chest, the one that felt far too close to a massive misstep, would disappear.

twenty-seven

Miranda's feet ached. She'd been on them since six that morning, taking phone calls about another pickup and then dealing with Rebel when she woke up early. The calls with lawyers hadn't gone much better either, and she was stuck in a state of *I don't know* and *I'm not sure I care*. She just wanted Rebel to have the best life she could growing up.

And since the girl in question had refused to nap that afternoon at daycare, she was a brute to drag through the grocery store. But Miranda had no food in the house. And she really didn't want to order in again. She probably should have placed a grocery order for pickup, but again, time was not her friend that day.

Rebel struggled against the seat in the cart, screaming as if she was a caged animal. Miranda had given up on shushing her and resorted to just trying to get out of the grocery store as quickly as possible. Anything to save face from the disaster that was a second trip there with a wild child in tow.

The first time had been just as bad.

Damn, that seemed like forever ago. It was nearly four and a half months since she'd walked into the store, frazzled with Rebel on her hip and upset because Tierney had left with no warning. Just a call during a layover of *Hey, pick up my kid for me, will you?* Miranda looked down at the out-of-control kid in front of her. They had made so many steps, leaps and bounds, and yet here they were, rehashing their first night together.

"Rebel, baby, you've got to stop screaming."

That didn't help anything. Miranda cringed, finally giving in to her maternal instincts. She pulled Rebel out of the seat and cradled her. Miranda pressed Rebel to her chest, cupping the back of her head as she rocked slowly and shushed her. Rebel was so tired. They probably wouldn't even make it through dinner before she crashed. Hell, the car ride home.

With one hand, Miranda steered the cart as she went down the next aisle and stopped short. Her breath caught in her throat. A pulse repeatedly pounded in the center of her forehead. Her entire body tensed sharply.

Tori stood at the other end, laughing and smiling. Her hair was around her shoulders in waves, loose curls that begged for Miranda to rake her hands through them. The woman she was with didn't look like her type at all. She had blonde hair, cropped short on one side and longer on the other. They were definitely the same age.

At first Miranda would have said they were friends, but the flirtatious tone in Tori's voice, the random touching of hands to arms, to sides, to backs—way too low to be friends. A growl erupted in Miranda's chest, and she bit her tongue to keep the sound at a minimum. She was just about to turn and leave when Rebel perked up.

"Ri! Ri!"

"Fuck," Miranda muttered.

She put her back to Tori and started turning the cart around. *Leave. Run away.* Those were the only thoughts that ran through her brain. She had to get out of there.

"Rebel?" Tori's voice was clear as it reverberated down the aisle.

Rebel squirmed, pushing against Miranda's arm that held her tightly. "Down, Mama. Down!"

Stunned, Miranda stopped immediately. She stared at Rebel, who still fought with her, tears clogging up her throat. She set Rebel down, and without hesitating, Rebel ran straight for Tori. Miranda had no choice now, but at least she could wear the best damn mask that she had around. Couldn't she?

Sucking in a deep breath of air, she bolstered herself and faced down Tori. The woman stood directly behind Tori, a curious look in her face as she waited for Tori to stand back up. Tori crouched close to the ground, her arms out as Rebel ran straight for her. Scooping her up, Tori spun in a circle before flipping Rebel's feet back and forth.

"What are you doing here, Rebel?"

"Mama. Eat."

"Right, I bet you need food for dinner, don't you?" Tori was grinning down into Rebel's eyes.

Miranda's heart told her she was an idiot. Everything in her made her want to step closer and break up what was happening. But she steeled herself against those instincts because it wouldn't be in anyone's best interest for her to do that. She had to control herself. But why was her control so precarious?

"I'm surprised to see you," Tori said, holding Rebel close to her and pressing her nose into Rebel's wild curls.

"Likewise," Miranda said, raking her gaze down Tori's body. She was in tight jeans, an even tighter shirt, and a pushup bra that was perfect for her cleavage. Miranda wanted to drag her tongue down the V-neck line of Tori's shirt. Then she remembered the last time they'd been together and balked.

"I didn't realize you had more than one ex or kid." The woman stepped forward, her hand on the small of Tori's back.

"She's not my ex."

That's right. Miranda wasn't Tori's ex. The feeling in the pit of Miranda's stomach sank.

"And Rebel isn't my kid, though sometimes I wish she were." Again, Tori pressed her face into Rebel's hair, dropping a kiss onto the crown of her head. "Rebel's adorable and sweet."

Miranda wanted to smile at that. Tori had seen Rebel go from the worst to the best in such a short period of time. It was amazing to have someone else recognize all the progress she had made. Miranda tightened her stance, unable to let those happy feelings in right now. Tori was on a date, and she should snag Rebel back so she could let the two of them be.

"I'm sorry. I forgot introductions. Miranda, this is Haylee. Haylee, this is Rebel's aunt, Miranda."

Right. Aunt. She wouldn't be anything more than that, would she? Not that she wanted to be Rebel's mother, because she wasn't a mother. She didn't understand the ways of parenting.

"We were shopping for some dessert to make at home," Tori continued, as if unperturbed by the wrestling Miranda was going through every second she breathed.

At home.

Those words solidified it. There wasn't anything between them, and Miranda had been stupid to even think there was for that one brief moment. It was more than one moment. She would admit that now, but not before. Not when there was a fighting chance between them. Miranda stepped forward, ready to take Rebel back.

"She seems tired," Tori commented.

"She is. She avoided her nap today."

"Sounds like you're in for an interesting night." Tori smiled, always sunny no matter how much rain fell on her.

Miranda clenched her jaw. "Yes. Seems like I'm not the

only one." She flicked her gaze to Haylee. She was curvy, her hips flaring, her breasts large, her eyes bright with a deep brown color to them. She wasn't Tori's type. Miranda cringed inwardly. She had to stop thinking that! Neither of them were Tori's type. Definitely not Miranda.

She didn't believe in soulmates.

She barely believed in love.

Her entire focus up until that point had been work and making herself comfortable in life. Doing her job to the best of her ability. And now, being the best replacement parent that she could be for her niece. Couldn't Tori see that?

"We just got done with dinner at The Met. Have you been there?" Tori interjected.

Miranda wondered briefly if Tori was worried about what she'd do or say in front of Haylee. Perhaps Tori hadn't told her what had happened between them. It would probably barely be a fleck in Tori's memory. But Miranda would never forget it. She couldn't. She'd already tried.

"Yes." Miranda's reply was short, but she tried to keep the bite out of her tone. She was unsuccessful, like normal. "I've had a few dates there." She put an emphasis on the word *date*, calling Tori and Haylee out on what they had been doing.

Would Tori let Haylee fuck her like Miranda had on their first—she stopped. They hadn't been on a date. They hadn't dated. Miranda flicked her gaze back to Tori, eyeing her up and down. They had done so many things wrong.

"I loved it. I've never been before."

Tori wouldn't have gone there. It was a decently expensive place, and no doubt her financial sensibilities would have kicked in with one look at the menu. Which meant Haylee must have paid, which meant she probably had a nice cushy job. Or maybe she was older than she looked.

"Where's Harley?"

"With Siena." Tori's smile faltered. "We switched weekends again."

"You two do have a good relationship like that." Miranda didn't know why she was being so obstinate, so hard when Tori was making every effort to have a nice conversation. She was looking back at Haylee again, and she couldn't stop herself from talking, her control tanking in a second. "I'm sorry, but you don't seem like Tori's type at all."

"And what's her type?" Haylee was smiling, but Miranda detected the waver of concern.

"Tall, dark, and handsome." She flicked her gaze to meet Tori's eyes. She raised an eyebrow at Tori, wondering if she remembered. "And older."

"Oh, I'm older than her."

"Not by enough." Miranda didn't bother to look back at Tori. "She likes mature women, someone who has been around the block a time or two. An experienced woman."

Tori's lips thinned—the only noticeable sign that she was upset. Miranda hated herself a little more for doing it. But she still couldn't stop herself.

Tori forced a grin, looking over her shoulder at Haylee. She bounced Rebel a little on her side and brushed her nose into Rebel's hair again.

Miranda wished Rebel was in her arms. Then she could walk away and leave. But without Rebel, she didn't have an escape.

"How was work?" Tori asked, swaying with Rebel now to that beat she constantly had in her body.

"Busy." Miranda frowned. "We had four services to juggle today. Two in-house and two at the cemetery." As she said the last bit, she looked at Haylee, wondering how much of this would surprise her. How it would offend her good life-focused sensibilities like it did most people. No one wanted to think about death, not unless they had to. Miranda was convinced that was why so many people were shocked when someone died, and so ill-prepared for it.

"Cemetery?" Haylee asked.

Tori nodded, not taking her eyes off Miranda. "Yeah. She's a funeral director."

"And you're a life coach." Haylee snorted, her lips pulling into a cocky smile. "That's amusing that you'd be friends."

The gut punch was hard this time. They were barely friends. Miranda had done everything in her power to avoid deepening that relationship in the last few weeks, and it had worked. Tori had pulled away just like she had. And when they had gotten together that once—something clicked. That had been it, hadn't it? Miranda was such a fool. She'd been the one to make that night a disaster from the start. She'd been the one to ruin what they had.

And now it was too late.

Tori was with Haylee, and there was no chance that Miranda could change her mind. Squaring her shoulders, she moved into Tori's space and held her arms out for Rebel. "We should get going. Rebel will need to go to sleep soon."

"Seems like she's almost there already." Tori stepped forward and turned to her side so Miranda could reach easier.

Miranda tried to keep her hands away from Tori's body as she slid the half-asleep toddler terror from Tori's grasp into her own. But she didn't manage at all. The backs of her fingers moved against Tori's side, the heat from her skin pushing through her shirt. The scent of her soap filling Miranda's senses. She sucked in a deeper breath, telling herself she wouldn't regret it.

Tori's arm got caught in the circle of Miranda's as she pulled back, and Tori let out a little nervous chuckle as she tried to wiggle loose. But Miranda didn't want to let her go. Not yet. She stepped in closer and pulled her lower lip between her teeth. She looked directly into Tori's baby blue eyes when she transferred Rebel's weight to her own body.

When she had Rebel in her arms, Miranda stayed as close to Tori as possible. She balanced Rebel on her hip and looked Tori over once more. Her soft curves, her innocent face, her sweet lips that were so damn kissable. Miranda had made the mistake of not going after what she wanted. Not in the right way at least. She was too late to realize exactly who Tori was to her.

Coming to her senses, Miranda stepped away, her heel clacking loudly on the floor. She didn't dare look at Haylee. She didn't dare give up any more time with Tori because she knew this was going to be the last moment they ever shared. She would make sure that Tori had every chance to get what she wanted in the end. A soulmate. And that wasn't Miranda.

"I'll see you around, Tori." Miranda tried to smile, but it didn't even reach her lips. She said nothing to Haylee as she put her back to them. Now it was time to protect herself, to draw herself back together and rebuild what she'd broken.

Miranda grabbed her cart with one hand and steered it around the couple. With her back to them, Miranda blinked away her tears and buried her face in Rebel's hair. She could still smell Tori lingering there if she tried hard enough. Miranda went down the next aisle and headed straight for the register. She couldn't stay in the store with those two any longer. She had to escape.

When she had Rebel strapped into her seat and was sitting in her car, she pressed her forehead to the steering wheel as she was racked with guilt. What had she done? She'd ruined everything she'd had going for her. All for what? Rebel? She didn't even know if she could get custody yet or if Tierney would swoop back in and take Rebel away from her. But she didn't want to go through that alone. She needed Tori to walk side-by-side with her in those ups and downs.

Miranda let out a shuddering breath and tried to pull herself together. She didn't have another choice. She'd pushed Tori away and made her choice. Life didn't give second chances. Backing out of the parking spot, Miranda headed for home with only one thought running through her mind.

Tori was her soulmate.

twenty-eight

Tori's hands shook as she placed the dessert items onto the conveyor belt at the checkout. Haylee's face had taken on a contemplative look, but all Tori wanted to do was forget running into Miranda and Rebel. Of all the times to see them out shopping again. But the interaction had been so different from that first time. She smiled as she pulled the last item from the basket.

She hadn't lied about wishing Rebel were her own child, but she hadn't meant for it to slip out the way it did, or at all, especially on her date with Haylee.

Despite what Miranda said, Siena had been far more on the money. Haylee may not be a lot older. Eighteen months hardly counted. And she definitely wasn't tall, dark, and handsome, but she was absolutely amazing.

Tori looked up and smiled at Haylee, making the other woman's cheeks pink just a little.

Adorable.

"Are you okay?" Tori reached out and gently brushed her fingertips along Haylee's forearm. Tori watched as Haylee's smile spread with the length of her stroke against her skin.

"Yeah." Haylee nodded, the strange air between them crackling just a little.

"Good. I can't wait to make you these when we get home." Tori bounced lightly on the balls of her feet and turned to the cashier who smiled shyly and told her the total.

"Oh, I should pay for this." Haylee pulled out her wallet, but Tori waved it away.

"Don't be silly, you got dinner, and I asked you out."

"Um actually, your ex-wife did that for you." Haylee laughed, and Tori caught the wide eyes and the now amused smile of the cashier.

"Okay, that's true." Tori laughed, swiped her card and grabbed up the bag of groceries. "But really, who's going to know me better than my ex-wife?"

Haylee's smile stretched wider, and Tori hoped that she understood what she was saying, without having to say Miranda's name again.

Haylee threaded her fingers with Tori's as they stepped out of the grocery store. There was a pretty good chance the encounter hadn't entirely ruined Tori and Haylee's date after all.

The drive went by too quickly for Tori's liking, though she didn't understand why.

They chatted, and it was easy. Almost as though Tori and Haylee had known each other for years, not days. Like old friends.

Tori swallowed the lump in her throat at the thought as she pulled the keys from the ignition and got out, racing to Haylee's door to open it for her.

No, not friends. More than friends. Haylee was easy to be around, and she was damn sexy.

"Come on, let's get dessert cooking." Tori smiled with fake coyness, ensuring Haylee understood the innuendo.

There were no doubts in Haylee's eyes as they roamed up and down Tori's body.

Warmth flooded Tori, and she bit her lip, laughing a little. She hoped it came out as a flirty chuckle and not the wash of relief that filled her. She'd be lying if she said she hadn't been worried she might be just a little too broken so soon after everything with Miranda had happened.

They linked fingers until they got to the front door, and Tori dug out her keys.

Fissures of tension that had opened earlier mended themselves, and she wouldn't let the unexpected encounter change the trajectory this date had been on before Rebel called out to her.

"You first."

Haylee smiled and stepped over the threshold. Tori followed, closing the door quickly with a sharp turn of the lock.

A flash of fear lit up Haylee's eyes, but whatever she saw on Tori's face turned that fear quickly into desire.

"And here I was worrying you might actually be a serial killer and do something bad to me." Haylee stepped forward.

"Oh I plan to do many bad things to you." Tori smiled, took a step forward and met Haylee halfway.

"I sure hope so." Haylee's voice had taken on a roughness that Tori found all levels of arousing.

Their lips met, and for a moment, Tori's mouth remained still. She was with Haylee, why had her body still expected the gentleness of Miranda's familiar lips?

"Tori?" Haylee pulled back enough for her breath to tickle Tori's lips.

"Sorry." She lifted her hand that carried the groceries for a dessert she never really intended to make. Or maybe make for breakfast instead. "I should probably put this up."

"Oh," Haylee nodded and stepped back. "Yeah, of course."

Tori wanted to reassure Haylee, as she ran palms over her hips and upper thighs as though trying to rid them of sweat and nerves. But her tongue, usually so free with words and joy, remained still.

Tori gave her a smile and headed toward the kitchen. "Come on, I'll give you the tour as well."

"Okay." Haylee smiled a little wider, her thumbs hooking into the belt loops of her pants.

"So, this is the kitchen." Tori laughed and threw a look over her shoulder. She really did like Haylee. They had talked about so many things during their date. Things that went beyond just the mundane favorite colors, movies, and songs. They talked about their lives and their worlds. Just like old friends catching up.

Tori opened the fridge door, hand poised to start pulling out the cold items from the bag one by one.

Fuck off with the friends thing. That's not what this is about. Miranda already broke your heart. She isn't going to ruin your chance to find your real happily ever after.

Tori nodded, a firm hard thrust of her head down as she pushed everything but Haylee from her mind. She threw the bag of groceries into the fridge and turned toward Haylee, grabbing her hand with more determination.

"And that's the rest of the house."

Haylee laughed, and Tori looked back and smiled, no need for false happiness or enjoyment. Her body was more than ready to explore the curves and skin of this gorgeous woman.

Tori had cleaned up the bedroom, just in case. She used to worry about rushing into bed with women, but she had never taken a woman home who didn't have the potential in her heart to be the one.

"You have a nice room," Haylee said when Tori stopped at

the end of her bed. But Haylee's eyes remained glued to Tori's lips.

Tori laughed and lifted her hand to Haylee's cheek on the side where the hair was longer, and brushed the back of her fingers against her soft skin. Haylee looked up, and Tori smiled, shoulders relaxing. Because there it was, the connection she had felt before they had left the restaurant.

"Hi," she whispered.

"Hi yourself," Haylee whispered, and this time when they kissed, Tori knew what to expect and let her body relax into the taste and feel of Haylee's body pressing against her own. Haylee was gentle, almost as though she knew Tori needed to be handled with care, eased into the entire evening.

The kissing grew hotter, and while Tori's body seemed to have no problem with the way things progressed, her mind apparently had other ideas.

Miranda's eyes flashed through her mind. The gasps she would make when Tori's fingers were buried deep inside her. The way she would cry out when Tori's mouth was against her, sucking, tasting. Her scent as she came hard, every single time.

Tori closed her eyes to block it all out, but she couldn't. Miranda was in that room with her whether she wanted her to be or not. Tori gasped and clenched her eyes tight. She pulled away, both hands cupping Haylee's face, and rested her forehead against Haylee's.

"It's okay, you know." Haylee didn't whisper, but her voice was softer than it had been earlier in the night.

"It's really not." Tori didn't like anything about herself at that moment. She had once loved her life, loved who she had become and had known that while growth never ended, she was so happy with the path she was on.

"It is." Haylee's fingers were gentle as they moved Tori's hands from her face and stepped back.

"Please don't leave."

"Oh, I wasn't going to." Haylee laughed. "I don't think you need to be alone right now."

Tori blinked and stared at Haylee. This amazing woman was someone she could have easily fallen in love with just a few months ago, before everything she thought she knew about herself had been turned upside down and twisted until she found herself unrecognizable.

"I think we should make that dessert and talk."

"Really?" Tori's vision blurred as tears filled her eyes. The lump in her throat wasn't doing her any favors either.

"Yeah, come on. Teach me about these fandangled crunchy baskets you were just about salivating over so much that we had to immediately go out and buy the stuff to make them."

"Thank you." Tori wiped the devious tears that had slipped out from off of her cheeks and smiled.

"No need. I've had an awesome night. Sex isn't an expectation."

"I know. I'm so sorry." The guilt still swam in Tori's belly, and she wanted it gone faster than it had appeared. But she was pretty sure it wasn't going away any time soon. She was pretty sure she knew why it was there too. She just didn't want to think about it.

"Don't be. If she was the woman I was pining for and stuck on, I'd be far less head-screwed-on-the-right-way than you are."

Tori blinked, mouth dropping open a little.

Haylee laughed. "If you somehow thought either of you were being subtle, you are both just as delusional as each other. Now, come on, let's get baking."

By the time the baskets were in the oven, Tori had blurted out her tragic dalliances with Miranda and why running into her had gotten into her head so badly. And Rebel. Fuck, Tori melted every time she thought of that sweet girl.

Tori leaned on the kitchen side of her island while Haylee sat at one of the bar stools. Haylee swiveled the bowl of blueberries around in a circle as she thought, and Tori hated herself even more. Haylee was so interesting, and Tori would have loved to have gotten to know her before Rebel ran into her in the grocery store that very first time.

"So what are you going to do?" Haylee asked, looking up as she snuck a blueberry from the bowl and popped it into her mouth.

"Those are for the bowls." Tori playfully scolded and swatted at Haylee's hand, not quite touching her. She wasn't sure either of them could take that situation again.

"There are plenty left. Now answer the question." Haylee raised an eyebrow, her dark eyes locking on Tori's in a no-nonsense look.

"I don't want to give up on finding my soulmate."

"I don't believe in soulmates." Haylee popped another blueberry into her mouth and laughed as she pulled away from Tori poorly aiming a swipe with the tea towel at her.

"Wait." The tea towel fell limp in Tori's hand as Haylee's words registered. "You don't?"

"Nope." Haylee shook her head. "The simple naming of it puts way too much pressure on everyone involved."

"But that doesn't mean you can't believe in them."

"True," Haylee conceded. "But the fact I don't think there is only one person meant for you your entire life does mean that I don't really believe in them."

"Oh." Tori's stomach knotted as it seemed to do often when her goal came up in discussion.

"But if you want to call those people in your life that, then go ahead. You need those people who become your person for a time, everyone does. What's the harm in calling them a seasonal soulmate?" Haylee shrugged. "And if you do that... then yeah, I can live with that one."

"Multiple soulmates?" Tori lifted her eyebrows and tilted her head slightly. "Is that what you're talking about?"

"I guess so." Haylee smiled, and its lightness helped untwist the knots in Tori's stomach. "I believe there are definitely people who are meant to be together. But it's not always the *together forever* that is implied with the term soulmates. And we're not even beginning with people you love who are assholes that you really shouldn't stay with."

Tori smiled wryly at that. "So do you think I'm an idiot for trying to find that mythical one and only one?"

"Did you think Siena was your soulmate when you two were together?" Haylee snagged a handful of blueberries now that Tori was sufficiently distracted. She ate them one by one.

"Well, yeah. For a while at least." Tori shrugged. Haylee did have a point with that one. She'd thought for years that Siena was her soulmate, until everything started to go sideways. It still hurt to think about that time in her life.

"But now you don't?"

"Obviously, she can't be." Tori blinked—had she had more than just the one glass of wine with dinner?

"Unless…" Haylee smiled "…you believe in multiple soulmates. All who are absolutely destined to be your person. But maybe not all of them will be the forever-after you were taught to believe soulmates were."

"All right." Tori stood back up and narrowed her eyes at Haylee. "How old are you really? Because there's no way you are only thirty-one."

Haylee laughed and stood up, coming over to help Tori pull the baskets from the oven and get them turned upside down and cooling on the racks.

"These smell amazing." Haylee inhaled deeply, bringing her mitted hands that held the basket upside down up to her nose.

"Right?" Tori sighed as she copied Haylee's deep appreciation of the smell. "And they taste absolutely amazing."

With a flick of her hip, Tori shut the oven and brought the tray with the upside-down bowls over to the island.

The two chatted and enjoyed their date, knowing there wouldn't be a second, and sex was well off the table now. Tori wasn't sure she could force herself through it anyway. She would need time to forget what Miranda felt like against her, as she came with Tori inside her.

"Oh my god," Haylee moaned around the spoon.

Tori laughed and enjoyed watching as Haylee's eyes opened and stared from the bowl to Tori and back again.

"I told you."

"I get it now." Haylee nodded and dug in for another mouthful.

"They are amazing." Tori's eyes crinkled. She loved when people discovered something new, something amazing.

"Yeah, but I mean. I get you and Siena."

"Oh?" Tori asked before closing her eyes and indulging in the dessert.

"When she told me she was friends with her ex, I didn't entirely believe it. And then when she set up the date for us, that made me intrigued. But now, I get it."

"What do you get?" Tori laughed.

"I can see how easy it would be to stay friends with you." Haylee winked. "You're an amazing person, Tori. And from what I can tell, you lead with your heart, no matter what."

Tori stopped the spoon from scooping up the next mouthful. Fuck, Haylee was intuitive. "I try."

"You didn't do anything wrong tonight. Please don't be racked with guilt because it didn't go the way you thought it would."

"I think I did." Tori looked up. "And I'm so sorry. I mean, we definitely have a connection, and I didn't lie about that. But it wasn't right for me to go on this date with you while Miranda is still taking up space here." Tori tapped her chest.

"Okay, so I will ask again, since you brought it up. What are you going to do about it?"

"I don't know." But Tori bit her lip. Not from a nervous habit but from a desire to keep the crazy idea that had come to her during their cooking and talking from spilling out.

"I suspect, Ms. Frazee, that you know exactly what you are going to do about it." Haylee pointed her spoon at Tori with a quirk of her lips.

"But I don't think I should."

"Well, maybe it's time you stopped thinking." Haylee gave Tori a wink and moved the conversation on as they went to the living room couch to eat the rest of their dessert.

"Thank you." Tori brushed her lips against Haylee's cheek when the rideshare showed up outside.

"It's been a great night."

"It really has," Tori said. "And Haylee?"

"Yeah?" Haylee turned back just outside the front door.

"I'd like to stay friends. If you would like that, too."

"Girl, that was already a given." Haylee waved and walked toward the idling car at the front of Tori's apartment.

Tori watched until the car pulled away. She closed the door, leaned her back against it and slid to her bottom, pulling her knees to her chest. As nice as the evening had been, there was something a good cry could do that nothing else compared to.

twenty-nine

Miranda cringed as soon as she pulled into the parking spot. She didn't want to get out of the car. She certainly didn't want to talk to *her*. Grinding her molars together, she slowly got out of her car. What had Tori told her? Because the last thing she wanted was to be reamed out after running into Tori at the grocery store last week.

"Hey there!" Siena called over the roof of her car. "Good timing!"

Good timing? Miranda frowned. What did that mean? She wouldn't call any of this good timing. In fact, she'd call it awful. Everything in her life had spun out of control since she'd met Tori. Granted, Tori wasn't the cause, but she'd certainly been along for the ride.

Siena skirted around the back of the car. "I wanted to talk to you."

"Why?" Miranda bit her tongue. She should be nicer. Siena hadn't been anything but nice to her.

"Because I thought you might need a friend."

The skies opened, and a heavier rainfall started. Miranda wrinkled her nose and tightened her jacket around her waist.

"Let's go in and talk."

"Perfect," Miranda mumbled. She didn't want to be cornered where she couldn't get out.

They ducked their heads as they ran inside. Siena punched in the code for the door rapidly and held it open for Miranda to step through first. She shivered and brushed her jacket off before straightening her shoulders. She could see what Tori saw in Siena. She was strong, and a calm force of nature to be dealt with. Unlike Tori, her energy was the easy balm that surrounded and consumed whatever was around it. They would make a good match.

"Why did you and Tori get divorced?" The question was out of her mouth before she could stop herself.

Siena froze, her lips parted in surprise. She was just about to speak when Aili's voice echoed down to them.

"Oh good. You two. Come in here. I need to talk to you both."

Miranda stared into Siena's dark eyes. What had Rebel gotten up to now? Siena touched Miranda's arm and implored her. "Hold on a second, I do actually want to answer your question."

"What question?" Miranda huffed, like she had forgotten her outburst. So much for Aili's save on that one.

"Why Tori and I got divorced."

Miranda pursed her lips and looked directly into Siena's eyes. She had her whole list of assumptions she'd made about the real reason, but she'd never asked Tori directly.

"Tori is amazing," Siena started.

Miranda wouldn't disagree with that.

"But we stopped working on our relationship. Well, I did." Siena frowned. "It was hard when Harley was little. She didn't sleep, and we didn't take the time for each other like we should have. And to be honest, we were having issues before that."

Miranda said nothing. What was she supposed to say?

"It was easier to end it and stay friends than it was to work on our marriage. And I realized how I rushed into marriage with her. Not because love and attraction weren't there but because I felt like I was on a time clock. I know it sounds sad and pathetic, but that's the essence of what happened. It's not that I don't love her or that she doesn't love me, but we don't want to be together anymore."

Miranda could understand that. She'd broken up with plenty of people throughout her years, most notably her fiancé. She broke up with him because she saw no way that it would work out in the end. What they wanted were two entirely different things, and she wasn't willing to lose her identity by marrying him. But that didn't seem to be the case for Siena and Tori.

"I won't make the same mistake twice," Siena murmured. "And I don't think Tori will either, despite her aspirations to find a soulmate."

"Are you coming?" Aili called from her office.

Miranda looked down the hall at the daycare director. Aili stared at them, a stern look on her face. They were being called to the principal's office. The real question was why. Saying nothing to Siena, Miranda started down the hallway.

Aili held her hand out for them to take a seat and shut the door, that stern look never leaving her as she sat in her rolling chair and crossed her arms. "You all are pathetic."

"Excuse me?" Miranda nearly choked. This wasn't about Rebel. And her stomach sank as soon as she figured that out.

Aili shot Siena a look, her lips playing at a smile. "You and Tori. I swear if I have to see her moping around here one more day, I'm going to lock the two of you in a closet."

"A closet?" Miranda said dryly. "I hardly think that'll solve anything."

"Oh, it will," Siena chimed in. "And Aili isn't wrong. Do

you want to know the one thing I really learned since my divorce?"

Miranda did, so she remained silent in the hopes that Siena would continue.

"No woman is an island."

Frowning, Miranda folded her hands together and crossed her legs. "I don't understand, I'm sorry."

"I'm not surprised," Siena answered with a smile.

Aili chuckled lightly.

"No woman is an island. In other words, we all need someone, a family of sorts, a village. We can't do this alone. Especially when we're raising kids. Especially when we're women in this world. We need that support system, and you need one just as much as Tori does."

"Tori has a village." One filled with her exes. That had never been more clear.

"Yes, but you don't," Aili chimed in. "And we want to give you one. Today."

"Tonight," Siena corrected.

"I don't think I understand." Miranda was being ganged up on, there was no doubt about that, but she still wasn't sure she understood what it was all for. Tori and she weren't anything to each other, that much was clear, especially with the last time they had been together. "Tori has a support system," she repeated.

"She does, but we think you need to be added to it," Siena stated, as if that was obvious.

"That's amusing." Miranda rubbed her lips together. "We haven't talked in a week. No real conversation in weeks. So what are you proposing? That I can come to you both about problems with the perfect Tori?" Miranda blinked, her mouth not quite closing as she wondered where that had come from.

"Tori *is* amazing." Aili nodded, a small smile touching the corners of her lips, "But she isn't perfect. No one here thinks that."

"Except maybe you." Siena's face crinkled in a less subtle smile.

"Fine." Miranda had expected the word to leave her mouth in a snap, instead a rawness filled the office. "But it doesn't change the fact that she's off dating other people, searching for her soulmate, not thinking twice about me."

"And yet she's actually at home, pining for you, wondering if you are her soulmate and if she's missed the boat entirely."

"What?" Miranda's eyebrow lifted. She flicked her gaze from Siena to Aili.

"She is," Aili agreed with a nod. "It's actually been pathetic to watch her walk in here and haunt these halls. She wasn't even this bad after her divorce. No offense."

"None taken." Siena shrugged. "She loves you, Miranda."

"She doesn't." Miranda shook her head, wanting their words to be true but knowing they couldn't possibly be.

"Oh, she does," Siena reaffirmed. "And I'm not sure where the communication breakdown has happened, but it is very clear that you are the one for her."

"I don't believe in soulmates." Miranda's words were nearly a whisper.

"But Tori does," Siena whispered back. "And somewhere inside her, she thinks you're it."

Aili looked just as firm in her belief of that. "There's still a chance for you, if you want it."

Miranda swallowed hard, her head already shaking. "I don't know if I can do that."

"Why not?" Aili's question wasn't an accusation, but said with genuine curiosity.

For the first time since she'd explained it to Tori, Miranda decided to risk it. "I grew up with strict parents, and then when my sister was born I was sixteen, and they decided not to parent her. They were over the whole parenting thing."

Aili hissed. "So you did it."

"And I didn't do a very good job."

"Listen to me real quick." Aili leaned down, resting her elbows on her knees. She made eye contact with Miranda and held it. "You weren't supposed to raise your sister. It wasn't your job. It wasn't your responsibility. And just because your parents didn't love her enough to parent her or love you enough to do what they needed to do instead of shoving it all onto the shoulders of a kid, doesn't mean you don't deserve love. It doesn't mean that you can't be happy. And it doesn't mean that you aren't a good parent."

Miranda let out a shuddering breath. How had they gotten that from her one statement?

Siena reached over and touched her arm. "You're incredibly strong, Miranda. I don't think anyone who has met you would say otherwise. But sometimes that strength is a defense mechanism, and it doesn't do anyone good. Sometimes we have to be vulnerable in order to be strong."

"I told her all this." Miranda's eyes watered, and she hated it. "I told her I had to focus on Rebel, and that I had to do my best by her."

"But she didn't hear you," Siena said. "Which isn't unlike Tori. At least not when her heart is involved. She wants to see the very best in everyone, so she didn't hear that you were struggling to keep your head above water."

Miranda barely held back her tears. What had she turned into? She hated that she couldn't control herself, that all these people were coming out of the woodwork because they could see on her face what she was feeling.

"Answer me this," Siena started. "Do you love her?"

Miranda couldn't find the words.

"Or maybe this...do you love her enough to try again?

Because I can guarantee you that she will want to try again. Tori is nothing but a hopeless romantic, and like we said before, she always sees the good in people."

"I don't even know where to start," Miranda confessed.

"We do!" Aili clapped her hands. "First, Siena is going to take Rebel tonight."

"What?" Miranda tensed instantly.

"Harley's been asking for a sleepover since I guess the last one didn't quite pan out?" Siena gave Miranda a questioning look. "I haven't asked for all the details on that, but we'll get there eventually."

"A sleepover?"

"Yup." Siena looked like she was ready to stand up. "And then you're going to go to Tori's, and you're going to do what you did in here. Just repeat that."

"I can't do that."

"You can!" Aili jumped in. "I just watched you do it beautifully, and Tori is so patient."

"She had to be to put up with me." Siena laughed.

Miranda thought the same was true for her. "I can take Rebel to my parents." She still didn't want to rely on Siena, to have that burden with her.

"Miranda," Aili caught her attention. "No woman is an island. Let Siena take Rebel."

It would probably be better anyway. Miranda would know she likely wouldn't get called unless there was an actual emergency. Rebel would get to spend time with Harley, learn things.

"I still have some of Harley's old clothes, so I'm sure we can find some jammies for Rebel."

"Are you sure?" Why was she hedging? Miranda wasn't used to trusting people, not with things as important as this, as important as her niece.

"Yes." Siena smiled. "I promise Rebel will be my everything right along with Harley while she's in my care. But I'm only doing this if you go to Tori and pull her head out of her ass."

Miranda chuckled lightly. "I'll talk to her. I can't guarantee any outcomes."

"Oh, we can!" Aili slapped her thigh and laughed. "Because if she's going to be an idiot again, I'll come over and beat her ass myself."

"She won't." Siena shook her head. "But we'll have the same talk with her that we're having with you."

"Why haven't you? Had it with her, I mean." Miranda folded her hands together, warmth seeping through her chest at the thought that this might very well be a possibility.

Siena raised an eyebrow in Miranda's direction. "What makes you think we haven't tried?"

"Are you saying Tori is more stubborn than me?"

"No, I don't think that." Siena pressed her lips together tightly. "I think she's too hung up on definitions, and she's worried about what it'll mean to break those definitions down."

"I'm not sure I understand."

"Tori needs to give up the box she's trying to put herself in," Aili stated. "And we think she's almost there."

Miranda was still confused, but she was going to have to trust that these women knew what they were talking about when it came to Tori.

"Right. So are we doing this?" Siena looked at each of them, but her gaze lingered on Miranda. "Because I'm going to need the car seat."

Miranda grimaced. Transferring that from one car to another was always a pain in the rear. However, with Siena and Aili, it took no time at all. She said her goodbyes to Rebel, who looked happy as could be. Harley leaned over the middle seat and held Rebel's hand as Miranda walked away.

The drive to Tori's was quick, but she sat in her car for three minutes before she got up the courage to get out. She hadn't called or texted. She didn't want to warn Tori what was about to happen, that she'd have the chance to run away and hide. Straightening her spine, Miranda climbed the stairs to Tori's second floor apartment. She closed her eyes and blew out a breath, settling the nerves in her stomach for one last time.

It was now or never.

She knocked.

thirty

A knock reverberated, strong and to the point. Hope burst in Tori's chest that it was Miranda, but she tamped it down. It wouldn't be. She was way out of line to even think that. The only time Miranda came over was when she was angry, not resigned. Throwing the tea towel from her shoulder onto the island, she walked out of the kitchen.

The second knock on the door echoed louder around her too-quiet home. Whether it was because she was now closer or because of the impatience of the person on the other side, she didn't know. What she did know was that after a week of forcing fake smiles and making sure her daughter had a mother who was as present as possible, she had been looking forward to some solitary time to feel and be however she wanted and this person had no right to interfere.

With that frustration racing through her veins, she opened the door, mouth open and ready to give whoever it was a piece of her mind when her eyes met honeyed eyes.

"Hi." Miranda's voice was soft, and was that a warble in the word?

Tori's face dropped, and the words she had been about to say floated off into the ether, never to be retrieved.

"May I come in?" Miranda asked, gaze still fixed on Tori's and doing things to her she didn't want done to her. Okay, she did want them done, to her body and her mind and most definitely to her heart, but she couldn't keep doing this.

"Are you fucking kidding me?" Tori closed her eyes and turned on her heel. Walking back into her home, she called out without so much as a courtesy head turn back to Miranda. "Close the door after you."

Tori walked as far as she dared and stopped. She waited for the click of the door, followed by Miranda's soft steps approaching. She counted them—*one, two, three*—she had hoped to get to six. But when the fourth sounded in her ear, she whirled back around ready for blood.

"I can't fucking believe you." Tori's voice, or maybe the hard look she pinned Miranda with, stopped Miranda in place. "This is so unbelievably unfair."

"I'm so sorry," Miranda said slowly.

Tori believed it, but it wasn't enough, not anymore.

"Sorry for what exactly?" Tori paced, to the couch then to the TV. There weren't enough steps, but there was no telling Miranda to move so she could pace the length of the living room instead of the width. So back to the couch and then again to the TV would have to do.

"I'm sorry—"

"No, actually let me just list a few of the things you might be sorry for, but who knows. I sure as hell don't. Because that would require you to be brave enough to actually let someone in. So are you sorry for getting to know me? For leaning on me to help with Rebel? Are you sorry for fucking me?"

Tori rolled her eyes, fighting back shudders as memories of Miranda's touch flooded her body. She kept pacing. The pacing helped—at least she told herself that.

"Fucked me so many times I lost my mind over you. Or maybe you're sorry for ruining the first date with an amazing person? The first person I saw a potential future with since I met you, because you threw a two-year-old tantrum, afraid she was going to play with the toy you no longer wanted? I should let Rebel know she's trained you well."

"Tori." Miranda stepped closer, hand half-lifting from her side but not quite reaching out.

"No." Tori stopped pacing, and the tears that had been held precariously in place while she ranted fell freely from her eyes and down her cheeks. "Why, Miranda? Why'd you throw me away repeatedly just to come back and do it to me yet again?"

"I was drowning," Miranda said the words, a choke in her throat.

"Then you should've lifted your hand out of the water to show me where you were."

"I tri—" Miranda stopped what she was going to say and closed her eyes. Her next words came out much quieter. "I don't know how."

Tori took deep shuddering breaths in and out through her nose, her shoulders rising and her head dropping forward. She gulped at the air and more tears came, for all the confusion and the hurt, for the pain and twisted knots. And then she cried for all that she had said, and the words she couldn't take back. She cried for no longer feeling as though she knew who the hell she even was.

"It's not a partner's job to teach you how to lift your hand out of the water. They're there to help support you, but you have to raise it first." She couldn't lift her head. She couldn't speak louder. And she had no idea if Miranda heard a thing.

"Tori." Miranda's voice was so close, the hairs on Tori's arms rising as Miranda's fingers brushed around her without entirely touching her. "No woman is an island. I really do get that now."

Tori looked up and laughed. "What?"

"I had a very interesting talk with some of your exes this afternoon."

Tori blinked, the tears stopping as she looked at Miranda's face.

Miranda gave a quick lift of her eyebrows and a bob of her head. "That's about how I felt about it as well."

"Why are you here, Miranda?" Tori's voice wasn't much louder, but it was no longer a whisper.

"I want to give us a chance. A real chance."

"We already tried that." Tori's heart deflated like a week-old balloon forgotten in the corner of the room.

"No." Miranda shook her head, her cheeks taking on a pink tinge. "You tried it, and I fought you every step of the way."

"It's not like you suddenly believe in soulmates." Tori wiped her cheeks furiously, hating that there were still tears rolling down her face. She should be much stronger than this by now, have more defenses against Miranda. But even the idea made her so tired and sore to her bones.

"I never lied when I said I believe in love." Miranda's hand was on her arm, holding her lightly, as if she was too scared to really grip her.

"It's not enough." Tori was barely able to prevent another sob from tearing through her. She wouldn't do this again. The last week had been hell, and she couldn't let Harley see her like this again.

"Love isn't enough?"

"I've tried love. And it works for a while. But it's not forever."

"Maybe not, but do you regret any of the love you've

shared, the love you've tried?" Miranda looked at Tori, a stunning expression of confidence on her face.

Tori wondered what exactly was going on in Miranda's head. Had she found some secret Tori was searching for? She was so confused. This wasn't the Miranda who had left her cold and alone, battered from the relationship that was doomed to fail from the start.

It was all too much.

"Stop." Tori shook her head and stepped away. Her legs screamed at her not to start pacing again, and the fire within her that had fueled the short turns and struts was a pit of cold embers now. "Please."

Miranda didn't move, and a look that threatened to snap Tori's heart in half crossed her face.

Hurt.

Tori sat on the couch and rested her elbows on her knees. She leaned forward and allowed her curtain of hair to protect her as she tried to reach inside of herself and think through it all. As she tried to process the situation, not just the fact the woman she was in love with was in her living room, telling her she wanted to try again.

Wait. *In love?*

Tori looked up and blinked again. She looked around Miranda searching.

"Where's Rebel? Is Tierney back? Is that why you're willing to do this?" The thoughts jumbled through her in a second, so scattered that she wasn't sure if they made any sense at all.

"Rebel's with Siena and Harley."

"Siena?" Tori squeaked out the word, confused. "What?"

"She's having a sleepover with Harley. Tierney's not back. She may come back, and she may not. I don't know what I'm going to do yet. I know I want to remain a stronger part of Rebel's life. I want to help parent her, not just when I have no choice."

"I understand being a parent. I know it's hard, especially at the beginning, to remember they need you to also be a person, not just their parent. But we tried that, and that's when it went downhill." Tori couldn't break her gaze from Miranda. She looked stunningly perfect, like always. Her hair in soft curls around her shoulders, her jacket buttoned up to protect her from the cold rain, but her shoes pristine, as though untouched by the world outside.

"I'm not perfect, Tori. I don't always know the right way to do things. I've never been shown how to be both a person and a parent. Not until I met you." Miranda's shoulders dropped, her face falling. "I wasn't allowed to be a kid, which made me grow up too fast."

"I can still help you with that. We don't have to be together for that." Fuck, why did she offer that? She wasn't going to be able to do that. Not without feeling this same pain every time they were in the room together. It'd been why she picked Harley up early all week. To avoid this.

"I know," Miranda said, her voice so soft and sure. "But I don't want to be with anyone else."

"It doesn't have to be anyone else." Tori swallowed down the lump in her throat. "But I think maybe, we should just be friends."

"Friends." The word was repeated in an almost robotic tone by Miranda.

"I still believe in soulmates, Miranda." Tori grasped. She had to make her point come across. She wouldn't put herself on this line again, only to have her heart torn out of her and smashed once more.

"I know."

"And I know everyone thinks I'm entirely crazy because of it. And yeah, maybe demanding that I have it all wrapped up in a bow by the time I'm thirty is a lot crazy." Tori sat up straighter, running both hands through her hair, tugging a little with the frustrations warring inside her. "Damn it, I know it is. I don't like it, but I know it."

"Tori." Miranda took half a step closer. "Do you remember how you tried to convince me that soulmates existed?"

"I wanted a kiss, and it was the easiest, cheesiest way to get you to agree." Tori's cheeks burned. They'd both known full well what a crock that was when she'd asked it. But it had gotten them what they wanted—at least then it did.

Miranda smiled, her beautiful red-painted lips curling upward in a bow. "Can we try the experiment again? Please."

Shock reverberated through Tori's chest. She hadn't expected that. Miranda was barely even responding to her rant, which was fine because that's all it was. She wasn't making much sense anyway. Tori gulped. "You want to kiss me?"

"Yes." Miranda's smile blossomed into something else, something Tori hadn't ever seen before.

"The last time we kissed wasn't so great." Tori tried to put her defenses up, to lock them back in place, but she was so bad at it. She wasn't Miranda with all her walls and moats already built-in.

"I know. But it was never going to be great when I had already pulled back. I took myself out of what was happening between us." Miranda took another half step closer.

Tori dropped her gaze to her feet, those perfectly uncomfortable heels she always wore, the bright red toes on them that matched her lips and faded into black, the four inches of height added. She dragged her gaze upward, across Miranda's shapely calves, to her thighs hidden under that black and red skirt. Tori swallowed down the blossoming arousal. Nope. She wouldn't go there. Miranda always had herself together, not just in appearance but in how she acted.

"Why?" Tori asked, shaking her head.

"Because it scared me. I didn't want to abandon Rebel just to follow what I needed, to be just another grown-up who put themselves first. I won't do that to her."

"No." Tori laughed, with a slightly maniacal bent to it because this was all crazy, wasn't it? "Why do you want to try the experiment again?"

"Because no experiment is worth a thing without a follow-up test to ensure the control group wasn't damaged at the time. Every test needs to be replicated to determine if the results are true." Miranda smiled, the hint of a flirt flipping Tori's stomach. "Plus, we have a lot more data to rely on now."

"We aren't soulmates," Tori said.

"Perhaps not." Miranda shrugged and offered her hands to Tori. "But there's really only one way to find out."

"And if I say no?"

"That's up to you, chickenshit." Miranda smiled.

And Tori laughed, the sound bubbling up from her in an instant. There was no way Miranda would know what those words meant to her. Closing her eyes, Tori steadied herself. She took both of Miranda's offered hands, the smoothness of her skin sliding against Tori's palms. The touch brought her home. Tori smiled, releasing Miranda's hands once she was back up on her feet. "Okay."

Miranda stepped forward and, with both hands, tucked strands behind Tori's ears.

"Hi." Miranda smiled, hands moving gently over Tori's shoulders and down her arms.

"Hello," Tori replied, the lump in her throat growing while her heart decided to take up the tango inside her chest.

When Miranda's hands reached Tori's, they interlaced fingers, neither hesitating or flinching away from the touch. The mood turned somber again, settling into the top of Tori's chest, but it didn't hurt so much this time. It felt natural and, in an odd way, beautiful.

"I am so sorry for all the pain that I've caused you. I never wanted to hurt you, ever." Miranda's gaze dropped to Tori's lips before flicking back up to her eyes. "I was scared."

"Don't do it again." Tori mimicked Miranda's words from all those nights ago, but for the first time that night, they were actually talking. Tori opened her wound and let Miranda see it, and now it was her time to heal.

"Never." The right side of Miranda's lips lifted. Her eyes met Tori's as she sucked in a breath, the change in mood from seconds before startling but oh so welcome.

A shudder ran through Tori, as though Miranda's gaze looked beyond the surface and dove right into her, seeing her and all her flaws and still refusing to look away. Tori sucked in a trembling breath. Was she really going to do this? Put her heart on the line one more time for someone she was adamant wasn't her soulmate? Did the difference between a soulmate and someone she loved matter all that much?

"Tori," Miranda murmured, a hand on Tori's neck. "Tell me what you're thinking."

"I'm scared," Tori whispered.

"Me too."

Tori flicked her gaze up. Miranda, raw and vulnerable, stood right in front of her. But she smiled, as if this was exactly what both of them needed. Tori wanted to collapse into her arms, hold her. She'd crumbled in front of Miranda in ways she never did with anyone else, not even Siena—not anymore at least.

Giving in to temptation, Tori stepped into Miranda's embrace and pressed her nose into Miranda's neck. She took a deep breath and closed her eyes as she wrapped her arms around Miranda's back and held on.

"What are we doing?" Tori asked, needing Miranda's confidence more than she could admit.

"Whatever you want." Miranda combed her fingers

through Tori's hair as she held on. "Whatever it is that you want. That's what we'll do, but I'm here to try this out, to put in my full effort. And you should know by now, Tori, that when I commit to something, I go all in."

"Like Rebel?"

"Yeah, like with Rebel." Miranda's chuckle was low. "So what are we doing? You tell me."

Tori pulled away slightly, meeting those honeyed eyes. Her breath caught in her throat. Leaning in, Tori pressed their lips together. Tentative. Slow. Just the barest of touches. The kiss was soft and gentle. Something entirely different from every other kiss Tori had experienced before, with or without Miranda. It reached into her, and all that mattered was this moment.

She groaned into Miranda's mouth as she tasted the familiar flavor that was Miranda and hints of the coffee that would have gotten her through the day. This was home. Miranda was her soulmate.

Tori had no doubt about it now.

thirty-one

Tori clutched Miranda's sides with her fingers, holding tight and pulling her in closer. This was exactly what she'd wanted. If only it were just as easy to forget all that had happened in the last few weeks. Miranda parted her lips, dashing her tongue against Tori's and hummed.

It would be so easy to fall into her, to let Miranda steal away any of those nerves and frustrations in the next few hours while they were together. But still, Tori hesitated. Not everything unclicked inside her. Miranda cupped her cheeks, keeping their mouths pressed together, but she didn't push to take their kissing any further than what they were currently doing.

In fact, she slowed the kisses, pecking Tori's lips as she pulled away slowly. "I can't begin to tell you how sorry I am."

"Was it the date with Haylee? Was it jealousy?" Tori needed to know what had changed, what had pushed Miranda to show up that night, outside of Aili and Siena's intervention.

Miranda shook her head. "No, it wasn't that. I just couldn't avoid it when you were standing right in front of me."

Tori smiled at that. She understood completely the

extremes they would both take to avoid the tension between them if they could.

"I really didn't want to ruin your date. I promise. I want you to be happy, to find your soulmate and be in love." Miranda kissed Tori's lips again, but she didn't linger. "Rebel loves you and Harley, you know."

"We love her, too." Tori grinned before her face fell. "I was such a shitty parent this week."

"No one is perfect every day of their lives. Though I do think you try to be." Miranda curled a strand of hair behind Tori's ear again. "Want to tell me about it?"

Tori shook her head, tensing. Then she stopped. "What was it then?"

Miranda frowned, confused.

"That made you change your mind. If it wasn't my date, then what was it?"

"Oh." Miranda sucked in a deep breath and let it out slowly. "Let's maybe sit down for that one."

Tori would be glad to do that, but she really liked how much they were touching right now. She wanted to hold Miranda as close to her as possible for as long as possible. Now that Miranda was back in her arms, she wasn't willing to let go. Miranda pulled away and dragged her jacket off, laying it on the arm of the couch.

Giving in, they moved to sit, but Tori turned sideways, one leg curled up against Miranda's hip and her other one spread out over Miranda's thighs. Tori also refused to let go of Miranda's hand. She didn't want Miranda to have any doubts as to her commitment to this conversation.

"The last night that we were together was off, and that's entirely my fault. I wasn't me. I couldn't reconcile what I was feeling here—" Miranda pressed her hand directly over her heart "—and what I was thinking. I haven't grown up with good relationships, and my parents don't exactly have a good relationship either. I often wonder why they're still married, but they seem to make it work. Everything with you is so easy. And I don't believe for a second that relationships aren't work."

"I don't either." Tori folded their hands together, staring at the way they fit so nicely. "I know I talk a big game about soul-mates, but I was married, Miranda. I absolutely understand how much work relationships are."

"You don't ever talk about it." Miranda played her fingers on the inside of Tori's leg that was splayed over her lap.

"We weren't exactly in a relationship, were we?"

Miranda closed her eyes. "I deserved that."

"So do I." Tori reached across and tangled their fingers together, palm to palm. "I treated it like a relationship when we didn't actually have that conversation yet."

"I want that." Miranda's voice rang through the room, full of understanding and confidence. She looked Tori directly in the eye. "I want a relationship with you."

Tori grinned broadly, her heart picking up speed again. "I want that, too."

"Are you sure? Because I've been anything but kind."

"I wouldn't say that, but next time, can we try to talk about things before we become total assholes to each other? Or at least have hot make-up sex afterward?"

Miranda laughed lightly. "I'll try my best, but I have years of learning to unlearn."

"Good." Tori pushed up on her knee and slid so she strad-dled Miranda's lap.

Miranda let out a shuddering gasp, her hands suddenly on Tori's hips as she held on. Tori wove one hand into the hair at the nape of Miranda's neck and pressed the other against her chest, her thumb resting against her collarbone. "Does this mean I get to plan a date for us?"

"Yes." Miranda looked Tori directly in the eyes.

"And you won't be all pouty during it?"

"That I can promise you."

"Excellent," Tori dragged out the word, bending close to brush her lips against Miranda's. When Miranda moved in to kiss her, she pulled back and grinned, her eyes dancing all over Miranda's face. She did it again—as soon as their lips touched, she pulled back as Miranda tried to dive in.

"Now you're teasing." Miranda pouted.

"I think teasing is one of the best forms of foreplay. That and I get to see these lips in the most perfect pout." Tori kissed Miranda's cheek, dropping her crotch right into Miranda's lap.

Miranda groaned. "What have I walked into?"

"Communication. Relationship. Friendship. Some of the hottest sex around."

"I like that last part," Miranda murmured. "Can we skip straight to that?"

"Oh, we'll get there." Tori nipped Miranda's lip, sucked on it, and rocked her hips hard against Miranda's thighs. It sent a shiver of pleasure through her, but she could see it did the same for Miranda. "We're really good at communicating through sex, did you know that?"

"Yes." Miranda wrinkled her nose and wriggled under Tori as if she was suddenly uncomfortable with her own body.

Tori reached down and undid the buttons on Miranda's blazer and pulled the sides apart, splaying her palm fully against Miranda's breast. "So we need to take that a step further, if we're going to be in this relationship of sorts."

"Of sorts?" Miranda's lips parted.

Tori desperately debated about sucking on the lower one again. "Yeah. Like, I want weekly dates with you."

"My job doesn't have standard hours."

"I know, but I want you to commit to doing something with me—you and me alone—every week. Siena can watch Rebel."

"Way to volunteer your ex-wife for that."

"She'll love it. And I'd do the same for her if she found

someone." Tori gave into temptation and pulled Miranda's lip between hers.

Miranda sighed and reached up, moving Tori into her so they could properly kiss. Tori melted. Their tongues tangled, her eyes fluttered shut, and she did nothing but feel the elation coursing through her. This would be no-holds-barred, and so different than the last time. That was for sure.

"Miranda," Tori said through kisses.

"What?"

"One night a week."

Miranda stopped. "It may not happen."

"That's not the point. The point is the commitment to make it happen." Tori started on the top button of Miranda's shirt.

"Is your goal to seduce me while asking for things you're not sure I can give you?"

"My goal is to seduce you while we talk about what we want our relationship to look like." One button down, a million more to go, but Tori wasn't going to be deterred. "My goal is to start this on the right foot, unlike whatever we did last time."

"There isn't a last time, just a before."

"Fine. Semantics." Another button! She wanted to cheer as Miranda's lacy beige bra peeked from under the fabric.

"Tori."

"What?"

"My face is up here."

Tori's cheeks burned. "Right. I'm sorry. What were you saying?"

"I will commit to one night a week to be solely focused on you." Miranda slid her hand around Tori's thigh and right onto her crotch. She rubbed slowly and firmly. "I want you, in turn, to be very patient with my neuroses."

Tori laughed, which turned into a groan when Miranda hit

a particularly sensitive spot. "Yes, I'll be patient." Her voice was strained. "Fuck, don't stop that."

"Do you like that?" Miranda cooed, all that confidence right back in place. "Because I somehow managed to distract you from what you were doing."

"What was I doing?"

"Undressing me."

"Fuck." Tori couldn't open her eyes, her forehead pressed to Miranda's shoulder as she continued to rub through the fabric of her jeans. "Nope, that's going to have to wait a second."

"Only a second?" Miranda's voice dripped with control.

"Yeah, maybe a few."

Miranda turned her head, nipping at Tori's ear and flicking her tongue over the lobe. "What if I want it to take longer?"

"Keep doing that and you won't get your wish." Tori's hips moved in time with Miranda's touches. "God damn, woman."

"Going to come apart already?"

"It doesn't ever seem to take you long." Tori gasped. She was having a really hard time controlling herself, and then it hit her. Why was she? She should just let happen what was going to happen. Miranda wanted this as much as she did, right? So why was she still trying to grasp on the way she wanted?

Moving in, Tori took Miranda's mouth. She pressed her hips down more firmly into Miranda's lap, increasing the pressure of Miranda's fingers rubbing against her. She humped Miranda's hand. Fuck, she hadn't done that since she was a teen during a sleepover when they were exploring what sex meant. This was so much better because Miranda knew exactly what she was doing.

"I'm going to come."

"Good," Miranda dragged the word out, nipping at Tori's ear again.

"Fuck, Miranda." Tori gasped for air, her fingers digging into Miranda's shoulders as she held on. "Don't stop."

"Wasn't planning on it." Miranda kissed Tori's neck, holding onto her tightly until Tori crashed through what she hoped was her first orgasm of the night. But the next one she wanted to be naked for. And she wanted Miranda naked and against her.

Tori stilled, gathering herself as Miranda moved her hand. She ran her fingers up and down Tori's back as Tori evened out her breathing. As soon as she had gathered herself up enough, she moved off Miranda's lap, put her hands on her hips, and shook her head with a laugh. "Get your ass up."

"Are we jumping to the sex part?"

"You're incorrigible."

Miranda's lips pulled up in a knowing smile. "I've been told that before."

Tori grabbed Miranda's hand and led her straight to her bedroom. She didn't bother shutting the door as she spun Miranda around and pressed her into the wall. They melted together in a deep kiss. Tori worked the buttons on Miranda's shirt, this time successfully getting them all undone. But she couldn't wait. She was tired of waiting and figuring things out.

"I need you," Tori muttered as she pressed open mouthed kisses down Miranda's front. "I need you now."

"You have me," Miranda breathed her answer, her hips jutting out as her shoulders pressed against the wall. "Take me."

Tori dropped her hand and pulled up Miranda's skirt. She couldn't wait any longer. It seemed as though neither of them could. She slid her hand under the last barrier of clothing. Miranda dripped against her fingers. Tori kissed her quickly. "I'll commit everything I have to you."

Miranda shivered, a light moan on her lips.

"I'll be all in like you are. No more searching for soulmates while we figure each other out."

Miranda's lips parted, her eyes fluttering shut. "No one's ever done that for me."

Tori stilled. Surprise filtered through her, along with a deep need to protect Miranda. When Miranda wiggled, she started her slow strokes again, but the thought wouldn't leave her mind. This woman deserved everything, and no one had ever taken the time to give it to her.

Tori would.

"I'm going to do that." Tori kissed Miranda's neck, the tops of her breasts. "I'll be there for you no matter what. We break up? I'm still there."

Miranda let out a wry laugh. "I don't think I have any doubts on that one. You're best friends with all your exes."

"Yeah well..." Tori shrugged. "I don't give up on people easily."

"Stop talking and focus." Miranda moved her hips again.

"Is this too much teasing for you?"

Laughing, Miranda shook her head. This time when she opened her eyes, her pupils nearly took over the honeyed brown. "Never and always."

"What does that even mean?" Tori slid a finger in knuckle deep. She backed out and added a second.

"Fuck." Miranda breathed heavily, hitting her head against the wall. "I should have done this sooner."

"You won't hear any arguments from me on that one." Tori scraped her teeth against the soft, pillowy skin of Miranda's breasts. She wanted to taste and tease, but right now she was scared that if she moved either one of her hands, Miranda would collapse to the floor in a puddle. She pumped her fingers, curling them to give Miranda everything she needed.

"Tori." Miranda breathed. "I don't want to be with anyone else."

Tori's cheeks heated, warmth spreading through her at the genuineness in Miranda's words.

"I'm not just saying that."

"You never say things you don't mean." Tori pushed Miranda against the wall harder. "Look at me."

"I don't think I can." Miranda struggled to talk.

"I want you to see me when you come." Tori pulled her lip between her teeth. She was never this demanding during sex. Miranda must bring it out in her. When Miranda didn't comply, Tori stopped teasing her. She waited as the red drained from Miranda's cheeks, as her eyelids fluttered open. Tori smiled at her. "That's what I wanted."

Miranda snorted and rolled her eyes.

"Perfect." Tori resumed the pattern she'd had before, thrusting in slow, long strokes. She would make the most of this, not because it was their last time or their first, but because this time, they truly understood each other.

Keeping her eyes open, Miranda held Tori's gaze as she convulsed around her fingers, the tight squeezes exactly what Tori had wanted to feel. She kept her hand between Miranda's legs as she leaned in for a sloppy kiss. This had been what they were missing before. The openness, the connection, the relationship and understanding, and friendship, and yes, the sex. Tori stayed right where she was as everything around them slowed down.

"I'm so glad you're friends with your exes," Miranda laughed as she spoke. "They're good women. Really."

"The best of friends." Tori kissed her again. "Think you can stand on your own two feet yet?"

Miranda whined and shook her head. "Give me another minute."

"Of course." Tori moved her hand, holding on to Miranda's hips as she kept her plastered to the wall. "We need to do this again. Naked."

"I'd expect nothing less from you."

"All night?"

Miranda groaned. "I'm exhausted from whatever the drama was between us."

"See? Not communicating leads to exhaustion, and exhaustion means no all-night sex. What more proof do you need that communication is a good thing?"

"Shut up," Miranda muttered with a smile. "This whole *told you so* attitude is over the top."

"Is it, though?" Tori winked and kissed Miranda loudly. "I'm not giving you an option. Naked. Now."

Tori kept her hands on Miranda's hips as she stepped back. Miranda was steady, though the look she gave Tori was one of annoyance. Maybe Miranda really liked being pressed up against the wall, the control option taken away. That was something they would have to play with in the future.

"Get on the bed." Tori raised an eyebrow, giving Miranda a direct look. "I want you to sit on my face."

Miranda laughed as she stripped the rest of her clothes. "So all night it is, then?"

"Why would you think otherwise?"

thirty-two

"Excellent."

Miranda's heels clacked against the linoleum hallway of the daycare a few weeks later. Walking ahead of her, with a far more casual pace, hand-in-hand, were Siena and Harley.

"Siena," Miranda spoke the woman's name with all the purpose and authority imbued by her mission and her general way of life for many years. She swirled her finger in the air in front of Siena who was still a dozen steps away but had just passed Aili's office.

"What?" Siena laughed in reply, slowing her steps.

"Hi 'Randa." Harley smiled and waved her free hand.

"Hi Harley. You want to tell your mom to turn around? I need to talk to her and Aili." Miranda had gotten to the center early in the hopes of finally catching Siena at pick up. She had planned to be here at least half an hour earlier, coffees in hand, as some extra goodwill to get things started the right way.

"Say please." Harley stared at Miranda and waited for her response.

"Of course, please."

"Come on, Mommy." Harley pulled at Siena's hand and walked back toward Aili's office.

"Is this payback?" Aili called out from her office.

"How the hell did she hear us?" Miranda genuinely wanted to know.

"Eyes and ears everywhere—that's Aili." Siena laughed and allowed herself to be led to the director's office.

"Hey, Auntie Aili." Harley disappeared into the office, a giggle floating out moments later.

Miranda's mouth dried instantly, and now would have been a really good time to be able to hand over those coffees she never ended up having time to buy in her rush. She could do this, she managed people all day every day. She could organize this and get the help of these two in her sleep. This was no different from organizing a funeral, except it was nothing like a funeral. And her heart was involved. And this was for Tori, and she had to make sure she didn't fuck this up because she wanted Tori to know. She wanted Tori to know everything. Miranda was in love.

"All right, Harley. The toys are all yours. Time for the grown-ups to talk." Aili winked at Harley and ruffled her hair as Miranda and Siena stepped through the door.

"Okay." Harley skipped over to the corner of toys and plonked herself onto the carpet.

Miranda smiled at her for a moment, and heat rushed through her. She loved that kid. The realization sent her heart racing faster, even harder than it had already been going. Everything had changed over the months, and even more over the last few weeks, since she and Tori had gotten together. Officially. With Tori, things still came up and they had moments of tension, but it had gone more smoothly than Miranda could have ever hoped. She loved being able to see Harley and Rebel playing like sisters. She enjoyed knowing that at least once a week she got to wrap her arms around Tori and inhale her scent, become grounded and reminded of the things that mattered most in their world.

Her parents hadn't managed to make any more effort with Rebel. And it seemed like even less of an effort, honestly, but she found this whole parenting gig slightly easier, not easy but not as hard, when she asked for help from Aili and Siena.

"Miranda," Aili spoke up. "I don't mean to rush you, but I do need to get back to work soon."

"Right." Miranda shook her head a little. Yes, life had definitely become so much more than what it used to be. Having a whole village of supporters was often overwhelming, and Miranda did sometimes miss the quiet that had been her island. But this was better, and worth it. So why couldn't she find her words? And why the hell were her palms sweating?

"Is Tori okay?" Siena broke the tirade of overthinking going on in Miranda's mind in the only true way anyone could.

"Yes. Yes, she's great. But this is about Tori."

"What's going on?" Aili as always was direct and to the point. Miranda had decided she quite liked the woman. Getting to know her had been more enjoyable than she had imagined.

"Tori's birthday. Have either of you planned anything?"

"Tori's a tricky one." Aili leaned back in her chair as she spoke. "She loves being around people, helping people. It's why she loves her job so much, and why she's so good at it. But when it comes to being in the spotlight, she can get a little overwhelmed sometimes."

"Right." Miranda wiped her hands on her pants and nodded, trying to process the information as quickly as she could. "Does that mean a party is a bad idea?"

"Normally, yes," Siena said. "But the last time I did mention it to her, she told me to do whatever I'd like. She didn't mind."

"Really?" Aili and Miranda asked at the same time, surprise filling the room.

"Yeah." Siena nodded, eyes watching Harley as she spoke. "It was a few months ago. But you know Tori. Even if she wished she hadn't said it, she would never go back on agreeing to something if the other person wanted it. Plus, she rarely says things she doesn't believe."

Miranda smiled, and the last of her nerves and worries slipped from her shoulders. This could actually work, and not only work, but it could possibly go well.

"Uh oh." Aili said.

"Uh oh?" Miranda cocked her head to the side.

"Oh no, she's right." Siena turned away from watching Harley and focused on Miranda's face. "That's definitely an *uh oh*. One that means we are about to regret the amount of work we'll have to do by agreeing to whatever you're scheming up."

Miranda flushed, her cheeks heating. When had these two become her friends as well? She wasn't sure, but having them here was exactly what she wanted. "It's for Tori. She deserves it."

"Mom deserves everything," Harley piped up, and Miranda grinned.

"She does indeed, Harley. But you can't tell Mom about this. It's a secret," Miranda said in a loud whisper.

Harley's face paled, and her bottom lip trembled. Miranda's blood ran cold. What the hell had just happened?

"No baby. Miranda didn't mean a bad secret." Siena rushed out the words.

"We don't keep secrets," Harley said, angry eyebrows angled toward her nose as she glared at Miranda.

Miranda wanted to say something, but her mouth was frozen in a stunned O.

"Miranda didn't know that, Harley. And she didn't really mean a secret. She meant to say a surprise for Mom." Siena leaned forward, locking her gaze on her daughter. Thank God she was there, because Miranda was so lost about what to do next.

"Okay." Harley wasn't quite convinced yet.

"I was hoping we could throw Mom a big surprise party." Miranda crouched down beside Harley as best she could in her pinstriped pencil skirt, her knees together and pushed off to one side. She had to fix this. Whatever she had messed up, there had to be a way out of it. Maybe the hard part wasn't going to be wrangling the adults but the kid in the room. "What do you think? Would she like that?"

"Oh, she would love it." Harley warmed up to the idea now. Miranda hoped that meant Harley had already forgiven her the mistake of using the word *secret*.

"Will you help me?" Miranda asked. "Please?"

"Oh yes. I'm a great helper."

"Yeah, you are, Harley." Miranda stood back up and faced Siena and Aili, who looked at her with expressions Miranda didn't even know how to begin to process. "And what about you two?"

"So you're throwing her a party?" Siena asked.

"Yes. That's what I want to do. And I'll need both of you to help because this isn't my area of expertise." Her nerves were already rampaging through her at the thought of the party and all that there was to do for it. But mostly the people, and being surrounded by people she didn't know.

"Excellent." Aili nodded and swiveled toward her computer, quickly bringing up a calendar with a few clicks of her mouse. "We have one week until her birthday. When and where were you thinking?"

"There's really only one day we could do it." Miranda leaned over Aili's shoulder and pointed to the weekend which was a day before Tori's actual birthday.

"That makes it easier then." Aili typed in big capital letters,

Tori's Surprise Thirtieth. "Though a little more time might have helped."

Siena cut in before Miranda could start spluttering with apologies or explanations for why she hadn't come to them sooner. "Where and what exactly are you planning?"

"And what do you need us to do?" Aili took the hint.

Miranda opened her mouth to answer but was cut off by the intrusive ringing of her cell phone. She pulled it out of her pocket and stared at the name across the screen. "Shit."

"No-no word," Harley piped up from the corner, and Miranda threw her an apologetic look. Great, two strikes with Harley, and it wasn't even Tori's week to have her.

"It's my mother." Miranda looked back up at Siena and then Aili. "I've got to take this, I'm sorry."

"It's okay." Siena smiled. "We'll catch up and start planning soon."

"Thanks." Miranda slipped out of the office and back into the parking lot as she answered. "Mom, what's wrong?"

Her mother never called. Miranda was always the one who had to reach out first. The only time her mother called was in response to a message Miranda left. Miranda hadn't left any messages, not for the last two weeks.

"Oh, nothing, I just got a call from Tierney."

"Okay." Miranda pinched the top of her nose, closing her eyes. Annoyance radiated from her. She needed to get Tori's party planned. She'd been too nervous to approach Siena and Aili earlier, which meant she had left herself with very little time now. But as always, that tension in her shoulders strengthened. The tension never quite disappeared, because every day she fell more in love with parenting Rebel and she remained subject to the whims of her sister's intermittent calls and questions about her daughter.

"Is she okay?" Miranda might be annoyed at Tierney, but she couldn't stop caring about her baby sister either.

"She's coming home." Excitement rang through the phone.

"Oh," Miranda replied, having heard this exact phrase from her mother more than once. But for some reason her stomach sank and twisted into tiny knots. Her heart was in her throat. Fear. She was desperately afraid.

"She broke up with John."

Miranda had almost hoped this one would end up being good enough for Tierney. She'd been with him almost two months, and Miranda had even spoken to him on the phone.

"Yes. It turns out he's actually married and was just on vacation." Why did her mom sound so damn pleased?

"What?" Miranda's eyes flew open, anger swirling in her stomach. She'd spoken to the man and had even been willing to consider him genuine.

"Your poor sister is a bit of a mess." Now at least she sounded sad.

"Where is she?" Miranda's voice wobbled.

"She wants some time alone to think, so I've rented her a car so she can drive home."

"Mom, that's too dangerous." What she didn't say was that Tierney had never done something like that on her own before. That she'd barely managed to get an apartment on her own without help. How was she going to make her way home?

"Oh, you know, Tierney. She needs to do it her way." As always, her mom dismissed any of her concerns.

Miranda held back a growl. She would call Tierney soon and put something in place so she could know instantly if something went wrong.

"When will she be home?" Miranda didn't want to know the answer to that, but she had to find out. How much longer would Rebel be hers?

"I don't know the exact time, but Tierney did say she'd be sure to drop the car at the local rental place next Sunday."

"Of course." The only day they could throw the party for

Tori. Miranda had known what the answer would be before her mother replied, because it had always happened, she could easily rattle off a dozen things she had had to give up over the years to make her family the priority. But Tierney had given them a lot of dates over the last few months, so there was still a chance it might not actually happen. Miranda clung to that hope.

Miranda had also begun to truly enjoy the rhythm of her life and how it worked to weave a beautiful pattern together with Tori's. Neither's life or job took priority over the other. Miranda even saw Tori in her strength and guidance for others. Who knew she would ever consider a life coach a respectable profession?

Who knew she would ever see herself in a relationship that didn't suffocate her as a human being, or having that and the responsibilities of a small child?

"Miranda?"

"Sorry." Miranda shook her head. She needed to get her mind back on track. She wasn't usually so distracted. "What were you saying?"

"Your father and I are meeting with friends that day for lunch so we won't be able to pick Tierney up. You'll need to go get her and bring her home."

"I'll be busy." Miranda quickly bit out before the automatic agreement could spill from her lips.

"Oh, your father is calling. I'll talk to you later."

Before Miranda could respond, the call ended, and she squeezed the phone hard enough that her fingers stung and turned an alabaster white. She had to believe that this was just another of Tierney's stories and that she wasn't actually going to come home.

"Everything okay?" Siena asked, coming up behind her.

"Yeah, not a problem."

"All right. Well, Aili and I have sorted out a few details. I'll text them when I get a chance tonight."

"Thank you." Miranda's chest tightened, and she wondered if her lips pursed together as obviously as she thought they did.

"We won't take over." Siena's hand was gentle and warm against Miranda's forearm. "But we're excited to help out as well. Tori's part of our village after all."

Miranda smiled, breathing a little easier, the tightness in her chest loosening a little.

"And so are you." Siena made a pointed look at the phone before giving Miranda a quick wink.

"Thank you." Miranda's words were a little clipped at the edges, but they came easier than the first time she had said them.

Miranda knew Siena wanted to help. She had seen the genuine way Siena interacted with Tori and Harley and had no doubt she truly wanted to help Miranda as well. But it had only been a few months in the end, and it would take more than that for Miranda to discard a lifetime of holding everything close.

"I'll text you." Siena laughed as Harley pulled on her hand to get Siena walking toward their car.

Miranda nodded.

Once Siena left, Miranda had gathered herself enough to walk back inside, pick up Rebel, and wonder just what on earth she would do if Rebel was taken away. She couldn't fathom life without her niece curled up beside her, speaking more words each week, and expressing her humor and interest in ways that made Miranda smile more in a day than she had previously smiled in entire weeks.

She held Rebel close in her arms, taking a deep breath of her niece's hair. There would be very little she could do to ensure Rebel remained in her life. But she would remain in Rebel's corner, if nothing else.

thirty-three

"What are you two doing here?" Tori stared through her open doorway at Siena and Aili, both with shit-eating grins on their faces.

"Mommy!" Harley ran straight for Siena, who scooped her up and cuddled her.

"It's your birthday." Siena winked. "So we're going out."

Tori cocked her head to the side, not releasing the door handle. Her stomach was officially in knots. Something about this entire situation reeked of subversion. "Where are we going?"

"That, my love, is a surprise." Siena snorted, barely containing it as she looked down to focus on their daughter. "Harley, go pack up an overnight bag. You're going to stay the night with Gram."

"Weee!" Harley raced to her bedroom.

Aili stepped into the small apartment first. "You need to get dressed up."

"For what?" Tori laughed lightly, still trying to pry information out of them even though she doubted she'd get anything worthwhile. She hated surprise parties, and she hated being the center of attention even more.

"For your party," Siena barked out.

"Oh good lord." Aili shoved Tori toward her bedroom.

Tori let the two of them hash out what she was going to wear, and they settled on a nice pair of dark jeans and a suggestive black shirt that would cling to her curves provocatively. Tori laughed but booted them both out while she changed. When she emerged from the bedroom, they were snuggled with Harley on the couch and reading her a book.

"You both are going to have to tell me where we're going." Tori put her hands on her hips, refusing to budge until she had an answer.

"Absolutely not!" Siena chided. "It's a surprise."

"Yeah, Mom. Surprise. That means you can't know, but not like a secret. Secrets are bad."

"Right." Tori frowned at Harley like she'd missed something. There was a conversation happening she wasn't privy to, so she glanced at Siena for an explanation.

Siena waved her hand. "I'll explain that later."

"Sure." Tori walked to the kitchen and snagged herself a can of soda. She was going to need the caffeine if she was going to stay out late that night, and if Siena and Aili were taking her somewhere, it'd probably involve alcohol and getting home after midnight.

"Are we ready?" Aili asked.

"Nope!" Harley jumped up, coming over with one of those God-awful eye covers that Tori always made fun of women wearing to sleep. It even had fake sleeping eyes with giant curled eyelashes on it. "You need to wear this, Mom."

"Uh…" She took the item from Harley and stared at it. "I don't think this is a good idea."

"You have to." Harley giggled. "It's the rules for surprises."

Tori sighed. She'd wear it long enough for them to drop off

Harley and then she'd take it off. Giving a patented smile, Tori pulled the eye mask over her head and put it in place. "All right. Now what?"

She could hear the muffled sounds of people moving and walking and feel Harley's hand in hers. It was a slow walk out of the apartment with Harley's stuff, her drink, and the stairs. Aili carefully walked with her down them while Siena got Harley in her seat and settled. Tori didn't understand why she couldn't just put the mask on once she was in the car, but this was Harley's game, and so she would play by Harley's rules.

Aili helped her into the front passenger seat, and once everyone was inside and buckled up, Siena started driving. "Aili, would you text Gram and let her know we're on our way."

"Sure."

Tori frowned. She tried to figure out which direction they were going, but she was hopeless with her eyes still covered. Giving in, she rested and let them take her wherever they were going. Harley chattered in the back with Aili, glad to have someone sitting with her.

Siena found Tori's hand and gave her a tight squeeze. It was beyond comforting for what Tori was sure was going to be a wild night of experiences she wasn't ready for.

"Are you ready for this?"

"For what exactly?" Tori tried again, a fleeting hope that she might figure at least one thing out. She'd wanted to spend her birthday with Miranda, but Miranda hadn't mentioned anything about doing something for her day. Then again, she'd completely forgotten Rebel's birthday in the drama of her life. Tori shouldn't have expected they would be together for hers.

"For your surprise." Siena teased.

"I don't think I'll ever be ready for a surprise." She didn't lie. She hated surprises. Moreover, she hated the fuss and expectations that came with surprises.

"You're ready for this one. Trust me."

Tori couldn't tell what that tone was in Siena's voice. She'd heard it before, but it was rare. Letting the sense of anticipation fill her, Tori stayed still. They drove for what felt like hours, but since she couldn't look at the clock, she had no idea how long it was. But it was probably only twenty or thirty minutes.

The tires crunched over gravel as Siena slowed down and pulled to a stop. "All right, there's a surprise for you here, so we're going to need you to get out, but keep the blindfold on."

"At Gram's?" Tori hadn't thought this would happen.

"Just…go with it, T. Harley wanted to do this for you, okay? So we're going to let her stay here for this part." Siena's hand was on hers again. Even through their separation and divorce, Tori had always trusted her. So she wouldn't put that to the test now.

"Yeah, sure." She stayed put while everyone else got out and then waited as they brought her out of the car and led her slowly forward. Grass, wet and soggy, padded her shoes as they walked slowly, one foot in front of the other. She had to be careful, even with Aili and Siena on either side of her.

But they didn't go inside. Confused, Tori stayed silent as she followed along with whatever game this was. The ground moved from grass to gravel to stone. Siena had never gotten this elaborate with her gifts before, and neither had Harley. It was odd, but also endearing, and Tori savored every moment of it.

"Okay, you just stay right here. Don't move." Siena was close to her, her breath brushing Tori's neck and shoulder.

Harley clasped onto Tori's legs and gave her a huge hug. "I love you, Mom."

"I love you too, Pumpkin." Tori's eyes watered under the mask, and she didn't resist the urge to reach up and wipe them.

They left, the sound of shoes fading. Tori stood, breathing deeply the fresh scents of spring. Flowers bloomed, which said so much to her about life, and it was finally a nice, beautiful day that didn't involve rain. Those were rare in Portland in the spring, but she was thrilled to have it, especially since her birthday gift from Harley involved being outside.

Footsteps startled her. Tori closed her eyes to focus her attention on them. It was only one set of footsteps, unlike when everyone had left. She dragged in a deep breath and held still. She wished she could see what was going on, but she was left completely in the dark—literally.

"Hello?" Tori called, wondering if whoever it was would answer, though she doubted it.

A hand grasped her elbow, thin fingers curling around in a tight, firm grip. She smiled, instantly knowing who it was. Warmth filled her chest, comfort, and that excitement she'd been longing for was right back where she wanted it to be. This was the one thing she had wanted for her special day.

"Are you my surprise?" Tori asked.

"In a way," Miranda answered with a kiss to Tori's cheek.

Tori reached up to take the mask off, but Miranda pushed her hand to the side. "Leave it on."

"So you're not my surprise?" She was confused now. She just wished someone would give her a straight answer already.

"For once in your life, Tori, don't think you need to give a response. I don't want you to say anything unless you really feel like you need to. Okay?"

Oh, that commanding tone did things to Tori's insides. The power, the control, the pure desire dripping from each of Miranda's words that would put Tori right in her place. She had to squeeze her legs together to keep herself from falling at Miranda's feet and worshiping her.

"Yeah, sure." Tori's heart pattered. What was going on? She held still again, glad that Miranda hadn't let go of her hand. Having her there to root her to her spot kept her grounded, and it was exactly what she needed in that moment.

"Tori…" Miranda paused, the air between them filling with a tension that Tori didn't want to name. The spark of excitement was back, the anticipation and arousal she'd wanted to keep nestled inside her was threatening to burst out.

Why did this feel so monumental?

"Miranda," she finally said, breaking the tension. It was so uncomfortable that she could barely stand it. "Why can't I see you?"

"Shhh," Miranda shushed her. Her fingers flitted across Tori's lips. "I need you to hear me."

"Okay." Tori grinned. "I'll try my best."

"I know that." Miranda's fingers were back at her lips, trailing lines down her neck to the top of her shirt. She let out a little whimper, a moan perhaps, before scraping her nail lightly against the top of Tori's breasts. "This is sexy."

Tori's heart leaped. Her breath caught in her throat, and she struggled to make words, especially after being told to shut up. "Aili picked it out. She said I needed something special and sexy for tonight. We're not going to shag out here, are we?"

Miranda let out a low seductive chuckle. "No, definitely not. Not tonight anyway."

"Pity. Tomorrow?" Tori tilted her chin, trying to follow where Miranda's mouth was. Maybe she could snag a kiss at least.

"When summer hits." Miranda's fingers were back at her lips again. "It's your birthday tomorrow."

"See? Tomorrow would be a perfect day to shag out here."

Miranda laughed, the trill filling Tori with joy. "You're distracting me."

"I think I'm supposed to feel bad about that, but I don't." Tori's eyes crinkled as her lips turned upward. "What's this secret everyone's keeping from me?"

Miranda pressed a kiss to Tori's cheek, then her other one. "Nothing is a secret. Don't you know that secrets are bad."

Miranda had been the one to have that conversation with Harley. That had been what Harley was talking about, what Siena would fill her in on later. They were all in on this. The knowledge sunk into the pit of her belly, which lightened and fluttered. She moved toward Miranda, seeking her out and reaching for her. "You planned this."

"Of course." Miranda pecked her nose with a kiss. "Who else?"

"I thought Siena and Aili, but then again, I also thought this wasn't their style." Tori wetted her lips. What was really going on?

"This one is all me." Miranda leaned in close, her breath on Tori's ear and down her neck. Was that her tongue dashing out for a taste? Or was that too much to hope for? Siena did say Harley would stay for this portion. God, please say Harley wasn't looking at them.

Shivers of hope through her when Miranda's mouth definitely pressed against her neck, just under her ear, and when Miranda nipped her earlobe? Tori's knees buckled. Oh what she would give to have her way with Miranda right now. She hummed in pleasure, reaching out to grip Miranda's waist and hold on lest she fall. "If you don't get on with it, I'm going to make you scream right here and right now."

"I wouldn't do that, Tori. We're not exactly alone." Miranda bit her ear again, this time flicking the tip of her tongue against her earlobe, just like she'd done to Tori's clit last week.

"Fuck," Tori whined.

"Right." Miranda scraped her teeth down Tori's neck to her shoulder. Her hands were warm against Tori's back and side, her breath spreading hotly down the front of Tori's shirt and over her breasts to harden her nipples.

"Don't do that if we're not alone," Tori pleaded.

Miranda chuckled, full pleasure in that laugh as if she had

gotten exactly what she wanted. "When I met you, I didn't want to like you. You picked up Rebel in the grocery store like you knew exactly what to do, and I was left sputtering. I didn't even know how to get her to eat."

"You were new to this. I wasn't."

Miranda wrapped her arm around Tori's back and tugged her in close. "You embarrassed me by my inability, but you didn't make me feel like an idiot."

"Is that a compliment?"

"Shut up, Tori."

"Aye, aye, captain." They were clearly back to that first command, though Tori wasn't sure she could listen now. Her entire body thrummed with arousal, telling her to push Miranda to touch her any way possible.

Miranda dug her fingers into Tori's hip. "Listen."

Tori squeaked.

"I didn't want to like you when I met you, and then suddenly you were everywhere I didn't want to be, and you called to me. You held strong when I pushed you away."

"You were struggling."

"Tori," Miranda warned.

"Right. Shutting up now."

Miranda pressed a gentle kiss to Tori's neck. "I tried so hard to push you away, but every day I've gotten to know you since, I've fallen deeper..." Miranda paused, the words lingering in the air between them. "Deeper..."

Tori swore she knew what Miranda was going to say, she wanted her to say it, hoped she would. Those words had sizzled between them for weeks now, but neither one of them had taken the leap. And it was her birthday. Was this really her present?

"...deeper into an understanding of who you are and what it means to be a parent."

Tori bit her lip. That hadn't been what she thought

Miranda would say. It hadn't been what she wanted her to say. Because Tori was in love.

Flat out.

Hands down.

Fully in love.

She'd been convinced for so long that Miranda was her soulmate, and yet they hadn't talked about it. Miranda had pushed off conversations of the future, neatly avoiding them any time Tori got anywhere near them. But Tori just wanted to talk. She was so future-oriented that to think about only the present was impossible. Tori gasped when Miranda's mouth was on her neck again, this time with a tickle of tongue.

"As we started a different kind of relationship, a sexual one…" Miranda's tongue flicked up Tori's neck, ending with a kiss on Tori's lips.

This was torture.

Tori shuddered in pleasure. Her nipples hardened in an instant, and she clenched against nothing. Why did there have to be people nearby? Miranda was teasing her slowly into an orgasm that would never come or at least not for hours and hours—probably tomorrow. Fuck, on her birthday. Was that what this was all about? With the blindfold on, every touch, every sensation, every scent was intensified. Tori wanted to reach up and kiss Miranda, but she also desperately wanted to see what exactly was going to happen.

"…I couldn't get enough of you. Every touch, every sensation, every kiss…"

Was Miranda a mind reader now? Tori dragged in a shuddering breath, digging her fingers into the soft part of Miranda's waist.

"I wanted more. I craved you." Miranda pressed their chests together. "I still do."

"Miranda," Tori whimpered, unable to formulate any kind of words. What was this?

"And then I got scared, because what you taught me, very subtly, very swiftly, was that vulnerability isn't a weakness."

Tori's heart shattered. Miranda shouldn't have grown up with that understanding at all. She should never have felt the weight of vulnerability being wrong or undervalued or anything but precious and beautiful. Tori held her arms around Miranda, keeping Miranda close and not letting go. She wouldn't let go. If there was one thing she could do, it would be to continue to show Miranda that all of her was welcome into their relationship.

"It scared the living shit out of me." Miranda chuckled nervously, her voice floating through the air to Tori's ears. "And I ran. Which was expected, but you know what?"

"What?" Tori whispered, her breath quick as everything hinged on this moment.

"I came back." Miranda kissed her, their lips touching as she continued to talk. "You allowed me to come back. I was so wrong before. I shouldn't have let you go."

"You still have me," Tori murmured, moving to kiss Miranda but missing when she pulled away first.

"I know I do." Miranda skimmed her hands up Tori's back, against her arms, over her breasts, on her hips. It was like Miranda touched everywhere at once except exactly where Tori wanted her to touch. "Take your mask off."

Tori didn't want to now. She was so entranced by everything that Miranda did. When she didn't move, Miranda pulled the blindfold off. Tori kept her eyes closed.

"I love you, Tori. I thought soulmates weren't real. I thought I didn't believe in them. But if there's one thing you've taught me, and you've taught me a lot, it's that you were right. You're my soulmate."

Tori's eyes flew open. Her heart seized in her chest, tightening. Every fiber of her being was frozen on the spot. "What did you say?"

"I love you, Tori Frazee, and I'm not willing to give you up."

Without hesitation, Tori pulled Miranda to her. Their mouths connected, elation bursting through her. With the scents of flowers surrounding them, with Miranda fully in her arms—vulnerable, risky, daring—Tori knew without a doubt this was real. She swept her tongue against Miranda's, bringing her even closer as she bent back and kept Miranda's body tight against hers.

Miranda laughed, pulling away slightly. "You didn't let me finish."

"That was more than enough." Tori kissed her again, closing her eyes and smiling at the same time.

"But I love you, and I want to be with you."

"Yeah, I got that." Tori laughed, kissing her one more time. "I love you, too."

"I know it's a day early—"

"Fuck that. This was perfect." Tori pressed their mouths together, sliding her hands up and down Miranda's back. She wanted to jump around for joy and stay right here and never move. She wanted to tear Miranda's clothes off, make sweet love to her and run to the others and tell them what Miranda had said.

"Tori," Miranda murmured in between kisses. "There really are people here."

"Fuck that," Tori whined. "Torture me and then make me play nice."

"Well, I learned from the best." Miranda kissed her quickly before sucking in a long breath. "Come on, we have a future to plan."

thirty-four

"Now?" Tori squeaked again.

"No, not now. Tomorrow." Miranda grinned broadly, contentment swelling inside her.

"God, I love you."

Miranda didn't want to let Tori go. She wanted to keep kissing her and touching her, but she hadn't been lying when she said they weren't truly alone. Outside in the yard, where the party had been set up, it would be easy to forget that while none of the hidden guests could currently hear her confessions of love, she could feel sneaky eyes from around the corners.

"This is beautiful." Tori turned around in Miranda's arms, her back now pressed against Miranda's chest, while her ass pressed up against her crotch. Miranda stifled a groan. She had forever with this woman. A forever that would have many moments alone, without prying eyes.

The silence wrapped around them, and Miranda smiled, looking over Tori's head to the strings of fairy lights wrapped around the yard that held tables that would soon be filled with food. Chairs were scattered around the yard as well as large rugs and cushions for the more relaxed vibe that Miranda knew would help Tori and many of her guests enjoy the evening better.

"I'm glad you like it." A warmth of pride spread through Miranda's chest.

"I can't believe you did all of this for me."

Miranda kissed Tori on the temple and deeply breathed in her scent.

"I didn't do it alone."

"You didn't?" Tori leaned back into Miranda's embrace.

"No." Miranda chuckled at the surprise in Tori's words. "Someone very clever taught me that no woman is an island."

"I love you. And I love this." Tori wriggled around in Miranda's arms once more so they were face-to-face again. Tori's arms threaded around Miranda's neck.

Tori lifted up on to her tiptoes, encouraging Miranda to bend her head to meet her halfway. Miranda had no problems with that. She gladly pressed their lips together.

"Are you two done yet?" Aili's familiar voice called out from the shadows around the side of Miranda's house.

Tori laughed, dropping back down to her true height, and buried her head into Miranda's shoulder. It was time to face the music. "Oh hell, we really aren't alone."

"No. On such an important birthday, I thought it would be selfish to keep you all to myself." That and she couldn't very well ask them to help her set this up and not include them in the party.

"I'm not sure I would have minded," Tori murmured and trailed her fingers down Miranda's side.

"We have a lifetime of moments just for the two of us." Saying those words out loud meant everything, and Miranda was confident that Tori would take it well.

"A lifetime." Tori's smile was so wide. The sting of tears built in Miranda's eyes.

"Yes."

"All right then." Tori nodded and untangled herself, slowly and deliberately making sure Miranda knew without a doubt that Tori wanted to be in her arms just as much as Miranda wanted Tori to stay there all night.

"Ready to be the life of the party?" Miranda asked with a gentle stroke of fingers along Tori's cheek.

"No." Tori chuckled.

"It'll be okay," Miranda threaded her fingers into Tori's. "You aren't alone."

Tori lifted their entangled fingers and kissed the back of Miranda's hand. "All right."

"Come on out then, and let's get this party started," Miranda called.

"Please don't ever say that again." Tori laughed.

"Easily done," Miranda replied. "Felt stupid saying it that time."

"Thank you." The words were perfection to Miranda's ears.

The cheers drowned out Tori's laughter, and the rush of people flooded from multiple shadowed areas of her backyard. Miranda held onto Tori's hand, staying right next to her as the celebration began.

Soon, the tables were filled with food and drinks. Music played, and the sound and rhythm of people enjoying their time together washed over Miranda's backyard.

Miranda laughed as Aili and Siena dragged Tori into the open space and turned it into an impromptu dance floor. There were so many people, most Miranda had met for the first time only that day. Miranda still wasn't sure who the woman was who smiled as she watched them, raising a hand and giving a small smile. In a lot of ways, this was surreal. Miranda never would have this many friends, but Tori did, which meant they were her friends. She enjoyed it, a feeling of balance which she had never truly known, not once in her memory.

She was just about to grab a glass of wine when her phone vibrated in her pocket. She'd sworn off work for the day, so this nuisance call was going to cause an upheaval Monday morning when she got back to the funeral home. Someone's head would roll. The screen lit up as she lifted it to see.

Her mother's name.

Miranda took a deep breath. She hesitated to answer, and that itself spoke volumes of how far she had come. She wouldn't let her parents ruin a beautiful night, where the focus was solely on Tori.

She hardened herself as she pressed the red button and shoved the phone roughly into her pocket. Tori had taught her many things. That it was okay to be a parent and an individual. But what she hadn't told Tori was that she'd also been learning to recognize when she needed to put herself first, and not the responsibilities of others that had been pushed onto her shoulders.

Tori laughed, and the sound pulled Miranda away from thoughts of her family. Now wasn't the time to worry about them, and now wasn't the time to put anyone else first—well, other than Tori. This time was her own, and she was in love with the most incredible woman.

"Thank you so much for coming." Tori gave Haylee a huge hug, and Miranda smiled with a nod.

"You've got a great woman here, Miranda. Don't fuck it up." Haylee winked, and Miranda smiled, heat rushing to her cheeks.

"Not going to happen," Miranda said, determined that her actions would prove her words correct for the rest of her life.

"Good." Haylee leaned forward and gave Miranda a quick kiss on her cheek.

Miranda stiffened a little, unused to the tactile affections of those in Tori's life.

"You'll get used to it." Haylee laughed, waving. Miranda and Tori fell in step with Haylee. "I've got to get going." Haylee had a wicked grin on her lips. "I've got a bet to win."

"What bet?" Tori asked.

Haylee shook her head, her cheeks reddening. "I stupidly challenged my co-administrative assistant to a duel in a way. There's this thing about a gala. I'm not really sure but apparently it was bad last year."

"The gala for the Holbrook Foundation?" Miranda's stomach clenched hard. "If that's what you're talking about, then yes, it was a disaster."

Haylee stopped short, her lip pulled tight between her teeth. "Wait, you know what happened?"

"I was there. I have history with them, so I went to the gala to support their efforts."

"History?" Haylee's eyes crinkled. "Oh, this reeks of a good story, but I don't want to spoil my bet."

"What's the bet?" Tori interjected.

"Well, if I don't let our boss, Febe Aarts, fuck up the gala again this year, then my co-admin will help me with a pet project and tell me what happened at the gala." Haylee still looked like she wanted to ask.

"And if you lose?" Miranda questioned.

"I have to feed her donuts every week and a dinner for two at Le Rochelle's."

Miranda tsked. "You should have told her The Met." It was a dig on Tori's date with her, but it was one of the best date places out there.

Haylee frowned. "It's not that kind of relationship."

Miranda wasn't sold on that. "Well, if you lose the bet and you want to know what happened, give me a call. I'll fill you in."

"How do you know my boss?"

Humming, Miranda shook her head slowly. "To tell you that would be to tell you what happened at the gala. You can't have your answers and have fun. So which is it?"

They reached the gate to the front yard. Haylee stopped and looked both of them over. "My theory is it has something to do with sex, drugs, and rock and roll."

Laughing, Miranda gave nothing away.

"Fine. But I think the way to win this bet is to get my boss laid."

"What?" Tori stared at her in complete awe.

"She's really hot." Haylee at least had the audacity to look sheepish. "But I honestly don't think either one of us will win. Febe is an ice queen to the core, and she doesn't let anyone in."

Tori chuckled. "Never say never. So was Miranda."

Haylee raked her gaze over Miranda, a smile playing at her lips. "Oh, she still is. Just not for you. Got to run! It's my day to win, I can feel it." Haylee waved them off. "See you, Tori!"

Haylee was the first to leave. The fairy lights brought out the magic Miranda had tried so hard to harness for Tori's birthday celebration. She wanted everything for Tori tonight, everything that she wanted and more.

Rebel and Harley ran over, clinging to Tori. Miranda smiled down at Rebel and snagged her up onto her hip, tickling her belly. "Did you find something good to eat?"

"Yeah!" Rebel shouted and laughed again.

Miranda turned her head toward the house. She stiffened instantly. Her heart sank. Her breath sped up. Panic clawed its way through her chest as her jaw dropped. There she was. Standing on the back stoop like she'd never left.

"Miranda?" Tori asked, soft worry brushing her tone.

"Tierney." Miranda stepped forward just as Tierney moved onto the grass.

Miranda stared at Tierney, as if she was a ghost who'd just

appeared in front of her. Miranda never actually thought she'd come back. Something deep inside her told her the next time they saw each other would be at her funeral.

With Rebel on her hip, Miranda walked right for Tierney and wrapped her in a tight hug. "I'm glad to see you home safe."

"Yeah." Tierney had eyes for no one but Rebel. "Hey, baby."

Rebel shied away from her, pressing her face into Miranda's chest. Miranda flicked her gaze over Tierney's shoulder to her parents. "I thought you were both busy for the day."

"We were," Emmitt answered with pursed lips and annoyance in his tone. "You didn't pick her up like we told you, and you didn't answer when we called."

Oh, so they actually had to be parents. Miranda resisted the eye roll. "I'm glad you're all here, anyway."

"We didn't mean to interrupt a party." Sandra stepped forward, glee shining in her eyes at the prospect of a party, belying her half-assed apology.

Miranda couldn't find words. Had her parents really abandoned their own plans to get Tierney? When had that ever happened before? So many thoughts collided around in Miranda's brain, but she needed to focus. Tonight wasn't about her family, despite how many questions she wanted answered. And the last thing she wanted was drama that would ruin Tori's birthday.

Tierney stepped forward, her arms outstretched to take Rebel. Rebel curled in tighter to Miranda, who stepped to meet Tierney. She lowered her voice but made sure it was gentle and held no judgment or bitterness, "She's tired, T. And it's been six months since you saw her. Give her a day or two to catch up."

"She's my baby."

"She is, and she'll warm up to you, but right now, she doesn't know you. Please trust me on this."

Tierney looked like she was going to object, but instead, she stopped short. Also a first. She nodded and put her hands at her sides. "Okay. So what's the party for?"

Right. That. She hadn't told them. She was so grateful to find Tori looking directly at her from across the yard, keeping everyone away from them. Tori immediately came when Miranda nodded at her.

"It's a birthday party," Miranda answered.

"It's not your birthday."

"No, it's not." Miranda smiled as Tori stepped up next to her. "It's my girlfriend's birthday. Tori, this is Tierney, and my parents, Emmitt and Sandra. Everyone, this is Tori."

"Girlfriend?" Tierney squealed and raced forward, wrapping her arms around Tori. "Are you the reason Miranda looks so happy and isn't killing me for being away so long?"

Tori laughed, and Miranda reached her free hand out to squeeze Tori's forearm gently.

"I'm so glad you're home safe, Tierney. I really am." Miranda lowered the walls holding back her emotions and let relief fill her words.

"Has Rebel been very difficult?" Tierney let go of Tori, dropping her eyes to the ground and rubbing her left arm with her right hand.

"She's an amazing kid." Miranda's voice was gentle, and she saw the glistening reflection of Tierney's eyes when she looked back up. "We can talk about Rebel later when we all have some time to sit down and talk."

Tierney nodded, and Miranda was certain she could almost hear the lump her sister tried to swallow.

"Come join the party. There's plenty of food and drink."

"Perfect," Sandra said as she started toward the tables.

Miranda smiled as she and Tori exchanged a sideways

glance. She led the way to the tables still overflowing with too much food. She wasn't going to put Rebel down so long as she had a chance. Then again, maybe Rebel would go to her mother if she did.

Miranda took a deep breath and steeled herself for the pain.

She put Rebel down. Harley raced over and with words too quick for Miranda to understand led Rebel away to get up to some sisterly trouble.

The air was electric. The magic Miranda had harnessed for Tori couldn't explain all the emotions she could articulate right then. She knew they threatened to overwhelm her, but having faced so many fears over these last months, she took another deep breath instead. She could tackle them, one at a time, tomorrow.

"I'm so proud of you," Tori whispered into her ear after Miranda had ensured her family were all fed and busy mingling. She would give them credit, they had always found it easy to slip into a crowd, charming with their small talk and easy banter.

"Me?" Miranda leaned into Tori as they watched the laughter and enjoyment around them.

Rebel continued to follow Harley around, while Harley looked as though her chest might swell so much she would float away.

"Oh yes, I'm so proud of you."

"What did I do?" Miranda narrowed her eyes, trying to understand.

"You could have told them to leave, you could have been angry and yelled. I understand how hard the last few months have been for you. With being Rebel's only caregiver, with worrying about Tierney's safety, that doesn't just go away when she comes back."

"I guess I'm not as angry as I used to be."

"And why is that?"

"Because without them, without everything that's happened, I wouldn't have found you and Harley. Or this amazing though absolutely crazy village of women I'm now a card-carrying member of."

"Should we get matching rings or something?"

"Someday." Miranda chuckled, though the idea wasn't a bad one. Maybe she would get to work on that in the near future.

"Mama!" Rebel's squeal stopped whatever reply Tori might have given. They turned to see Rebel running with all her might toward Tierney. Tierney crouched down, arms wide, and bundled her daughter up the moment she reached her.

"Hey, baby. I've missed you so much," Tierney said, the sob evident in her words.

"Mama, mama, mama." Rebel wriggled to get put back down. But she grabbed Tierney's hand and dragged her over to Harley.

Miranda couldn't hear what Rebel or Tierney said to each other as they reached Harley, but she smiled, imagining Rebel's enthusiasm at introducing her mom to Harley.

Miranda pulled her eyes away, feeling a pull in her chest that mixed too many emotions, not all good but not all bad. She would have to deal with them later. Right then, a weight heavier than she realized slid from her shoulders.

"She's had a very tough time." Sandra made Miranda jump, speaking as she slid up to Miranda's side.

"I imagine so." Miranda nodded, eyes pulling away from Tierney and Rebel.

"I thought she could come back with us tonight and you could bring Rebel to see her in a few days, once she's settled."

"I don't mind having Rebel, Mom." Miranda smiled at her mother. "I think it's a great idea for you and Tierney to spend some time together."

"Well…" Sandra sniffed. "…she's my daughter, and she needs me right now."

"Yes, she does." Miranda gave her mother's hand a quick squeeze before moving back into the crowd of people, shifting between the smaller groups that had emerged organically. She had to escape that one while she could, at least for another day. Tonight was about the woman of her dreams, her soulmate.

thirty-five

"Hi." Tori smiled, opening the door wider for Miranda to come inside. It was the middle of the day, and the last person Tori expected was Miranda.

"Hello." Miranda stepped over the threshold with no hesitation. But Tori still sensed trepidation in her girlfriend's movements.

Her girlfriend.

It still seemed surreal, and she caught herself smiling at the thought. Apparently so did Miranda.

"What is that smile for?" Miranda asked, the one raised eyebrow doing some gooey things to Tori's insides. She could so easily fall into Miranda for the rest of her life.

"It's just nice to see you during the day." Tori's gaze wandered up and down Miranda's body. Today's outfit was a deep blue pantsuit, with a soft gray blouse beneath. The jacket was open, Miranda's right hand tucked in her pants pocket. The jiggling from within gave Tori the impression that was where Miranda had deposited her keys.

"Well, yes." Miranda's hand stilled as though she had heard

the tinkling sound for the first time and realized what she was doing.

"Miranda?" Tori held out her hand, and Miranda took it with her free hand. "Are you all right?"

"No," Miranda stated simply.

"All right. How about we have some coffee, and we can talk?" Tori tried to hold in the anxiety, because while her brain wanted to jump to problems between them, she didn't think Miranda would be acting like this if that were the case.

"I would love that."

Tori turned, and the instant loss of Miranda's hand in her own was startling. Miranda took one of the barstool seats at the kitchen island while Tori made them both coffee, not needing to ask how Miranda liked it.

She caught herself with the same goofy grin once again. But the tension that crackled from behind her pushed her concern for Miranda to the forefront and chased away the thrill of comfort and love.

"Here you go." Tori brushed her lips across Miranda's cheek as she set the white ceramic mug on the countertop. Her own mug, a bright yellow smiling sun surrounded by a rainbow pattern, looked garish in comparison, but Tori suspected she would need the extra happiness after whatever Miranda had come to talk about.

"Thank you." Miranda smiled and leaned forward, kissing Tori gently on the lips. Tori leaned in, almost toppling herself forward on her own barstool.

"Oh shit." Tori quickly shuffled back, getting all four legs of the stool on to the ground.

Miranda chuckled, her lips curled into a smirk as she lifted her drink and blew gently over the top of the hot liquid. Tori was completely entranced by the shape of her lips, Miranda's direct gaze, the things she wanted Miranda to do with that mouth.

For a moment they sat in the silence Miranda seemed to need. Tori took deep breaths of her own, knowing whatever Miranda had to say wouldn't destroy the future she had already created in her mind, especially since her birthday party. But fear didn't always listen to logic, so she continued to wait, though the skin on her legs itched as though she'd run up far too many flights of stairs.

"I need your advice," Miranda finally said, putting her coffee mug onto the counter.

"Oh?" Tori dropped her shoulders, which had slowly been rising with the lingering silence. "Advice about what?"

"Life advice." Miranda looked up as she spoke, those brown eyes all but glowing as they reached inside of Tori and landed with a thud inside her chest.

"Life advice?" she parroted, disbelieving.

"Yes." Miranda nodded along with the word.

"From me as…" Tori took a slow breath, trying to figure out if she would regret asking, regret checking, "…as your girl-friend or as a professional life coach?"

Miranda looked at Tori, head cocked with a look Tori hadn't quite mastered the understanding of yet. Her chest tightened, and she regretted it, instantly. Miranda had never pretended for a moment to have anything other than an obvious distaste in Tori's profession.

"Would it be too demanding to hope for a little of both?" Nonchalantly, Miranda reached for her coffee and took another slow sip. Did she realize how much of this was torture?

"Both?" Tori's smile beamed. She had tried to anticipate how she would react depending on which side of the question Miranda came down on, but she hadn't even considered *both*.

"Yes."

"Okay." The answer had thrilled her, no doubt about that, but still the situation twisted a little uncomfortably in her chest. "What advice exactly are you looking for?"

Would Tori be able to offer real advice as Miranda's partner? She couldn't be scared to stay true to her profession because it was Miranda. But what would she want Tori's advice on?

"About the situation with Rebel and Tierney."

"Ah." Tori nodded. She should have figured that out. It was the heaviest weight on Miranda's shoulders right now. Tori shook her head. She knew, despite Miranda not directly saying it, that the entire situation with Tierney's reappearance had thrown Miranda for a loop, and she had hoped Miranda would reach out to her. But she hadn't expected it to be in a professional manner. "All right. When were you thinking?"

"Oh." Miranda's eyes were wide as she looked up. "I thought you didn't have any clients this afternoon."

"I don't." Tori smiled. "But I like to give all of my clients the opportunity to go at their own pace. We can start now or at another time."

"Oh, well. I guess that makes sense." Another sip of coffee. Was Miranda using that as a distraction to pace herself?

"You should always have control over every part of your journey with a life coach." Tori smiled, failing to keep the veneer of pure professional mask in place. "And we know how much you like control."

Miranda's cheeks pinked.

"Just relax." Tori's eyes lingered on the angles of the woman who made all her dreams come true. She reached over and covered Miranda's hand, squeezing. Her skin was so soft, and she didn't miss the ragged breath Miranda took in just from that quick moment of comfort. "Talk to me."

"I don't want to lose Rebel." Miranda's words came out slightly choked, as if she was on the verge of tears. "Or Tierney."

Tori nodded, letting Miranda have the control of the situation, just as she would for any of her clients. But it was so much harder not to jump in, not to frame questions immediately, to let Miranda have this time to come to her own conclusions.

"Rebel's been back in my bed sleeping again ever since Tierney came home, and I'm scared." Miranda flipped her hand, lacing their fingers together as she looked to the ceiling. A sure sign she was trying to avoid crying.

"Have you talked to Tierney?" Every ounce of energy Tori had was focused on Miranda. That's what her love needed right now. Her attention, her listening skills, a comforting moment. Tori would give her all and more.

"Not really." Miranda broke their touch and sipped her drink. Her shoulders stiffened and squared, and she refused to make eye contact. "Tierney's asked all about what Rebel's been up to, and I've shown her photos and told her about how far she's come at daycare."

"And how did that go?"

"Every time I mention how much Rebel has improved in her speech or her behavior, Tierney gets quiet and then goes off to do something else." Miranda huffed out in frustration. "How am I supposed to suggest anything when she won't even talk to me?"

"What would you ultimately like to have happen?"

"With Rebel?" Miranda asked.

Tori nodded, letting the silence carry Miranda through her thoughts.

"I don't want to lose her."

"How would you lose her?"

"If Tierney takes her away," Miranda answered too quickly before taking a shuddering breath. "Or maybe worse, if Tierney keeps leaving without warning, keeps leaving for me to pick up the pieces, and I have to start from scratch every time, getting to know my niece over and over again, and having her resent me each time she's stuck with me instead of her mother."

"Oh, Miranda." Tori's heart shattered. "Is that what happened with you and Tierney?"

"What?" The skin between Miranda's eyebrows crinkled, her confusion evident.

"Is that what happened when you had to take on the parental role for Tierney?" Tori pushed. That was really what the whole problem was, wasn't it?

"I…" Miranda blinked at Tori and then slowly nodded. "I guess it is, yes."

"Then I understand why you're even more worried about what might happen with Rebel." Tori ran her fingers up and down Miranda's arm lightly, hoping that it added some comfort to this conversation. She knew it wasn't easy, especially for someone like Miranda, but she hoped she at least knew that Tori would hold this information sacred.

"I don't want her to be shuffled and shoved aside like Tierney was." Miranda placed her mug back down carefully on to the counter. "I wasn't good enough to be a stable presence for Tierney, but I can be for Rebel. I *want* to be."

"Miranda," Tori spoke and waited for Miranda to meet her eyes. This was going to be a hard point for Miranda to hear, and even harder for her to understand and take to heart. "Tierney wasn't your responsibility."

"She was," Miranda interrupted, but Tori didn't mind. She loved the fierce love and loyalty Miranda carried with her, even if her shoulders carried a far greater burden than she should have ever been asked to.

"She became your responsibility in a way, absolutely. But you need to stop blaming yourself, thinking you weren't enough for her." Tori cupped Miranda's cheek and dragged her gaze back.

"I didn't exactly raise a model citizen."

"She's lost, Miranda. She doesn't know who to lean on, she doesn't know how to be a parent, and that isn't your fault.

She needed her parents, not her big sister." Tori trailed her thumb along Miranda's cheek, the skin under her thumb pad soft.

Miranda fluttered her eyes shut, her face relaxing as she seemed to accept Tori's statement. "I tried my best. But she won't talk to me about things. She doesn't see me as her sister."

"Do you see her as your sister?" Tori asked. Her heart stammered a little as it revved up for a race. Was she overstepping her mark? She wondered how she might answer these questions if she didn't know Miranda. The thoughts sped through her mind, and she relaxed. She would have found out these things, and she would have asked everything.

"Miranda?"

"I don't know." The honesty was raw and real.

"What would you say is the most important factor in all of this going forward?"

"Rebel." Miranda didn't hesitate, and it warmed Tori's heart.

"Good. But can you make the hard decisions to ensure what's best for Rebel? Even if that means losing Rebel or Tierney, or estranging yourself from the rest of the family?"

Miranda stared at Tori, face stony. All the ice she'd melted away in the last few months came rushing back, and she hardened in an instant. Tori's back went up, and she regretted asking the question.

"All right, looks like time is up for today." Tori grabbed Miranda's now empty cup along with her own and quickly took them around the counter and placed them in the sink.

"What?" Miranda asked.

"Come here." Tori opened up her arms, and after a beat, Miranda stepped into the embrace. Miranda buried her face in the nook of Tori's neck, breathing in deeply. Her eyelids fluttered shut, and the ice that had come up to protect her before slid away slowly.

"Is this how you end all of your clients' appointments?" Miranda hummed.

"Not at all," Tori mumbled into Miranda's collar bone. "But you didn't need life-coach Tori anymore. You needed your girlfriend."

Miranda's arms tightened around Tori, and she breathed into the embrace.

"So what do I do?"

"I think you should talk to them, all of them."

"They don't listen when we are all together. The minute anything gets too close to home, they change topics and use Rebel as the excuse. Is she hungry? What is she playing with? Does she need a nap?"

Tori sighed and kissed Miranda's neck before pulling back slightly. "Then perhaps you need to see them without Rebel."

"I don't have a lot of time without Rebel. Tierney hasn't been up to having her home, and Mom and Dad don't seem to be pushing for that either."

"You're no longer an island, Miranda Hart. Did you tell me that?" Tori brushed Miranda's hair over her shoulder, looking directly into her eyes. She saw the moment it clicked for Miranda. Her lips parted, her gaze casting down to Tori's mouth before flicking back up.

"Would you mind looking after her for me?"

"Of course not. But make sure you let your parents and Tierney know that Rebel won't be with you, and where she'll be before you go over there." Tori tangled her fingers in the ends of Miranda's hair, tugging lightly.

Miranda groaned in pleasure, her cheeks flushing with arousal. "Why?"

"Because communication is key, and I hate to tell you, but you will probably have to be the one to start that."

Miranda nodded and stepped back, pulled her jacket down a little, straightening out the evidence of her mid-day meeting.

"Thank you," Tori said before Miranda turned to head back out of the kitchen.

"Aren't I the one who is supposed to thank you?" Miranda's brow crinkled in that cute way.

Tori shrugged but, as an afterthought, shook her head in the negative. "No. Thank you for trusting in what I do. For believing that what I offer this world is worthwhile."

Miranda smiled and nodded.

Tori understood how many words Miranda had already used today, how many emotions were wrapped up in every single one of them, and understood her need for silence.

"Can I drop Rebel off after daycare?" Miranda asked, wringing her hands together.

"Or you can call Aili and give me permission to pick her up. Whatever is easier for you. Just let me know."

Miranda leaned down and kissed Tori on the lips. It started as a gentle caress. Miranda leaned in, her hands wrapping around the back of Tori's head to cradle her. Humming, Tori fluttered her eyelids closed. She spread her legs and pulled Miranda by the hips to right between them. This was the comfort they had both needed minutes ago, the connection that would restore everything between them and deepen their love for each other.

Nipping Miranda's lip, Tori grinned as she dug her fingers tightly into Miranda's long locks and tugged sharply. If only they both didn't have to work today, she would drag Miranda to her bed right now and have her dirty way with her. Tori skimmed her hand under Miranda's blazer and against her blouse, then up higher, cupping her breast. She rolled Miranda's nipple under her thumb.

Miranda pulled back with a gasp. "You devious woman."

"Always." Tori grinned at her.

"I'll bring up the car seat."

Laughing, Tori moved her hands away. She knew Miranda wasn't going to push this. "I love you."

"I love you, too."

Tori watched Miranda walk back to her car after bringing the seat in. She leaned on the door frame and waited until the vehicle was no longer visible before pushing herself off and closing the door.

She hoped they could work it out. There were so many years of hurt and pain, but maybe now was the perfect time for all of them to begin the healing process. Maybe all they really needed was a rebel.

thirty-six

Miranda's hands beaded with sweat as she stood on the doorstep of her family home. Words had never been her strong point. Direct and to the point had always been her style. But this wasn't about her, not entirely at least.

She took in a deep breath, pushed back her shoulders, and gave herself a sharp nod of encouragement.

Even after steeling herself, she waited another beat, and then just one more for good measure.

"Oh for fuck's sake," she muttered and finally rang the doorbell.

There were no obvious sounds from inside, no voices or shuffling, and after waiting five minutes, Miranda pressed the bell again, holding it in for the count of three.

"Oh hey." Tierney opened the door with a yawn.

Miranda looked at her, eyebrows raising of their own accord. Was she just waking up?

It was five o'clock in the evening, and it looked as though Tierney had slept the entire day. A baggy shirt hung from her shoulders, shoulders free of any bra straps and far thinner than

Miranda remembered from before she left, while her legs were hugged by the black leggings Tierney seemed to sleep in no matter how hot or cold the weather got. Her hair was as wild as Rebel's had been the first day Miranda had picked her up from daycare.

Good, remember this is all about Rebel.

Miranda forced her eyebrows to relax, a far harder feat than she imagined it to be.

"Where are Mom and Dad?"

Tierney looked over her shoulder as though she had been expecting them to be standing right behind her.

"I, um…" She turned back around to face Miranda, eyebrows pulled in toward each other. "I don't actually know."

"And that's a surprise?" Miranda smirked, and Tierney smiled back, though it lacked the usual conspiratorial look they had often shared about their parents' absenteeism.

"A little bit." Tierney yawned again and then stepped back, as though only just now realizing she had been standing as gatekeeper to the family home.

Miranda wanted to ask if she'd slept all day, but she bit her tongue, grateful for a loud clatter coming from the kitchen.

She strode, legs taking her as fast as they could without breaking into a run, toward the kitchen. Tierney's own footsteps followed in her wake. "What's going on here?"

Before they reached their destination laughter echoed from within.

Miranda bit back another sharp retort, or something far less appropriate, as she stepped into the kitchen to find her parents standing in front of a stove with pans filled with various items sautéing, steaming, and frying.

"Miranda," Her father called over, waving one hand while lifting the other, spoon clasped between fingers, from a large pot. "Come and taste this for me. You have far better taste buds than either of us."

"Oh, we aren't so bad." Her mother tutted, though she smirked playfully with her husband.

Tierney laughed, and Miranda suddenly found herself on the outside of some joke that made no sense in her world. What was going on? Had her parents suddenly become different people? They seemed almost…happy.

"Tierney, how are you feeling?" Sandra met Tierney on her way to sit at the table, while Miranda obliged her father's request to taste the mystery dish.

Miranda pulled back from the spoon, waving at her partly opened mouth that was now filled with something spicy and yet lacking flavor. Her entire tongue and throat burned as though she'd eaten straight hot sauce.

"What are you trying to make?" Miranda asked, trying to figure out the tastes on her tongue.

Her father looked crestfallen, and Miranda found her own heart squeezed at the sight. She should have been more considerate in how she'd phrased that, but she'd been so taken aback by what was happening.

"It's a curry of some sort, right, Sandy?" His eyes were wide as he looked to his wife.

"Yes."

Emmitt clung to a hope he obviously found in her words.

"All right, good start." Miranda could do this. She had time and didn't want to rush any of them. "We just need to balance the herbs and spices a bit. Any more coconut milk?"

"I did exactly what the recipe said." Indignation dripped from Emmitt's words.

Miranda saw herself in him. She had grown up in such an odd house. She'd never been able to explain it, but what her parents were doing now was *not* normal.

"All recipes need a little tweaking for personal tastes," Sandra chimed in, like she was almost flirting with him.

"Oh." Emmitt's chest puffed up, and Miranda wondered

what had gotten into him. As she adjusted the items in the dish, she watched her mother talking to Tierney, her fingers gently stroking her younger daughter's arm. Had Miranda slipped into another world where she wasn't the sole responsible grown up? The feeling didn't sit well with her. She was so thrown for a loop, and this wasn't how she'd thought tonight would go.

Once dinner was ready, the four of them sat at the table as though it were just another standard day in their lives. Miranda looked at the three in turn and wondered if any of them sensed the shift in the air or understood the changes she saw glaring at her.

"So, why is our little Rebel not here with us?" Emmitt asked, sounding almost disappointed.

Miranda couldn't decide if he meant it or if it was for her benefit.

"I wanted to talk to you all—about Rebel." No time like the present, though she had been enjoying the facade of family bliss.

Tierney looked up, and Miranda's throat clogged with a lump of dread. Tierney's eyes were glassy, as though tears were held back by sheer force of will. Miranda had all the power in the room. It hit her in an instant. Miranda was the one who had control when it came to Rebel, even though Tierney was her mother. This wasn't about a power play anymore. It was about teaching Tierney how to hold that same power in her own life.

"She's trying, Miranda," Sandra spoke up for Tierney.

"I know." Miranda's voice was so gentle, the entire shift of her tactics happening in an instant. She smiled at Tierney, who couldn't meet her eyes for longer than a second. "You have an amazing daughter, Tierney."

"But not because of me," Tierney whispered, guiltily.

Miranda's chest tightened, and she wished to have even a

fraction of the people skills Tori had. How Tori and Tierney were the same age still blew Miranda away. Tori was so much more mature.. Miranda was about to speak, but her dad jumped in first.

"So you're wanting to take Rebel away from Tierney?" Emmitt asked with such a placid tone, shoveling a forkful of curry into his mouth as he waited for an answer. Miranda might have mistaken the words as him asking about the weather if the hiss of quiet hadn't rippled through all three women sitting at the table with the man.

"No," Miranda snapped out. "I don't want to take her away." She knew that as absolutely true the moment the words were out of her mouth. She'd thought about it, wondered if she'd have to, but ultimately, she had avoided the paperwork and calls that would get the ball rolling. She didn't want Rebel to be without her mother, not like Tierney had been when she was growing up.

"You don't?' Tierney asked, her jaw dropping in surprise.

"No, I don't." Miranda leaned back in her chair, shaking her head, her fork abandoned on the table beside her bowl. She couldn't eat. Not right now, not when there were so many emotions swirling around in her belly that she could barely drag one out at a time to label it before diving in for the next.

She supposed she couldn't really be that insulted by the idea they would think that. The thought had occurred to her so many times throughout the years, and especially since this latest stunt started. But she couldn't do it. It was the last thing Rebel needed. It was the last thing Miranda wanted.

"Tierney, I just want to help."

Tori's words rang in her ears. Miranda swallowed the words she didn't want to speak but knew she had to. Why were emotions always so hard for her family? They were damn good at avoiding them, but look where that had landed everyone.

Hurt. And barely able to have a civil conversation with meaning attached to it.

"I thought taking her away might be the way to help at the beginning. But I don't think that now."

Silence reverberated around the table, her dad still lazily eating but both Tierney and her mom staring at her with wide eyes. Miranda guessed she hadn't told any of them this. She'd avoided it herself for so long, but Tori was right. They had to learn how to communicate with each other. One way or another.

"How can you help?" Tierney's will broke, and the tears washed over her cheeks. Sandra's hand rested on Tierney's arm, as if she was suddenly the parent she'd never been before.

"I know it won't be easy, and we'll have to set down some ground rules, but I would love for you and Rebel to move in with me." Miranda looked directly in Tierney's eyes, wishing she would hear exactly what Miranda was saying.

"So you can monitor me?" Tierney's voice rose slightly, the accusation fully there.

"No," Miranda said calmly. She could do this. "Because I can help, and because Rebel deserves the best environment she can have in order to grow and learn."

"I don't understand." Tierney threw her napkin onto the table, anger rippling from her. Miranda had expected this, but she still wasn't entirely sure how to deal with it.

Miranda bit back her initial words. But if she let the silence linger much longer she was pretty certain her parents, who were currently not interrupting, would soon fill the gap.

"I'd like to help you find your village."

"My what?" Tierney sneered.

Miranda bit back a chuckle, wondering if she had given the same reaction to Tori when it had first been suggested to her.

Honesty. I have to be open and honest.

"Look, parenting is hard, especially if you're trying to do it alone. I didn't understand that before, not really. But no one should have to do it alone. And this is a way I can be there for you and for Rebel."

Tierney's sneer dimmed a little, and Miranda tried to process what was going on inside her sister's head.

"I want to help you and Rebel find the stability you both need and deserve."

"Me?" Tierney cocked her head.

"Yes." Miranda reached over and placed a hand over Tierney's, gave a quick squeeze, and then returned it to her lap. "If you need to go on a date, or to go away to see if he's the one, then you can. You and Rebel will always have a place with me. She won't have her home or routine disrupted, and you can be her parent, knowing you have backup."

"This sounds like you're trying to control me."

"I'm not, Tierney. I promise. You're free to have your own place if you want, but I think Rebel needs to remain in my care until you settle down." That's really what this was about, wasn't it? Tierney needed to calm her life down before Miranda would allow her to have Rebel full time.

"Settle down?"

Miranda bit her tongue. "That was a poor choice of words. We all have some learning to do, so let's do it together. But Rebel needs to be our priority. I want you to be a part of her life, as much as possible."

Tierney blew out a breath. "Since when do you believe in *the one?*"

Miranda couldn't tell if the roughness in her words was from a scoff or a choked hope.

"Since I met Tori." Miranda picked up her fork. She scooped up some of the curry but halfway to her lips she knew she had to say this last bit before she could move the evening on. "It's up to you. I will always be here to help you and Rebel. It's just an option that I thought might make things a little easier. In the end, I'll support whatever you want to do so long as Rebel's best interest is the priority."

The silence slowly disappeared under the sound of utensils hitting crockery, eating, and everyday banal conversation.

As far as things went, Miranda couldn't have hoped for much more. After they'd cleaned up, Miranda was at the door, ready to head out and get Rebel when Tierney stopped her.

"How would it work?" That babyish tone Tierney had was nearly gone.

"How would what work?" Miranda stilled, wanting to give her full attention to her sister.

"Me living with you."

Miranda stilled. "Come outside, let's talk about it."

"Sure." Tierney grabbed her jacket.

Miranda sat on the bench on the front porch, letting the chill in the night air hit her fingers and cheeks. "I think Rebel should continue to live with me, for now. I think you need to prove to me and her that you're able to take care of her, but more than that, I think you need to prove it to yourself."

"I miss my baby."

"I know you do." Miranda gave a sad smile and covered Tierney's knee with her hand briefly. "I want you to have the best relationship possible with Rebel. I just think you need some support to do that. Right now, that is."

Tierney nodded, silent tears rolling down her face. Her breath shuddered, and she couldn't look Miranda in the eye, as if to do that would be too much. "You don't want to take my baby away?"

"No." Miranda did something she never thought she would. She reached around Tierney and pulled her in, tightening her arms in a hug. "No, I don't want to take her away. I want to help you so that you can raise her like you want to."

Tierney sobbed. "Okay."

"We got this. Together. Okay?"

"Yeah. Okay." Tierney hugged her back.

Miranda's eyes were wet as she closed them, holding her sister tightly. She never thought the night would go like this. She never thought they could work together to raise Rebel.

thirty-seven

"How about we skip dessert?" Miranda asked with a smirk on her lips and eyes that Tori's body reacted to instantly.

"Harley is at home with Siena." Tori regretted having to say the words.

"My house is empty." Miranda's sly smile hadn't left, and the movement of her toes against the inside of Tori's thigh was distinct.

Tori shuddered, canting her head to the side. "Where's Rebel?"

"With her mother and grandparents. Their trial overnight run." Miranda pressed her fingers together, popping her pointer fingers off her lips. "Tierney moves in this weekend, and then my house will always be full."

"Oh." Tori's body cheered with renewed enthusiasm for where the night would lead them. "So does that mean we have all night? By ourselves?"

"Why, yes, yes, it does, Tori." Miranda finished her wine, her gaze never leaving Tori's face except to drop to her breasts.

"God, you're horny, aren't you?"

"When you're around? Always." Miranda moved her foot

up higher, right into Tori's crotch.

She groaned. "You better drive fast."

Miranda had her hand on Tori's thigh throughout the entire drive. Tori dragged in a deep breath. This felt so right. They had been together nearly two months now, and it was so much easier. Maybe not the relationship itself, but just knowing that they were both committed to even trying. They might not see each other every day, or sometimes even every week, but they talked every day, and that was what mattered. Miranda was there for her, no matter what.

"What do you think Rebel's doing?" Tori asked, giving voice to her wandering musings.

"Tori?"

"Hmm?" Tori turned her head in the seat to look directly at Miranda.

"I don't want to talk about Rebel tonight."

"Okay. What do you want to talk about?"

Miranda let out a little sexy grunt, and Tori grinned in response. She'd been thinking the exact same thing. Miranda didn't want to talk at all. Leaning closer, Tori pressed her palm flat against Miranda's knee, sliding her dress upward as she went.

"Your skin is so smooth here."

Miranda whimpered.

"I love to run my fingers over it." She did exactly what she said. "I can't wait to touch you tonight." Tori slid the pads of her fingers over Miranda's crotch, heat radiating from her. She teased slightly before moving back down Miranda's leg.

"You're going to be the death of both of us," Miranda muttered sharply.

Tori laughed lightly. "You're a good driver."

"Not when you're distracting me." Miranda grabbed Tori's hand and brought it to her lips, kissing her fingers. "Hands to yourself for right now. I need to concentrate."

Tori relaxed into her seat. "Should I touch myself?"

"Here?" Miranda squeaked. "We're in the car."

Tori shrugged. She dropped her voice to nearly a whisper, lowering her tone so her next words would be seductive. "Somehow I think you'd like a bit of a show."

"Oh, I would, but not here. Not when I can't watch… everything…you're going to do."

"I guess we can wait then."

"Some night for Rebel to be gone."

"Are you nervous because it's her first night away?" Tori grabbed Miranda's hand, offering comfort.

Miranda had tensed, the lines in her neck tight, and her thigh muscles so rigid that Tori was tempted to massage them right there. "Yes."

"They'll be fine."

Miranda grunted. "Maybe."

"You'll have to trust that Tierney can handle her own child."

"I trust Rebel to make a mess of things, like she normally does."

Tori chuckled. "We should have stuck her with Siena. She could handle both of them."

"Perhaps." Miranda pulled off the highway. "Tierney's ready."

"Are you saying that to convince yourself?"

"No." Miranda shook her head. "I really think she's ready. At least for one night."

"Perfect."

Another five minutes and they were at Miranda's house. The lights were off inside, but the porch light was on. Miranda didn't park inside the garage. Instead, she shoved the car into park and grabbed Tori by the chin, dragging her forward so their lips connected.

"I could really use the distraction," Miranda breathed the

words against Tori's lips.

"Coming right up, boss."

Tori went to leave the car, but Miranda dragged her back. Tori melted into Miranda's kisses. Miranda's fingers were in her hair, holding tight, a hand against Tori's back to keep her in place. Their lips brushed endlessly, tongues tangling before pulling away and starting again. Every nerve in Tori's body was telling her to climb over the center console and take Miranda right there, but car sex had never been her favorite.

She wanted a bed.

She wanted Miranda laid out flat on her back, hair around her in a halo, and unrestrained by anything. She wanted to watch as Miranda touched herself, brought herself pleasure, had her fingers buried deep inside herself as she came around them. But tonight would be Tori's turn for that. She'd give Miranda anything that she wanted.

They barely got inside before Miranda leaned against Tori, pressing her up to the closed front door. Miranda's breath danced on Tori's lips, their mouths not quite touching, while their eyes blazed at each other. The silence hummed through Tori's body. She could feel Miranda's hunger for her, the heat of her body where it touched her own.

Miranda's fingers danced up Tori's sides, not quite tickling with their gentle touch.

"I love you," Miranda said, taking Tori's mouth before she had a chance to reply.

This hunger was gentle and deep. There was no bruising of lips or clashing of teeth, though it took Tori's breath away faster than any of their previous kisses had. She melted into the embrace, allowing it to happen in its most natural and easy form. She wouldn't stop Miranda, wouldn't deny her what they both desperately wanted.

Tori moaned into Miranda's mouth and was rewarded with the press of Miranda's breasts against her chest.

"Please," Tori whined.

"Please?" The smile was evident in Miranda's question as she moved her lips from Tori's and nibbled down Tori's jaw and neck, taking her time to lavish the skin with teeth and tongue.

"Please take me to bed."

"I want to watch you." Miranda delayed the walk to the room as she returned her lips to Tori's, her tongue teasingly exploring the inside of Tori's mouth. Tori felt around Miranda's back, desperately trying to find the zipper on her dress, anything so she could feel Miranda's skin against hers and not just her mouth.

"Miranda." Tori wanted everything at once, even though she knew that was impossible. She wanted Miranda to touch her but also to watch her. She wanted to be fucked hard right now, but she also wanted the slow calm of making love in a soft bed, in comfort not just physical, but emotional as well.

Miranda laughed and turned around, entwining her fingers with Tori's and leading them toward the bedroom. Her feet were sure as she went, Tori dragging behind her. The click of Miranda's heels against the hardwood was so distinct in Tori's mind. She would remember this forever. Whatever was happening tonight was monumental, and it would last in her mind for eternity.

Tori wrapped her arms around Miranda's waist, pressing up against Miranda's perfectly round ass. She pressed her breasts against Miranda's strong back, the muscles in her shoulder blades making Tori's nipples harden into pebbles. She pressed a gentle kiss to Miranda's neck before sliding her hand around to toy with Miranda's nipples.

"Wait," Tori muttered as she realized they had just passed the bedroom.

Miranda didn't wait. She didn't stop until she reached a second door on the left.

She opened it, and Tori watched, eyebrows pulled tightly together, as Miranda leaned her back against the frame and waved her arm, with the same flourish that a TV game show host might use to display the grand prize.

And what a prize it was.

Tori didn't need to be told this was Miranda's actual bedroom. It was warm, lived in, and absolutely Miranda. Everything was in its place, shoes stacked under a small bench at the bottom of the bed, a bench Tori was definitely going to use in an entirely different way the next time they did this. The comforter was rumpled, Miranda not having made her bed that morning, and the idea that Miranda would leave something so simple and easy filled Tori with admiration.

It had never crossed her mind to question the lack of personality in the room she had previously thought was Miranda's. It hadn't entirely registered—probably because she'd been so distracted by the woman in front of her, and they had only ever been in there for one thing.

But now, as she looked into Miranda's actual bedroom, she noticed the things that had always been missing. On the bedside table was a book, a tassel hanging out the end about a quarter of the way in, an empty water glass, and a wireless charging station for Miranda's phone.

"Are you okay?" Miranda asked, taking Tori's hand firmly in hers.

Tori looked up into those honey eyes.

"This is your bedroom." It wasn't a question, and it wasn't an accusation.

"It is." Miranda nodded. "Rebel's bed used to be in that corner, not that she slept in it nearly as much as she slept on me."

"And that's why." Tori nodded. She understood the logic of never having used Miranda's actual bedroom before, but still something shifted inside her. The way Miranda looked down at her, love shining through even more than the lust that sparked around them. It made Tori's love swell to new heights.

Love had so much more power than even she, a serial romantic, had ever truly understood.

"That's why?" Miranda asked, even as she led Tori over to the foot of the bed and slid her hands beneath Tori's shirt.

Tori breathed in sharply at Miranda's cool touch. Her hands were sure and confident, like they'd done this every night since they'd met. They'd definitely never shied away from this part of their relationship, but something about tonight was so different from before.

"Why we've never used your room before." Tori pulled at the hem of her shirt.

Miranda stopped Tori's movements instantly. Had she said something wrong?

"I guess so." But the look on her face wasn't convincing. "I think it was a convenient excuse to keep me from falling in love with you."

"Oh." Tori laughed and pressed into Miranda's body, trying to entice her back to what they had been doing before. "And how did that work out for you?"

"Wonderfully." Miranda slid her hand expertly up Tori's stomach to cup her breast. Her thumb rubbed over Tori's nipple until it hardened despite the material still between skin to skin.

"Clothes. Off." Tori didn't even attempt to string more words together. Everything rushed over her. Her heart and mind met in agreement with her body that grew steadily warmer at each stroke of Miranda's thumb.

"Yes," Miranda chuckled confidently. "Take your clothes off. I want to see what you can do."

Tori moaned. Miranda was going to torture her through a slow pleasure tonight. This was so similar to their first time together, except instead of Tori telling her what she wanted, she was willing to do whatever Miranda wanted. She reached for the hem of her shirt again and pulled it over her head, dropping it to the floor.

Locking her eyes on Miranda's honeyed ones, Tori decided to give her a bit of a show. She trailed her hands over the skin on her stomach, her breasts, and up to her neck before going back down again. She moved her hips back and forth, anticipating the feeling of Miranda against her, in her. Miranda's eyes lit up, understanding fully what Tori was doing. She leaned against the foot of the bed, her arms crossed, one ankle over the other, and she waited to see exactly what Tori was going to do next.

Which left Tori in the precarious position of having to figure out what to do next. She'd never done this before. But she wanted to give Miranda everything possible, let her know just how much Tori was getting out of this.

"I feel like we need music for this," Tori said as she reached behind her back and flicked the clasp on her bra.

"I like the silence," Miranda answered, her gaze dropping to Tori's newly revealed skin. She looked so stoic, standing there, as if nothing could move or sway her.

Tori was determined to make that happen. She touched her breasts, moving circles around her nipples with her thumbs, licking her fingers to increase the sensation on her hardened nipples. Tori imagined it was Miranda's hand instead of hers, the slight tease that Miranda would give her as her entire concentration was focused on Tori and nothing else.

"I like the way you move, and I'm not talking about during the throes of passion." Miranda's gaze was intense as she spoke, her cheeks reddening.

Tori continued to tease her body, but now she couldn't stop looking at the woman in front of her.

"You move with such a quiet understanding of the world, not always around everyone but with them." Miranda's grip on her elbows tightened, as if she was really struggling not to reach forward.

Tori dropped her hands to her waist and pulled at the button on her pants. Miranda's eyes were glued to her fingers. Tori didn't push her pants over her hips. Instead, she slid her hand between the fabric and her body, finding out just how wet and ready she was. She had to bite back her groan.

"You have such a way of understanding the world, understanding people," Miranda's voice cracked. Tori could see her self-control snapping slowly, but she gathered herself back and continued. "You truly listen and guide those around you to whatever is best for them."

"And what's best for you?" Tori asked, her words filled with breath. She hadn't realized just how turned on she was by this. She slid her middle finger inside her, heat and pulsation surrounding her before she dipped back out. She couldn't do that yet. She was way too close for that kind of tease.

"You are." Miranda wasn't looking at Tori's body anymore, but at her face, deep into her eyes. "And I hope, with time, that I'll be what's best for you."

Tori whined. She wanted to wrap Miranda up in her arms and hold her, tell her that she'd never found someone like Miranda before, that she'd never fallen so hard for someone, never found a woman as strong or dedicated. She wanted to shout at Miranda that they were perfect for each other, that Tori couldn't imagine her life going forward without Miranda in it.

"Don't stop touching yourself," Miranda commanded.

Tori hadn't realized she'd stilled. She immediately pushed her pants and underwear over her hips, toeing off her shoes and stepping out of her clothes completely. Instead of touching herself again, she walked forward and pressed against Miranda. The tug of fabric against her heated, warmed, and sensitive skin was beyond enticing. Their mouths melded together in a deep kiss, but Miranda didn't move other than to kiss her back.

Tori took exactly what she wanted, pushing Miranda against the footboard, fingers skimming down her body to her hips, her ass. Miranda nipped Tori's lower lip hard. "Enough."

"Miranda," Tori protested.

"I want to watch you."

Tori kissed her again lightly this time. "Where?"

"On *my* bed." Miranda still didn't move.

Stepping back, Tori took deep breaths to calm her raging body. Miranda clearly wanted this slow and teasing tonight, and Tori would oblige. She skimmed her hands over the flare of her hips, around and between her legs for a quick dip, and then up, over her breasts. She walked with full confidence around the side of the bed and climbed onto it, shoving the covers to the side with her feet.

Tori's heart raced. She lay on her back, her knees parted, and her head far away from Miranda. She could barely see Miranda over the rise of her breasts, but she knew Miranda could see everything. Tori was completely vulnerable, rendered to Miranda's whims.

"What do you want me to do?" Tori flitted her fingers around her body, teasing lightly, and waiting for Miranda's next demand.

"Touch yourself exactly like you want to."

Tori raised her head up, finding Miranda gripping the wrought iron of the foot board, her knuckles white, and her eyes glued right between Tori's legs. "When will you join?" It wasn't a question of whether Miranda would or not, and Tori wanted to make that clear. "I want your mouth."

"Not yet." Miranda dragged in a breath through her nose. "Touch yourself, Tori."

"But I want you." Even as Tori said it, she slipped her pointer finger around her clit in a decisive circle. Her hips bucked, her body finally getting exactly what it wanted. "I want you to be with me, every time, every moment."

"I'm right here," Miranda cooed, still from the foot of the bed.

"Miranda, I love you."

Tori covered one breast with her palm, teasing her nipple. She chose the simplest way to do this. With the flat of two of her fingers, she gathered up some of her juices and flicked rapidly over her clit. Back and forth. Back and forth. Biting her lip, her back arching off the bed, Tori closed her eyes. Using her imagination, she pretended her hand was Miranda's hand, and Miranda's intense stare as she watched was exactly what she needed to get her going.

"Miranda," Tori called again, wishing the damn woman would just come around and touch her already.

"Don't stop, Tori." Miranda's voice filled her, ringing through her ears as if she was right next to Tori's head.

Popping her eyes open, Tori looked down to find that Miranda hadn't moved. She stood completely still at the end of the bed, her eyes glued between Tori's legs, to the movement of her fingers. Tori gasped.

"Miranda."

"Come."

Tori released her breath, pleasure flowing through her in an instant. She clamped her legs together, hand between them, and turned on her side. With her eyes clenched shut, Tori tried to steady her racing heart, her overheated body, the power of whatever had just happened. Hands at her ankles turned her, and she allowed the movement. She trusted that Miranda would take care of her, whatever she needed.

Miranda pressed her knees back open, and shoved Tori's hands to the side. Tori's head spun. But when Miranda's mouth was against her, tongue sliding through her swollen and sensitive slit, Tori cried out. She dug her fingers into the sheets on the bed, tilting her head back as Miranda's entire mouth covered her clit, her fingers sliding deep inside her to curl.

Words flew through Tori's brain, but none of them reached her lips. She wanted to curse Miranda, tell her to never stop, ask for a few seconds, while at the same time demanding more, faster, harder, calling out that this was exactly what she wanted.

"Harder or softer?" Miranda murmured.

Tori wasn't even sure how to answer that. Her mind drew a blank. Drawing in a deep breath was so hard, and concentrating was impossible.

"Tori." Miranda's voice cut through the floaty feeling. "Harder or softer?"

"Harder." The word burst from her. She hadn't even known what she was going to say.

"Slower or faster." Miranda sounded so pleased with herself.

"Faster." Tori opened her eyes, locking her gaze on that honeyed one, the one between her legs that was filled with sweet satisfaction.

Miranda said nothing as she dove back in, doing exactly what Tori had told her to. In an instant, Tori was digging her fingers into the sheets, trying to find anything to keep her rooted to the spot. Her heels dug into the soft mattress, her hips raising up as she undulated against Miranda's mouth. Miranda sucked hard. A burning pain rushed through Tori, but she held it tight in her chest, closing her eyes and breathing through it. She clenched her jaw, moving again and again. Miranda's hair tickled her thighs. Heat built within her.

Tori grunted as she continued to move against Miranda. She reached forward, her hand planted on the top of Miranda's head, increasing the pressure between her legs even more. She was so close. All she had to do was hold this space for a little longer. Tori rocked her hips against Miranda's mouth, tensing her fingers in Miranda's hair.

"Now," she breathed out the word as her entire body tightened. A moan ripped from her lips, and her head spun.

Miranda stayed between her legs, slowing her licks into long languid movements. Tori couldn't speak. She was still so completely taken with what had just happened, her mind washed of thoughts and concerns. Eventually Miranda pressed kisses to her thighs, her hip bones, a chuckle quietly reaching Tori's ears.

"Did you stop thinking?"

"Fuck you," Tori said with a grin and a laugh. "But yes."

"Good." Miranda moved onto the mattress, still perfectly made up from her day and their dinner.

"I'm a goddamn mess compared to you."

"Hardly." Miranda kissed Tori's lips, her mouth still damp and Tori's flavor lingering on her. "I think our messes complement each other."

Tori chuckled, running her hands over Miranda's sides after finally finding herself again. "You're still dressed."

"I enjoyed that." Miranda kissed her again.

"Why are you still dressed?" Why was Tori repeating herself? Maybe she really had lost her mind.

"I wanted to enjoy you."

Tori pressed her lips together. "That was hot."

Miranda laughed, her lips curling up into the most beautiful smile. "It was."

"But you're still dressed."

"My, my, who's the demanding one now?"

"Miranda," Tori whined.

"Patience." Miranda kissed her again.

Tori fell into it. She could barely move, but she wrapped her arms around Miranda's back, pressing their bodies together, smooshing Miranda against her. She intensified the embrace, scraping her teeth against Miranda's lower lip. Their tongues touched, and Tori could taste the lingering wine mixed in with her own flavor. It was so sexy. Her entire body hummed.

"I'd ask for the same show from you, but I'm not sure I have the self-control to just watch."

Miranda giggled. She buried her face in Tori's neck, the laughs rocking through her body. "I love your enthusiasm."

"Get naked already." She knew she was whining, but she wanted desperately to have Miranda against her, naked, warm, enticing. And she needed another minute or two to gather her wits again.

The strip tease Miranda gave her wasn't as good as the one Tori had done, but that wasn't the point. Tori just wanted Miranda naked, against her, as fast as possible. Miranda stood at the edge of the bed, her dusty pink nipples already hard, her chest flushed with color.

"Move back."

Tori did as she was told, sliding into the center of the large bed. Miranda climbed on top of her, the green beads from her necklace bouncing with each move she made. Tori was completely entranced. She lifted her hands, fingering the beads before dropping lower to brush slightly over Miranda's nipples. Miranda hummed.

Moving in, Miranda kissed Tori lightly. "I love you, Tori Frazee."

"I love you, Miranda Hart." Tori grinned, unable and unwilling to contain the happiness that filled her now. She really couldn't have asked for anything more than this. Honesty. Connection. Desire. Vulnerability. "God, I love you so much."

"Then show me what that looks like."

Tori skimmed her hands down Miranda's body to her hips, ready to give Miranda everything she asked for and more. "Forever and always."

epilogue

SIX MONTHS LATER...

Miranda stood at the window waiting. Rebel played on the floor behind her. The rain had eased up that summer, but they were nearing fall again, and Miranda knew they didn't have many nice weekends left. She dragged in a deep breath, keeping her eyes glued to the street corner that she could barely see out of her front window. Where were they?

Tori had said they'd left forty minutes ago. They should have been there already. Miranda tightened her grip on her elbows. She hoped nothing had gone wrong in the meantime, that Tori hadn't had an accident or anything like that. She was debating whether or not to text because that could easily add another distraction and potentially cause Tori to have an accident.

The U-Haul rounded the corner, and Miranda sighed in relief. She shouldn't have worried so much, but this was huge for her. In some ways, it was bigger than letting Tierney move into the house with her, although she only lived there about half the time anyway.

Miranda glanced at Rebel. Her hair was almost to her shoulders, the tight ringlets tamed sufficiently now that Miranda understood how to handle curly hair. "Rebel, Tori and Harley are almost here."

"'Arley!" Rebel jumped up and raced for the front door.

Her speech had gotten so much better in the last six months, and she was making short two- and three-word sentences. Tierney had given permission for Miranda to pay for some early intervention with speech, and that was helping in so many ways.

Stepping out onto the front porch, Miranda's cheeks warmed from the breeze. They'd been planning this day for a couple months now, and it was finally here. As soon as Tori parked the truck, Harley jumped out of the front seat and ran toward Rebel, scooping her up. Then she raced to Miranda, wrapping her arms around Miranda's hips and burying her face into Miranda's side.

"Hey, Harley." Miranda carded her fingers through Harley's hair.

"I'm so excited!"

"I am too."

Looking up, Miranda saw that Tori was already frazzled. She couldn't stop the smile from blooming on her lips as Tori came around the front of the truck and pocketed the keys. She walked right into Miranda, a hand on Miranda's waist and their mouths against each other in a quick but hot kiss.

"Please tell me we're having beer and pizza tonight."

"Sure, if you want." Miranda skimmed her hand down Tori's arm. "What's wrong?"

"Moving is stressful. The crew will be here in about twenty minutes to get everything moved in. Want to tell me where it goes?"

Miranda canted her head to the side. "I think we get to figure that out together, don't we?"

"Right, but until we do that…" Tori turned around and motioned to the truck "…we still have to unpack this beast and put everything someplace so we're not tripping over it."

"Makes sense." Miranda hadn't moved since she bought the house ten years ago, and this was going to be the adjustment of a lifetime. Well, she probably would have thought that before Rebel had come to live with her. But now this was just one more step toward what she really wanted—life, family, love.

Tori took Miranda by the hand and started toward the house. "Come on, girls. Let's figure out your bedroom."

Miranda followed dutifully, stopping at Rebel's bedroom that would soon become her shared room with Harley. Rebel was already pulling out toys, and as much as Miranda had the urge to jump in and tell her to stop, she knew it wouldn't do any good. In fact, it'd probably keep the two of them entertained while the adults moved everything in.

"Did you get the beds?" Miranda asked.

"Should be delivered in a few hours. I figured what's one more thing to add to the chaos that we can accomplish today." Tori leaned into Miranda's side, holding her close.

"Still, we need them."

"We do." Tori winked and kissed Miranda's cheek. "Any news on Tierney moving out?"

Miranda shook her head. "Not permanently. She is renting a studio in Vancouver, but she still stays here two nights a week."

"When she's not working," Tori said, like a statement.

"She's kept the job for three months. Longest one she's had in years." Miranda tightened her clasp on Tori's fingers. "I just hope she continues to work at it."

"It seems like she's trying."

"You know, it does." Miranda had comforted herself with that thought many times over the last few months. Tierney was taking on parenting roles in ways she never had before, and holding down a job and remaining single was a good step toward that.

"Hello?" Aili's voice rang down the hall.

Harley's ears perked up instantly, and she ran when Tori nodded at her. Rebel was quick to follow. Tori took the chance and had Miranda pinned against the wall and their mouths melding together in an instant. Miranda moaned, clutching Tori's sides as she held on for dear life. She hadn't expected this, the suddenness of what Tori would do. She'd experienced it before, but for some reason, she'd anticipated that when they lived together it would calm down. It still might as the days dragged into months.

"Stop thinking," Tori muttered and kissed her again, this time sliding her body against Miranda's in an intoxicating way.

Miranda laughed lightly and lifted her arms to wrap them around Tori's neck and keep her close. If she could get full kisses like this now whenever she wanted, then she would take it.

"Oh, you two are gross." Siena's voice might as well have announced her rolling her eyes. "Get a room."

"I think they're adorable," Aili said.

"Mommy!"

Miranda winced and tried to pull away, but Tori stayed put. Eventually, she pushed Tori with a kiss and broke the embrace. Turning her head, she found Siena and Aili standing at the end of the hall with the kids next to them.

"Like I said, get a room!" Siena laughed, her comment coming off not harsh but joking.

"That's what we're doing." Tori flicked her middle finger up at Siena before hiding it behind her back where the kids couldn't see.

Miranda straightened her back, determined not to step into

the middle of that. She smoothed her hands over her pants and couldn't figure out where to even start.

"Let's get this truck done." Aili walked away with Rebel.

Tori chuckled and snagged Miranda's hand again. "Where do you want us to stash everything?"

"I honestly don't know." Miranda hadn't done this before. Ever. And that age-old panic started to swell in her chest again.

Tori reached up and cupped her cheek, bringing her chin around so they faced each other. "Take a breath, Miranda. I'm right here."

"I know." She did as she was told, calming the fear that threatened to burst out of her. "I've never moved in with anyone before."

"I know." Tori kissed her cheek. "That's why I feel so special to have the honor."

"You are special," Miranda countered. "I wouldn't do this for anyone else."

Tori melted right in front of her. This time the kiss didn't have the same heat as before. It was full of warmth. Miranda parted her mouth, sliding her tongue along Tori's lips and closing her eyes. This was what she had wanted. This was what they had worked toward. She just had to keep reminding herself of that.

"Again?" Siena's voice boomed down the hall.

Miranda jerked back. Tori snorted. "Yes! Again! Shut up. We were there once."

Siena rolled her eyes. "I know. You locked the back of the truck. We can't start unloading without the key."

"Right. Here." Tori reached into her pocket and threw the keys at Siena. "And yes, get used to it already."

"I will. Just give me a few weeks to make gross sounds at how cute you two are together. And I'll remind you—repeatedly—that you wouldn't be here without me."

Tori sighed. She was just about to say something else, but

Miranda grabbed her wrist and pulled it back. This conversation was useless and wouldn't get them anywhere. Miranda kissed her cheek. "And we will be eternally grateful to you for that."

"And for moving the heavy crap."

"That too." Miranda walked in front of Tori, sending Tori a scolding look over her shoulder. "Because there's no way Tori and I could move her entire apartment here without you."

Siena looked over Miranda's shoulder and pointed. "She learns fast. You could learn faster."

"Shut up." Tori broke the space between them, her arm over Miranda's shoulder. "Let's get this truck empty. I think the priority needs to be the girls' room. We can set up the bunk beds when they come."

"Bunk beds?" Siena stopped, frozen in space. "We never talked about bunk beds."

"There's no way to fit two beds, even twin beds, into that room. There isn't another option."

"I assume Harley will be on the top." Siena had gone pale.

Miranda flicked her gaze from Tori to Siena and back again. She stepped around them, snagging the keys to the truck from Siena's hand as she went. "I'll let you two argue this out while I open the truck."

She was never happier to be out of a conflict, and this was one she could gladly say she didn't need to be a part of. The girls raced around Aili in circles until Miranda showed up. For the next three hours, they and all of Tori's closest friends unloaded the truck and went back for a second and third load.

By the end of the day, Miranda was exhausted. Her feet hurt, her arms hurt, and all she wanted was a hot bath and a good night's sleep. Instead, she was rounding up the girls to sit down at the table when the pizza was delivered while Tori and Siena built the bunk beds in the girls' room. Tori was determined to have that room done before the end of the night, or really, before bedtime, which was fast approaching.

Siena and Tori worked through dinner, but Miranda brought them each a beer when the snippy comments escalated. When Rebel yawned, Miranda started their nightly bath routine, which Harley wanted in on instantly. They were going to have to figure this out with both kids in the house. That was the one thing they hadn't done since they were together.

Finally, Tori came and found her, dragging Miranda into the girls' bedroom to show off their handiwork. To say Miranda was impressed was an understatement. The girls' room was completely finished. The bunk beds made, and two dressers side by side. Tori gave her a quick tour, ending with a kiss.

"I think this is going to work," Tori mumbled.

"Think?" That same old panic started again.

"Know! I know this is going to work. What's between us." Tori kissed her again.

Miranda remained dubious. "Think we'll get any sleep tonight?"

"I think we're all going to crash after the excitement of the day."

Miranda had woken up with Tori in her bed several times over the intervening months, but this would be different. This would mean so much more because Tori wasn't leaving. This was her home as much as it was Miranda's. And instead of panic at that thought, she was warmed by it. Clasping Tori's hand in her own, Miranda kissed her cheek.

"Go get something to eat. I'm going to get the girls to sleep, and then you and I can talk."

"Talk?" Tori's brow furrowed. "That sounds serious."

"We need a routine."

Tori laughed heartily. "Oh, are you going to create schedules for everyone now?"

"Aren't you the one who told me children thrive on routine?"

"I think that was Aili." Tori walked out of the bedroom. "I'm going to tell Siena goodbye."

Miranda watched her walk down the hall before heading back toward the bathroom. She got the girls out of the tub and brought them into their new room. It took longer than it should have to get them dressed for bed, because Harley barely let go of Rebel's hand. This was going to be an adjustment for every single one of them involved in this little family they were creating.

The girls raced down the hall toward the kitchen to give Tori goodnight hugs and kisses. All in all, it took Miranda another hour to get the girls to settle into their new beds, and Harley ended up on the bottom bunk with Rebel pushed against the wall to keep her from falling. But they were both asleep, which Miranda was calling a win.

She dragged her feet as she went out to the living room, flopping next to Tori on the couch and stealing her beer for a sip. Tori pulled Miranda against her side. This was what she had wanted. Everything was fitting together well, and Miranda didn't want to give this up, ever.

"What are you thinking?" Tori asked, tangling her fingers in Miranda's hair.

"That I'm happy, and that this is exactly what I want."

Tori grinned broadly. "You know what? Me too. A house full of kids, my soulmate next to me."

Miranda stilled. "You know that the goal is for Rebel to live with Tierney."

"Eventually, but not tomorrow."

"No, not tomorrow." Miranda looked into Tori's eyes, trying to get a read on the conversation, but she was so bad at this. She'd gotten better over the last few months, but this still wasn't something she'd consider herself proficient at.

"Do you want kids?" Tori tentatively asked.

"Don't you think that's a discussion we should have had before you moved in with me?" Miranda shifted, putting some space between them and setting the beer onto the coffee table.

"Miranda...I—how do I say this? I wouldn't mind having another kid. I know Harley would love a sibling, but it's not a deal-breaker for me."

Miranda nodded, more to herself than Tori, as that knowledge settled into the pit of her stomach. "We can talk about it."

"Yeah, we don't have to talk about it today." Tori wrapped her arm over Miranda's shoulder. "Tonight I want to sit here with you, snuggle into you, and pass out like a drunk college student."

Miranda laughed. "I want a massage."

"That can be arranged." Tori winked.

Miranda groaned. "Not one of *those* massages."

"Oh. Well. Fine. Rain on my parade."

Miranda kissed Tori softly. "We can do that kind of massage another night."

"In the morning?"

"You're insatiable."

"I have free access now."

"Hmmm...you do." Miranda stilled. Then she did something unexpected. She pushed up on her knees and straddled Tori on the couch. Leaning down, she pressed their mouths together. "We have all the nights and all the mornings together."

Tori grinned up at her. "I'm so glad that I met you."

Miranda kissed her again. "It's a good thing I had a Rebel who needed taming."

Laughing, Tori shook her head. "What will we do without her?"

"I have a feeling she'll never be too far away."

"Auntie?" Rebel's small voice broke the moment.

Miranda dropped her head onto Tori's shoulder with a sigh. "See?"

Rebel crawled up onto the couch and tried to slide herself between them. Miranda laughed and pulled away, snagging Rebel up in her arms. She dropped a kiss into Rebel's hair and sent a look to Tori. "Let me put her back to bed."

"You do that. I'm going to take a shower, and maybe, when you're done, you can join me."

Miranda laughed as she walked away. Who would have ever thought this would be her life?

———

thank you!

Dearest Reader,

Thank you so much for reading this beloved story. It means the world to me! I absolutely fell head over heels in love with Miranda and Tori and especially little Rebel. This whole story and series started because I wanted to write stories involving childcare.

Which means there's a lot of single parents, there's a lot of chaos when kids are involved and whole lot of moving parts. But kids are a huge part of my life with the ones I have at home and the ones I've taught in various daycares and camps and programs.

I really hope you enjoyed these three as much as I did. Since this is my first book out under this name, I'd love it if you'd leave a review or a rating.

You'll get a free copy of **Made You Look** when you do sign up for my newsletter, a novella all about Aili and Rebel's teacher, Birch and just how their love story starts.

If you haven't signed up for my newsletter yet, you can by going to: https://qrco.de/MYLnewsletter

or scanning the QR code with your phone

SCAN ME

I love keeping in contact with readers, so send me emails or get hold of me on social media anytime.

And I always love a good dad joke. Send me your best!

Til the sun shines again,

Eada

about the author

Eada Friesian is an author of snarky sapphic women who fall in love hard. She loves all the characters and relationships she gets to play with and the best friends she makes with each new book she writes. She fell in love with the genre years ago and could never leave it. Who would? Now that she's authoring her own books, she hopes to bring a fresh flair to the sapphic book world.

Eada lives in the mountains, camping her life away with her partner and horde of animals. She has her family right by her side as she strives to live her best life authentically as an author, a parent, a spouse, and weird person. She loves the smell of campfire, the taste of a completely charred marshmallow for a s'more, and living off the land with very little people around her. Of course, none of this last part is true, because Eada is a pen name, and the identity of the person(s) behind her remain hidden.

instagram.com/sapphicsnarks

love & cherish

**One reserved professional. One bubbly long-term temp.
One gala to unite them.**

Haylee Coleman can't lose another job. Flat out broke, she's
desperate to turn her life around, pay her bills, and keep her job. But
more than that, she's found a place she might belong for the first time
in her life. She can make a difference here. If only Cherish would like
her. If only Cherish would help her figure out how to not get fired. If
only Cherish wasn't so distracting.

With a bark that rivals the boss's, Cherish Barkley lives and breathes
her job. She's loved Febe Aarts for decades. When the annual gala for
the Holbrook Foundation looms, Cherish begs for Haylee's help. It
has to go off without a hitch, unlike last year, when Febe…Cherish
can think about that later. Right now, she has to protect Febe.

Will they put aside their differences long enough to ensure their boss
survives the gala unscathed? Or will the mounting tension between
them erupt in unsuspecting ways?

*Find out what happens in this sapphic age gap, workplace romance, with an ice
queen in love with her boss and a curvy new assistant that won't give up on her
dream.*

Releasing July 2024

or

Join my Ream and start reading **Love & Cherish** today!

https://reamstories.com/sapphicsnarks

spicy sapphic christmas

Will it be a white Christmas when four singers join together for the charity event of the year?

Bea's band is taking off. With authenticity as their backbone, they climb the ranks in the music world. When her sister, Jo, begs a production manager to check them out, Bea is shocked to find an undeniable attraction to the famous Bunny. Unwilling to be in the closet and taking every opportunity to advance her career, Bea won't back down from the chance of a lifetime.

Bunny has worked hard to reach the charts with bandmate Piper and won't risk it for a one night stand. Bea might be attractive, talented, icy, and everything Bunny is looking for in a woman, but to date would require Bunny to come out. When her production manager teams up the two bands, Bunny's caught between fear and love. With the Christmas charity event drawing closer, Bunny must keep her attractions hidden.

Piper and Jo team up to bring Bunny and Bea together, wanting their best friends to find love. They're willing to go to any length to make that happen, including faking their own engagement.

Will Bunny risk her career for love? Will Bea get out of her own way to open her heart? Will Piper and Jo admit their fake relationship might be real?

Spicy Sapphic Christmas is a story of finding love in unexpected ways and allowing yourself to be loved unconditionally. Join Bunny and Bea along with Piper and Jo in this modern, queer White Christmas reimagining.

Releasing November 2024

Printed in Great Britain
by Amazon